Jack & Harry

no turning back

'A refreshing, delightful and thoroughly Australian book, full of adventure, courage, humour and *surprises*. It made me review my own life and agree – wryly – that there is indeed "no turning back". And – so rare these days – it's a great "feel good".'

Rosemary Crooks, BA

AUSTRALIA
1950's

Map by Resource Mapping Pty Ltd - based on published maps of the period

0   400

Scale of Miles

KEY TO MAP

▄▄ ▄▄ ▄▄   Jack & Harry's route

--------------   Railways

Acknowledgements

I was introduced to Jack Ferguson and Harry Turner in March 2003 by two mates, Mervyn Davis and Murray Meyer who brought the lads to my home for a barbecue. I learned, during the course of the evening, that both boys were accused of theft and, fearing the worst, had decided to scarper into the outback to avoid going to goal and had dreams of 'striking it rich' digging for opal in the tough outback mining town of Coober Pedy.

I became intrigued that night with these two young men and their naive but determined plans. They had no money; only some hair-brained scheme to get some, and they didn't even know where Coober Pedy was! I should explain here that Jack and Harry are fictional characters but during the months that followed as I lived, worked, worried, rode, sweated, sat around the campfire, and laughed and cried with them, the line between fiction and reality often blurred - they became my friends.

It is often said that writers can live a lonely existence, closeted in solitude with only the whirr of a processor for company but that was not my experience. I was never alone, I had the lads to keep me company, and Uncle Warri and Paddy O'Brien and Reynold and Tom Cooper and ... well ... you'll meet them all soon.

The cover credits state, 'written by Tony McKenna and Mervyn Davis' but No Turning Back is the fusion of idea contributions from several people. The words are mine but the concept and initial story framework belong to Mervyn Davis. Many plot ideas and characters were birthed from 'brainstorming sessions' when Mervyn, Murray and I would devise challenging situations and ask how the boys would react? What emotions would they experience? What would they do next?

At the end of these sessions we would have some story bones that I would then add flesh and substance to. While the story is fiction the places they visit exist and there is a degree of truth in every situation as we drew deeply from the wells of our own varied knowledge and experiences.

There is also some legitimacy in each fictional character as they are composites of people met on our own journeys over time across this incredible land we live in.

Murray Meyer deserves special credit for his valued contribution to this book and all three of us; Murray, Mervyn and I, are more comfortable on a stump around a campfire than we are in suburbia.

Others, too numerous to name, deserve our sincere gratitude for their input, support, patience and encouragement including many people who contributed unwittingly by just having crossed our paths at some time.

— Tony McKenna

Jack & Harry

no turning back

Australian Arts and Entertainment Pty. Ltd.

Published and distributed by
Australian Arts and Entertainment Pty Ltd
96 Wanneroo Road Tuart Hill, Western Australia 6065

Cover image photography and design by Graeme Bond
Birdsong Press, Mandurah, Western Australia

National Library of Australia Cataloguing-in-publication data:

McKenna, Tony, 1944 –
Davis, Mervyn, 1940 –
Jack & Harry – no turning back

ISBN 0-9757850-0-1

Printed and bound by Griffin Press, South Australia

Trade Enquiries to
Birdsong Press
Studio 2/ 9 Birdsong Grove
Riverside Gardens, Mandurah WA 6210
Ph: (08) 9581 2577 - Email: graeme@birdsongpress.com
website: www.birdsongpress.com

Chapter One

It was November 3, 1950 in Perth Western Australia. The hot afternoon dragged on at Ashmorton public school. Jack Ferguson was restless, fidgeting with his pencil, drawing doodle circles on his workbook as the teacher droned on about polygons and fractions - not Jack's favourite subject. He glanced at the wall clock above the teacher's head. It was almost three o'clock and he willed the large black hand on the clock to move more quickly to the magical 'bell' time. His mind wandered to the coming weekend when his mate Harry would be staying over.

Harry and Jack had been inseparable friends since they met in primary school. With the same interests in football and cricket, fishing and just having fun, Jack knew the weekend would be a great time. They planned to go down to the creek to catch yabbies. These small freshwater crayfish were delicious cooked and eaten with fresh crusty bread and a dash of vinegar. Even more fun was catching them with a hunk of red meat, or a lamb chop, tied to a piece of string. It was a skilful art to gently pull them to the bank and scoop them up with a handmade net, usually made from Jack's mum's discarded stockings, and Jack and Harry considered themselves master 'yabbie catchers'.

After what seemed like an eternity to Jack, the hand eventually crawled to the '12' at the top of the clock and the bell signalled the end of the school day and - more importantly - the school week and two whole days of fun.

There was a scramble as the students spilled from the classroom along the passage and into the schoolyard. Jack searched for Harry in the bustling throng. Harry was in a class behind Jack being exactly one year younger, their birthdays being within two days of each other which meant they usually had a combined party.

'Jack, Jack!'

'Hey, Harry! Over here.'

Harry, a tall gangly kid with a shock of sandy coloured hair and a mass of freckles on his angular face, ran to where Jack was standing. Smiling, he slapped Jack on the back and they feinted in a mock fight for a few seconds.

'Got your gear with you?' Jack queried.

'Yeah, in here.' Harry indicated his school bag. 'Don't need much, just a change of clothes and me toothbrush. I left the schoolbooks in the desk 'cause I guess we're not doin' any homework this weekend are we, Jack?'

'No way! Let's go then.'

As they walked from the schoolyard, another boy caught up with them. 'Hey, you blokes, what are you up to this weekend?'

'G'day, Billy, not a lot,' Jack replied. 'Harry's staying over and we'll probably go down to the creek tomorrow, see if we can catch some yabbies. Might have a game of cricket or somethin' this arvo.'

'Can I come over and join in?'

'Yeah, suppose so, but you'll have to bring your bat as we only got one.'

'OK, see ya.'

'See ya, Billy.' The boys continued walking.

'Hey, did you know it's my birthday tomorrow?' Billy called after them.

'That right? You havin' a party, Billy?'

'No, my dad says I can't have a party *and* a bike.'

'You gettin' a bike for ya birthday, Billy? How do ya know, aren't presents supposed to be a surprise?'

'Dad let me go down and pick it out at the shop. It's a Malvern Star racer. I'll bring it over to show ya tomorrow.' Billy turned on his heel and was quickly lost in the gaggle of bustling school children.

'There's somethin' about him I don't like, Jack.' Harry glanced over his shoulder at Billy Munse's, retreating back. 'Not sure what.'

'Billy's all right, Harry, just a bit spoiled I reckon. His old man's a snob but.'

'A Malvern Star racer for his birthday lucky bugger, and a *new* one.'

'Yeah, well his dad *is* a solicitor so I suppose he can afford it.'

'My dad says you can't trust solicitors.'

'Dunno, Harry, never had anythin' to do with 'em, don't even know what they do really except it's somethin' to do with law and criminals and stuff.'

'You ever been over to Billy's house, Jack?'

'No. You?'

Harry shook his head.

Ashmorton, a subdivision on the eastern outskirts of Perth with rows of neat three and four bedroom brick houses set on quarter acre blocks of land, bordered natural bush parklands with a creek, that was called a 'river' meandering through it. The park separated Ashmorton from the more affluent suburb of Kelsborough.

The Fergusons lived in one of Ashmorton's red brick houses with a white picket fence behind which was a rose garden that Alice Ferguson, Jack's mother, tended with loving care. A concrete driveway ran down the right-hand side of the house that led to a single timber-framed garage. The backyard was spacious with grassed areas, shady trees and the inevitable wood fuelled brick constructed barbecue around which most of the Fergusons' social events took place. Jack's father, Jack Senior, was proud of his home, his wife Alice and family of six children. He had worked hard to achieve his success and was a Stock and Station agent with Elder Smith Goldsbrough Mort, having joined them when he was thirteen years old as a yard hand at the saleyards. Eager to learn he had shown natural ability to evaluate sheep and cattle and worked his way up the ranks reaching the position of Buyer, travelling to remote stations and sometimes interstate on behalf of clients to purchase stock. Forty-five years old, he had a tanned face and arms, a result of hours in the open at the saleyards. He was considered an honest, no-nonsense bloke you could rely on; he was steady, liked a beer, a barbecue with his mates and enjoyed a bet on the races although he was never known to wager beyond his means. Tall and muscular with black curly hair and brown eyes, everyone said that young Jack was the spitting image of his father.

'G'day, mum,' Jack called as he and Harry entered the kitchen from the back verandah.

'Hello, son. Oh, Hello, Harry.' Alice Ferguson turned from the kitchen sink and wiped her hands on a floral apron she was wearing.

'G'day, Mrs Ferguson.'

'How was school today, boys?'

'OK I guess,' mumbled Jack.

'Yeah OK,' Harry added.

'What time's dad gettin' home mum?'

'He called to say he was stopping off for a couple of beers on the way home as it's Friday but said he'd be here about six o'clock. I've got tea planned for about seven. What are you boys up to?'

'Not much, probably have a hit of cricket; a couple of kids are comin' 'round. Got anythin' to eat, mum? You hungry, Harry?'

'You bet.'

Alice smiled, taking a plate of sandwiches from the refrigerator and placing them on the kitchen table. 'Thought you might be a bit peckish. This should keep the wolf from the door until teatime. There's a billy of milk in the fridge too if you want it.'

'What's for tea, mum?'

'Growing boys!' Alice mused, 'always thinking about tucker. Lamb's fry and bacon tonight and there are stewed quinces with custard for afters. You eat lamb's fry, Harry?'

'Eat anythin', Mrs Ferguson.'

'OK boys, make sure you let the littlies join in the cricket and don't bowl too hard at them.' She looked at them with mock sternness.

'We won't, mum.'

Alice could soon hear the kids playing cricket out in the street. Fortunately they lived in a 'No Through Road' and only resident traffic used the street. Not everyone owned a vehicle and those that did knew that most of the kids living in the street played outside after school and on weekends, so they kept a watchful eye out for them.

◆◆◆◆◆◆◆◆◆◆◆◆

The front bar of the Exchange Hotel was packed to overflowing. There was a lot of laughter and a buzz of rowdy conversation as workers unwound after a busy week and planned the weekend ahead.

'Another beer, Jack?'

'Better not, Eric.' Jack Ferguson glanced at the bar clock 'Told Alice I'd be home by six. How about we get a couple of bottles and take 'em home to my place, have a beer there. How about you pick up Eve and stay for a feed? What about you, Jim?'

'No I can't, Jack,' Eric said, 'I promised Eve I'd take her to the pictures tonight. Maybe tomorrow though.' He stubbed his cigarette butt into a glass ashtray.

'I'm a bit tied up tonight too, Jack,' Jim answered. 'How about we have a barbecue tomorrow though?'

'Sounds fair to me.' Jack drained his glass. 'Let's have it at our joint though 'cause young Harry Turner's staying over with Jack for the weekend so I'll invite his folks too. You know Claude and Jean don't you?' They nodded.
'We'll make an arvo of it then. Come 'round about three or thereabouts.'

They agreed to meet at Jack's house the next day and left the smoke filled bar.

◆◆◆◆◆◆◆◆◆◆◆◆

Jack Junior and Harry woke early on Saturday morning. The house was quiet, with Jack's siblings and his parents still sleeping. Jack opened the vents on the slow combustion wood stove and fanned some kindling alight. When the stove was hot he filled an iron kettle with water from the tap and placed it on the stove to boil. Harry busied himself making toast. The younger children started to stir, laughter and noise filling the house.

'Quiet you lot!' boomed a voice from down the hallway. 'Your mum's trying to sleep.'

Jack laughed. 'That'd wake mum anyhow, dad yellin' like that. How about we take 'em in a cuppa and some toast?'

They knocked on Jack and Alice's bedroom door.

'Yeah, come in,' Jack's father bellowed.

'Thanks boys, what's this in aid of then, Jack?' His father pointed to the pot of tea and plate of heavily buttered toast.

'We want to head off early dad to go down to the creek.'

'So this is to soften us up eh?' His father took a bite of toast. 'All right, Jack but don't get up to any mischief you blokes and don't forget that your parents are going to be here for a barbie, Harry. Be good if you boys could chop some wood and set the fire. That'd save me some time as I want to go down town and get some ice to keep the drinks cool then to the butcher's for some snags and chops.'

'Be careful too boys, down at the river.'

'Yeah, mum, but it's only a creek not a river and not all that deep except for a couple of holes. We'll be all right. Stop worrying.'

'Yes, Alice, the lads'll be OK. Don't get carried away and forget the time though.'

'No, dad.'

'See ya, Mr Ferguson.'

Across the park in Kelsborough there was excitement at number 29 Lawton Drive as William (Billy) Munse woke from a restless dream-filled sleep. It was his birthday and even though he had chosen the bike at the shop, he couldn't quite remember every detail of it and was anxious to see the bike again and to ride it out to show off to his schoolmates.

He paced impatiently around the lounge room waiting for his parents to come downstairs. They had been out to dinner the previous night to a restaurant in the city. Billy hadn't really wanted to go but his father had insisted, saying that it was only proper for a young gentleman to go to dinner with his parents on his fifteenth birthday. Billy now waited for his parents to wake. He didn't dare disturb them as his father would probably be in a bad mood anyhow after drinking too much wine at dinner and Billy didn't want to make matters worse by antagonising him further. He knew the bike was in the garage but it was locked and he didn't have a key so he would just have to wait. He made himself a cup of Milo and nibbled at some toast to pass the time

After waiting restlessly for almost an hour, Billy was joined by his parents.

'Good morning, William, happy birthday, dear.' His mother brushed her lips against his cheek.

'Happy birthday, son.'

'Thanks, dad, mum.' Billy moved from one foot to the other expectantly. 'Can I have my bike now?'

'Shortly, William.' His father glared at him over the top of his thick horn-rimmed glasses. 'There's something you need to be aware of though, it's important and concerns your new bike.'

'Yes, dad, what?' Billy was mystified.

'You know that bike was not cheap, it cost me a lot of money and you have to learn to respect things of value, William.'

'Yes I know, I really app …' His father cut him off with a wave of a hand.

'That bike is for you only. I don't want you letting any of the local riff raff ride it do you hear?'

'Yeah, er … sure, dad,' Billy stammered.

'I mean it, son! I'm not going to pay good money to have other kids whose families can't afford it, ride your bike. You have to be aware that we are a little better than they are and if I see you letting any of the other kids riding it then I'll lock it up in the shed and no one will ride it. Do you understand?'

'Yes, dad,' Billy agreed with his father. *Agree to anything so that I can get the bike.* He smiled sweetly. *He'd never know if I let someone ride it anyhow.*

Billy was presented with the bike and spent the next hour riding it around the driveway and a short way down the footpath outside his home so he 'could get used to it' as his father advised before he would be allowed to take it further.

'You were a little harsh on him, William, it is his birthday after all,' Mrs Munse said.

'Harsh nothing and I meant what I said. He's better than those other kids, especially those ruffians from the other side of the park. They're just a blue collar mob, not professional people like us.'

'I know, dear but he does go to school with most of them and you know I didn't agree with that from the beginning. He should be in private boarding school, we can afford it.'

'It's not a matter of money. I never went to boarding school but I slogged hard to get a scholarship to go to university. William has to learn to mix with the ordinary people of this world but not to be part of them. That way he will learn what they are like, what makes them tick so that when he eventually graduates from the bar and comes into the firm with me he will understand their mentality more. After all, they're the ones who are usually in trouble with the law and need a solicitor to defend them. Makes sense to me.'

His wife smiled weakly and agreed. She had learned over the years that submission was the key to peace in the Munse household.

Chapter Two

Jack and Harry were walking up from the creek through the park towards Jack's home with a bucket full of yabbies when Billy Munse rode into the park and swept speedily toward them down the bituminised pathway.

'Get a look at this for a bike! Told ya I was getting one for me birthday.' Billy yelled as he approached the duo.

'Gee, Billy, sure is a beauty.' Harry stared in amazement at the shining chrome and blue Malvern Star with the racing handlebars and pedals fitted with straps so the rider's feet wouldn't slip off.

'She's flash all right, Billy,' Jack agreed. 'Look at them wheels, got racing tyres too. Bet she goes fast.'

'You bet she does,' Billy quipped proudly. 'She's got front and rear brakes too. Stops on a sixpence.'

'Come on, Jack,' Harry started to walk off. 'We have to get back to your place to chop that wood for ya dad.' The last thing Harry wanted to do was look at the bike and watch Billy gloat.

'Yeah, catch ya, Billy.' The boys walk off up the path but Billy rode beside them. He certainly wanted to get more glory out of this encounter than the brief discourse so far. 'Wanna ride?' Billy asked.

'Nah, better not,' Jack said. 'We've gotta get home.'

'Yeah, OK. I don't suppose you *could* ride it anyhow.' Billy reverted to sarcasm. 'You have to know what you're doin' to ride a bike like this. You've only got that old thing that your dad used to ride eh? Was it your granddad's or did Noah have it on the ark with him?' Billy laughed sneeringly. 'Got flat tyres now hasn't it? Rusted out in the shed.'

'I could ride it no worries.' Jack started to bristle with indignation.

'Me too,' Harry said. 'I could ride it easy. My cousin's got one similar and I've ridden his before … lotsa times.'

'Well have a ride then.' Billy was anxious to have the boys ride his new bike because he knew that would make them even more envious of him and his birthday present. He also figured they would talk about it at school so Billy would get the glory and not even have to mention a word about it himself.

'Are ya sure you're allowed to lend it, Billy? Jack asked. 'Bein' so new and everythin'.'

'It's my bike, I can lend it to whoever I like. Do ya wanna ride or not … last chance?'

'A little turn on it'd be good eh, Harry?'

'Yeah, maybe, you go first though.' Harry was still reluctant to give Billy anything further to gloat about but was busting inside to get a ride on the bike.

Billy dismounted and proudly handed the bike to Jack who tossed his leg over it and after a slightly shaky start, got the feel quickly and rode off down the path toward the river. It was exhilarating. Jack couldn't imagine what it would be like to actually 'own' a machine like this. He braked, turned the bike and pedalled strongly back up the slope to where Harry and Billy were standing.

'Wow!' Jack couldn't think of anything more appropriate to say. 'Your turn, Harry.'

Harry hopped on board the racer and headed off at speed down the path to the river. He too braked, spun the bike around expertly and rode full pelt back to where the two boys stood waiting.

'What do ya think, Harry?' Billy asked.

'Hhmm, not bad.' Harry was reluctant to give too much praise although he was green with envy of Billy's bike.

'Have another turn then, Harry.'

'No I'm right.'

'How about you, Jack, like another turn?'

Yeah, I reckon one more'd be good, Billy, thanks.'

Jack rode off along the flat beside the river and Harry, unable to restrain himself, ran after him shouting encouragement. 'Go faster, Jack, give it to her, she can take it.'

Billy was ecstatic with pride as he watched Jack ride his bike with Harry running and skipping alongside trying to keep up and yelling for Jack to go faster.

The pride quickly turned sour and a sinking feeling hit the pit of his stomach as he glanced over his shoulder and saw his father striding purposefully through the park entrance towards where he was standing. Panic took hold as he realised that his father must have come to watch him ride the new present and where was it? About two hundred yards away along the track with Jack in the saddle and Harry running beside it.

There goes the bike, he thought. *My dad's gonna kill me and hang the bike in the shed.*

Tears welled up in his eyes as he realised the mistake he had made and the consequences he would have to pay for being so stupid. He could see the anger on his father's face and the grim set of his mouth was enough for Billy to recognise that this was no mere temper but a rage that his father was in.

Jack was laughing and Harry yelling so loudly that at first they didn't hear Billy screaming to them. Then they heard the urgency and panic in Billy's voice and looked back in amazement to see Mr Munse striding down the path and Billy jumping up and down waving his arms wildly in the air.

'Give my bike back you thieves. My dad's here so you won't be so brave now eh?' Billy screamed accusingly.

'What's he yellin' about?'

'Dunno, Harry … let's go and find out. Doesn't sound too good though and there's his father the solicitor. Billy must be in some sorta trouble.'

'What the hell do you think you're doing, William. I told you not to let anyone ride your bike and you've disobeyed me almost immediately, that bike will be going to the shed, believe me!' Munse's was red faced with anger.

'I didn't lend it dad, honest, they stole it from me,' Billy lied.

'Stole it! Stole it! Did they now? Well I'm not surprised, I told you they were riffraff. This is going to be reported to the police. You won't get away with this you young hooligans.' Munse shook his fist at Jack and Harry who had arrived at the angry scene and slowly began to understand what was happening.

'We didn't steal the bike, Mister.' Jack was defensive 'Billy wanted me and Harry to have a ride.'

'Did not, liar,' Billy yelled tearfully. 'You forced me to let you ride it, stole it you did. They did, dad, they did, they stole it, honest.'

'We did not!' Harry yelled back at Billy.

'My William wouldn't lie to me and say you stole the bike if you didn't. You stole it all right and the matter is going to the police, You will both go to jail for this my lads, mark my words.' Munse reached out and grabbed the boys by their shirt collars holding them in a tight grip. 'William!' he directed. 'Run up to the police station now and bring the constable back while I hold these two thieves here until he arrives, get a move on, lad.'

Billy Munse ran at top speed, still sniffling, up the hill and out of the park toward the police station on the corner.

♦ ♦ ♦ ♦ ♦ ♦ ♦ ♦ ♦ ♦ ♦ ♦

Jack and Alice were getting ready for their guests to arrive for the barbecue. Alice had been making salads from fresh lettuce, apple cucumbers and tomatoes that had been home grown in the vegetable garden behind the garage. 'These tomatoes are firm and sweet, Jack. Good crop this year.'

'Mmm. It's the sheep manure I fertilised them with. Best thing for vegies. Wonder where those bloody kids are? They promised to be back and chop some wood for the barbie.'

'Young Timothy will do it dear; he loves to help with the barbie.' Alice called out to Jack's younger brother. 'Timmo, come and help your father, dear. Jack and Harry are a bit late.' A shadow of worry flitted over her usually smiling countenance as she hoped her son and his mate Harry hadn't gotten into any trouble at the river. She had an irrational fear of water, especially when it came to her kids. 'Hope they're OK, Jack.'

'They won't be OK when I get 'em, Alice. They're just forgetful and havin' too much of a good time that's all.'

'Oh, Jack, you know you aren't really cross with them. They'll be home shortly.' She still couldn't shake the feeling though that something could be wrong. It was unlike young Jack to be late when he said he would be home at a certain time. He idolised his father and wouldn't let him down intentionally.

The arrival of Eric and Eve with their children, followed closely by Jim and his family interrupted her thoughts as she greeted them all warmly. The men moved to the backyard area where Jack had set up a rescued concrete wash tub filled with ice to keep the drinks cold.

'Gotta have cold beer, boys,' Jack said.

'Never a truer word said,' laughed Eric. 'Did you say that young Harry's parents Claude and Jean are coming today too?'

'Should be here shortly,' Jack replied as he carefully placed kindling on top of newspaper under the steel barbecue plate. 'They'll be here before their son gets back the way things are. Jack and Harry are a bit late. Went down to the creek this morning … should be home by now.'

'Ahh you know what kids are like, Jack. They'll be here shortly.'

Alice ushered the children onto the verandah where she had set up a trestle table with plates of sandwiches and trays of sliced rockmelon. 'There's homemade ice-cream in the fridge, Eve, would you mind getting it out for the kids?'

'You've been busy, Alice,' Janet said. 'Can I help?'

'Thanks, Janet, I kept a good job for you. Can you slice up those onions there?' She pointed to some peeled white onions on the bench. 'For Jack to cook on the barbie. I'll help Eve get the kids something to go on with. You know what they're like if they have to wait for the meat to be cooked. Jack'll throw some snags on for them soon but I suppose he and the boys will want a couple of beers first.'

Claude and Jean then arrived and after greeting everyone looked around the yard. 'Where's Harry and Jack?'

'Not back from the creek yet, Jean. Shouldn't be long now though.' Jack put a match to the wood.

At this point Timothy, Jack's younger brother, came out to the back yard and said that someone was knocking at the front door.

'Why didn't you see who it was, Timmo?'

'I dunno, dad … didn't think.' Timothy went back inside as Jack put his beer glass on the table and went to see who was at the door.

'Keep your eye on that fire will you, Eric, should be hot enough soon to start cooking.' Jack checked the flames then disappeared inside the house. When he opened the door he was shocked to see a uniformed policeman standing with his son Jack, Harry Turner, young Billy Munse and Billy's father William, who looked extremely angry.

'What's this then, Bob?' He knew the constable from investigations over stolen stock from the cattle yards some months ago.

'Your son and his mate stole my William's new bike,' Munse said accusingly.

'What? Jack is this true?' His father turned to him with a puzzled look.

Both boys spoke at the same time, hotly denying the accusation. Young Billy skulked in the background standing off the front porch on the pathway, his eyes lowered.

'No way, dad, we didn't steal the bike. He …' Jack pointed to Billy who refused to look up, '… let us ride it and then said we stole it when his dad turned up. He's lyin', dad.'

Munse started toward young Jack, his fists clenched. 'Don't you dare call my son a liar, you scoundrel.'

Jack's father was about to lunge forward when the constable intervened. 'That's enough of that. There's enough trouble now without you two blokes making it worse.' He glared at Munse. 'Sir, if you don't mind, I'll handle this my own way.'

'Nothing to handle, constable. The boys stole William's bike and I want them charged.'

'Nobody is going to be charged until I get all the facts and I want to talk to each of the boys involved alone. It's the weekend and I want you to go home now with young Billy here …'

'His name's *William* not *Billy*,' interrupted Munse.

The constable ignored the rebuff and went on. 'Take *Billy* and the bike home, sir. I'm sure there must be some explanation for all of this and I'll get to the bottom of it. Take the weekend to cool down … all of you!' This comment was directed mainly at William Munse who stood menacingly on the verandah facing young Jack and Harry. 'I'll be back around on Monday afternoon after school to get statements from you three boys.'

'I will bring William to the station after school. There's no need for you to come to my house.' Munse was horrified at the thought that a police car might be seen parked outside his home.

'Whatever you prefer, sir,' the constable replied

'Don't think because you happen to know the constable that your boy will get away with this, Ferguson. I'll make sure there is a charge, I have better contacts than you, you know.'

Before Jack could respond Munse stepped from the verandah with his arm around his son and they went out the gate together wheeling the bike.

'I don't believe this!' Jack stared after the Munses running his hand through his hair. 'You're accused of stealing a bike, Jack, that's serious you know? You too, Harry.'

'I know it's serious, dad,' Jack replied for both of them 'But we *didn't* steal it. He let us ride it then his dad turned up and he started yellin' that we stole the bike.'

The policeman intervened. 'Look, I know it's a serious accusation, Jack, but there's no point in everyone getting upset and ruining the weekend. Forget about it until I get the statements and sort a few things out early next week.'

'Yeah, I guess you're right, Bob, but you blokes are grounded.' He glared at the two boys. 'For the whole weekend and I've a good mind to send you packing off home with your parents, Harry.'

'Dad! That's not fair,' Jack pleaded. 'We didn't steal the bike and even you believe that Mr Munse and his kid instead of us.' Young Jack was close to tears. He was frustrated and felt cheated by the injustice.

'He's right you know, Jack.' The constable supported the boy's defence. 'Nothing is proven at this point.'

'OK, OK! I'm just upset that's all and what right has that Munse to come around here wavin' his bloody fists around and threatening us. Anyway you boys are still grounded. You'll have to amuse yourselves in the yard if you still want to stay over, Harry, until this thing is sorted out. I don't want either of you out in the street. Is that clear?'

'Yes, dad.'

'Yes, Mr Ferguson.' Harry mumbled.

'We're havin' a barbecue, Bob, but I guess it wouldn't be right under the circumstances to invite you to stay?'

'That's right, Jack, not good timing and I got to get back to the station anyway. We'll catch up some other time after this episode is out of the way and have a couple of coldies then.'

The constable left. Jack went to explain what was going on to Alice and Harry's parents. The two boys decided it would be prudent to stay out of the way for the time being so they went around the side of the house to where Jack had fashioned a swing from an old tyre slung by a rope to the limb of a mulberry tree. They wanted to discuss what had happened, as they hadn't had a chance to do so since the debacle in the park.

'Do you think we'll go to jail, Jack?' Harry was clearly concerned.

'Nah, don't think so. We didn't steal the bloody bike, Harry, so how could we go to jail for somethin' we didn't do?'

'What if they don't believe us, Jack?'

Jack had no real answer for this so they just sat, each consumed by his own thoughts until Jack's dad called out to them. 'Come on you two, better get something to eat.' Then he added with a wink and a smile to the people gathered at the BBQ. 'You won't get good tucker like this in the lock-up.'

It was a joke that was totally lost on the two boys who stared at each other in horror.

After a while, with a few beers, and friendly conversation, the tension of the bike episode began to fade and everyone relaxed around the barbecue. Alice and the wives set salads out on the trestle table and Jack put a big metal tray of cooked lamb chops and burnt sausages in the centre. 'Help yourselves, folks, don't stand on ceremony around here.'

When they had all eaten their fill and the kids had demolished all the sausages, bread, icecream and rockmelon and consumed gallons of raspberry cordial, the wives retreated inside. They said they would 'do the dishes' and get a cup of tea so the men settled back in the shade on the lawn to sink a few 'cleansing ales' as Jack liked to call them and have a yarn together. Young Jack and Harry, being grounded, sat on the verandah and listened to the adults talk. Jack liked this time when his father relaxed with his mates and shared tales and experiences. Jack often picked up a few pointers for life as they talked about where they had been and the people they met.

'You were up in the Territory recently, weren't you, Jack?' Claude asked.

'Yes, that was interesting but the most interesting part of the trip was coming back down and through Coober Pedy.'

'Coober Pedy? What was that like? I've heard about it.' Alice and the women by this time had completed the washing up and now joined their husbands with cups of tea in hands.

'Hang on.' Eric reached into the ice tub to get another bottle of beer, opened it and began to fill the glasses. 'Once Jack gets going with one of his stories we could all die from thirst.' Everyone laughed at his good-natured ribbing.

Jack took a long draught from his glass. 'Ahh, that's good, Emu Bitter, can't beat it. Travel all over and try lots of beers but it's good to get home to a *real* beer.'

'Get on with the story, Jack,' Alice prompted.

'Well,' Jack continued. 'We were up at Anna Creek station buying cattle and decided to come back through Coober Pedy just for a look. It's an amazing place, like somewhere from another planet. Everyone lives underground up there.'

'Is that because of the heat?' Queried Eric.

'Certainly gets hot up there and it's a lot cooler to live underground but it's also practical in that you can dig for opal and build a home at the same time. Bugger of a place to get building materials into anyhow.'

'Must be interesting. What are the people like there, are there families?' Eve asked.

'A few I guess but mostly blokes of all sorts and nationalities. Mostly on the run from something they say. Alimony payments, broken homes … the law.'

'Bad lot then?' Claude's comment was more a question than a statement.

'No, not really. They have a pretty tight unwritten law of their own up there and everyone keeps to themselves. They ask no questions and give no information about where they're from or about their past. No one seems to mind that, in fact it's expected. Part of the culture.'

Jack and Harry were listening intently to this information as they sat quietly in the shadows on the verandah. 'Did you hear that, Harry?' Jack whispered.

'Do they make much of a living, Jack, up there in Coober Pedy? Opal, isn't it, they dig for?' Jim leaned forward and stubbed his cigarette out in the jam tin ashtray on the table.

'Some don't but others make an absolute fortune. Some of the best opal in the world is mined there and it brings big quids that's for sure. Overseas buyers pay lots for quality stone.'

'I saw some opal jewellery in a shop in the city last week.' Jean joined in the conversation. 'Blue, very beautiful.'

'What were you doing looking at jewellery, dear?' Mock anger from Claude.

'Only looking, only looking,' she laughed.

'You could have brought me some back, Jack, I wouldn't have minded an opal necklace. Mind you, I wouldn't have anywhere to wear it out to.' Alice stood and gave Jack a good-natured clip across the head. 'Better start to clear things away.'

'Didn't have time to dig, dear and couldn't afford to buy any,' Jack replied. 'It's not just the blue that's worth the big quid you know although that's very popular. The black opal … that's the prized find.'

'Black opal?' Jim and Eric said in unison.

'I've never heard of that, Jack,' Claude added.

'Pretty rare but worth a fortune and they reckon it's up there somewhere. 'Fire in the Stone' they call it.'

'Fire in the stone eh? Sounds sort of mystical,' Janet said wistfully.

'More *magical* than mystical, Janet.' Jack went on. 'If I was a young bloke with no responsibility that's where I'd be headed. Coober Pedy diggin' for opal.'

'Yeah,' Eric added thoughtfully. 'Jim and I talked about going out there years ago but of course with the depression the market went out of opal, worth darn near nothing for the effort.'

'That was the case all right but then you know about the aboriginal lady, what was her name?' Jack paused thoughtfully. 'Dottie Bryant, yes that's it. She made a big find about five or six years ago just after the war and now there's a big rush out there.'

'Its a young bloke's game though, Jack. Lot of hard yakka and there's always the chance you might not find a thing.'

'That's what I mean about 'magical', Eric,' Jack said. 'You just never know ....'

'Did you hear that, Harry?' Jack leaned close to whisper in Harry's ear. 'Best opal in the world at Coober Pedy and my dad's been there eh?'

'Sounds pretty good, Jack. Maybe when we leave school we could head up there and make a fortune. Buy *two* bloody bikes each.'

'Yeah!' giggled Jack. 'That'd show that Billy Munse a thing or two.'

'I'm thinkin' of showin' him a coupla things on Monday, Jack. Me fists.'

The womenfolk began to clear away the remaining glasses and the few plates that were left and the visitors made moves to pack their things saying that it was time to get the kids home to bed.

'Hey, Jack, who do you reckon'll win the Cup next Tuesday?'

'The Cup? Do you mean the Melbourne Cup?' Claude asked.

'What *other* Cup is there?' Jim had a surprised tone in his voice.

'Claude doesn't know much about horse racing do you, dear?' Jean reached over and patted her husband's knee, springing to his defence. 'He's a real cricket buff though, knows a lot about the tests.'

'I know enough about horse racing to know that anything can win the Melbourne Cup. There's never any 'sure thing' when it comes to the Cup.'

'There is this year,' Jack stated. 'Comic Court will win the cup.'

'Comic Court? Cripes, Jack,' Eric laughed. 'Have you gone crackers, mate? Not a chance.'

'Yeah pull the other leg,' Jim agreed. 'My money's on Chiquita.'

'Mine too.' Claude glanced at his wife. 'Just a few bob though. Not a betting man you know but I like a flutter on the cup.'

'Then you'll both do your dough. Comic Court is already past the post and'll go down in history as the winner of the 1950 Melbourne Cup,' Jack said with finality.

'OK, you boys.' Alice came out of the house. 'Stop arguing,' she laughed.

That night in bed Alice turned to Jack before she switched the light off. 'That was a good day, Jack, despite the problem with the police and the boys. You don't think they stole that boy's bike do you?'

'No I don't. I know Jack wouldn't steal anything and I'm sure that Harry is just as honest as Jack is. There's got to be some misunderstanding. It'll get sorted out. Are you going to turn the light out?'

'There's no chance they'd go to jail is there?' she persisted.

'No, Alice!' Jack sounded exasperated. 'Even if they did steal it, which they didn't, they're too young to go to jail. They'd just get a good talking to from the sergeant. After all, that Billy still had the bike so it's not like it was stolen and sold or lost or whatever.'

'But his father said that he would have them charged and he's a solicitor.'

'He's just a red-faced bag of wind and the fact that he's a solicitor doesn't put him outside the law, Alice. It'll be all right … believe me. There's something fishy about this and I think that that Billy is lying. Bob will get to the bottom of it when he takes the statements and examines it all.' Jack rolled onto his side but Alice continued.

'Shouldn't we let the boys know to take the pressure off them as they seem very upset about it all and were very quiet today …not their usual boisterous selves.' Alice had her head cradled on her arm facing Jack.

'Good to have 'em quiet for a change. No, let 'em sweat a bit longer. I don't believe for a minute that they did it but it won't hurt for them to be aware of the sort of consequences that can happen and if they were ever tempted in the future to pinch something. I'm sure this experience will make them think twice.'

Jack leaned across and kissed his wife on the cheek. 'Now *please* go to sleep. Good night, Alice.'

'Good night, dear.' She turned out the light.

◆◆◆◆◆◆◆◆◆◆◆

In the sleepout attached to the back of the house where Jack and Harry were in bed both boys were still awake but the house was quiet so they whispered so as not to disturb anybody.

'What a day, Harry. That Billy's a lyin' little shit.'

'Do ya reckon we'll go to jail, Jack?' Harry asked, for what seemed to Jack to be like the hundredth time.

'We can't go to jail for pinching somethin' we didn't pinch. It wouldn't be right. We're innocent, Harry.'

'Yeah, I suppose so. I'm gonna kill that Billy though when all this has died down.'

'Then he'll be twice dead 'cause I'm gonna kill him too.' They sniggered quietly at Jack's comment.

'What'll we do tomorrow, Jack? Can't go to the creek seein' as we're grounded?'

'We'll just hang around here, mate. You can help me build a billycart. I've got a box and wheels and everythin' we need.'

'Have ya?'

'Yep and we can use dad's tools in the garage. He won't mind as we'll be doin' what he wants and stayin' in the yard.'

'Good idea, Jack. She'll be a beauty.' Harry yawned. 'G'nite, Jack, I'm pretty tired.'

'Me too. See ya in the mornin'.'

◆ ◆ ◆ ◆ ◆ ◆ ◆ ◆ ◆ ◆ ◆ ◆

Sunday morning dragged on for Jack and Harry. Normally they would be down the creek early or out in the park playing with some of their mates but as they were grounded they moped around the house, played some card games, listened to the wireless and waited for lunch. Jack's brothers and sisters were pleased to have the two older boys at home for the day but their childish games and noise made Harry and Jack even more bored.

After lunch that consisted of left over chops, sausages and salad from the previous day's barbecue they went into the garage to start putting the billycart together. Jack's father reversed the car out onto the front lawn where he proceeded to give it its weekly wash. Jack was proud of his car, a near new cream coloured Holden FX sedan with red leather upholstery, even though it belonged to the company.

Alice had a small Austin Ten that she somehow managed to cram all the kids into to take them to school and do the shopping when Jack was away on a buying trip. It was old but honest and Jack couldn't bring himself to upgrade it as they had owned it for many years and it was almost part of the family.

The boys tinkered in the shed with much banging of nails and sawing of wood and by mid afternoon the cart was beginning to take shape. Jack had rescued four wheels from an old pram that was destined for the rubbish tip and with a piece of rope attached to the front cross piece for steering the boys were keen to try it out down the slope in the road outside the house.

'Dad?' Jack asked tentatively. 'Would it be OK if we just gave the billycart a trial run down the road?'

Jack stood up from where he was crouched beside the car cleaning the wheels and thought for a minute. 'Yes, I suppose so. You've been pretty good and haven't whinged about stayin' in the yard … but just a couple of runs though then it's back behind the fence.'

'Thanks, Mr Ferguson,' Harry said.

'Thanks, dad.' They wheeled the cart down the driveway through the double wooden gates and onto the road. 'I'm goin' first.' Jack exercised his priority as owner/builder.

The first run with Jack on board and Harry push-starting him down the slope revealed some adjustment was needed to the steering so they sat on the footpath at the bottom of the hill and began to make some modifications to the rope attached to the steering.

'I thought you blokes were grounded. Did ya pinch that cart too off some other kid?' Billy Munse swept past them on the other side of the road and pulled up some distance away, one foot on the pedal to make a hasty departure if it was necessary.

'Piss off, Billy, you dobber,' Harry responded. 'Come over here if you're game and say it again.'

'What are ya doin' over here, Billy, why aren't ya at home makin' up more lies to tell to ya dad?' Jack threw at him.

'They were not lies. My dad says you'll both be in big trouble with the coppers and will probably end up in jail for what ya tried to do.' Billy edged his bike even further away as insurance to avoid any possible attack the boys might launch at him.

'It's just your word against ours, Billy,' Jack said. 'There are two of us and only one of you so we have a better chance when it comes to makin' statements and *we'll* be tellin' the truth. Yours will be just a pack of lies.' Jack turned back to the billycart on the nature strip.
'I've got witnesses.' As soon as he said it Billy felt a hot flush of remorse colour his cheeks. His father would kill him if he knew what he had said. 'Keep this between us, William,' His father had warned. 'The element of surprise.'

'What witnesses?' Jack stood up from the billycart. 'There wasn't anyone else there.'

'Yeah ... and how can someone witness somethin' that didn't happen anyway?' Harry added.

'There was people there.' Billy was committed now. Having spilt the beans prematurely he had left himself no option but to continue.

'People? What people? We never saw anyone except your father, did we, Harry?'

'Friends of me dad were walkin' their dog by the river and saw the whole thing. You two grabbin' the bike off me and runnin' away with it even though I was pleadin' with ya not to steal me birthday present.'

Billy thought he would practice some of the lines his father had primed him with in preparation for the statement he would have to give to the police on Monday and Jack and Harry were struck dumb. They stood with slack expressions as Billy kicked his bike into action and rode off.

'See ya in jail,' He yelled with a sadistic laugh as he pedalled away.

'Geez, Harry, we're in big trouble now.'

'But he's lyin', Jack.'

'*We* know that but who's gonna believe us now that his father's lined up some friends to lie as well.'

'You're right, Jack. What're we gonna do?'

'Dunno but I'm not goin' to jail.'

'Me neither, Jack. You only get bread and water to eat in jail so I've heard.'

'Yeah and ya have to break up big rocks with sledge hammers.'

'Only one thing for it, Jack, and that's to bolt. Head off somewhere, but where?'

'I know.' An inspiration hit Jack. 'Coober Pedy. Let's run away to Coober Pedy. You heard what me dad said last night? People don't ask where you're from or what you've done out there.'

'Mmm, he did, didn't he? But how would we get there? We haven't got any money … not enough to get to Coober Pedy that's for sure and where is it anyhow, is it in the Territory?'

'Not sure, don't think so though, think it's in South Australia somewhere. We'll look it up on a map. How much money have you got, Harry?'

'Nothin' on me but I've got a few bob in me moneybox at home. Four bob or thereabouts.'

'Four Bob have ya? I've got about five or six bob saved up at home.'

'Ten bob isn't much to run away with, Jack, what can we do?'

'Don't know, Harry.' Jack shook his head despondently. 'We'll think of somethin' though ... got to.'

Chapter Three

Jack yawned and stretched. *Another day, Monday already,* he thought. It took a while for it to dawn on him that things had changed, it wasn't *just* another Monday. As the memory of the weekend started to flood back there was a vague feeling of uneasiness and Jack realised that things would never be quite the same again. He couldn't put his finger on it but knew in his inner being that life had changed for him and Harry … forever!'

'You awake, Harry?' Jack leaned over to the single bed beside him and gave Harry's inert shape a nudge.

'What?' Harry sputtered and sat bolt upright in bed. 'What? … Oh, g'day, Jack, musta been dreamin'.'

'What about?'

'Oh nothin' really. What's the time?'

'Time to get up and get ready for school.'

'School?' Harry paused and looked around him, 'Oh, yeah, it's Monday but what about our plans from last night, you know … runnin' away and all? You still game, Jack?'

'Not a matter of *game*, Harry, it's a matter of *have to*.' said Jack.

The boys dressed quickly and went to the kitchen where they could smell bread toasting.

Jack's mother had eggs cooking in a pan and was busy at the bench buttering toast. 'Morning, boys. You're up nice and early.' She looked at Harry. 'Normally I have to wake Jack up on a Monday.' She laughed and continued, 'but that's good, you boys can finish off your lunches while I make some sandwiches for the kids and get their school books ready.' She went off down the hallway calling to her younger children.

She returned to the kitchen to find Jack and Harry sitting at the table staring into space. 'What's up with you kids? You haven't even started on your sandwiches.' She sounded irritated.

'Sandwiches?' said Jack. 'Oh, sorry, mum, just tired I guess. We'll get on with them now. Harry, wanna give me a hand? Get the vegemite out of the fridge will ya, mate?'

'You OK, Jack?' Alice was concerned at his vagueness. He just didn't seem to be himself. 'Something on your mind, son?'

'Nothin', mum, I'm all right.' Jack glanced at Harry who stared at the table.

'Come on, son, you aren't telling me everything, I can see there's something heavy on your mind ... is it the bike thing?'

'Yes, mum, it is.' Jack became animated, his arms flailing the air in exasperation. 'It's that bloody Billy Munse and his lies and ...'

Alice interrupted. 'Jack! You know I won't have swearing in this house.'

'Sorry, mum, but it gets me so mad to think that that mongrel Billy can lie about me and Harry and get away with it and we could end up goin' to jail just because he lied and everyone believes him and not us.' It was a long sentence from Jack.

'Jack.' His mother reached out putting her hand on his shoulder. She wanted to hold him in a close hug but knew better than to embarrass him with Harry in the room. 'Just stick to the truth, son. The truth always wins out you know.'

Jack threw a look over the table at Harry who was still engrossed in the tabletop. Jack didn't want to alarm his mother any further by telling her that Billy Munse's dad had apparently found witnesses to say they stole the bike.

'I'm sure it will all be all right, boys; your father thinks so too, Jack. Just forget about the bike and Billy Munse and his pompous father and concentrate on your lessons. Dad will be back on Wednesday and he'll sort a few things out. Don't forget though that the constable will be around after school to talk with you so as I said before …just stick to the truth. You better go straight home after school today, Harry, so the constable can see you too.'

The hours dragged on through the morning. Neither Jack nor Harry could concentrate on any schoolwork, enduring the lessons as they thought through plans for their departure to discuss with each other at the lunchtime break.

During lunch they moved away from the main body of milling students to a remote corner of the schoolyard where they sat on the ground in the shade of a peppercorn tree to eat their sandwiches. It may have been their imagination but they were sure everybody was sniggering at them. It didn't help when a crowd of boys and girls with Billy Munse in their centre laughed and pointed at them.

'I'm gonna kill that Billy.' Jack started to stand up.

'No, Jack, not now.' Harry grabbed his shirt. 'It'd only make matters worse. We'll get him though, don't worry about that.'

'Yeah, guess you're right. We gotta concentrate on our plans. How we gonna do it? We only got ten bob between us and we'll need a lot more than that to get to Coober Pedy.'

'I looked it up in the atlas this morning, Jack; Coober Pedy, it's in South Australia … in the outback.'

'Good! They'll never find us there.'

The three o'clock bell eventually rang marking the end of the school day. Planning to meet down at the creek later in the afternoon after the policeman had been around for his statements, each boy hurried home. They were eager to avoid any contact with Billy Munse or have to field accusations from many of the other kids who took delight in stirring for any reason.

Constable Bob Peters carefully questioned the boys about the Saturday incident and wrote down their statements. As they were telling the truth their accounts of the incident didn't vary all that much from each other's and the constable knew in his heart that they were innocent but maintained an impartial attitude. When he finally closed his notebook at the Ferguson's, put it in his tunic pocket and left, Jack headed off to the creek, telling his mother that he was going to meet Harry to see what the policeman had said to him.

'Don't be late home, Jack, you know how I worry and tea will be ready soon.'

The boys sat beside a river gum and threw stones into the creek. No yabbie fishing today as they had too much to discuss and plan.

'OK!' Jack got down to business. 'We decided then? We're gonna go to Coober Pedy?'

'Nothin' else for it, Jack, but we need more money; any ideas?'

'We got ten bob between us and if we can convince our mums to give us some lunch money, say two bob, that'll be fourteen bob.'

'Not enough, Jack. That's only pennies and we need to get hold of more. A quid won't get us as far as Northam let alone Coober Pedy.' Both boys were silent, staring into the sluggish moving water at their feet.

'Jack?' Harry turned to him. 'What was the name of that horse your dad said'll win the Melbourne Cup?'

Jack pondered for a second. 'Comic Court,' he said. 'Yeah, that's it, Comic Court.'

'Let's have a bet on it then.'

'Need lots of money to bet on a horse though don't ya?'

'Nah.' Harry sounded knowledgeable. 'My dad's only havin' ten bob on Chiquita so we'll put ten bob on Comic Court. If it wins we'll have heaps of money.'

'What if it loses?' Jack threw in a negative.

'Won't make a lotta difference, Jack, we haven't got enough to run away with now so if it loses we'll just have to think of somethin' else. Worth a chance though but.'

'OK let's do it! Better get home now as we don't want anyone gettin' suspicious. See ya tomorrow and don't forget to get some lunch money from your mum.' They shook hands solemnly to seal their agreement.

Tuesday, November 7, 1950, Melbourne Cup day. The Melbourne Cup was an institution when almost the whole nation came to a standstill to listen to the race on the wireless. Workplaces downed tools, schools suspended classes and people who never bet on horses had a small wager either at courses around the country that held race meetings, with the SP off-course bookmakers or in office sweeps.

Jack met Harry as normal but instead of going to school they went down to the creek to count up their money and plan a strategy for getting a bet on Comic Court for the afternoon's race at Flemington in Melbourne.

'Got the extra money, Harry?' Jack pulled a handkerchief from his pocket and undid the knot that secured his small change. 'I told mum we needed to buy lunch as we had swimming practice at the baths.' He held up a pair of togs and a towel he took from his school bag. 'Had to bring these,' he laughed.

'Mum could only spare one and sixpence, Jack, so I got five and six so with your seven bob we got twelve and sixpence. How we gonna get a bet on, Jack? We can't go to the bookie ourselves.'

'No, we'll go down to the Exchange and try to find someone who we can trust to put it on for us.'

'Bit of a risk.' Harry was thoughtful. 'But it's the only way I suppose.'

The boys wasted time playing around the river until about ten thirty then walked down the main street and waited outside the Exchange Hotel trying not to look conspicuous. It was common knowledge that, although illegal, the SP bookie operated out of the pub on race days. Many people were going in and coming out of the main bar entrance so they knew that the bookie must be working from there.

'Gotta pick an honest lookin' fella, Harry, what about him?' Jack indicated a small man dressed in work clothes wearing a tweed cap walking toward the pub entrance.

'No he looks a bit shifty, Jack. How 'bout him?' They looked at the well-dressed man who had just parked his car and was crossing the road toward where they were standing.

'You go, Harry.' Jack held out the cash.

'No way, you do it.' Harry was nervous and looked to Jack as if he was about to turn tail and run.

'Excuse me, mister.' Jack stepped up to the man as he stepped onto the footpath. The man hesitated then stopped, looking quizzically at Jack with Harry standing behind him.

'Me dad's sick in bed and asked me if I could find someone to put a bet on the cup for him … could you help?' Jack showed the man the money in his hand.

'Did he now?' The man stared hard at Jack who shifted uneasily under his gaze. 'And what horse did he want a bet on?'

'He gave me a note.' Jack pulled a piece of crumpled paper from his pants pocket that he and Harry had composed and written at the creek that morning.

'Ten bob on Comic Court eh?' The man glanced at the note, a smile edging his mouth.

He examined the note again then looked at each of the boys in turn. Jack felt his stomach tighten as he waited expectantly.

'All right then, wait here a minute.' He took the money from Jack's hand and walked into the bar.

'Pheww.' Jack let out his breath. 'I thought he was onto us, Harry.'

The boys paced up and down outside the hotel feeling self-conscious but after about ten minutes the man emerged and walked over to them. 'Here you are, son.' He held out a betting ticket.

'Thanks, mister. Dad'll be happy about that.' Jack reached for the ticket the man held.

'Will he now?' The man glanced at Harry, then back at Jack. He held the ticket firmly as Jack took hold of it.

'Today you will learn a big lesson in life, boys.' He still held the ticket as Jack looked at Harry who again appeared like he was ready for flight. 'Betting is a mug's game, son, and that horse has no chance of winning so you lose ten hard-earned bob but that'll make you think twice about doing it again.' He let Jack take the ticket, grinned to himself and walked off to his car.

The boys crept close to the bar window to listen to the race on the wireless that was blaring inside the pub. They knew the cup was about to begin when the hubbub of voices died down, then there was a shout and they were off in the 1950 Melbourne Cup.

Soon there was enthusiastic shouting as people in the bar began to urge their horse on and the boys had some anxious moments, as they couldn't make out the caller's voice over the noise. Then they heard it …clear as a bell. 'Down the straight and it's Comic Court. Comic Court takes the lead, it's Comic Court coming to the post. Comic Court wins the Melbourne Cup.' The rest of the broadcast was drowned by shouts from within the bar.

Harry looked at Jack, a huge smile on his face. 'We've done it, Jack.' They grabbed each other by the shoulders and started to dance around in a circle oblivious now to the stares of people passing by them.

'We've done it, we've done it!' They chanted. 'We're on our way.'

While they were exuberantly leaping around, a middle-aged shabbily dressed man stepped from the bar and eyed the two youngsters. 'You two look happy.' His voice was slurred. 'Anyone'd think you'd backed the winner,' he chuckled.

'We did!' Jack replied then quickly corrected himself. 'Well … me dad did.'

'Lucky bugger!' The man stood unsteadily before them. 'I lost the lot and I'm broke, can't even buy m'self another beer.'

Jack looked at Harry who shook his head but Jack turned to the man. 'Would you like five bob, mister?'

'How would you have five bob?' His eyes had trouble focusing.

'Me dad's sick at home and another bloke put the money on Comic Court for us … er, for dad.' Jack held out the betting ticket. 'If you could collect the winnings for us …'

Harry interrupted. 'As we can't go into the bar.'

'Dad said whoever did us a favour, to give them five bob,' Jack continued.

'Well five bob's five bob, more than I got now. I'll collect it for you.' He took the ticket from Jack.

'We'll be right here, mister … waiting.' Harry tried to sound as grown up and menacing as possible.

'Don't worry! I won't run off with your dough, tempting as it is.' He gave a wry smile then walked unsteadily into the bar as Jack and Harry waited anxiously for him to return, hoping they hadn't made a mistake in their choice of courier. The man didn't notice the relief on their faces as he came out of the bar some time later and walked over to them.

'See!' He held his fist aloft with a wad of notes in it. 'I'm a lot of things but not a thief, boys. I've got your money … oh, I mean your dad's money!' He emphasised the word 'dad's'. 'Now about that commission.' He fixed them with a steely gaze. 'I reckon ten bob'd be fair.'

'His dad said five bob,' Harry quickly replied.

'Well then, I'm sure that if I took the money to his dad that he'd give me ten bob. Where do you live, son?' He turned to Jack. 'I'll come home with you to make sure your dad gets the money and you two don't spend any of it on the way.'

'No! No, mister! He's really sick and can't see anyone.' Jack was desperate now. 'What he's got is, is … ahh, *contagious,*' he added. 'You could catch it too. I'm sure he'd agree to ten bob wouldn't he, Harry?'

Harry looked crestfallen but nodded agreement.

'OK then, here you are.' The man peeled off a ten shilling note from the wad and placed the rest of the money in Jack's outstretched hand. Without another word he turned and weaved his way back inside the bar with his new found wealth.

'Gee, Jack, how much we got?'

'A fortune,' Jack laughed. 'Let's go count it, Harry.'

Down at the creek the two boys excitedly counted the money, three times, just to be certain they were right. 'Twelve pound, ten shillings plus the bit of change we had over.'

'OK. You still want to do this, Harry?' Jack looked at his friend suddenly. "You know … run away?'

Both boys stopped smiling as the significance of the moment hit them. It was now decision time. Up to this moment it had all seemed like a bit of a game but now they had the money and they glanced at the packs holding their clothes that they had sneaked out that morning and hidden by the river, the seriousness of their actions made them uneasy.

'Nothin' else we can do, Jack.'

'Guess not, Harry. We'll be OK, it's just mum and dad I'm worried about.'

'Me too, Jack. My folks are gonna to be mad as hell … and worried sick.'

'We'll send 'em a note down the track in a couple of days, Harry. Then they can stop worrying.'

They stood, picked up their bags and glanced around to make sure they hadn't left anything behind.

'Let's go then.' They shook hands to seal the deal and walked purposefully from the river toward their new life on the run from the law.

Chapter Four

The snub-nosed Commer truck laboured up the hill as the driver changed down a gear. It was cramped in the cabin with the smell of exhaust fumes that made the two boys a little queasy in the stomach.

The boys feigned sleep, not wanting to engage in too much conversation with the driver in case they gave an answer to one of his conversational questions that made him suspicious of their motives for wanting a lift to Northam.

It had been relatively easy to get the ride on the milk truck from Perth to Northam. The boys knew that the truck left each afternoon loaded with bulk milk in 20-gallon cans and crates of bottles for delivery to the dairy in Northam.

After leaving the creek they had gone to where Mr Bodini, the milk cart driver was loading up for the trip. They both figured that it would be a remote chance that their parents would check the dairy, as they wouldn't know which way they had planned to head and Mr Bodini wouldn't normally run into their parents. There was a possibility he could mention it to his friend Eric Chambers but that was a risk they would have to take. They would be far gone anyway by the time that happened ... if it did.

Jack had walked up and introduced himself. 'Mr Bodini?'

'Yes, what can I do for you?' The man had paused, a crate of milk bottles in his grip.

'My dad's name is Jack Ferguson. I think you know of him don't you, he's a friend of Eric Chambers?'

'Yeah, I know Eric well and I've met your father a couple of times.' He had then glanced at Harry. 'Who's this then?'

'Harry Turner.' Harry hadn't reached out to shake the man's hand as he was still holding the milk crate.

'My dad's a stock and station agent with Elders,' Jack had explained. 'He's up at the sale yards in Northam buying some cattle and said if we could get a lift up after school we could meet him and he'd show us around a bit and then bring us home. Any chance we could get a lift with you … dad suggested we ask?'

Bodini had thought for a second then agreed, telling them he would be leaving in about an hour and if they wanted a lift they would have to be at the depot right on time as he couldn't wait due to his timetable.

The boys had then gone down the street and bought a hot dog and some lollies for the trip to Northam.

'Maybe we should buy some new gear for the trip, Jack; we got plenty.'

'This is travellin' money, Harry,' Jack had said. 'But we have to eat. When we get an idea of how long it'll last then we'll look at some gear for us but for now let's be real careful with it. It's gotta last.'

They had eaten their hot dogs, a real treat for them, and then made their way back to the depot to make sure they didn't miss the truck and their ride to freedom.

'Right on time, boys.' Bodini had indicated the truck. 'Climb aboard and make yourselves comfortable; we'll be off in a minute or two.'

After checking the load for a final time Bodini had climbed into the driver's seat, turned the key, pressed the starter and when the motor had fired he warmed it for a couple of minutes before driving from the yard onto the road heading to Northam.

'On our way, lads!'

Both boys glanced at each other and settled back quietly in the cramped cabin.

Gus Bodini had driven this route many times alone so fortunately for Jack and Harry he didn't feel the need to talk much as he was not used to conversation as he drove. He whistled quietly to himself as the truck wound its way through Midland and slowly up through the Darling Ranges, Bodini expertly working the gears to keep the power on up the hills.

'Should make good time,' he said as Jack stirred. 'Not much traffic on the road today.'

'Why's that, Mr Bodini?'

'Cup day. Lot of people stay home or go to the pub, take the day off work.'

'Cup day?'

'Yeah, don't tell me you don't know about the Melbourne Cup. I thought everyone knew about it.' Bodini sounded incredulous.

'Oh, I know about the Cup, just didn't know it was on today that's all.' Jack nudged Harry. 'Did we, Harry?' Harry murmured and pretended he was still asleep. He didn't like the way the conversation was headed.

'Come to think of it, Jack, I'm surprised your dad is out buying today, didn't think anyone'd be doing much.'

'Who won, Mr Bodini?' Jack quickly steered the conversation away. 'The cup?'

'Comic Court. Amazing! Long shot it was, not many picked it. Beat Chiquita. Wished I'd put me money on it, paid a good dividend.'

'Country looks pretty dry up this way.' Jack changed the subject completely, his mouth as dry with nervousness as the land looked.

'Hmm, could do with some rain.' Bodini glanced at the brown paddocks as they slipped by the truck window. 'You boys seen the swans up in Northam?'

'Seen plenty of swans haven't we, Harry?' Jack nudged Harry more firmly in the ribs needing some support in the conversation.

'Plenty of swans, yeah,' Harry mumbled.

'These are white swans, have you seen white swans?'

'White swans! Come on Mr Bodini, you're pullin' our legs.'

'No I'm not,' he laughed. 'White swans on the Avon River. You can feed 'em if you've got some bread, very tame they are. You can almost pat 'em but sometimes you've got to be careful 'cause some of them get a bit nasty. You could maybe see 'em while you wait for your dad to finish his business at the saleyards.'

'That sounds like a good idea, we'll tell him first though.' Harry at last joined the conversation. 'Don't want your dad worrying that we didn't get to Northam, Jack, eh?'

'I stop out of town a bit, boys. If you hang on I can maybe find someone heading into town and they could drop you off at the saleyards.' Bodini liked the boys and thought he would help them get to Jack's father without having to waste time walking the rest of the way.

'That's OK, Mr Bodini.' Jack was concerned. 'We can walk, be good for us and you've done enough already.'

'No trouble really but if you want to walk then it won't take you too long. Been here before … to Northam?'

'Only once, drove through it with dad.'

'Well if you head down this street …' Bodini braked the truck to a stop outside the dairy depot, pointing through the windscreen. 'Three streets down you turn right and go down a ways and you'll see the saleyards.'

'Thanks, Mr Bodini, we really appreciate the lift.'

'Yeah, thanks a lot it's been great.' Harry climbed from the cab followed quickly by Jack.

'Have a good day, boys and don't forget to have a look at those swans if you get time. Say hello to your dad for me, Jack.' He put the truck in motion and waved as he entered the depot yard.

Bodini thought to himself what well-mannered kids they were. Not for one minute did he suspect that they were lying about meeting Jack Ferguson at the saleyards. He sounded the truck's horn in farewell to the boys as he watched them walk down the road, bags slung over their shoulders.

'Stage one, Harry, we made it to Northam.'

'Where to now, Jack?'

'Let's find the railway station. We can buy two tickets to Kalgoorlie.'

Their tickets purchased on the 'Kalgoorlie Miner', an overnight steam train that ran from Perth to Kalgoorlie, they checked the departure time with the stationmaster then stowed the tickets safely in their bags.

'We gotta bit of time, Harry, let's see if those white swans are real or not.'

Finding a bakery they bought a small loaf of bread and two large poppy seed rolls then, passing a fish and chip shop, purchased sixpence worth of chips that the shop assistant, a pretty dark haired girl with vibrant green eyes, wrapped in newspaper.

Down at the river they saw that indeed Mr Bodini was right, there *were* white swans. The boys had never seen them before and commented that they seemed more graceful than the black ones. They broke off pieces of bread and threw it out for the swans and laughed as a number of black ducks darted in to get their share, flapping out of the way of the swan's savage beaks as they fought for the soggy morsels.

'Wonder if there are yabbies in here, Jack?'

'Sure to be although it's runnin' a bit faster than the creek at home.' Harry glanced at Jack when he mentioned *home*. 'Probably perch and yellowbellies, though.' Jack missed Harry's look.

'Pity we haven't got time to throw a line in, a good feed of yellowbelly'd be good, eh?'

'We didn't bring any fishing gear, Harry, and where would we cook 'em. Can't take a fish on the train,' he laughed.

Both boys then sat down on the riverbank, tore the rolls in half and crammed the hot chips into them. 'Be good if we had some butter,' Harry mumbled through a mouthful of chips and bread.

'Yeah, we always have butter with them at home.' Jack fell silent as the reality of their seeing home again for a very long time sunk in.

'Wonder if they know we've gone yet?' Harry looked gloomy as his thoughts drifted back to home and his parents.

'Don't know, Harry.' Jack stared into space, consumed by his own thoughts.

◆◆◆◆◆◆◆◆◆◆◆◆

Panic began to grip Alice Ferguson. It was almost six o'clock and young Jack wasn't home from school. She had even gone down to the river to search for them as she knew they spent every moment they could down by 'The Creek' as they called it. There was a favourite spot that the boys thought nobody knew about but of course they were wrong and Alice looked for them there. She asked some other children that were fishing if they knew Jack or Harry and if they had seen them or anyone like them down by the river.

Her searching was fruitless and her enquiries drew blank responses so she went to Jean and Claude Turner's house. She had telephoned them earlier but the boys were not there, but she thought they might have turned up by now and she might have missed them somewhere on the way.

They were not at the Turners' and Jean was beside herself with worry although Claude seemed to be less concerned. 'Boys will be boys; they'll turn up sooner or later,' he said.

The two mothers sat down at the kitchen table with a cup of tea as they wondered where their sons might be. Jean had freshly baked scones on a plate but neither woman ate anything. 'They've never done anything like this before, Jean.'

'No, they're always pretty much on time, maybe a half hour or so late but now it's almost three hours and still no sign of them.'

'I bet it's got something to do with that Billy Munse and the bike.' Alice was angry as well as concerned. 'Perhaps we should telephone them, Claude ... the Munse's, they might know.'

'They wouldn't be over there, Alice, I can assure you but I'll give a call anyhow just to put your mind at rest. They're up to something but I can't guess what it might be. Did you call the school?' he asked.

'It was too late by the time I realised they weren't home.' Alice stood up from the table and began to pace around the kitchen. 'If only Jack was here, he'd be able to help I'm sure. Not that you aren't a help, Claude.' She smiled at him. 'Having Jack home would make me feel a lot better though.' She looked at the clock hanging above the stove. 'I have to get back to the other children, Jean.' She walked to the back door. 'Keep in touch and let me know if anything happens. I'll call you if they turn up at our place.'

'I'll drive you home, Alice,' Claude offered but she declined saying that walking might give her a better chance of seeing the boys. There was no sign of them on the streets however and they weren't at her home when she got there so she busied herself getting tea for the other children.

The telephone rang. Alice rushed to answer it. 'Hello, yes?'

'Alice, it's Claude. Do you know if any of young Jack's clothes are missing? We've just discovered that Harry seems to have packed a bag of stuff as a lot of his gear is gone. Jean's awfully upset.'

'Hold on, Claude.' Alice put the telephone receiver down and rushed to Jack's bedroom and threw open his cupboard. A cursory glance revealed that most of his 'non-school' clothes were missing. The boots that his father had bought him to wear when he sometimes helped out at the saleyards were also missing from the bottom of the wardrobe.

'You still there, Claude?' She picked the telephone up. 'Yes some of his clothes *are* missing; what does all this mean?'

'Not sure at this point, Alice, but don't worry over much until we find out. Jean and I are going to get the kids and come over to you for a while as Jack's away and you have the other children to consider. Jean can give you a hand to get them to bed, and then we'll get *our* mob settled.'

A short time later Alice heard Claude's car pull into the driveway and she welcomed their company. 'Did you call the Munse's, Claude, any news there?'

'I spoke to Munse Senior, he wasn't too chatty but said he'd ask Billy if he knew anything. I told him that it seemed the boys might have taken off somewhere.' Claude didn't tell Alice or Jean that William Munse had added that the fact that they had run off went a long way toward proving their guilt.

'I'll call the Elders manager at his home, Alice, and find out if he can get in touch with Jack, get a message to him to call you, eh?'

'Thanks, Claude, that would be good. I'm a little confused right now, not handling things too well.' She burst into sobs. 'Where could they possibly be, Jean? They're so young and never been away before except for the odd school camp.'

Jean took her in her arms and began to cry too. Claude, embarrassed, hurriedly left the room to find the telephone and call Peter Forbes, the Elders manager.

The shrill whistle of the steam engine at one of the level crossings where the line crossed the road on the way into Northam jolted the boys back to reality. 'The train, Harry. We gotta run, don't want to miss it.'

They grabbed their bags, threw the last of the bread into the water and ran up from the river toward the railway station, running panting onto the platform as the train pulled to a stop with a screech of metal brakes on steel wheels. The platform, deserted earlier when they had purchased their tickets, was now bustling with passengers as people said farewell to friends and family. The display of families hugging and shaking hands made the boys even more conscious of what they were about to do.

Harry looked about him and there was sadness in his eyes and his shoulders drooped.

'You OK, Harry?'

'Guess so, just a bit homesick I suppose, Jack.'

Jack was about to reply when the conductor blew a shrill whistle. 'AAALL AAABOOOAARD,' he yelled.

'Well, Harry …this is it, mate. We don't have to get on you know, there's still time to change our minds. If we get on we'll be in Kalgoorlie in the morning and even further away from home.' Jack looked at his friend who was fighting back tears and felt a lump begin to choke in his own throat. 'Do you want to go back home, Harry?' His voice was croaky when he asked the question.

Harry looked him in the eye and straightened his shoulders as the train whistle blew, signalling its departure. 'Can't ever go home, Jack, not ever, you know that?' There was a catch in his voice. 'There's no turnin' back.'

'You're right, Harry, there *is* no turnin' back so let's make a pact never to get homesick again.' They shook hands solemnly and leaped onto the train.

Chapter Five

It was six o'clock on Wednesday morning. Jack Ferguson had driven through the night after getting a message from his manager and telephoning Alice to be told the news that Jack and Harry were missing.

He held his wife gently, caressing her hair as she sobbed against his chest.

'There, there, Alice, settle down, dear. I'm here now and we'll find the little buggers. Can't believe they'd do this, so there must be a very good reason and a simple explanation. They can't have gone too far as they haven't got any money, so they'll be in the city somewhere with one of their mates, no doubt.' Jack wasn't to know that some five hours earlier, as he was driving through the night and had stopped at a level crossing in Merredin to wait for the 'Kalgoorlie Miner' to pass, that his son and Harry were fast asleep in their carriage, just feet from the bonnet of his car.

♦ ♦ ♦ ♦ ♦ ♦ ♦ ♦ ♦ ♦ ♦

As the train grunted and wheezed through the Avon Valley, the boys watched the sun set, then had tea in the dining car. They had both selected roast beef and vegetables that were served with rich dark gravy followed by apple pie and icecream washed down by a large glass of lemonade.

'This is the life, Harry, eh?' They had returned to their compartment in the second class carriage toward the rear of the train and Jack stretched out on the comfortably upholstered bench seat.

'Yep! Really livin', Jack.' Harry sat opposite him. Both had window seats as the train wasn't carrying many passengers that day and they had the compartment to themselves. They were pleased at this stroke of luck as they didn't have to talk to anyone or explain why they were on a train travelling to Kalgoorlie alone without adult company.

'We'll each of us write a note to our parents from Kal, Harry, don't ya think? Let 'em know we're all right.'

'Good idea. That'll stop 'em worryin' but we won't tell 'em where we're headed but.'

'No way! We'll just say we're off to make our fortunes.' Jack laughed and Harry joined in.

Much brighter in spirits now as the journey on the train had gotten off to such a good start, they were not to know that the luxury of the night on the train was something they should have savoured more. There were many nights to come when they would wish for the comfort and security of the rocking train.

With the excitement of the day, thoughts of what lay ahead and full bellies, they were soon fast asleep serenaded by the 'clackety clack, clackety clack' of the wheels as the 'Miner' steamed on into the night toward Kalgoorlie and adventure.

♦ ♦ ♦ ♦ ♦ ♦ ♦ ♦ ♦ ♦ ♦

The train hissed to a wheezing stop and the screech of brakes woke Jack. 'Harry?' He gave the sleeping form a nudge. 'Wake up, Harry, we've stopped somewhere.' He stared out of the window trying to see where they were.

Harry was quickly awake and at his side. They depressed the metal catch at each side of the window and pushed it up to open it. Harry put his head out and could read the sign on the station building. 'Some place called Southern Cross.'

Just then he saw a figure amble toward their carriage door. 'Quick, Jack, some bloke's headin' to our carriage.' They slammed the window shut and sat hoping the man would find a different compartment. To their annoyance the door slid open and a man with a hat placed jauntily on his head and a large smile on his ruddy face stepped into the car.

'Top of the mornin' to you, lads,' He bellowed. 'Name's Patrick O'Brien but you can call me Paddy … everyone else does.' He held out his hand in greeting.

Each boy shook hands in turn hoping the man would just sit quietly and not ask any questions.

'Hello, Mr O'Brien,' Jack said

'Morning,' Harry mumbled.

'Mister? I said to call me Paddy, lads. Mister makes me sound too old. And what are your names then?'

They said their names.

'Headin' to Kalgoorlie then are ye, what's the reason for the trip then?'

'Visiting our auntie,' Jack said quick as a flash. 'We're cousins me and Harry.' He pointed to his friend

'Cousins ye are! You don't look alike but that's all right, I don't look like anyone in my family that's to be sure.' He took a flask from his coat pocket and took a long swig from it. 'Arrgh, good drop that, me lads, mother's milk it is.' He chuckled and stretched his short legs out in front of him.

The boys looked at each other and giggled. It seemed to Jack that the man who had joined them looked just like a leprechaun that he had seen a drawing of in a book at school. They both began to relax though as there was something about the little man that they liked. He was jovial and smiled a lot even though he sounded funny.

'So, Kalgoorlie is it? Been there before have ye?'

'No, our auntie's just moved up to there and our parents thought it'd be good if we would go up and give her a hand settle in.'

'Go *out*, lads, go *out*. Kalgoorlie is not *up*, it's *out*,' He laughed loudly and took another swig on the flask.

'That's a funny lookin' bottle, mister … sorry, I mean, Paddy.' Harry pointed to the flask. 'What's in it … tea?'

'Tea!' Paddy roared with laughter. 'It's whisky, lads, but not just *any* whisky.' He looked suddenly serious. 'It's Irish whisky, the finest little drop of the doin's you can get, to be sure.'

There was silence for a time as Paddy seemed to reflect on the merits of fine Irish whisky.

'You goin' to Kalgoorlie too, Paddy?' It seemed strange to Jack to address an adult by his Christian name.

'That I am, that I am.' The boys thought it funny that Paddy always seemed to say things twice.

'You boys ever seen a game of *two-up*?' Paddy said suddenly

'Two- up? No, what's that?' Harry asked. 'Is it a type of footy?'

'Football? Football?' Paddy roared again. 'No, me lads, it's a bettin' game it is. You take two pennies and place 'em on a piece of wood called a kip.' Paddy took another swig from the flask then looked sadly into the neck, shaking his head before placing the cap back on it and continuing with his explanation. 'The pennies must be placed on the kip tails up and then you spin them in the air and if they lands heads up like you called you win but if they come down as they went up, that's tails up, you lose. Simple it is, but a grand game, a grand game.'

'Do you win much if they come, what is it … heads up?' Jack asked.

'Oh, to be sure you do, lads.' Paddy shook the flask near his ear.

'I'd like to play a game like that,' Harry said.

'Me too.' Jack sat forward eagerly in his seat.

'Aahh, boys, it's for adults it is, not for lads and you need to have money to play two-up.' Paddy looked wistfully out of the window at the passing bush.

'We got money, Paddy,' Harry said.

Jack looked sharply at Harry. 'Only two pounds.'

'Two quid have ye, lads?' Paddy looked thoughtful then a smile spread across his impish features. 'Tell you what, me lads, if you want to trust me with yer two quid I could take you to see a two-up game. You'd have to hide in the bush but it'd be a grand experience for ye both. And we, er … you, could make a quid or two as well if I won. But you'd have to be aware that ye can sometimes lose. You the types of lads that can take that sort of chance?' He gazed steadily at them.

They looked at each other, knowing they had only yesterday taken a big chance with their money by having a bet on the Melbourne Cup.

'I think we are, Paddy, don't ya reckon, Harry?'

'No doubt about it, Jack.'

'Well, that's grand then. Just wanted to make sure you were serious, lads, 'cause let me tell ye, Paddy O'Brien never loses at two-up, Paddy O'Brien only ever wins.' He winked at the boys and took a final swig at the flask holding it high to drain the last drop from it. 'It's a deal then, is it?' He was suddenly serious. 'You stand me the two quid and when I win you get your two quid back and we share the winnin's, that a fair deal, lads?'

'Seems fair,' Jack answered not sure if they should be agreeing to any new gambling game with this stranger.

'Let's shake on it then, lads, and then I'll have a little snooze to prepare me mind for the game. Have to be clear headed ya know and that's for sure. Don't be makin' a lot of noise now.'

They shook hands with the little man who then sat back on the seat and was instantly asleep, snoring loudly over the sound of the train.

'Jack, look at that.' Harry pointed excitedly out of the window at a big mob of kangaroos that bounded away from the passing train. 'Gee, there must be hundreds, Jack.'

The train sped steadily on through a changing landscape, mostly flat but with varying vegetation. There were thickly treed areas giving way to grassed plains dotted with spinifex. Emus were also plentiful and at one stage Jack pointed a wombat out, scurrying from the track. Soon there were low hills with rocky outcrops standing above the dense bush.

A wedge tail eagle flew from the sky into their view from the carriage window. 'Look, Jack, he's divin' on somethin'.' The eagle descended like a bullet from the sky and just when it seemed it would crash headlong into the ground it pulled back and with legs stretched, cleanly picked a rabbit from beside a grasstree. Flapping its great powerful wings the huge bird returned to the sky, rabbit securely held in its talons.

'Wow! Jack, did you see that?'

'Sure did. Hey we're comin' into a town, Harry, wonder what it is?'

'I think it must be Coolgardie, Jack.'

'What's all the noise about?' Paddy O'Brien snuffled and rubbed his eyes. 'Oh, looks like Coolgardie it is.'

'Coolgardie,' whispered Jack reverently. 'One of Australia's wealthiest gold mining towns once.'

'Certainly was, and still plenty to be found.' Paddy had now stirred and was sitting up straight in his seat looking from the window. 'See that tree over there? He pointed. 'Ernest Giles, the great explorer once camped under that tree and in the mornin' they found him dead from pneumonia. I think he was one of Australia's finest explorers. You must have learned of him in school.'

'What? Er … not sure, Paddy.' Jack was too excited looking at the gold mine headworks that sped past their view from the window to think about school or explorers or anything.

Paddy looked at them and thought about when he was their age and new things fascinated him as they were discovered. He wondered about these two boys and if this trip might not instil wanderlust into them like travel at an early age had done to him so many years ago. *Not much new now,* Paddy thought wryly. *Next great adventure is meetin' me maker.'*

'We'll be in Kalgoorlie soon, lads; you enjoy the trip?' he said aloud.

'Yeah.' They both replied breathlessly. 'Seen kangaroos and emus.'

'And a wombat,' threw in Harry. 'And what about that eagle, Jack?'

'Haven't you lads ever seen yer own wildlife before?'

'Only seen 'em in the zoo, Paddy, not a lot of wild kangaroos or emus around Perth.'

'Zoo, eh?' Paddy said, a tinge of sadness in his tone. 'Shouldn't be no such things as zoos, lads. Poor bloody animals and birds and things locked up in cages. Just like they were in jail ya know. Did nothin' wrong those animals, lads, so why should they be locked away when they didn't do anythin' wrong?'

The boys looked uneasily at each other.

'I suppose people got to see what they look like and all but to me it's a shame it is to see those creatures caged up when they should be free to roam about the land. All animals, and men, should be free and not locked away somewhere.' It was quite a speech for Paddy and the boys saw a seriousness to him they had not seen before. It was a sensitive side that Paddy kept well hidden behind his jokes and jovial smile.

The train eventually steamed to a stop at the Kalgoorlie station and passengers disembarked to be met by family or friends on the platform. Most lugged heavy cases with them but Jack and Harry were travelling light with only a bag each. Paddy had a small sugar bag tied with a rope that he put over his shoulder. The unlikely trio left the station together and stepped into the searing heat of a Kalgoorlie summer day.

'Now, me lads.' Paddy stood looking thoughtfully at one of the many hotels that serviced the thirsty mining town. 'What are ye plans now, goin' off to see your Aunt I suppose?'

'Er ... that's right, Paddy.' Jack had almost forgotten the story he had told.

'Where's she live then?'

'Oh, don't worry about that, Harry's got her address on a note in his bag and there are directions on how to get there. Me dad sort of drew a map.' Jack didn't like this subterfuge but they had to keep their secret or be discovered and maybe turned in to the police. He shuddered at the thought that like the animals they could be locked away behind a cage and never get to be *free* like Paddy had said.

'Well, me lads, about the game?' He lowered his voice and looked suspiciously around him. 'Can't let on about it now you know, it's illegal and the police crack down on it now and then. Bloody spoil sports they are, can't be lettin' a few blokes have a bit of fun and win a few quid. It's a shame it is, a shame.'

'Yes, what about it?' Jack also whispered as he looked at the people passing them on the street.

'It'll be on this evenin' but I have to find out where. Now can you meet me back here later in the afternoon?'

'Suppose we can.'

'All right then, lads, we'll be winnin' some money tonight I can feel it in me bones I can, we'll be rollin' in it.' He appeared excited at the prospect and it was catching. Soon both boys were excited and looking forward to the evening with the chance to increase their kitty.

'Now, lads.' Paddy was suddenly serious again 'Would you be standin' me a small advance on the winnin's'? Just ten bob so I can get me'self a little drink and talk to some old friends to find out where the game is at. It has to be moved regular like so the coppers don't get wind of it.' He licked his lips in anticipation.

Harry looked at Jack and they didn't answer Paddy.

'I know what you're thinkin,' lads, that I'll take yer ten bob and disappear. I'd think the same, lads, if it weren't me that was involved. You can trust me, lads. You meet me back here on this street corner at five thirty this evenin' and your old friend'll be here, mark my words or me name's not Paddy O'Brien.'

The last phrase made the boys even jitterier. The thought that his name might *not* be Paddy O'Brien went through their minds.

'Don't you trust me, lads?' Paddy stood with a hurt expression on his face.

'Yeah, I suppose so.' Jack was hesitant but took ten shillings from his pocket and handed it to Paddy, still unsure if he would ever see it again.

'You won't be regrettin' it, lads, not at all, not at all. See you back here at half past five then.' Paddy hurried across the street to the hotel and the two boys walked away to fill in time and explore Kalgoorlie.

Chapter Six

They looked at the huge clock in the tower on Hannan Street and saw it was well after five o'clock. They hurried back toward the agreed meeting place wondering if Paddy would be there or if they would have to look for him somewhere and try and get their ten bob back. Not that it was likely because they knew Paddy would have well spent it by now on 'the doins.'

Rounding a corner of the street they were pleasantly surprised to see the small figure of Paddy O'Brien, hat set at a jaunty angle on his head, leaning on a lamppost on the corner outside the hotel.

'Paddy, Paddy,' they called excitedly as they ran to where he stood.

'Ahh, me lads; Said I wouldn't let you down now didn't I then? Let's go, it's a bit of a walk. Have you got the two quid on you?'

Paddy grunted satisfaction when they said they had the money with them.

'How's your Aunty then?' Paddy asked as he walked quickly ahead of them.

'OK,' Harry replied quietly not wanting the conversation to continue.

Paddy led them to the outskirts of town and down a lane toward a large corrugated iron machinery shed surrounded by trees. There were a few cars parked in the bush and saddled horses tethered nearby.

'This is the place then.' Paddy walked purposefully toward the shed only to be stopped by a man who stepped from the bushes beside the track to bar their way.

'So it's you again, Paddy, but you can't take those kids into the game; they'll have to wait here.'

'Now look.' Paddy was soulful, 'These lads are me mates, we're travellin' together. It wouldn't be right to be leavin' 'em standin' out here in the paddock now would it? They don't plan to come in they'll just wait outside for me. No harm in that is there?'

The man scratched his head then reluctantly agreed but said that they had better not cause any trouble. Paddy just waved his hand and shook his head to indicate that there would be no trouble at all so the man let out a low whistle as a signal. As the three of them moved on there was a replying whistle from closer to the shed.

'What's goin' on, Paddy?' The boys were mystified.

'Oh, they're the cockatoos,' Paddy responded and kept walking.

'Cockatoos?' Both boys said in unison 'What do ya mean by cockatoos?' Harry asked.

'Well, they're the lookouts. They call 'em 'cockatoos' because just like those big white parrots, that screech warnin' to their mates when danger is approachin', these blokes let the players know if there's a raid or if anyone suspicious might be comin'. That way the blokes can put the kip and the pennies away and bolt. Now you be quiet, lads.' Paddy closed the subject as they neared the big shed.

Instead of going in the main entrance he circled around the back of the building, the two boys at his heels. 'Here, lads.' He indicated a small door at the back. 'Sneak in here, but be very quiet. You should be able to hide amongst the machinery in the shadows but still see what's goin' on.'

The boys stumbled their way through the conglomeration of old farm and mining equipment that littered the shed until they were at the edge of a cleared space at the front of the building. They could see a group of men assembled in the dim light of the kerosene lanterns.

The men were standing in a circle and looked up as Paddy joined them shouldering his way to the centre. 'Head 'em up for ten bob,' Paddy called

'Show us the colour of your money, Paddy.' It was obvious that he was known to most of the men in the circle.

Paddy proudly waved the two one pound notes above his head. 'I've hit a pot of gold I have, I'm flush, lads …now head 'em up.'

'Heads are good,' called the ringmaster.

Paddy smiled broadly. 'Head 'em up again.'

'Heads are good,' called the ringmaster a second time.

The boys looked on in awe as time after time paddy called and time after time won the toss. There was a murmur from the crowd as Paddy collected his winnings at the end of the game. 'Told you I'd hit a pot of gold.' He laughed loudly, stuffed the money in his pockets and left the circle. The boys scurried out the back door of the shed to meet the Irishman who beamed at them as he came around the corner.

'Lads, we made a killin' we did. I told you Paddy doesn't lose didn't I. I just need to have the money to bet with that's all, haven't always got it though.' He pulled his now refilled flask from a pocket and took a long swig. 'I deserves a little drink I do and that's for sure now.'

'Twenty two quid plus the two pound you gave me to start with.' They had just counted the money and Paddy gave Jack the two pound notes.

'Now let's divvy up the winnin's. I'll be takin' eight quid if it's all right with you, lads, as me commission like. That'll leave you with fourteen quid between you. That fair enough?'

Paddy counted off eight pounds and handed the rest to the boys who were wide eyed with astonishment. They had never seen so much cash.

'Paddy, you're a champion.' Harry clapped the little man on the shoulder.

'Now don't go getting' mushy on me lads and let me give ya a little tip. Don't be thinkin' because this was easy that ye should start gamblin'. Will ye promise me that? He waited until they nodded in agreement. 'I needed a float and I'm sure you blokes could do with a quid and that's why I did it. I know what I'm doin', lads; if you tried it those blokes'd bleed you blind in a second. Do you understand me now?' He fixed them with a steady gaze. 'Promise me now, go on I want you to be sayin' it.'

Both boys made a promise that they wouldn't gamble and added that they would be extra careful with their money.

'OK, me lads, now, it's gettin' on and your Aunt will no doubt be wonderin' where ye are. I'll walk you to her place. Not good to be wamderin' the streets it is especially with money in yer pockets at this hour. Now where does she live?'

The boys stared at the ground for some minutes as Paddy stood by waiting for them to answer. 'What is it, lads, and come to think of it, how come you still got your bags with you? I would've thought you'd have been leavin' 'em at your Aunt's instead of cartin' those heavy ports all over town with you?'

'He's proved his trust,' Harry said when Jack asked a silent question with his eyes.

'What's this trust you're talkin' about? What's goin' on, lads?' Paddy stood with his hands on his hips facing the boys.

'Paddy,' Jack began shakily. 'We trust *you*, now you have to trust *us* and that what we tell you is the truth. We got no Aunt here in Kalgoorlie. Harry and I aren't even cousins.' Jack gave Paddy a brief outline of what had happened over the past few days starting with the accusation that they had stolen Billy Munse's bike.

Harry concluded by telling him that they had run away from home and were on the run now from the law. It felt good to be able to talk about it and the words tumbled from them both as they unloaded the guilt of what they had done onto their new found and unlikely friend.

'I thought it strange, lads, that you were travellin' alone but it wasn't up to me to be knowin' yer business and all, unless you wanted to tell me. Have ye anywhere to be stayin' the night then?'

The boys shook their heads. 'Righto then, come with me,' Paddy said. 'I'll get ye bedded for the night somewhere safe and we can all talk about it in the mornin'.'

'Where we goin', Paddy?' Jack asked as they headed off beside the little man.

'To a great friend of mine, a kind and godly man who'll be takin' good care of ye that's for sure. His name's Father O'Malley. He's the catholic priest here.' He pronounced it *praste*.

'But we aren't catholic, Paddy,' Jack said slowing back a pace.

'You're God's children, lads and that's all that matters. Don't be worryin none about catholic or non-catholic or whatever. If it doesn't worry you it won't be worryin' the good Father and I'm sure it won't be worryin' the Lord at all. There'll be a warm place to sleep and a good feed in the mornin' I'll be guessin'. Mrs Lacey, his housekeeper, comes in to the presbytery and cooks for Father O'Malley and any guests he has and he has some most of the time, I can tell ye.'

They arrived at a large stone building behind a tall fence. Paddy led them through the gate and up a neatly packed gravel path past some statues washed ghostly in the pale moonlight and banged loudly on the door with the brass knocker.

After some time, as the boys stood nervously on the porch and Paddy leaned on the verandah post whistling softly, the door opened and a shaft of light fell on the trio on the porch. Jack couldn't see the man who stood there clearly because the light was behind him but he was tall, slightly stooped and looked ominous in the darkness.

'Patrick? That you?' The figure spoke with a gentle warm brogue much like Paddy's 'It's good to be seeing you, Patrick, my son, and who then are the young men you have with you?' He motioned for them to come inside and Paddy introduced the boys to Father O'Malley.

Both boys were shy when confronted with the tall man. They had never been so close before to a 'praste', as Paddy called him, and certainly never spoken with one so were a little daunted by his presence. The fact that he was dressed from his neck to his ankles in a long black robe which was buttoned down the front, made him seem sort of sinister. When he spoke, though, it was gentle and reassuring.

'You must have a story as to why you brought them here, Patrick, but it's getting late and the boys must be tired and probably hungry as well?' He looked at the boys and raised his eyebrows questioningly.

They nodded tentatively, so the priest led the trio into a large, stone-floored kitchen where he took bread from the larder and a plate of corned beef from the fridge.

'You make yourselves some tea and I'll go and see that there are a couple of beds for you. You know your room, Patrick, it's always made up in case you call in, you old scoundrel.' The priest smiled warmly at Paddy as he left the room.

They ate hungrily and drank cordial that Paddy poured from a large jug he took from the fridge. 'I told ya, lads, didn't I? No need to be worryin', and we'll sort a few things out for you in the mornin.'

The priest returned as they were finishing washing the plates and led the two boys down a long timber-floored corridor to a small room that was sparsely furnished with two single beds and a wooden dressing table with a small mirror attached.

The only other thing in the room was a large wooden cross on the wall with a figure of Jesus Christ hanging forlornly from it and, while this was an alien thing to the boys, it was somehow strangely comforting. The priest bid them goodnight and closed the door. They climbed wearily into bed and, with their money tucked safely under Jack's pillow, fell into a deep, dreamless sleep.

◆◆◆◆◆◆◆◆◆◆◆◆

The morning sun filtered through the thin curtain into the room where the boys slept. After a while Harry stirred and called softly to Jack, 'You awake yet?'

'Yeah, I'm almost awake. Gee, that was a good night's sleep; we didn't sleep much on the train and yesterday was pretty exciting.' Jack stretched and pulled back the covers; noticing two towels on the chair with a cake of soap.

There was a note on the dressing table. It read 'Didn't want to wake you. The bathroom is down the hall to the right and breakfast will be ready after you have bathed. You know where the kitchen is.' It was signed 'Mrs Lacey.'

'Must be the housekeeper.' Harry concluded as Jack read the note aloud. 'This is incredible, Jack; we've been pretty lucky so far, eh? Just hope it keeps up.'

Breakfast was set out on a large scrubbed pine table in the kitchen when the boys entered. There was toast with jam and corn flakes and a large jug of milk covered with a net cloth with little beads around the edge. Eggs were sizzling in a pan on the large Metters wood stove set in the brick wall beside what appeared to be an oven for baking bread.

Mrs Lacey was a rotund lady dressed in a short-sleeved cotton frock and large blue apron. Her greying hair was tied in a bun and she wore tiny silver spectacles perched at the end of her nose so that she constantly held her head down to peer over the top of them. She bade the boys 'good morning' and nodded when they thanked her for the towels and soap. Other than that, she didn't talk and busied herself with duties in the kitchen.

When they had finished eating she removed her apron. 'Now boys, Father would like to see you so I'll take you to him.' She led them from the presbytery across the lawn to an office at the side of the large church.

Father O'Malley was seated behind a well-polished wooden desk. There were tall shelves lining the walls filled with many bound books and journals. The place smelled pleasantly of pipe tobacco, leather furniture and Old Spice aftershave.

'Come in, boys, come in.' He waved them to two chairs. 'Take a seat. Did you sleep well? How was breakfast?' He smiled warmly at them.

'Fine, thank you, sir,' Jack answered.

'Fine, thanks,' added Harry. Neither boy knew how to correctly address this kindly but unfamiliar man seated before them so figured that 'sir' would fit the bill.

'Patrick said to say goodbye. He said he would see you sometime along the track.'

'Paddy's gone! Where?' Both boys looked nervously at each other then back at the seated priest.

'Patrick, or Paddy as you know him, comes and goes.' The priest waved his hand vaguely in the direction of the town. 'He's an itinerant man with a heart of gold but too much of a liking for the 'doins' I'm afraid … I've known him for many years. He calls in every now and then and I keep a room for him but he only stays overnight and is gone the next morning. We usually sit up for some time talking into the night as we did last night. Now tell me, boys, can I help you in anyway? Patrick tells me you are running away from home for some good reason but left it for you to tell me if you want to.' He leaned back in his chair, filled his pipe and patiently lit it with a match as he waited for them to talk.

The boys thought if the priest was friend of Paddy's and had been so kind to them then they should trust him and come clean. Jack, however, prefaced their tale with the remark that they wouldn't be going home no matter what.

The priest listened intently to their story and when they had finished he sat thoughtfully for some time, drumming his long fingers on the desk, the now cold pipe still in his mouth.

'Hmm.' He leaned forward in his chair. 'I understand your dilemma. I believe that you didn't steal the bike but what about your parents, they must be worried sick? Let me call them to let them know you're OK. Better still, boys, I know the police sergeant well here in town and I'm sure I could persuade him to help you out.'

'No!' Jack started from his chair. 'We thought we could trust you but now you're gonna dob us in to the coppers and we'll go to jail.'

'Sit down, son, I'm not about to 'dob' you in at all; I'm just concerned for your welfare and about both your parents.' He nodded to include Harry. 'They must be going through a very tough time not knowing where you are, or if you are OK or not. Do you think that's fair?'

'No, sir,' Harry agreed. 'Will you help us write notes then and you can post them, one to each of our parents, that way they'll know we're all right. We really want to continue on our journey, sir.'

'We've made up our minds,' Jack said with finality, holding the priest's eyes with a firm look. 'We're not goin' home.'

'You are a determined couple of young men I can see that. I believe what you've told me and I'm sure you will do what's right.' He thought again for some time, looking at the ceiling before he spoke.

'Tell you what I'll do. You write notes to your parents and let me read them before you seal them up, then I'll post them to make sure they've gone. Then, and this goes against my better judgment, and may the Good Lord forgive me if I'm making a mistake, but I'm not going to just let you head off into the distance alone with no guidance.'

The boys thought the priest was again about to betray them in some way but relaxed when he continued, 'I'm going to Mt Margaret in the morning, taking a young lad about your age back to his family; he's been here recuperating from a broken leg. You can come with me if you like. That way you can get a taste for the outback without being abandoned to it and if you want to return with me to Kalgoorlie you can.'

'That's more than fair, sir,' Jack said.

'Thank you, sir,' Harry smiled. 'Where's Mt Margaret?'

'A fair drive. It's between Leonora and Laverton, north of here.' He produced a lined pad from a drawer. 'Here's something to write on, and there are pens and ink on the desk. You write while I go and arrange a couple of things for tomorrow.' The priest went to leave the room but paused at the door, his long black robe rippling in the wind. 'There's just one thing I ask, please stop calling me 'sir', it sounds so formal.'

'What do we call you then?'

'Just plain, *Father*. He closed the door.

The boys sat in silence in the office and then began composing notes to their parents. 'Looks like another lucky break has happened, Harry, we're now off to Mt Margaret. I wonder what it's like?'

'Darned if I know, Jack, it sounds pretty good but eh? Mt Margaret,' Harry said almost reverently.

Both boys edged closer to the desk and began to write their letters home.

Chapter Seven

It was Wednesday mid-morning at the Fergusons. Jack had been home for some hours, having driven through the night, and the Turners, Claude and Jean, had come around to be with them to plan the next course of action in finding their two sons. Eric, Jack's best mate, had also turned up to see if he could help in any way and to just be there for them in this crisis time. They were all seated around the kitchen table, a large pot of tea brewing in the centre. Eric pulled a tobacco pouch from his pocket and began to roll a cigarette.

'Well.' Jack refilled his cup from the pot, 'I've been in touch with the school and the boys wagged lessons on Tuesday, so they must have planned all this over the weekend while they were here and on Monday. I'm sorry, Claude, that Jack has got young Harry involved in this.'

'Not just your boy's fault, Jack; they're both in this together. Been like it since they were little tackers, in everything together.'

The two mothers were visibly upset, their eyes red and swollen from a night filled with tears and lack of sleep.

'Have you reported to the police that the boys are missing?' Eric puffed thoughtfully on his cigarette, smoke swirling lazily around his head. 'Wouldn't be a bad idea, Jack … they could put a bulletin out for them.'

'Not yet, Eric. I thought we'd wait for bit before involving the police.' He looked at Claude who nodded in agreement. 'There's a good chance they'll turn up today when they get hungry enough and run out of money.'

'Got much with them, Jack?' Eric asked.

'Only a few bob.' Jean joined in the discussion. 'They both conned us out of a couple of shillings didn't they, Alice? They told us they had to buy lunch yesterday from the tuckshop and Jack said he had swimming lessons. Their money boxes are empty too but there wasn't much in them so at most they would only have a bit over ten shillings between them, if that.'

'Won't last them long, that's for sure.' Claude took a sip from his cup. 'They'll spend up big on lollies and soft drink, probably go to the pictures and be back for tea tonight I'd wager.' He smiled encouragingly at the women.

'Yes, there's no sense in getting all het up about it, I suppose.' Alice took a deep breath and forced a wan smile. 'They're sensible kids and can look after themselves and our worrying won't bring them home any quicker.'

'That's better, Alice.' Jack reached out and patted her hand. 'I'll go over to the Munse's though later this afternoon when he's home from work, to see if they can throw any light on what's happened. You want to come with me, Claude?'

'Try keeping me away. What say we have another drive around, Jack; you never know, we could get lucky? We'll go down to the shops and check out the milk bars and maybe the picture theatre.' He got to his feet.

'I've got a better idea.' Jack looked determined. 'While we're out let's go to Munse's office and talk to him there.'

'What if he won't see you, dear?' Alice was concerned.

'He'll see us.' Jack said with authority.

'Don't you two go getting into trouble there; you know what that Munse is like. Keep your fists to yourselves, it'll only make matters worse,' Jean pleaded.

'We'll be right.' Jack took his hat from the hallstand and he and Claude left the house.

Eric left shortly after them saying he would take a drive around the shops down the main street as well, on the off chance that he might spot them. 'I'll call you later, girls.'

Eric was a plumber, operating his own business, so could spare some time to help search. Claude had taken a couple of days off from his work at the factory where he was foreman and Jack's boss just told him to take as much time as he needed. It made the two women feel more confident knowing that there were now three men scouring the neighbourhood and outlying areas. They were sure that the boys would be found, or come home by nightfall.

◆◆◆◆◆◆◆◆◆◆◆◆

Billy Munse was a nervous wreck at school and couldn't concentrate on any work. He was aware that the boys had not turned up at school the day before and his father had asked him, following Claude Turner's telephone call, if he knew anything about the boys running away.

It seemed that things were getting really out of hand and all he had wanted to do was make sure that his father didn't hang the bike in the shed for letting the other kids ride it. That's why he had lied in the first place, but now it seemed that he would have to own up and get a thrashing from his father, or plan something else to get him off the hook. His father was a very hard man but he didn't like lies. The fact that he arranged for some people to say they had witnessed the boys stealing the bike was based solely on the fact that he believed that Billy was telling the truth. 'It's just a precaution, William,' he had said. 'Those boys will lie like pigs in mud and you're telling me the truth aren't you?' He fixed his son with a practiced courtroom look that made Billy wince inside.

'You know I am, dad.' Billy had to look away.

'Well then ... I've arranged for those people to back up the truth of what you have said so those two can't get away with stealing, and then lying their way out of it. It's my job to see that truth and justice are carried out, William, and as I said, this is a precaution, an insurance policy if you like, to ensure that truth prevails.'

Billy couldn't quite see how what his father was setting up was any different to what he had done to avoid punishment, so he figured that maybe *he* should have an 'insurance policy' in place to confirm his previous actions. An idea began to form in Billy's mind and the more he thought about it the better he liked it.

Billy hadn't been riding his bike to school since the incident. After he had been to the police station with his father and told his version of the Saturday bike episode, his father had told him to leave it at home so as not to incite any further problems. 'You can ride it around after school, but keep it safe at home and don't go near the park, William, until those boys are charged.' There was no room for argument.

He had ridden it a couple of times but felt a bit guilty when he was on it, although he had almost convinced himself that Jack and Harry *had* stolen it. It was amazing, he thought to himself, how, after telling the same lie time after time, it gets confused with the truth until the lie almost *becomes* the truth.

The idea Billy had conceived now hatched in his mind until he thought it was the best idea he had ever had. His father had been going to work early and never got home until almost dark, so he hadn't seen the bike in some time and his mother was vague and wouldn't even know if it was in the yard or not. Billy had parked it at night in a small shed at the back of the garden as putting it in the garage wasn't an option because his father always kept it locked, carrying the key on him. 'I've got important papers stored on the shelves in there, William, archives you know, got to keep it locked … you can use the small shed.' Billy didn't know what 'archives' were, but didn't care.

At lunchtime Billy left the schoolyard and ran quickly to his home. He knew his mother would be out at the Wednesday Bridge game and his father would obviously be at work.

With great haste, as he only had an hour, he grabbed his bike from the shed, jumped on it and pedalled as fast as he could down to the river. He knew Jack and Harry's 'secret spot' and when he reached it he dragged his bike up the bank and into the bush beside the river. He stood back and surveyed the spot from the bank and, convinced that it wasn't visible, ran as fast as he could back to school, arriving just as the bell rang. The teacher looked quizzically at him as Billy was puffing and sweating profusely but made no comment.

When Billy arrived home from school his mother was arranging flowers in a tall glass vase she always kept on the hallstand with fresh flowers from the garden. She greeted him and asked if he wanted something to eat. She was a little surprised when he declined but was soon engrossed again in the blooms, standing back to admire her work.

'Mum, mum!' Billy's voice, edged with panic, broke into her thoughts.

'Whatever is it, William?' She called out as she went quickly to the back yard to meet her son running up the path. 'Mum, mum … me bike's gone!'

'What! It can't be, where did you have it?'

'In the small shed at the back.' Billy was telling the truth at this point.

'Well …where is it now, William, did you ride it to school?'

'No, mum, dad said not to. I haven't ridden it for a couple of days.' He was amazed at how easily the lies flowed off his tongue. He waited for some minutes before continuing with his planned story, while his mother helped him fruitlessly search around the garden.

'Whatever will your father say, William?' Mrs Munse was concerned at her husband's reaction to this latest news. It seemed that this bike was nothing but bad luck.

Billy waited for the right time. His mother took a deep breath and looked at her son, shrugging her shoulders in an expression of hopelessness. 'Bet those kids stole it for real this time, mum,' he said.

'What kids? You don't mean that young Ferguson and his friend do you?'

'Must be. Nobody else'd steal me bike, mum, and they must have been angry when they didn't get away with it last time and came 'round here while we were out and stole it again.' He emphasised 'again'.

'But when, how? … this is awful.' His mother was flustered now so Billy pushed the advantage.

'Well, they've run away you know, never been to school for two days and Harry's father spoke with dad yesterday on the phone to find out if I knew where they might be or if I'd seen 'em.'

'Good Lord. We better call your father and let him know. He's going to be very angry.'

'But it's not my fault, mum … honest,' Billy said with anguish in his tone. 'I didn't know, I had it safe in the shed. They must have jumped the fence and taken it.' He was flushed from the lies, but his mother took it for concern.

'Of course it's not your fault, William. Your father will know what to do.' She hurried inside and reached for the telephone.

◆◆◆◆◆◆◆◆◆◆◆◆

William Munse didn't offer Jack or Claude a seat when they entered his office. He had initially refused to see them saying he was busy but when his secretary mentioned that they were determined to speak with him he relented, mainly out of curiosity.

'Thanks for taking time to see us.' Jack felt uncomfortable standing, his hat in his hand, before the large desk behind which William Munse sat, his face expressionless.

Munse didn't speak, so Claude explained the reason they had come to see him. He went on to tell Munse that they were concerned that the boys had run away and that it must have something to do with being accused of stealing the bike. Had he spoken with his son, he asked, and was there anything at all that Billy may have said that could help them?.

The telephone rang. Munse ignored it at first but when it persisted he picked it up. 'Yes,' he said irritably into the mouthpiece.

Jack and Claude stood, ill at ease on the plush carpet, their eyes roving across the panelled walls and to the view of the Swan River from the large picture window behind Munse's desk. They didn't notice Munse smile as he listened intently to the caller.

'Very interesting, my dear, I'll attend to it immediately.' Munse put the telephone receiver back on its cradle and slowly stood to his feet, the smile on his face even wider.

'I think it's time we all went to the police station.' He was enjoying this. 'It seems your boys have not *run away* but have *ridden away*. My William's bike has disappeared from our house and it's my conclusion that your boys have taken it to make their escape. There is probably some other unfortunate young victim around town who has also had his bike stolen because they both couldn't travel on *one* could they?' He glared at the two men in his office who were dumbfounded by this latest news and further accusation. 'If you would be so kind now as to leave my office, I will meet you at the station, when I make additional charges.'

◆◆◆◆◆◆◆◆◆◆◆◆

Constable Bob Peters took notes as Munse reported the bike missing but didn't record that it was Munse's belief that the boys had taken it to use as transport to leave town and avoid the initial charge of stealing. His face was impassive as he wrote while he thought to himself that there was something very wrong here but his position wouldn't allow him to comment.

When Jack and Claude entered the station, Munse ignored their presence and strode from the building.

'Is it true that your boys are missing?' The policeman looked up from his notes.

'Why didn't you report this to me before?' The policeman asked when they nodded. 'They now have a head start and it'll be more difficult to track their whereabouts.'

A search of the immediate area was organised, the park and creek being the first locality concentrated on as everyone knew the two boys were often there fishing and playing by the river. After a short time one of the officers located the blue Malvern Star bicycle in the bushes beside the river.

◆◆◆◆◆◆◆◆◆◆◆◆

'This throws a very different aspect on the situation.' The sergeant in charge of the station was speaking to both the boys' parents in one of the interview rooms. Alice and Jean were crying softly and their husbands sat beside them stony-faced with shock and disbelief.

'There's no point in being overly concerned.' The sergeant paused, taking a deep breath. 'But we are going to drag the waterhole in the river near the bend where the bike was found.' He held up his hand as Jean and Alice gasped 'It's only a precaution, but we have to eliminate all possibilities.'

Chapter Eight

Alice was at the Turner house. Alice's sister had come to collect the younger children and Jean's parents had taken her children back to their house. Both fathers were down at the river where the police were putting a boat in the water and officers clad in overalls were arranging ropes with grappling hooks. A crowd had begun to gather to watch the activities but the police had dispersed them and roped the area off. There were radio news people and newspaper journalists there, cameras flashing. It seemed bizarre to Jack and Claude who didn't think for one minute that the boys would have either taken the bike or gone swimming in the river. Fortunately they had been able to convince their wives of these facts, but it was unnerving for them to watch the grim event taking place as the men in the boat threw grappling hooks into the river searching for possible bodies.

♦ ♦ ♦ ♦ ♦ ♦ ♦ ♦ ♦ ♦ ♦ ♦

Gus Boldini parked the milk truck in the dairy yard, locked it and went into the small office at the front of the building to complete his paperwork. He had just returned from his regular run to Northam and was looking forward to getting home but had to leave the delivery dockets on the bookkeeper's desk so the invoices could be attended to early the next morning before he came on duty again.

He switched the radio on, tuned the dial to the ABC and whistled quietly along with the orchestra playing. He glanced at the clock on the wall and saw that that it was almost seven o'clock. The familiar news theme filled the office as Boldini worked and he figured he should be finished the end of the news bulletin.

He didn't pay a lot of attention to the items but his ears caught the mention of 'Ashmorton River' so he turned the volume up to concentrate more closely on the broadcaster's deeply modulated voice.

> 'Police this afternoon dragged a section of the Ashmorton River following the disappearance of two teenage schoolboys and the discovery of an abandoned bicycle beside the river. The boys, missing since Tuesday, have not been seen since they left for school that morning and there are grave concerns for their whereabouts. The boy's parents declined to be interviewed but a police spokesman said …'

Gus Boldini didn't wait for the rest of the broadcast. It hit him like a ton of bricks that the two missing boys must have been Jack Ferguson and Harry Turner that he had driven to Northam in his truck on Tuesday afternoon. It added up now, two teenage boys, missing since Tuesday … He rushed from the office, not bothering to switch off the wireless, slammed the door shut behind him and ran to his car.

◆ ◆ ◆ ◆ ◆ ◆ ◆ ◆ ◆ ◆ ◆

The Turners were now at the Fergusons, relieved by the result of the police river search but confused, nonetheless. They had just heard the ABC news item and when Jack switched the wireless off they sat silently in the lounge room not knowing what else to say when there was a frantic knocking on the front door.

At first Jack didn't recognise the swarthy man standing on the porch but invited him in when he said who he was and that he had news of the boys.

They sat listening, without interruption, as Gus Boldini relayed what had happened on the Tuesday. 'I'm sorry, Jack.' He shook his head when he finished the story. 'I believed everything they said. Bloody stupid of me it was, but they were so convincing.'

'Not your fault, Gus,' Claude replied.

'Thank goodness they've come to no harm.' Alice couldn't stop sniffling but smiled through her tears.

'What do we do now?' Jean asked.

'First thing we do is let the police know that they are in Northam so they can look for them tomorrow. Who do they know up there? Alice … Claude? Any ideas?'

They shook their heads.

'I've always thought there was something fishy about this bike business. I just knew they couldn't be involved in leaving that bike down by the river. That bloody Munse kid is going to be in a lot of hot water now for sending the police on a wild goose chase.' Jack was angry, his teeth clenched.

'Forget about the Munses for now, Jack.' Claude anxiously paced the floor. 'Have to find those silly young buggers before they get into any major trouble.'

Jack telephoned the local police station and reported what Gus Boldini had told them.

'Let's all try and get a bit of sleep now, as hard as that may be,' he said when he hung up. 'You and I will drive up to Northam at first light in the morning, Claude.'

'Righto, Jack.'

'Shouldn't you go *now*, Claude?' Jean wiped her eyes with a crumpled handkerchief.

'No point,' Jack answered kindly. 'We couldn't do much at this time of night anyhow, Jean. We'll get there early in the morning and find them. Northam's not that big and someone will have seen them. With the police looking as well we'll have them back home safe and sound in no time.'

The Holden was pushed to its limits as Jack headed toward Northam in the early hours of Thursday morning. He knew he was driving fast but was experienced in travelling on the open road.

'Need to keep an eye out for roos, Jack.' Claude concentrated on the road and surrounding bush ahead of the car as dawn broke over the Avon ranges.

Arriving in Northam they drove to the police station and knocked on the door as it was well before office hours. When there was no answer the two men went to the house next door A man answered their knock with a not too pleased expression on his face. He held a mug of steaming tea in his hand. 'What can I do for you? I'm Sergeant Mitchell, the office isn't open yet. I hope this is important.'

They explained who they were and why they were in Northam and the policeman apologised for being gruff and said he had received a call from the Ashmorton station the night before. He invited them in but they decided to wait until he had breakfasted and then they went into the station when he opened up a short time later.

The policeman said he would get a couple of his men to make enquiries around the town and see what information they could turn up on the boys. 'Not too hopeful though,' He told the two men. 'We usually know when anyone strange comes into town and is seen around the streets. I'm sure if your boys had spent a couple of days here someone would have seen them by now and my blokes keep a pretty close ear to the ground. Still, we'll have a look around; what are your plans?'

'Thought we'd ask some of the shopkeepers if they might have seen them, maybe go to the school. Not sure where to start really but just couldn't sit at home and do nothing.'

Claude nodded in agreement with Jack 'You don't mind if we ask a few questions around do you?'

'Not the usual thing to do but under the circumstances I can understand your concern. The more the merrier as they say.' The sergeant picked up the telephone. 'I'll let my senior constable know and he can have a check on his way to the station. Do him good to get an early start too as I'm *already* up.' He smiled at the two men. 'We'll do our best, I'm sure something will turn up.' He began to spin the handle on the phone to reach the exchange. 'Call back here around lunchtime.'

Jack and Claude drove to the main street, parked the car and stepped onto the footpath. Shopkeepers were opening their doors, placing advertising boards on the street and sweeping paths in front of their shops, readying themselves for the day's trading.

'No point doing them all,' Jack reasoned. 'They'd only go to places that sell things like food or clothes or such. Waste of time going to all the shops.' They passed by a furniture retailer and a haberdashery store and went into a bakery enticed by the smell of freshly baked bread and pastries.

♦♦♦♦♦♦♦♦♦♦♦

Back at the station just before noon Jack and Claude excitedly told the sergeant that two boys answering their sons' descriptions had bought a loaf of bread and some rolls at a bakery on the main street and asked for directions as to where the white swans were. 'Then we went a few doors up the street and went into a fish and chip shop,' Jack explained. 'It seems the girl there remembers a couple of young boys, who she didn't know and carrying bags with them, bought sixpence worth of chips. It had to be them, eh?' Jack was animated and couldn't stand still

'It's a possibility, yes.' The sergeant was non-committal.

'We went down to the river but of course they weren't there, but at least it's a start,' Jack said hopefully. 'Those boys just love a river … don't they, Claude?'

'Trail's a bit cold, gents.' The sergeant didn't want to raise their hopes too much. 'But, yes, at least it confirms they were probably here but I wonder where they are now? Do they know anyone in the area?'

'Not that we know of.' Jack scratched his chin thoughtfully 'I know a few people here because of work but I'm sure the boys know no one here though, do they, Claude?'

'We've racked our brains on that question, sergeant, no luck there. I can't imagine why they would come here to Northam, it's a mystery to us.'

A uniformed officer came to the door and motioned to the sergeant to join him out of the room. He glanced at Jack and Claude and the sergeant excused himself and stepped from the room, closing the door behind him.

'Wonder what that's about?' Claude queried.

'Don't know, mate, could be anything. I guess these coppers have more on their plates than just worrying about our two young runaways. Little buggers, I'll tan Jack's hide when I find him that's for sure.'

'That's what I feel like too, Jack, but quite honestly I'll be just so pleased to see them that I'll probably forget to yell at them.' He looked up as the sergeant returned with the young officer at his side.

'Well, Dave, better tell them the news then.'

'News! What news?' Concern showed clearly on the two men's faces. 'You got some news about the boys?'

'Dave here,' The sergeant indicated the constable, 'was down at the railway station checking on some vandalism there and mentioned your boys to the stationmaster. It seems two boys answering the description you gave us bought tickets on the train that left on Tuesday night bound for Kalgoorlie.'

'Kalgoorlie! What the hell would they be going to Kalgoorlie for and where did they get the money to buy tickets?' Jack was puzzled.

The young constable looked at his sergeant who nodded. 'Ahh, sir?' The young man addressed Jack. 'The stationmaster said that the boys never queried the price of the tickets and paid cash for them. He got the impression that the cost was of no concern to them and he also noticed they had a few quid on them.'

'I don't believe it, Jack.' Claude sounded troubled. 'They have money on them! Where did they get that? Why would they be heading to Kalgoorlie?'

'I'm not sure, Claude, but those Munses have something to answer to, that's for sure. Those boys are on the run for something I'm sure they didn't even do. They've obviously convinced themselves that they would go to jail over that bloody bike.'

The sergeant looked baffled so Jack explained to him and the constable what had led up to the boys' disappearance. 'I'll put a call through to the Kalgoorlie station, gents, and alert our boys there to be on the lookout. They'll turn up,' he encouraged.

'Kalgoorlie … on the train.' Claude said mainly to himself.

'Yeah and do you know what, Claude?'

'What, Jack?'

'On Tuesday night when I drove back to Perth after I got the message about the boys I stopped at Merredin at the level crossing to let a train go through. Do you know what bloody train it was?' He continued without waiting for an answer. 'The 'Kalgoorlie Miner'! I was yards from my boy and didn't know it, Claude. Just yards from them both.'

Chapter Nine

Writing the letters home was a disturbing experience for both boys. When each of them had composed the one page rough note they compared what they had written to ensure neither one had divulged anything in the letters that could reveal their exact whereabouts or give a clue to any future plans. They made some minor edits then carefully, in their best handwriting, wrote their final messages to their parents.

Father O'Malley returned to his office as they finished writing and seating himself at his desk, read each note in turn, smiling occasionally to himself as he did so.

'Well done, boys.' He looked up from the cautiously composed notes. 'Now if you would address the envelopes I'll get these in the mail for you.' He took two white envelopes from a drawer and handed them to Jack and Harry. 'The sooner your parents get these the better, as it will ease their concern. I dare say they will continue to worry about your welfare though, but at least they will know you are safe, to some degree.'

He stood and motioned them to follow him from the room. Walking into the bright noon sunlight the boys squinted from the glare, marvelling at how much hotter it was in the Goldfields than at home in Perth even though it was only about three hundred miles east of the coast.

'You plan to be away for some time I imagine, what preparations have you made for suitable clothing?' The priest looked at their light cotton shirts and gabardine trousers.

He noticed Jack's elastic-sided boots and grunted satisfaction but then noticed Harry's thin-soled, laced school shoes. 'You will need some better footwear, Harry, and both of you will need hats and some harder wearing clothes if you still plan to head into the bush. It's very inhospitable and tough country out there.' The boys looked uncomfortably at each other aware that they were ill prepared for the journey.

'What can we do about it, Father, can you suggest where we can get what else we need?' Jack was pleased that *his* boots were obviously acceptable.

'Let's go and get some lunch, boys, and we can make out a list of things you will need, keeping in mind that you will have to travel light though. Don't want to be carting heavy loads with you.'

Mrs Lacey had set out a platter of cold chicken, a loaf of bread and a bowl of fresh salad on the large table. The boys weren't all that hungry having had a substantial breakfast but the housekeeper hovered over them. 'Eat up boys; growing young men need to be well fed.' She piled more meat onto their plates.

The priest began to list items they would need for the trip. 'I take it you have some money with you to purchase some goods?' He looked across the table. 'I can lend you some if you're short.'

The boys were amazed at this generous offer. Nobody had ever treated them quite like this before, as grown men but they assured the priest that they 'probably had enough.'

Father O'Malley smiled to himself and nodded with satisfaction at their honest, but wary, acknowledgment. He was not about to reveal to them that Paddy, after a few too many nips of Irish whisky they had taken together the previous night, let slip that they had had 'a bit of a windfall, Timothy, me lad' at the two-up game.

After lunch they went with the priest to the shed at the rear of the presbytery and climbed into his ancient black Chevrolet when he backed it out of its shelter. Both boys looked anxiously at the priest as he scrunched the gears and drove off jerkily down the street with a trail of blue smoke behind them.

'There's a camping store that belongs to one of my parishioners,' he explained. 'I'm sure he'll be taking good care of you with what you need and will be kind with the prices.'

The store was crammed with every type of gear from swags and tents to picks, shovels, kerosene lanterns, a large selection of work clothes, boots, shotguns, rifles, blankets and various items of army surplus goods. Father O'Malley handed the man in the store the list. They each got a swag, an enamelled mug, plate, knife, fork and spoon, packets of waterproofed matches, a waterbag and canvas haversacks to replace their school bags.

They bought some heavy cotton work trousers, long-sleeved shirts, woollen socks and broad brimmed felt hats each. Harry tried on some work boots and settled, on the shopkeeper's advice, for a pair of elastic-sided riding boots similar to Jack's. 'Easy to pull on and off,' he advised. 'And the flat heels are good for walking.' The priest also insisted that they would need some warm clothing as the desert could get extremely cold so they added heavy woollen jackets to the growing pile of goods.

Both Jack and Harry were enthralled by the selection of firearms chained to a rack on the wall but knew they were too young to buy a rifle so each chose a Bowie styled hunting knife in a leather scabbard. When Father O'Malley saw them he wisely suggested that a knife was an essential tool but that they should consider something a little more practical and multi-purpose. They were at first disappointed but when the shopkeeper explained its features they took his advice and settled on bone handled, multi-bladed Stanley Rogers pocket knives. This purchase meant they also had to buy belts so they could carry the knives in the pouches for that purpose.

Father O'Malley suggested they purchase a small pocket watch each, which they did. The watches also came with a sturdy leather pouch and these were attached to their belts as well. They left the store proudly wearing their newly purchased clothing and with swags and backpacks slung over their shoulders and hats pulled low over their eyes, imagining they were prospectors or stockmen. Their pockets were much lighter but they knew they needed the equipment they had bought if they were serious about where they were headed and they still had some cash reserves.

Father O'Malley said he would take their gear back with him to the presbytery and suggested they spend some time having a look around Kalgoorlie. He told them he had some tasks to attend to and suggested that they come back later in the afternoon to the presbytery so they could help him pack the car ready for the journey to Mt Margaret the next morning. Jack and Harry watched the black Chevy depart, a pall of smoke trailing behind it and wondered if it would even get to the end of the street let alone undertake a trip into the desert.

♦♦♦♦♦♦♦♦♦♦♦♦

The first thing the boys noticed about Kalgoorlie was the width of the streets, nearly three times wider than anything they had seen in Perth. They made their way down Hannan Street, named after the Irish prospector who was credited with making the first major gold discovery in the area, and gawked wide-eyed at the buildings, many still as they were in the gold rush days.

They paused for a time to examine the statue of Paddy Hannan on the corner of Wilson Street. 'Maybe one day there'll be a statue of us in Coober Pedy eh? Harry. After we find all that opal!'

'Yeah, but let's hope we get richer than poor Paddy here.' Harry pointed to the bronze figure seated on a rock. 'I learned in history that he never made a lot of money out of the gold even though others made fortunes. He ended up on a pension from the government and eventually moved to somewhere in Melbourne. Died about twenty five years ago.'

They continued down Hannan Street past the town hall and huge Government Building complex that once housed the Warden's court, the Mines Department and the Telegraph Office. 'Gee, Harry, look at that ... pink stone!' They both looked up at the large impressive clock in the building's tower.

They were standing on the footpath admiring the impressive structure of the Palace Hotel with its verandahs and wrought iron decorations when they heard a voice calling to them.

'It's Jack and Harry it is to be sure, how are ye, me lads?'

They spun around to see the familiar figure of Paddy O'Brien crossing the street toward them ignoring the traffic and oblivious to the angry yells from irritated drivers. He waved enthusiastically to them and they returned his greeting with equal zest.

'Paddy!' They called with genuine pleasure. 'Good to see ya, how've ya been?' Jack asked as Paddy leapt onto the footpath.

'Never been finer, me lads, never been finer. Sorry I didn't say goodbye when I left the other mornin' but I had tings to do and that's for sure.' He danced a sort of mini jig, his face beaming with delight at having seen the boys. 'Didn't think I'd be seein' yer though, thought you'd have moved along by now. Grand it is though, grand.'

'What sort of things did you have to do, Paddy?'

'Ahh, Jack, a few friends to be catchin' up with and a little bit of 'the doins' to share with 'em. Which brings me to a question, lads that I wouldn't be askin' an all except we're mates?' He swept his hat from his head, holding it with both hands before him as he bowed his head in a humble pose. 'You wouldn't be lendin' me a few bob now would yer? Just till I get m'self straight you see.'

'A few bob, Paddy!' Jack sounded surprised. 'What did you do with the money you won from ...' He lowered his voice and looked around before continuing, '... the two-up game?'

'Ahh ... that's another story, it is.' Paddy looked remorseful. 'You see I met a colleen I did and that's for sure.' He smiled wistfully.

'What's a *colleen*, Paddy?' Harry was mystified.

'A *colleen*, me lads, is a beautiful young Irish lass. Well, she wasn't exactly a colleen and not exactly Irish either but she did have dark hair and sparklin' blue eyes, I'll be tellin' yer.' Paddy winked at the boys.

'She a friend of yours, Paddy? You didn't tell us ya knew a lady here.'

'Well, Jack ...' He shifted from one foot to the other. '... I've not actually been knowin' her like but she was a fine lass.' His eyes sparkled at the memory. 'Met her down in Hay Street.'

'Where's Hay Street, Paddy?'

'Hay Street?' Paddy suddenly looked serious. 'You don't need to be knowin', lads, not at your tender ages but with that and a few drinks I've sort of run m'self a little short of the foldin' stuff. Anymind, not to be worryin', lads, I'll be fine and that's for sure. Now what about you, what are your plans? Has the good Father been takin' good care of ye now?'

They explained what had transpired with Father O'Malley and the equipment they had bought for the trip. They also told him that they were heading to Mt Margaret with the priest the following day.

'Not goin' in that old rattle trap he calls a car are ye, heaven forbid, lads?'

'She does seem like she's in need of some lookin' at, that's for sure, blows a lot of smoke,' Harry agreed. 'He should take it to a garage for repairs.'

'A garage! I don't think even the good Lord himself could be fixin' that beast of a car. Be sure to be takin' plenty of water with ye, lads, it's sure to break down out there somewhere on a lonely stretch of road. I'll be askin' the Lord to be takin' good care of yer on the trip.' He placed his hat back on at a jaunty angle.

'I should be off then.' He stood hesitantly for few seconds. 'You be lookin' after yourselves now, lads, stay out of trouble and keep in mind to stay in touch with yer parents.' He held out his hand. 'It's been a pleasure meetin' yer, lads, hope we catch up again someday.' There was sadness as he spoke and the boys were moved by the genuine tone in his voice.

'Paddy, we want to thank ya for takin' us to Father O'Malley and for all the help you've given us and ...'

'Nothin' at all, nothin' at all.' Paddy waved a hand to dismiss their gratitude then shook hands with each of them and turned quickly to walk away.

'Paddy?' Jack called, after seeing Harry nod his head 'Wait up.'

The little Irishman turned back to see his two young friends standing side by side and Jack holding a pound note out to him. 'No, lads, I couldn't be takin' it from yer. You'll be needin' it down the track.' He turned again to walk away.

'Paddy ... please ... we want ya to.' Harry called to him.

Paddy hesitated before walking back to the boys. 'Well, I'll only be takin' ten bob then, have ye got a ten bob note?'

Taking the money he pushed it quickly into his coat pocket. There was a catch in his voice as he looked into their eyes. 'You're good lads ye are and that's for sure. This is a loan and I'll be getting' it back to yer one fine day or me name's not Paddy O'Brien. God bless ye, lads.' He spun on his heels and walked quickly away.

Jack and Harry failed to see Paddy's eyes mist over as he left them standing in the heat outside the Palace Hotel on Hannan Street and went off in search of more of 'the doins'.

♦♦♦♦♦♦♦♦♦♦♦♦

Returning to the church complex they were not surprised to see that the priest's old car had the bonnet open and a grimy, shirt-sleeved Father O'Malley, sweating profusely and muttering under his breath, was bent over the motor.

'What's the problem, Father?' Jack asked.

'Not sure, boys, not sure at all.' The priest straightened and stretched his back, concern clearly on his face, 'Seems the old girl has decided to play up a bit. Can't understand it, she's been tickin' over like a clock.'

The boys concealed their grins.

'It seems I'll have to make some other arrangements for tomorrow's trip. It's too late in the day to be getting her looked at now and I'm sure it's a little more than a tune she'll be needing.' Father O'Malley looked soulful.

'What sort of arrangements, Father?'

'There's a mail run that leaves in the morning early. It gets to Mt Margaret but calls in to a few places on the way so the trip will be a slow one I'm afraid. Still, better than no trip at all I suppose and the mailman is a good bloke. We'll be a bit cramped for room but I best be off to telephone him and see if he can accommodate us. He takes passengers when there's room.' Father O'Malley took a final look under the motor, climbed into the cabin and pressed the starter. The motor turned over, coughed once then backfired loudly but refused to start. 'Can you help me get her in the shed, boys, take your gear out first though and we'll take it up to the house.'

They unloaded the goods then pushed the heavy vehicle into the shed with Father O'Malley behind the wheel. The car smelled of burnt oil and the boys doubted it would ever get back on the road again.

'Come on up to the house. You can have a bath and get ready for tea.' The priest picked up a swag and a parcel of clothes. 'The young lad that's travelling with us will be here a little later in the evening to stay overnight so we can get an early start. You'll meet him then and I only hope the mail truck can fit us all in. I'll go and call now.'

'Good news, boys,' Father O'Malley greeted the boys when he came to the table. 'Ted Johnson, the mail truck driver, said he has a fairly light load tomorrow so can take us all. You three boys will have to ride in the back though but that's OK. It has a tarp over the tray and Ted never drives all that fast so it'll be safe. Just need to keep the dust out of your eyes is all.'

When they had completed dinner, the boys went out onto the verandah where it was cooler. They sat in two wicker chairs to watch the sun, a fiery red ball, sink behind the low hills in the west while they waited for the other boy to arrive so they could meet him.

They were sitting quietly, conversation exhausted for the moment, when they heard the crunch of feet on the gravel path. They peered into the gloom of the evening to see Father O'Malley's tall stooped figure walking toward them, accompanied by a shorter slim youth walking a yard or so behind.

'Jack, Harry,' the priest called to them. 'This is the young man I was telling you about.' He turned to the figure behind him. 'Come on, son, no need to be shy, these are good lads and you'll all get on well I'm sure.'

The two stepped from the darkness onto the verandah into the dim shadowy light spilling from the window. 'Harry Turner and Jack Ferguson.' The priest pointed to them in turn, 'this is Reynold.'

It wasn't the unusual name that surprised the boys and caused them to hesitate briefly, a point not missed by the priest nor by the youth beside him, but the fact that he was aboriginal, something they had never considered, nor had Father O'Malley mentioned.

Jack recovered quickly and stepped forward with his hand outstretched. 'G'day, er … Reynold did you say, Father?'

The boy nodded slightly as he took Jack's outstretched hand in a soft grip. 'G'day to you too. That's right … Reynold.' He pronounced it 'Rennol.'

Harry took Jack's lead also holding out a hand tentatively in greeting to the aboriginal boy. 'G'day.' They shook hands briefly.

'You boys like some lemonade?' The priest stood up without waiting for an answer. 'I'll go and get some and see if Mrs Lacey left any biscuits out. You boys can get to know each other. I'll be back shortly.' He left the three boys standing awkwardly together on the verandah each with his hands pushed deeply into trouser pockets and Reynold staring shyly at the wooden decking beneath his feet.

Reynold had not had a lot of exposure to whites having been born on the mission and grown up there. His schooling had been minimal, only briefly attending mission schools with his own people. Jack and Harry were in no way prejudiced and Jack's father spoke highly of the aboriginal stockmen that he had met on his travels, but they had never been in close contact with aboriginal people and were unsure of how to communicate. A distinct division existed between whites and blacks, particularly in the suburbs where they had been raised and there were no aboriginal children that attended their school. They did play against them sometimes in the odd football match and were in awe of their prowess with a ball and their determination on the field, so they were a little intimidated by them. Reynold, on the other hand, was wary of the two white boys expecting, as he had experienced previously, to be ignored at the very least.

He was therefore surprised after what seemed like an eternity of silence on the verandah, when Jack initiated conversation with a question. 'You been crook, Reynold?'

'Yeah, got throwed from a horse, broke me leg.' He still stared at the verandah beneath his bare feet.

'You been in Kalgoorlie long then?' Harry ventured

'Nah, coupla' months.' He paused for a few seconds. 'Yu boys, yu goin' out to the mission then?' he asked.

'The mission?' Harry looked puzzled.

'Yeah, Mt Margaret. I live there at the mission sometime. When I'm not out drovin' wit' me uncle Warri that is.'

It slowly dawned on Jack and Harry that where they were headed in the morning with the priest and Reynold was to an aboriginal mission station.

Until then they had though that Mt Margaret was some ordinary outback mining town. They were confused and a little apprehensive. 'What would it be like? What would the people be like, would they be friendly or not? Were they doing the right thing?'

Father O'Malley appeared carrying a tray with four glasses of fizzing lemonade and a plate of Anzac biscuits that he placed on a small low wooden table. 'Here you are, help yourselves, boys.' He took a biscuit and bit into it.

Reynold hung back in the shadows so Jack picked the plate up and held it toward him. 'Here, Reynold, better grab a couple before Harry here eats 'em all, he *loves* Anzac bikkies.'

Reynold smiled, his teeth flashing white in the light from the window. He took a biscuit and bit it in half.

That night, in the small room dominated by the large wooden crucifix on the bare white wall, Jack and Harry discussed the developments of the day and the inclusion of Reynold into the equation.

'Seems OK, Jack, Reynold?'

'Bit if a shock eh? But yeah, he's quiet, but seems OK.'

'Do you think we're doin' the right thing headin' out to this Mt Margaret, Jack?'

'Not sure but we don't have much choice now, do we?'

'Suppose not. Anyhow, we don't have to stay there for long.'

'No, that's for sure. I'm not too keen about spending time with a bunch of aboriginals, Harry, regardless of how friendly Reynold seems. We'll just get there on the mail truck and then move on, get a lift with someone, eh?'

'Sounds fair, Jack, maybe there's a train from there or somethin' do you think?

'Sure to be, Harry.'

The boys examined their equipment again and went to sleep on the beds without getting undressed; only taking their boots off and removing belts for comfort.

It was a novelty for them to sleep in clothes because at home it was a fact that one only slept in pyjamas. 'Only swagmen sleep in their clothes,' Jack's mother often said. Even on school camp they had had to put their *jammies* on. 'Uncouth to sleep in your clothes and unhealthy,' the teacher had stated emphatically.

In the future, however, sleeping fully clothed would become so much a part of their lives that they never for an instant imagined that night that there would be many times when they would yearn for a hot bath, clean sheets, soft mattress, fluffy pillows and loose-fitting pyjamas.

Chapter Ten

Father O'Malley knocked on the bedroom door to wake them. 'Come on, boys, need to get an early start, the mail truck will be along shortly'.

After splashing their faces with water to wash the sleep from their eyes they packed their gear and went to the kitchen where Father O'Malley had a pot of tea brewed and toast buttered. Reynold was already there and nodded to Jack and Harry as they entered.

Breakfast completed they collected their luggage and went out into the yard as a large tray-bodied Ford truck pulled in, its lights dim in the pre-dawn half light. They could see that the truck was heavily stacked with all sorts of merchandise even though Father O'Malley had said it would be a light load that day. There were drums of petrol, oil and sheep dip, rolls of netting, coils of fencing and barbed wire, steel posts, wooden crates and cardboard boxes, all roped firmly into place. There was a moderately clear space directly behind the cab where the mailman indicated that the boys could sit and he took their bags and swags and threw them unceremoniously onto the tray.

'Climb on, time's getting away. G'day, Father'

'Good morning, Ted, glad you could fit us in. My old car seems to have given up the ghost.'

'What! The Chev? Never!' He grinned and winked to the boys.

The priest climbed into the truck's cab and slammed the door shut. After telling the three boys to 'hang on' the driver engaged gears and drove from the yard.

Neither boy spoke as the truck drove through the awakening town. They could see the sun beginning to creep into view and already feel the promise of another blistering day as the streets and buildings slipped by and the truck began to gather speed as it hit the open road and headed toward Menzies.

It was noisy on the back of the truck with the engine hum, the whistling wind flapping the canvas tarpaulin and some piece of machinery that was also clanging rhythmically against a metal drum at the rear, so conversation was difficult. Each boy welcomed the noise that rendered talk unnecessary so they settled back as comfortably as possible in the confined area and dozed.

The truck slowing and changing down a gear stirred the boys. They woke to see ruined remnants of buildings, lonely chimneys pointing forlornly into the morning sky. There were some occupied cottages and old, but solid, brick town buildings, some boarded up and others seemingly tenanted.

'What's this place, Reynold?' Harry asked

'This place called Menzies … got cuzins 'ere eh?'

'I read about it at school, I thought it was bigger than this.'

'Used to be, years ago. Nuttin' 'ere now just a pub, post office 'n a coupla shops.'

The truck stopped outside the post office, unloaded some parcels and a canvas mailbag then moved down the street to the hotel where Ted drove the truck down the side of the building and pulled to a stop in the rear yard. He switched off the engine and he and Father O'Malley exited the cab. 'Jump down, boys,' the priest said. 'Stretch your legs, we'll be here for a few minutes.' He and Ted went into the building.

A short while later Father O'Malley came out of the rear door with three tall glasses of raspberry cordial and lemonade. 'Thought you might like to whet your whistles, boys. Ted and I are just finishing some business with the publican and we'll be with you shortly.' He walked purposefully back inside.

Reynold grinned and said 'They havin' a pick-me-up for the trip.' He sat down cross-legged on the ground leaning his back against the truck wheel, 'Yu bloke better sit down too, they gonna be a while.'

'What are they doin', Reynold?' Harry took a sip from his glass.

'Yu boys been nowhere, eh?' Reynold drained his glass. 'They havin' a little drink wit' the man what owns this pub. They be out in little while.'

Jack and Harry decided they would go for a short walk to have a look at the buildings in the main street and maybe buy some lollies if they could find a shop. 'You comin', Reynold?' Harry asked

'Nah, Rennol wait for yu boys 'ere eh?' He leant further back against the wheel of the truck and pulled his weather-beaten felt hat down over his eyes to shade his face from the ever intensifying heat of the sun.

The two boys came to a general store that sold petrol and had some signs leaning against its walls that advertised Craven 'A' cigarettes, Arnott Biscuits and Plume kerosene. They bought a jar of boiled humbug sweets and three peanut bars from the lady behind the counter.

'You boys new in town?' She placed the lollies in a brown paper bag and pushed it over the timber counter to them.

'Just on our way through.' Jack looked up from the comics piled on a shelf beside the cash register.

'You read 'em you pay for 'em.' The woman pointed to the comics.

'What? Oh, no … I was just lookin' at the covers.' Jack closed the magazine he was browsing and placed it back on the pile.

'OK then. It's just that I have to be very careful here as they get pinched as quick as you can say Jack Robinson.' The woman busied herself with a feather duster, brushing it over rows of canned vegetables and Camp Pie neatly shelved behind her.

'Not a lot here is there?' Jack commented. 'The town, you know.' He pointed vaguely out the door. 'I thought Menzies would be bigger than it is.'

'No, not now.' The woman looked thoughtfully into space. 'There was a time … long before I came here,' she added hastily. 'At the turn of the century when this town had over ten thousand people living here. There were a couple of breweries they say and, believe it or not, thirteen pubs! Now it's just the one pub and the town hall, still without its clock,' She chuckled 'The clock's somewhere on the bottom of the ocean, ship sunk on the way out from England and they've never ordered a replacement and that was fifty-odd years ago. Council hasn't changed much over the years.' The woman laughed to herself as she went on dusting the shelves and seemed to forget the boys were present.

They left the shop and began to walk toward the hotel when they were confronted by four young aboriginal lads of roughly their own age who barred their path.

'What yu white boys doin' 'ere then, eh? Yu don' live 'ere, mate, do yu?' The bigger boy poked Jack menacingly in the chest.

Jack, taken aback at this unprovoked aggression, looked to Harry for support.

'We're just travellin' through, mate,' Harry explained. 'On the mail truck.' He reached out and nudged Jack's elbow to guide him forward.

'Where yu tink *yu* goin', white boy?' The apparent leader of the group stepped in front of them. His companions moved up beside him, their fists clenched. 'Yu come inta town lookin' for trouble, eh?' The leader spat on the ground at Jack's feet.

Harry looked sideways at Jack who nodded in agreement. They knew this was a threat that no talk would get them out of. They would have to fight to get past the four young men standing between them and the hotel where the truck was parked, so Jack put the jar of humbugs on the ground behind him knowing it was dangerous to fight with glass in a pocket. Harry tucked the peanut bars in his shirt, sniffed loudly and took a step backwards bringing his fists up in a defensive move. Both Jack and Harry were nervous. They had never encountered this type of belligerent behaviour before and although they knew they could both handle themselves under normal circumstances, to face four unknown assailants was disconcerting.

They didn't see Reynold appear but heard his voice behind the four boys facing them. 'Hey, Winston! What yu doin' fightin' wit' me mates, eh?'

A look of surprise came over the leader's face and he spun around to see who had spoken to him. 'Rennol ... what you doin' 'ere?' He was now obviously confused.

'These boys they named Jack 'n Harry. They mates, travellin' wit' me back to the mission. What yu go doin' takin' 'em on for? They do nuttin' to yu.'

'We did'n know they yu frens, Rennol.' Winston licked nervous lips and looked from Jack to Harry then back at Reynold. Winston's three supporters took a step back from the confrontation.

'Yeah, well they are 'n if yu wanna fight them yu gonna 'ave to fight me too.' Reynold stepped passed the four young aboriginals and stood beside Harry and Jack. Reynold spat on the ground in the same manner that Winston had done earlier.

'Hey, Rennol, we jus' make mistake, eh? No need to go get angry 'bout it.' Winston looked to his three friends. 'That's right, eh?' The boys nodded in agreement, looking nervously at Reynold.
The threat was over. Jack and Harry stood alone together as the five boys greeted each other with much hand shaking and back slapping then Reynold introduced them to the boys who just minutes before had been threatening to assault them. Cautious handshakes were passed around and then Reynold said they had to go to catch the mail truck.

They never mentioned a word of the encounter to Father O'Malley or the mailman. The boys were already seated in the rear of the truck when they came from the hotel, climbed into the cab, started the motor and drove from the hotel yard. As the truck turned onto the main road leading out of town Winston and his friends waved cheerily from where they were standing. Reynold waved back but Jack and Harry didn't feel it was necessary.

'Thanks, Reynold,' Jack said. 'Coulda been a bit nasty.'

Reynold just shrugged his shoulders as the truck gathered speed heading toward Leonora on its way to Mt Margaret Mission.

Jack took the humbug mints from his pocket, unscrewed the lid and held the jar out to Reynold, 'Take a few, Reynold.'

Harry then retrieved the three peanut bars from his shirt pocket. He handed one each to Jack and Reynold.

'Yu buy me one *too*?' Reynold was stunned.

'Yeah, why not, we're together aren't we?' Harry replied ripping the paper from the bar of chocolate.

'I tink I laik yu boys.' Reynold took the paper off his chocolate, screwed it into a ball and threw it out to be snatched away by the wind 'Rennol 'e laik yu a lot.'

They grinned at each other as the truck rattled on into the day, tarpaulin flapping and V8 motor throbbing. The three boys sat silently together on the rear tray of the truck and devoured the peanut nougat bars covered in rich dark chocolate, the seeds of an unspoken bond beginning to take root between them.

It was late in the evening when the truck pulled into Mt Margaret. The last part of the trip had been uncomfortable as they were thrown about on the tray from the rough and rutted road leading into the mission. Choking dust had blanketed everything and filled their throats and noses. They felt with every breath that they were sucking bucket-loads of red sand into their lungs and were glad when the truck slowed and a few pale lights indicated they had, at last, arrived at Mt Margaret.

Even though it was late, the truck was greeted enthusiastically by a group of people of all ages and what seemed like a hundred barking dogs. There was laughter and rapid-fire talk, much in a language that Jack and Harry couldn't understand although they knew the joy was due to Reynold's return to his family. They didn't get to speak with Reynold after he jumped down from the truck. He was swiftly enveloped in a large group of people and whisked away followed by a group of excited children skipping along behind the group, with the inevitable barking dogs darting around the perimeter, dodging the odd kick aimed at them by the children.

'Let's bed down for the night, boys,' Father O'Malley said. 'Grab your swags and crawl up near the truck there. I'll be staying in that hut just over there.' He pointed to a small fibro sheeted building with a corrugated iron roof, just visible in the starlight. 'Ted will be sleeping in the truck cab and we'll sort a few things out in the morning, Not much can be done tonight as everyone's too excited to have Reynold home again.' He bade them goodnight and faded into the darkness.

The boys found it almost impossible to sleep in the unfamiliar swags, the strange environment and being bedded down out in the open with the occasional dog sniffing at them and growling as they melted back into the night, after being yelled at, to, 'Get away, you mongrel, shoo!'

The night sky was ablaze with more stars than they had ever seen before and they watched them from their swags for a time. The noise from the nearby dwellings eventually subsided, broken only occasionally by a shriek of laughter and the odd barking dog but as they were exhausted, they eventually drifted off into a restless slumber.

Chapter Eleven

Jack was not sure exactly what woke him. It might have been the heat of the early morning sun and at first he thought he must still be asleep and dreaming but it happened again. A soft tinkling sound followed by silence then the noise again, louder this time. He opened one eye slowly and peered out of the swag to see a bunch of small children sitting not more than five feet away staring at him and Harry in their swags.

The children, dressed only in an assortment of shorts and ragged pants, consisted of both girls and boys of between what he figured to be about two and six or seven years old. Two little girls held completely naked babies and there were three dogs lying quietly beside them. The children were staring intently at the two boys and then they whispered softly among themselves and giggled. This was the tinkling noise that Jack had heard, the soft gentle sound of children's laughter. At first he didn't know what to do or why they were there but when he reached out and nudged Harry's still form in the swag next to him and sat up there was a shriek from the children. They leapt to their feet and ran away screaming and laughing followed by three barking dogs.

'Yu bloke awake at last, eh?' Reynold appeared before him. 'Them kids bin watchin' yu for 'ours.' He rolled his eyes in mock exaggeration and laughed. 'Come on, git up, day 'e almos' gone. Yu come now 'n meet some fam'ly. I tell 'em yu mates from Kalgoorlie 'n we travel up 'ere together.'

Jack and Harry stretched. They were sore from the pounding of the truck and stiff from sleeping on the hard ground, their bodies not yet used to the rigours of bush life.

They followed Reynold over to a group of men, women and young men about their own age. There were no girls in the group seated around the ash grey camp fire but they did catch a glimpse of two girls some distance away who quickly turned their faces when Jack and Harry glanced in their direction.

Reynold introduced them proudly to his family. 'These boys they me cuzins, this one 'e me brother, Nigel, this woman she me aunty 'n these …' He went on pointing to the group gathered around the fire, not mentioning anyone by name except his brother. Nigel stood and held out his hand to Jack and Harry but the others remained seated or squatting around the fire and only nodded a greeting as Reynold pointed them out in turn.

Introductions over, a tall thin woman of indeterminate age, dressed only in a faded cotton dress and with tousled hair and broken teeth, stood and picked a steaming billy from the coals. 'Yu laik tea?'

'Yeah, they laik tea, eh, boys?' Reynold answered for them. 'Go get yer mugs 'n we 'ave some brekfas.'

The boys took their cue and left to get the pannikins from the haversacks beside the truck, welcoming the break from what seemed to them to be a very awkward time. When they reluctantly returned to where Reynold and his family were Reynold poked a blackened lump of something from the fire with a stick and after blowing ash from it broke it into large pieces 'Yu share our tucker 'cause we mates. Yu laik damper?'

The thin woman poured steaming black tea into the pannikins and threw a handful of sugar into each one. 'Yu stir 'im wit' a stick,' she said.

They held the damper tentatively and were self-conscious realising that everyone was watching them silently. When the boys bit into the damper and took a sip of the strong, sweet black tea however it was like a signal and all gathered at the fire began to talk animatedly to them and ask them questions.

'Rennol 'e tell us yu share yer choclat wit' 'im,' one of Reynold's 'uncles' said. 'Good to share tings wit' frens.'

The damper was surprisingly tasty washed down with the hot tea and certainly filling. Breakfast over Reynold led them, his brother and three other boys away from the fire to a large dead log under the shade of a tree. 'Now we work out what we gonna do, eh? Where yu boys goin' from 'ere, Jack?' He straddled the log, his bare feet dangling in the dust.

'Well, we're goin' to Coober Pedy.'

'Coober Pedy, eh?' He pronounced it *Kupa Piti.* 'Never bin there but I 'ear 'bout 'im from me uncle Warri. Best darn drover yu ever meet, me uncle Warri. 'Ow yu gonna git there?'

'Not sure, Reynold, but that's where we want to go. You able to show us how to get there?' Harry queried.

'Well ....' He looked thoughtfully at his feet while scratching his ear. 'I know 'e long ways out, this Kupa Piti, Harry. Way out, 'cross 'im border in Sout Stralya.'

The boys began to wonder if they had made a mistake heading northeast to Mt Margaret instead of going directly east from Kalgoorlie. 'Maybe we shoulda caught the train over, Jack?' Harry wore a worried expression.

'Tell yu what, boys, me 'n Nigel we off t'morra to Warburton, meet uncle Warri, 'e know 'ow to get to Kupa. Yu can come wit' us, that'd be good, eh?' He smiled broadly at his solution to the problem and slid from the log. 'Warburton, that where I *really* come from.'

'How you gettin' to Warburton, Reynold?'

'On the supply truck. Big truck 'e come thru 'ere 'n go up to Warburton. Yu come too, it'll be OK.'

Jack groaned at the thought of another rough truck journey. 'Harry and I'll have a talk about it, Reynold, and then see what Father O'Malley thinks. We'll let you know in a minute. Thanks for the invitation though.'

'Sounds good, Reynold,' Harry added as they walked off. 'See ya in a bit.'

They left the group at the log and walked off to where Ted was readying the truck for his return journey to Kalgoorlie, having unloaded all the supplies for the mission. Father O'Malley was leaning against the bonnet dressed in black trousers and a short sleeved white shirt, his thin pale arms folded across his chest, smoke curling from the pipe clenched in his teeth.

The boys outlined Reynold's idea of travelling to Warburton on the supply truck with him and Nigel.

'Well, boys, you've come this far and you are green to the bush.' He blew smoke from the pipe. 'Inexperienced,' he explained when they looked puzzled when he said they were 'green'. 'I couldn't think of a better way to become skilled about survival out here than to travel with Reynold. I've never met his uncle Warri but I've heard about him. Bit of a legend he is, been a drover in the outback since he was a lad about your age. If you want adventure, boys, I think you've found it.' He took the pipe from his mouth and tapped it against the heel of his shoe.

'The other choice of course is to come back with Ted and me to Kalgoorlie, there'd be no harm in that you know. We could talk about where you go from there and …'

'No, Father,' Jack said firmly. 'We're not goin' *back*, we're goin' *on*. aren't we, Harry?'

'Yes, goin' on.' Harry sounded a little uncertain.

'Very well, boys, but you have to promise me one thing.' He fixed them with a serious stare.

'Yes, Father … what is it?

'Jack, you too, Harry, I want you to keep in touch with your parents, let them know where you are and that you're OK.' The boys shifted uneasily under the priest's hard stare.

'Not *where* we are, Father, can't do that or the police would find us and we'd end up in jail.' Jack thought for a minute and continued. 'Father …when you posted those letters home for us did you keep a note of our addresses from the envelopes?'

'What makes you think I'd do a thing like that, Jack?' The priest hedged.

'Did you, Father, we need to know?'

'Yes, Jack, I did.'

'I want *you* to promise us something now, Father.' Jack sounded more grown up than he felt. 'If you promise us you won't write to our parents or tell them where we are, we promise that we'll write regular to them but we'll send them to you to forward on for us.' Jack looked at Harry who nodded and squared his shoulders in support.

'Hmm …' Father O'Malley put the cold pipe back in his mouth and considered the boys standing before him surprised at the resolve they displayed. *I think they'll make it,* he thought to himself.

'We don't want to sound ungrateful for everythin' you've done, Father, but if you can't promise us that then we can't make a promise to you.' Harry reinforced Jack's argument.

'You drive hard bargains, boys.' His voice was warm when he smiled. 'But, yes, I'll make that promise to you.'

Relieved, Jack and Harry relaxed and smiled back at this tall friendly man knowing that they had made a friend of the priest. A friend they could trust, like Paddy and Reynold.

Ted fired the truck into life and blew the horn, signalling he was about to depart. All the residents of the mission, young, old and in between plus all the dogs appeared and milled around the truck to say goodbye to Father O'Malley. He shook hands and patted children's heads before turning to Jack and Harry standing with Reynold, who held the cabin door open.

'You boys take care of each other now, won't you?' The priest said farewelling each of them with a smile as he took their hands in a firm warm grip. He folded his tall frame into the cabin. 'Now, Reynold, you learn to ride a little better all right? No more falling off your horse.' He laughed and slammed the truck door shut.

Reynold hooted with laughter and the entire gathering of people joined him as the truck pulled away, horn tooting and both Ted and Father O'Malley waving wildly from the windows.

'Thanks, Father, fer lookin' after me ... and bringin' me back,' Reynold shouted to the priest as the truck drew away, and Father O'Malley responded by holding his hand up in a victory salute.

The truck, now raising clouds of powdery red dust, disappeared down the corrugated track chased by a gaggle of shouting children and barking dogs.

The crowd dispersed and the children returned from their chase. The dogs settled down in the shade and life reverted back to normal at Mt Margaret Mission, except for two white boys who stood silently for some time watching the dust trail diminish into the distance until all that was left was a settling cloud on the horizon.

◆◆◆◆◆◆◆◆◆◆◆◆

The dogs were the first to announce the arrival of the supply truck into the settlement. This truck, a Dodge, was much bigger than the mail truck and was heavily loaded with goods roped down under tarpaulins.

The driver jumped down from the cabin and walked to the front of the bonnet to retrieve a canvas waterbag that was tied to the bumper bar. He took a long swig, replaced the cap and strapped the bag back securely in place, wiping his stubbled chin with the back of a weather beaten hand. 'G'day, gotta pick up a couple of young blokes to go to Warburton … they here?'

'Yeah, that me.' Reynold stepped forward. 'I'm called Rennol 'n me brother, Nigel, 'e be 'ere dreckly.'

'Not too long I hope, have to get goin'. It's a long trip and the road is as rough as guts out there.' The driver walked around the truck checking that the ropes were still tightly in place.

'Mista?'

'Yeah, Reynold.' He didn't look up from the ropes.

'Yu got room fer two of me mates, they wanna come to Warburton wit' me?'

'What? No way, this isn't a bloody bus, mate! I'm helpin' out by takin' you two.'

'We'd really appreciate a lift, Mister.' Jack walked up to the man. 'I'm Jack and this is me friend, Harry.'

The man was taken by surprise to see two young white boys dressed in bush clobber standing before him. 'What the hell *you* doin' out here?' He stood, pushing his hat back off his head with his right hand and scratching his hair. 'How did ya get here?'

They explained how they had come with the priest on the mail truck but didn't go into any other detail.

'Where ya headed then?'

'Just to Warburton?' Harry replied.

'That so? What's at Warburton that'd interest you blokes?'

Jack glanced at Reynold. 'We got family out there at Warburton, need to go and see 'em.' Reynold nodded enthusiastically with a grin at Jack's explanation.

'Ya don't say?' The man was unconvinced.

'Sir?' Jack decided to try once more as he couldn't imagine what they'd do if they were left alone at the mission. 'Father O'Malley only brought us here because he thought there wouldn't be a problem with getting a lift on your truck. He wouldn't have brought us all the way here if he didn't believe we needed to get to Warburton.'

'There's no problem about gettin' a lift, young fella, but I've already got two passengers. I can't fit four into the cabin.'

'We'll ride in the back sir, on the tray, we won't be any trouble.' Jack was desperate now to get on this truck and leave with Reynold and his brother.

'You'll choke from the dust and it's a bumpy ride even in the cab.'

Jack felt he was making ground so pressed the advantage. 'We'll pay you, sir, we got a little money, not much but we could give you somethin'.'

Reynold, who had been standing back listening to the exchange ,said, 'These boys they good fellas, they don' cause no trouble 'n won' grizzle 'bout no dust. Any'ow, we take 'im in turns, eh? On the back, me 'n Nigel.'

'Well, it's against me better judgement but if you promise not to whinge then it's up to you. There's no need to give me anythin' for the trip though as I'm goin' there anyway and I couldn't take money from a coupla kids sittin' on the back in the dust.' He shook his head in resignation. 'Grab yer stuff then, let's go.'

Chapter Twelve

Jack insisted that he and Harry ride on the back first, as Reynold and his brother were the legitimate passengers. Reynold didn't put up too much of an argument as he was looking forward to impressing his relatives by riding in the cab of the big truck, so he jumped onto the running board and hauled himself into the cabin, having pushed Nigel in first to sit in the middle.

Reynold smiled and waved importantly from the window as the truck moved out of the mission on to the Warburton road followed by the inevitable bunch of children and mangy barking dogs running behind obscured by the dust. Jack and Harry were amazed at how, once again, the entire population of Mt Margaret turned out to farewell them.

It was more of a track than a road and, although the ride was uncomfortable with the truck shuddering from the corrugations and jolting frequently as it encountered wash outs and dry creek crossings, it was relatively dust-free for Jack and Harry. Nestled behind the cabin on their swags the dust trailed behind and it was only when the driver slowed and changed down gears to negotiate one of the many crossings strewn with loose gravel and rocks did the dust catch up with them and envelop the vehicle.

They were fascinated by the varying landscape as it slipped past them hour after hour. Stunted mulga trees, low scrub and saltbush gave way to vast areas of claypan then changed to gibber stone flats and sandy ridges bare of vegetation. The redness also captivated them. The sand was red, the rocks were red, even the bush near the road had a reddish tinge from a coating of dust.

The driver eventually slowed and parked the heavily laden vehicle beside a small clump of tall spindly gum trees with smooth white trunks. The trees offered only enough shade for the cabin so when the truck was at a standstill with no breeze created by its momentum, the heat was stifling.

They climbed down off the freight onto the ground as the driver came around, again checking the ropes. 'You blokes OK?' he asked.

'Yeah, no problems.'

'You wouldn't say even if there was would ya?' He glanced at them, a grin on his stubbled face. 'Thought we'd pull in for a bite of lunch … boil the billy. You want to collect some wood.' It wasn't a question.

'We already got 'nuff.' Reynold and Nigel threw down a bundle of sticks and started arranging them in a pile over handfuls of dry grass between some large stones that had obviously been placed there for the purpose of providing a makeshift fireplace by a previous traveller.

'My name's George Fuller anyway, boys. Sorry I was a bit gruff back there but ya sorta took me by surprise.'

'G'day, Mr Fuller,' Harry replied

'Call me George.' He heaved on a rope and, satisfied it was still taut, moved off toward where Reynold and Nigel now had a small fire blazing. The timber was so tinder dry that very little smoke rose from it although the scent from the burning wood was pleasant as it drifted in the still midday air.

Both Harry and Jack were surprised at being invited to call the driver by his Christian name. It was something they weren't used to, having been taught that adults should always be addressed as *Mr* or *Mrs* and it would take them some time to become accustomed to this familiar habit existing in the bush.

'You boys bring anythin' to eat?' George asked, aware that they probably hadn't done so.

'We all right ... not 'ungry,' Nigel answered.

'Neither are we.' Jack avoided using the name *George*.

Without argument George lifted a cardboard box down from the truck cabin and placed it near the fire. He reached in, took a billycan, two tins containing tea and sugar in them and placed them beside the carton then lifted a tea towel wrapped bundle from the box..

'Just as well the missus always gives me far too much for these trips, I dunno;' he laughed. 'You'd think I had an army to feed. Just as well you're here to help me eat it though, 'cause she gets pretty upset when I come home with left-overs.'

The last thing out of the box was a large newspaper wrapped parcel that George placed on top of the now empty carton. Removing the paper carefully the boys could see that the inner wrappings were damp and when the paper was off George reached into a cheesecloth bag and took out a large chunk of salted beef.

'OK, fill the billy from that orange drum on the tray there, Jack, the one with the tap.' He pointed as Jack walked to the truck. 'Yeah that's the one. You make tea OK, Reynold?'

'Best darn' billy tea yu ever taste! Me uncle Warri 'e learn me good 'ow to make tea,' Reynold responded proudly, taking the billy from Jack.

'You slice up some of that corned beef then, Harry, and, Jack …?' George unfolded the tea towel and handed him a dark honey coloured crusted damper. 'You're the bread man, mate.'

Nigel felt left out standing off to one side until George turned to him. 'Now, mate, you run over to the cab and behind the seat you'll find a paper bag with a few tomatoes and a coupla onions.'

With the four boys now occupied and involved in preparing lunch George knew that they wouldn't feel it was a handout so he sat back on his haunches, pulled a leather pouch from his shirt pocket and began to roll a cigarette. 'This is the life,' he said as he watched the lunch preparations. 'Wish you blokes were with me every trip. Don't have to do too much then, just drive ol' Betsy over there.'

When they had all eaten, George poured the billy dregs onto the coals, kicked sand over them to snuff out the fire and glancing at the low dark clouds gathering on the distant north westerly horizon said, 'Let's get movin' then.'

They packed the things back in the truck. Reynold and Nigel climbed onto the tray and Jack and Harry jumped into the cabin beside George, as it was their turn to ride up front.

George Fuller took in the new clothes the two boys were wearing and was curious as to what they were up to out here in the outback heading for Warburton but knew not to ask too many questions. Although he had only just met them he felt that they would only tell him what they wanted him to know.

'You boys ever been out this way before?'

'No, first time.'

'You're well kitted out, plan to travel a fair way do you … be out here a while?'

'Maybe, just see what happens.' Jack was cautious.

'It's OK, boys, I don't want to know yer plans, it's just that I can see that you're city kids and I thought maybe ya could do with a bit of advice ... you know, a few tips on survivin' out here. I know ya haven't got any *family* out here.'

The boys glanced at one another but didn't respond.

'The thing to do, boys, is hang in with Reynold, he seems like a good bloke ... genuine. I've heard of his uncle, Warri, he's a legend out this way having droved stock for many years. He knows the country like the back of his hand and if he takes a likin' to ya he'll take ya under his wing and teach ya lots of things.' He wrestled with the steering wheel guiding the truck around a washed out section of the track and slammed it back a gear. 'It won't be no picnic boys, life is gonna be hard and the country ...' he pointed through the windscreen '... is unforgivin'. If ya don't know what yer doin' out here, ya can die easy but I think ya both have the determination that'll stand up through the tough times. Just be like a couple of sponges, soak up everythin' ya can learn, but be wary too, there's blokes out here that'd cut yer throat for a shillin' and not lose a wink of sleep over it either.'

After a couple of hours, George pulled the truck up on the track saying they needed to fill up with petrol. He took a hand pump with a hose attached and, opening a 44-gallon drum roped near the side, filled the truck tank from it using the pump. He was sweating heavily when he finished.

'Hard work that,' he said. 'But better than a few years back during the war with petrol rationing when all we had were gas producers. You know ... charcoal burners, to fuel the trucks.' He waved his hand at the surrounding desert with its stunted mulga. 'Used to be more trees out here than yer could poke a stick at but they cut 'em down to make charcoal. They, together with the sandalwood cutters, have depleted thousands of acres of timber so now the sands blow. Further south around Leonora a lot of timber was also felled to fuel the steam trains hauling ore for the mines'

'Don't like the look of those clouds, boys.' He stood for a minute looking at the mass of dark grey clouds now much larger than before building menacingly toward them. 'Get stuck out here in a big wet, we could be here for days.'

'Little rain maybe.' Reynold looked at the clouds. 'Tonight, later on but no big rain.'

'Fair enough, Reynold, but let's get on the track anyhow.'

'Doesn't look like it ever rains out here.' Jack kicked at the red dust.

'When there's a low or cyclone off the north west coast they sometimes come inland. Often they turn into rain depressions and can drop heaps of rain on the Kimberley, down through here and into the Goldfields.' George climbed into the driver's seat.

'If we were stuck out here for days we wouldn't have anythin' to eat.' Harry sounded concerned. '

'Not with Reynold and Nigel around,' George said with a grin. 'That's what I meant, boys, about learnin' from 'em on how to survive out here.'

It got darker as the clouds intensified late in the afternoon obscuring the lowering sun. A short time before dusk George pulled the truck to a stop once again. There was no need to pull off the track, as there was no other traffic on the lonely stretch of dirt track.

'Need to pump more petrol in before it gets dark. May as well light a fire and have a cuppa and a bite too 'cause we won't outrun this rain and if it comes a fire'll be impossible ...and I do like me cuppa.' George jumped from the cabin glancing at the mass of clouds. 'We could be in for a long wet drive through the night.'

It started to drizzle as they finished the damper smeared with Golden Syrup washed down with strong, sweet billy tea. 'Time to hit the track.' George packed the supplies away. 'There's a spare tarp, small one, up there.' He pointed in the general direction of where the boys had been travelling on the tray. 'Might keep a bit of rain off.'

'Where *you* goin?' Jack asked as Reynold and his brother started to climb onto the back of the truck.

'It gonna rain, Jack, yu 'n Harry yu ride up front. We used to bein' wet.'

Jack reached out and took hold of his arm. 'Reynold,' he said firmly, 'a deal's a deal, mate. It's our turn to ride on the back. You and Nigel jump in with George.'

'But you'se all dressed up 'n stuff ...' He was baffled by Jack's way of thinking.

'We'll have to get wet sometime, Reynold,' Harry added. 'May as well be now.'

'Yeah, and besides,' Jack agreed. 'These clothes look too new anyhow, need a bit of weatherin' in.'

Reynold held Jack's firm gaze for a moment then grinned. 'Yeah, guess yu do look sorta green don' they, Nigel?' The four boys laughed in the rain.

'Come on, you blokes, get a bloody move on and make up yer minds.' George's tone was gruff, concealing his thoughts as Jack and Harry clambered up onto the tray and huddled down under the green canvas tarpaulin. *They'll make it*, he smiled to himself. *Looks like my bit of advice sunk in.* He let the clutch out and drove off into the increasing darkness, wipers sweeping in arks across the windscreen.

The truck lurched on through the night. The rain was intermittent and didn't pose too much of a problem. It wasn't as heavy as George had expected and he shook his head silently in the darkness as he glanced at Reynold across the cab. *How do they do it?* He thought.

The rain did make the trip more hazardous however as George had to reduce speed and engage second gear on many occasions to traverse sandy creek crossings. There hadn't been enough rain for the creeks to run, fortunately, but exiting them was hazardous as the tyres sometimes spun, making the rear slide out.

The truck pulled into Warburton on Monday morning as the sun rose in a now cloudless sky, casting long shadows over the red soil.

George was relieved that, apart from a flat tyre that had wasted an hour and the rain that had slowed them down, the trip was otherwise uneventful.

'Here we are, boys, Warburton, end of the road.' He thought about Jack and Harry still perched on the back having declined to swap along the way as they said they were more than settled and already wet anyhow. *End of the road for me but just the beginning for those two young blokes on the back,* he added to himself.

Chapter Thirteen

Alice sat dejectedly at the kitchen table, staring into space. Normally uncluttered, the table was now littered with discarded newspapers. The sink, usually sparkling, still had last night's plates and cooking pots piled on it. Alice, a proud housekeeper had not been able to concentrate on housework over the past few days. Try as she might and even with her husband's positive encouraging comments that the boys would be home soon, she was despondent and missed her son terribly. Not knowing where he was and if he was safe was what nagged her most of all, her imagination painting disturbing pictures of her son and Harry in all sorts of perilous situations. It was now Monday and the fact that there had been no contact from either of them worried her. She couldn't understand why they hadn't at least written a note or telephoned.

The police had turned up no leads other than that the boys had caught the train from Northam to Kalgoorlie, beyond that ... nothing. She was even more distressed that a warrant had been issued for their arrest over the theft of the bike. William Munse had insisted that charges be layed, adamant that they had taken his son's bike for a second time and abandoned it by the river.

Jean talked with her every day and they both cried together on and off. Claude and Jack had driven to Merridin and Southern Cross making enquiries in addition to the police efforts but had returned on Sunday, their labours in vain. When Alice had been angry with her husband for not going directly to Kalgoorlie he explained, quite logically, that there was a chance that the boys had left the train en route and as those places were much smaller, it made sense to search them first.

She heard the postman's whistle in her subconscious, as he worked his way along the street delivering mail, but it didn't register. Jack came out from the bathroom after showering. He had slept late that morning, tired from the driving and emotionally drained. He looked haggard, dressed only in grey trousers and a white singlet. He filled the kettle from the rainwater tap over the sink and placed it on the stove, looking up as he heard a knock at the door. Alice jumped at the sound but remained seated, a look of apprehension on her drawn face.

'I'll get it, dear.' Jack walked quickly to the door.

'Tom?' Jack was surprised to see the postman standing on the front porch, his bike leaning against the front fence beside the gate.

'G'day, Jack. Sorry, mate, but I couldn't help thinking you may want to see this as soon as possible.' He handed an envelope to Jack. 'Figured from the writing it might be from your young Jack.' Tom the postie had been delivering mail to the residents of the suburb for a number of years and knew everyone on his round. He had seen most of the kids grow up.

'My God it *is* his writing. Alice, Alice …' Jack called excitedly. He went inside, slamming the wire door behind him, forgetting about the postie standing on the porch.

'What ever is it, Jack? What's the matter?' Alice stood up, alarm in her voice.

'It's a letter … from Jack.' They stood side by side staring at the envelope with Jack's distinctive juvenile scrawl on its face, both too apprehensive now to open it.

'Go on, Jack, you open it.' She was shaking, one hand to her mouth.

He picked up a knife from the table and carefully slit the envelope, retrieving the single page of tightly written script Alice started to cry softly and Jack put his arm tenderly around her shoulders as he read.

Dear mum and dad'

'By the time you get this letter we will be a long way away. I couldn't stay home and go to jail for something I didn't do and bring shame on you all. I want you to know that we didn't steal that bike, never stole nothing in my life. Billy Munse told us that his dad had witnesses or something that we pinched it but that's a lie.

Sorry to cause you so much trouble but don't worry about us, we'll be alright. We have met some beaut people and are off to make our fortune. Harry is writing to his parents too so they should get a letter about the same time.

Sorry mum that I lied about the lunch money. We put that with our pocket money and had ten shillings on Comic Court in the cup. It won so thanks dad for the beaut tip. We been real careful with our money and still have quite a bit left. We bought some work clothes and hats and stuff so are OK.'

'I will write again soon, don't try to look for us as we don't want to go to jail and don't tell the police that you heard from us. I reckon I'm the luckiest kid in the world to have a mum and dad like you. Sorry again for worrying you so much.

Love
Jack xx

Alice wiped tears from her eyes, noticing that Jack also had a catch in his voice as he read the closing lines.

'There's no address, Jack,' She sniffled. 'They don't say where they are.'

'It's postmarked Kalgoorlie.' Jack examined the envelope. 'They're not that clever, Alice. I don't suppose they realised we would work that out from the envelope.'

The telephone rang, interrupting their thoughts. It was Claude calling to say that they had also just received a letter from Harry postmarked Kalgoorlie. Claude said he and Jean would come around and work out what they should do next.

Both parents read each other's letters. The notes were essentially the same in content, both boys stressing their innocence about stealing the bike.

'Better let the police know, Jack,' Claude suggested. 'They'll be happy to know the boys are OK at least.'

♦♦♦♦♦♦♦♦♦♦♦♦

Constable Bob Peters and his sergeant read each of the letters. 'Seems like we need to have another talk with the Munse family, Bob.'

'Certainly do, Sarge, I'll get over there straight away. Hope all their neighbours see the car out the front.' He smiled wickedly as he left, placing his cap squarely on his head.

'Don't be too pushy, Bob,' The sergeant called after him.

'I won't but I aim to get to the truth this time,' he shot over his shoulder as he left the station.

'You go home, folks,' the sergeant said. 'I'll come 'round after Bob gets back. Will you be together?'

'We'll be waiting for you at our house.' Jack glanced questioningly at Claude who nodded assent.

◆◆◆◆◆◆◆◆◆◆◆◆

William Munse Senior opened the door and was disconcerted to see the police constable in full uniform standing on the verandah. Munse looked past him and his expression tensed. 'Did you have to park out there? ... Bring the car onto the driveway, Constable, if you have to come here. What is it you want anyhow? You should have telephoned, this is most inappropriate.'

'The car's fine where it is, sir. Is young Billy home?'

'William is studying, constable, you can talk to me if you have something to say.'

'Let's not make this more difficult than it needs to be, sir. There have been some developments and I need to talk to Billy.' He was satisfied to see Munse scowl at the use of *Billy* rather than William. 'Perhaps I should come inside?' He inclined his head in a questioning manner and Munse reluctantly stepped aside and ushered the policeman through the door.

Billy was summoned and came sheepishly into the room where they were waiting and looked fearfully at his father standing with the constable.

'Now, Billy, I think we need to have an honest talk here about the bike episode and your accusations that Jack and Harry stole it. You know they're missing?'

'William has told you all there is to know constable. You're wasting your time here, I'm going to call your sergeant now and complain that you are harassing my son. Everyone knows you are a friend of the Fergusons.' Munse moved toward the telephone.

'Good idea, sir, the sergeant would welcome the chance to come around to be a part of this interview. Do you know the number? It's ...?'

'That won't be necessary.' Munse was unnerved by the policeman's attitude. 'Just get on with it and be quick about it.' He attempted to assert himself again, unaccustomed to not being in control.

'Tell me again, Billy.' The constable spoke quietly in a friendly manner. 'Why did you say Jack and Harry stole your bike?'

'Because they did, that's why.' Munse senior butted in. 'What is the purpose of your line of ...'

'Sir!' It was said firmly, the policeman holding his hand up to silence William Munse. 'Let Billy speak for himself. Billy, answer the question.'

Billy Munse licked his lips, eyes darting between the policeman and his father, unsure of what to say. He felt trapped because either way he was in trouble, if not from the police for lying then certainly from his father.

'Billy ... this thing has gone far enough.' The policeman could see the conflict in the boy's eyes. 'There are two young kids missing out there somewhere and their parents are worried sick about them. They were your *friends*, Billy, why would they steal your bike? They've run away because they were scared to death they would go to jail. Don't you care what's happened to them or if they're all right?'

Billy's mouth opened and shut a couple of times but no sound came out. He looked at his father, tears beginning to well up in his eyes.

'William, you don't need to say anything. Constable, this is most irregular and I'll have your ...'

'With due respect, sir ...' Bob Peters paused and turned to face William Munse. '...Shut up!'

Munse spluttered, his eyes bulging but he remained silent.

'Dad?' Billy was visibly shaking with fear. 'Dad, I'm sorry.'

'Go on, son, let's clear this thing up once and for all.' The policeman gave Munse a sidelong glance.

'I just didn't want you to hang my bike away, dad, you said you would and ...' He broke into sobs.

'What's this, sir? You were going to hang his bike up ... what for?' Bob Peters looked hard at Billy's father.

'Well, I ... er.'

'Yes, go on, sir.'

'Dad said if I let any of the other kids ride it he'd hang it up in the shed and nobody would get to ride it. I didn't mean to get 'em in no trouble, honest,' Billy blurted out.

'I see. So you said they stole it to stop your father from taking your bike away did you?'

'That's enough, constable, can't you see you're upsetting the boy.' Munse however had lost his belligerent tone.

'No, dad, it's OK. I know I'll be in trouble for lyin' and you'll probably take me bike away forever but that doesn't matter now. *I'll* probably go to jail now instead of Jack and Harry.' He sniffed and wiped his nose with the back of a hand, fighting to keep from sobbing.

'Nobody's going to jail, son, but there is a warrant out for the boys' arrest. Do you think that's fair?' the constable appealed to Billy.

'No, it's not I guess. I made it up about them stealin' the bike, they didn't do it.' Billy felt a great weight lift off his shoulders but shivered inwardly when he saw the look in his father's eyes.

'Good lad, Billy, takes a man to admit he's made a mistake. Doesn't it, sir?' The policeman turned and faced Munse squarely.

Munse didn't reply immediately but then tried to regain command of the situation. 'What about the time it was found down at the creek, on the Tuesday? They must have taken it that time and …'

Billy went to speak but the policeman interrupted him. 'That's OK, Billy, I don't think we need to go into that episode do we?'

'I still insist that …' Munse was blustering and the policeman spoke again, directly to him.

'There's also the matter of the costs you know?' he said, pausing for effect before continuing. 'Very expensive having boats and officers dragging a river for nothing. Serious offence really, but then you'd know that wouldn't you, sir, being a solicitor?'

Munse looked deflated as the policeman continued. 'There's also a little matter about some *witnesses* that were mentioned in the initial statement. I'll have to investigate that also. I should go around and have a talk with them I suppose. Anyhow, must be off, back to the station to make out my report.' He turned back to the young boy standing forlornly in the centre of the room. 'Billy, thanks.' He held out his hand that Billy took weakly after hesitating and glancing at his father.

'I reckon you deserve a ride on that new bike, Billy, sort of a reward for your honesty. Take a spin down to the park eh?' The policeman gave William Munse a meaningful glare. 'I'm sure your father won't mind as he didn't mean it when he said he would take your bike away … did you, sir?'

Munse said nothing so the policeman continued. 'He just said it, son, to make you more careful with your bike that's all. Bring it past the station one of these days, Billy, I used to race bikes once so I could maybe give you a couple of tips.' He left, letting himself out the front door.

Back at the station, the sergeant looked up as the constable entered. 'What ever did you say over at the Munse's, Bob? Munse telephoned a minute ago and said he wanted all the charges against young Ferguson and Turner dropped!'

Bob Peters smiled innocently. 'I'll put it all in my report.'

◆◆◆◆◆◆◆◆◆◆◆◆

The sergeant had just left the Ferguson house after telling them and the Turners that all charges against their sons had been dropped and therefore the warrant would be withdrawn. He also told them he couldn't officially list them as 'missing persons' either because realistically they weren't as they had now made contact. He would let his colleagues in Kalgoorlie know to keep an eye out for them he said but beyond that could offer no further assistance.

'Nothing for it then, Claude, we'll have to go and look for them ourselves. They can't be too hard to find as we know they're in Kalgoorlie.'

'Little buggers,' Claude replied. 'But at least we know they're safe.'

'Or at least were when they posted the letters on Thursday.' Alice was unconvinced. 'That was three days ago.' She looked anxiously at the two men. 'When are you leaving?'

'First thing in the morning. That OK with you, Claude? I'll telephone a couple of the Elders men there and arrange somewhere to stay for a couple of days. At least our trust in them has been confirmed, they're innocent and now there's no warrant.'
'Yes, that's a Godsend, Jack. Once they find that out they'll be busting to get home.' Alice tried to sound cheerful but failed.

'Hmm ... that's if they haven't made their fortune.' The four of them laughed, a little too loudly, at Jean's attempt at humour.

Chapter Fourteen

Jack and Harry were at a loss as to what to do in the Aboriginal Community of Warburton. They had again witnessed the turnout of what seemed to them to be the entire population, both human *and* canine, to welcome the arrival of Reynold and Nigel. The boys wondered how the people knew the two young aboriginals were coming as they doubted there had been any contact from Mt Margaret but this was to be a phenomenon they would witness many times in the future. The ability of the Aboriginal people to communicate almost telepathically about many things, births, deaths, danger, comings and goings.

Their two friends were enveloped in a mass of swarming relatives as soon as they had stepped from the truck. They were almost immediately whisked away leaving Jack and Harry standing alone beside the truck in the increasing heat, surrounded by hordes of small black annoying bushflies that blanketed their backs and explored their eyes and mouths.

'Don't worry, boys.' George saw their uncertainty. 'That's pretty usual. Everyone knows you're here and you aren't being ignored but Reynold and Nigel are family and they come first. After things settle down in a while and the boys tell their relatives about you they'll be back. Give us a hand to unload while you're waitin'.' He began to untie ropes.

George was right. After about forty minutes an ancient vehicle came clattering up to where they were unloading boxes onto the verandah of a corrugated iron building that doubled as a post office, general store and, by the old rusty glass-bowl topped bowser, a petrol garage as well.

Reynold and Nigel waved to them over the top of the windscreen from the front seat of what appeared to be an old Model T Ford. What had once been a tourer had been converted into a rough tray back utility. It had no top, the headlights were broken and the bonnet cowlings were missing. There were three young children perched on the wooden floor at the back.

'This bloke 'ere me cuzin.' Reynold pointed to the driver as way of introduction but ignored the kids in the back, the boys again noting the lack of name exchange. 'Trow yer stuff on, we goin' to meet me uncle Warri now. Got good camp out little way.'

They climbed onto the back of the small tray, squeezing in with the kids who avoided looking at them, and the old Ford jerked to a start. About two miles down the red gravelled track Reynold's cousin swung heavily on the steering wheel, hauling the old vehicle onto an almost invisible trail toward a rocky red bluff. Before they saw any habitation the vehicle slowed and stopped.

Reynold turned to them with a serious expression on his face. 'Yu two fellas jump out 'ere, eh? Wait by that tree there.' He pointed to a stunted mulga offering a little shade. 'Rennol go in first 'n see uncle Warri. Come back for yu bloke shortly.'

His tone left no room for argument and the boys were mystified as they watched the old car move off through the low scrub and disappear round an outcrop of rocks about half a mile away. They could hear the distant barking of dogs a couple of minutes later so figured that the camp must be just beyond the rocks. They sat on their swags and waited, swatting the ever-present flies from their eyes.

Jack checked his pocket watch, then slipped it back in the pouch. 'He's been gone nearly forty minutes.'

Harry was about to respond when they heard the old Ford coming and saw the dust cloud rising behind it. It passed, did a U-turn and pulled up beside them, Reynold alone and at the wheel.

'Come on then,' he shouted as if it was they who were responsible for being there. 'Jump on, uncle Warri 'e waitin' fer yu.'

They rounded the bluff and drove for a few hundred yards to be met by three dogs running toward them. The boys thought that Reynold would run over them as he didn't slow down but the dogs dodged aside and spun around to chase the car, barking furiously behind it.

'This uncle Warri's camp,' Reynold yelled over the noise of the motor and pointed as they came into a clearing in the scrub. The 'camp' consisted of a large tattered canvas tarpaulin slung with ropes between four trees that had two wooden fruit crates with some planks on top as a makeshift table placed under it. Smoke curled lazily skyward from a campfire with an iron tripod over it. A blackened billy was suspended from it and there were three or four upturned kerosene tins doubling as chairs. An assortment of cooking pots and an iron frypan were dangling from the trees. A short way off to the rear, close to the bluff and under a rocky overhang for shelter, was a large fenced yard constructed from bush poles that held three horses.

Reynold's 'cuzin' jumped behind the wheel of the old truck and whistled for the kids who came running and clambered on the back. He waved his hand and drove off down the trail, soon lost from sight.

'This me uncle Warrinidding,' Reynold said proudly. 'These bloke the mates I tell yu 'bout, uncle. This one Jack, and this one 'e Harry. Yu can tell which is which 'cause Harry 'e got them freckles, eh?' he stood aside smiling as the two boys stepped nervously forward.

The man before them was tall. He wore only denim trousers and a battered felt hat with a wide brim, curled at the edges in a western style. He was barefoot; his skin the colour of ebony, and the boys noticed tribal scars on his muscled chest and arms. There was grey stubble on his cheeks and his eyes were dark and intelligent. He smiled broadly and shook each boy's hand in greeting. His voice was deep but strangely quiet when he spoke.

'Rennol, 'e bin tell me all 'bout yu fellas. Rennol say yu good mates. Travel wit' 'im all the way from Kalgoorlie.'

'Nice to meet you, Mr Nidding.' Harry said.

The tall man slapped his thigh and burst out laughing. Reynold hooted with him. They continued to laugh and the boys joined in with no idea what the joke was about.

'No ...' the man laughed again before explaining. '*Warrinidding* jus' *one* name not two name. Ev'ry one call me jus' plain *Warri* though.'

Harry was embarrassed, his face turning bright red. 'Er ... sorry, Mr Warri,' he stammered, again triggering more gales of laughter from the two aboriginals.

Jack was concerned for Harry but glad that he hadn't spoken first because he would have probably said the same thing. 'Well, what do we call you then? Harry didn't mean no harm?' He defended his friend and looked at Reynold for support.

The old man stopped laughing and was suddenly serious, his laughter replaced with a warm smile as he held his hand out again to Harry who took it hesitatingly. 'No one ever call me Mister *Nidding* before, it jus' soun' funny.' The boys could see he was fighting to stop from laughing again.

'Yu good fellas, Rennol tell me so. Yu frens of 'is so yu frens of mine. Rennol 'e tell me yu laik brothers to 'im so yu call me uncle Warri jus' laik 'e do, eh?'

'Thanks, uncle Warri.' Harry began to relax with Warri's friendly explanation.

Jack also calmed down and both boys, seeing the funny side of the recent exchange, started to laugh. Uncle Warri and Reynold joined with them and the tension lifted.

That night lounging around the campfire with the stars a brilliant mass of light above them and the bush hushed in silence, uncle Warri sat back on his haunches, and lit a cigarette dangling from his lips with a glowing stick from the coals.

'How long have you been a drover, uncle Warri?' Harry asked.

Warri thought for a while, eyes squinted due to the smoke circling his face. 'Long time now.'

'How long, uncle Warri?' Jack joined the conversation.

'Bin drovin' since I was a little fella, boy drover. Bin drovin' all over, bin drovin' for Sidney Kidman.' He paused, thoughts drifting back to times long ago. 'Took big mob of cattle for Mista Kidman up there to Quinsland, you know, way up to Normanton. Long way up.' All three boys now sat listening intently, fascinated by the unfolding story.

'We pick 'nother mob up down in Mt. Isa 'n come back wit' 'em all way down to Peterborough in Sout' Straylia. Sidney Kidman 'e say to me once 'Warrinidding, yu best boy drover ever.' I laik that Sidney Kidman, 'e good fella ... never forget me.' Warri flicked the butt into the coals.

'Go on, uncle Warri,' Jack urged.

'I do lotta trips for Kidman. Other fellas too but Mista Kidman 'e laik me special. When I drovin' I wear boots ... not *no* boot laik this.' He held up one bare foot. 'I wear boot that Sidney Kidman give me. He get 'em special for Warri. Special so they fit good, not pinch feet laik other boot I wear.'

Jack and Harry were mesmerised by Warri's accounts of droving and sat wide-eyed encouraging him to continue.

'I bin work for Boss Drover, Matt Savage in me time too. Very 'ard man that Matt Savage but 'e good drover. Also work wit' Paraway once ... long time back.'

'What's *Paraway*, uncle Warri?' Jack asked

'Not what, Jack ... who.' Warri smiled and explained. '*Paraway* a bloke. 'Is name Matt too but not Savage, 'is name Matt Buchanan.' He chuckled to himself remembering back. 'Funny fella but 'e top drover that one. Paraway 'e carry big green umbrella all time, shade 'im from the sun. We all laugh at that, eh? Not so 'e could 'ear though.' He gazed silently into the fire for a few seconds lost in thought.

'Warri getting' ol' now, Rennol maybe take over from uncle Warri one day. Rennol 'e *good* drover, I learn 'im ev'ry ting 'e know 'bout drovin.'

'We'd like to learn drovin' too, uncle Warri,' Jack stated.

'Take long time to learn 'im good but yu could 'elp out little bit I s'pose. Yu ride a horse, Jack? Yu too, Harry?

Both boys shook their heads realising that this admission could probably exclude them from the trip with uncle Warri and Reynold over to Docker River to meet up with a big mob of cattle on the way down from Katherine in the Territory. Reynold had told them earlier that that was the plan and that they could come too, if uncle Warri agreed.

Uncle Warri was silent for a time, stirring the fire with a stick. He looked over at Reynold who said nothing then turned back to face Jack and Harry. 'Yu can't go drovin' if yu can't ride no horse. Yu gotta ride good to be a drover, eh, Rennol?'

'Yeah, uncle, ride horse, crack a whip, round up strays, yu gotta be *very* good rider.'

'Never seen no drover that couldn't ride good. Jus' don' happen.' Warri said with finality.

The two boys were crestfallen. It seemed that all their plans had come to a sudden halt just when they thought they were on their way. They had come so far and now it was all over just because they couldn't ride a horse. They would now have to hitch a ride back to Laverton or somewhere and start all over.

'I think I might turn in then.' Jack stood up to walk from the fire, disappointment obvious in his tone.

'Me too, Jack.' Harry stood with him. 'G'night, uncle Warri, 'night, Reynold.'

'G'night, boys,' uncle Warri called as they walked from the firelight. 'Better yu get good sleep, boys, up early tomorra. Yu can't drove if yu can't ride so we better learn yu to ride, eh?' They didn't see Warri and Reynold grin at each other over the campfire.

Chapter Fifteen

Jack woke early with the sun an orange glow on the horizon and a deceptive chill in the dawn but he knew the day would be hot. He was not first up as Reynold was already at the fire, flames devouring the twigs he had thrown on the coals, blue smoke hanging listlessly in the morning air. Leaving Harry cocooned in his swag Jack crossed the clearing to speak with Reynold.

'Yu up at last, Jack, day 'e almos' gone,' Reynold chuckled without glancing behind him and Jack wondered how he knew it was him and not Harry, but refrained from asking.

'Yeah! OK for you, Reynold, this is your life, mate; we've to get used to it. Where's uncle Warri?'

'Bin long gone, Jack, gone to bring ol' Brehardie back. Brehardie 'is best 'orse once but 'e old now. Uncle Warri was gonna spell 'im this trip but 'e reckon 'e be good 'orse for yu or Harry to learn to ride on.' Reynold threw a handful of tealeaves into the bubbling billycan and moved it to the edge of the coals to brew.

'I really thought we were goners last night when he said we couldn't drove if we couldn't ride.'

'That jus' uncle Warri's way of jokin'.' Uncle Warri 'e wouldn'ta let yu come inta camp first time if 'e 'adn't decided yu could stay. We 'ave long talk 'bout yu 'n Harry. Warri 'e little bit wary of white fellas. White bloke drovers out on the track OK mos'ly but some don' laik us much. Warri 'e never 'ad much to do wit' town folk 'n yu bein' from the city it even worse. I tell 'im 'ow yu treat me 'n Nigel laik we brothers, sittin' inna rain 'n all 'n 'ow yu buy me a choclat bar 'n Warri 'e say, 'Good 'nuff, Rennol, yu say so, they OK.' Warri 'e was wonderin' though why yu'd even wanna to be wit' us blackfella as not many would, yu know, but I tell 'im you'se runnin' from them policemans 'n 'e understan' that. I tell 'im I don' think yu done nuttin' bad so uncle Warri 'e say, 'if yu believe 'im, Rennol, I believe 'im too.' Uncle Warri 'e trust Rennol.'

'How did you know about us runnin' from the police, Reynold? We didn't say anythin' to you about it.' Jack was baffled.

'Dunno … jus' guess I s'pose.' He was silent for minute and then closed the subject. 'Yu wanna cuppa, Jack?'

Warri returned about mid-morning, riding one of his horses bareback and leading two others, one on each side. Reynold walked out to meet him and took the two ponies he was leading. Warri slipped from the horse and led it over to where Jack was standing near the fire, a mug of tea in his hand.

'I bring me ol' 'orse Brehadie for yu to learn on, Jack. Brehardie 'e bin top 'orse once but 'e bit tired now, teeth not so good. Brehardie 'e 'appy to be 'ere though I can tell.' He reached up and fondled the horse's ears. 'Brehardie treat yu good, Jack, yu treat 'im good too, eh? We start learnin' yu in a little while. Where's Harry? I brought 'nother quiet 'orse for 'im to ride.'

'I'm here, Uncle Warri, just puttin' me boots on.'

'This one she called Dolly. She know drovin' too and she quiet laik a baby, eh? She learn yu to ride good, Harry.'

Jack was nervous and it showed. The horse sensed it and snorted, pawing the ground when Jack took the reins as Warri had shown him.

'Yu jus' settle down now, ol' fella.' Warri leant close and whispered in the horse's ear in his native tongue and Brehardie settled immediately. 'Yu learn these boys to ride good, Brehardie. Come on, Jack, yu cock 'im one leg by yu knee laik I show yu, keep 'im stiff now.'

Jack put his left foot in the stirrup and bent his right leg. Warri took his upheld foot and lifted him quickly into the saddle, placing his right boot into the other stirrup. Jack felt insecure so far up from the ground in an unfamiliar situation so he clung firmly to the reins and also had a grip on a piece of the horse's mane. Glancing quickly sideways he saw that Harry was also seated on the grey mare Dolly with Reynold standing beside him.

'Now, yu jus' sit easy, I'm gonna walk 'im, ol' Brehardie.' Warri clicked his tongue softly and the horse moved off with Jack clinging for dear life to the saddle pommel and the tuft of mane. 'Let go 'is mane, Jack, 'e not laik that much eh?' Warri advised.

After a few minutes Jack, realising he was not going to fall headlong to the hard ground, relaxed slightly, beginning to feel the horse's rhythm beneath him. Warri, holding lightly to the bridle, talked to the horse softly as he walked beside its head, reaching out to pat the horse's neck now and then. 'Yu good 'orse, Brehardie, yu learn Jack good. Jack, 'e good fella, Brehardie.'

Jack was sweating heavily but knew it wasn't only from the heat as Warri walked the horse. Warri also spoke to Jack giving him little tips on balance and controlling the animal. They had walked up the track some distance and returned to the yards three or four times and Jack was beginning to enjoy the experience. 'Yu take 'im on 'is own now, Jack.' Warri stepped back.

'But … but.' Jack began to panic. 'I don't think I'm ready to do that just yet, Uncle Warri. What if he takes off on me?'

Warri chuckled. 'Jack, yu bin ridin' 'im you'self last two times 'round. I jus' pretend to lead 'im. Brehardie won' take off on yu, Jack, unless yu kick 'im. Make sure yu don' kick 'im. When yu get to end of the track jus' pull little bit on the rein which way yu want to turn, left or right 'n Brehardie 'e know what to do.'

Warri watched Jack take the horse out, turn him easily and walk back, a huge smile on his face, to where he was waiting. 'Yu got it, Jack, no trouble. Yu do that three, four time more 'n we stop for some tucker. Give Brehardie a spell, let 'im have a drink. I show yu 'ow to get 'is saddle off 'n then me 'n Brehardie teach yu little bit more in the afternoon when it cooler.'

Harry returned at the same time having walked Dolly in the opposite direction to Jack. He was smiling broadly too, and called 'Yahoo,' to Jack as he reigned to a stop and slid awkwardly from the saddle. The two boys then led their mounts into the yard where Reynold and Warri instructed them on removing the saddles that they then slung over the top rail of the yard.

'That was great, Jack, wasn't it?' Harry was thrilled at the ride. 'Beats ridin' a bloody bike. Billy can keep his bike.'

'You bet, Harry. I was a little scared to start with but it's beaut all right. Trouble is I only feel about three feet tall after gettin' off Brehardie.'

'Me too,' laughed Harry. 'It's a funny feelin' all right.'

When they had eaten they all took some time to lie down in the shade until the extreme heat of the fiery sun had subsided. Jack and Harry stretched out on their swags but Warri and Reynold just lay down on the ground with their backs against a tree trunk, hats over their faces to ward of the flies, arms folded across their chests, and dozed.

The late afternoon was spent on the horses. Both boys became more confident as the day wore on and by the time Warri said it was enough for the day they had learned to canter leisurely up and down the track. They did slow to a walk to turn around though, not yet confident enough to do it at a canter. 'That'll come tomorra' wit' practice,' Reynold said.

Around the campfire that night uncle Warri sat back with his usual rolled cigarette and contemplated the coals. The two boys were exhilarated but weary, legs aching from gripping the saddle. When they closed their eyes they could still feel the rhythm of the horses beneath them.

'Did we do OK, Uncle Warri?' Jack asked.

'Yu do really good, Jack, I very good teacher yu know, learn yu to be drover in no time.' He turned to Harry. 'Yu do good too, Harry, Rennol 'e good teacher laik me. I learn him ev'ry ting 'e knows. Yu bot' quick learners, yu boys. After coupla' more days we ready to 'ead off to Docker River. Yu learn more on the ride too 'cause it take a few days to get there 'n by the time we meet the big mob, yu ready to 'elp out well wit' the drovin, by crikey.'

The next two days were spent on the horses and by the afternoon of the second day Jack and Harry were becoming quite confident and had learned to canter and even galloped for a few hundred yards. They could mount and dismount easily and learned to put the bridles on and saddle up without help but still couldn't get the hang of moving up and down in time with the horses' gait when they trotted. Warri and Reynold showed them how to rub the horses down with a bag at the end of the day and to feed them. They carried buckets from the waterhole in the rocks to fill the cut down oil drums in the yard so the horses had a drink.

On the morning of the third day Warri told them to saddle up and ride with Reynold into town to stock up on some supplies for the trip from the general store. 'Yu know what to get, Reynold 'n cuzin Wally 'e drive it back eh? Then we pack it right for the 'orses to carry. We'll leave at sun up tomorra' all goin' well.'

Jack and Harry felt important riding beside Reynold as they came into Warburton and slid from the saddles near the general store, tying the horses to a hitching rail in the shade of a couple of gum trees close by. They selected items from the shelves and put them in a pile near the door where the manager noted each of the items and wrote them in a large tattered book, licking the pencil regularly as he did so.

There was canned meat, beans and peaches, tins of golden syrup, condensed milk, bags of flour, salt, sugar, packets of matches, some 'Havelock' tobacco and cigarette papers for Warri and, of course, a box of tea.

'How much is all this gonna cost, Reynold?' Harry asked. 'You got enough money? We can put in a little for our share.'

'We have to, yes.' Jack reached into his shirt pocket.

'No need for that.' Reynold put his hand out to stop Jack. 'Uncle Warri 'e put all this on tick, pay when 'e come back.'

'But we have to pay our share, Reynold,' Jack insisted. 'It's not fair otherwise and we'd feel bad eatin' your tucker and not payin' for it.'

'That all right Jack. Uncle Warri 'e tell me yu boys can 'elp out on the drove and travel wit us but yu don' get no wage jus' your keep. That way yu don' owe nothin' … yu earn it.'

Both boys were astonished at this generosity and knew from what Reynold said that they were obviously accepted by uncle Warri as part of the crew so determined in their minds to be as good as they could be at helping out on the trek.

'Looks like we're real drovers now, Jack.'

'Can't believe it, Harry. We've come a long way since leavin' home haven't we? Seems like months ago.'

The mention of home sobered the boys somewhat and they wondered if their parents had received the letters they wrote and what their reaction had been to the news that they had no plans to return to Perth.

'What would our parents say if they could see us now, Harry?'

'Not sure, Jack. Don't think they'd be too happy even though they'd be proud that we can now ride.'

Even though the boys had no idea when cousin Wally had been alerted or by whom, the old Ford rattled to a dusty stop outside the store just as they finished checking that they had everything they needed. They loaded the goods onto the tray and mounting up, followed the vehicle on horseback down the track toward uncle Warri's camp, wondering what adventures the next few weeks held in store for them.

Chapter Sixteen

Disaster struck four days out of Warburton.

They had risen early on the day of departure and helped load the two packhorses that Warri had turned up with the evening before and distributed the balance of the supplies between them. Swags were roped behind the saddles and they had discarded their bags, leaving them for Wally, and rolled their clothes and personal belongings in a blanket secured with rope. Warri had explained that a *bluey* was easier to carry than a haversack on a horse.

The ride had been easy except for the stifling heat and, of course, the bush flies, but they were even getting used to them now and had developed the bush 'wave' which they now did unconsciously to keep the flies off their faces.

It was customary to start off each day in the first light before the sun had risen and then to camp for a couple of hours during the intense midday heat under whatever shade they could find before heading off again in the afternoon. They hadn't followed any defined track but trusted that uncle Warri knew where he was going through the arid desert country. They learned to sip sparingly at the water bag, wetting their lips and swilling a mouthful of water around before swallowing it rather than gulping large quantities. This method kept thirst at bay, moistened their lips and also conserved the precious liquid.

Warri, quite uncannily it seemed to Jack and Harry, always found a waterhole each day where the horses could drink and they could top up the waterbags. The boys were not aware that there were markers in the bush known only to the aboriginal people that pointed to where water was. Over thousands of years of nomadically wandering through the arid, seemingly waterless deserts of outback Australia with no capacity to carry water it was essential for survival to know where water could be found. Quality and quantity varied from hole to hole but it was these holes that Warri either knew from previous journeys or could find by reading the markers, visible to a learned eye from miles away. The markers, or 'trigs' as white settlers knew them, could consist of a pile of strategically placed rocks or possibly a tree with bark marked a certain way.

Reynold had shown the boys how to make damper from flour, salt and water then to bake it in the coals. They had dined on canned meat and beans for the first two nights and breakfast and lunch consisted only of damper washed down with strong black billy tea. 'This damper, 'e OK.' Warri took another bite. 'Yu boys gettin' to be good cooks, eh?'

They were stiff and sore for the first two days, hardly able to walk at the end of each day but gradually the aches eased and the stiffness receded from their muscles. By the third day on the road they felt fit and were both aware that they had trimmed pounds from their bodies and were becoming tanned from exposure to the sun. Harry had burned a little at first due to his light skin but soon his arms and face turned a golden brown highlighting his freckles, while Jack's skin became like mahogany. Reynold had commented jokingly one morning that Jack was turning so dark that nobody would question him when he called Warri, *uncle*.

Days spent continually in the saddle had been good for their confidence on the horses, both gaining experience and able to ride reasonably well. Reynold had even begun to coach them in using a stock whip, something he said they would need to master for the cattle drive. Both boys felt like seasoned bushmen and Warri was pleased with their progress but knew they had a lot more to learn before they were competent enough on horseback so that he could safely let them ride out alone.

When the billy was filled on the third evening Warri had commented that they were getting short of water as the last hole was dry, yielding only damp clay. He said he knew there was a waterhole not far from where they were camped and Reynold could head off to it early the next morning and suggested that the boys go with him for the ride.

Jack woke and looked over to see that Harry was not lying on his swag. Curious to know where he was he got up and rolled his swag, tying it ready for slinging over his saddle, and went to find him. The sun had not yet risen but there was a pre-dawn light in the east. The fire was not alight and he could see Reynold and uncle Warri stretched out beside the fire, heads resting on the saddles that they used for pillows.

He was baffled that Harry was not around then, to his surprise, he noticed that Dolly was missing so he quickly walked back to Harry's swag. There was a note pinned to it that he had previously missed in the darkness. He read and re-read the note before running to where Warri and Reynold were, calling out to them as he ran. They woke asking what he was yelling about and he told them that Harry was missing. Jack held the note out to uncle Warri.

'Yu read 'im out, Jack,' Warri said. 'Eyes 'e not so good for readin' yu know.' Jack was unaware that Warri had never learned to read and could only just write his name. 'What 'im say?' He sounded concerned.

Jack read the note aloud.

> Gone to find the waterhole. Took the two big waterbags. Thought I would earn me keep and save Reynold a trip. Get the fire going Jack. Be back soon.

It wasn't signed.

Warri said nothing, just stood and went to the fire and started to stir the coals and throw twigs on it.

Reynold looked at Jack, his eyes clouded with concern. 'Jack, this not good. He could get lost easy out there.'

'But uncle Warri said the waterhole was close by; he should find it shouldn't he?'

'But what direction 'e go, Jack?' Warri asked from the fire. 'Yu see 'im leave?'

'No, I just found the note, I didn't see him leave. I suppose we better go look for him.'

'No point in that, Jack.' Reynold sounded older than his years 'We could ride 'round in circles for hours 'n still not see 'im.'

'We jus' wait 'n see if 'e come back soon.' Warri didn't look up from where he was fanning the fire into a blaze. 'Maybe we lucky 'n 'e not get lost. Harry no fool really 'n should be able to backtrack to the camp if 'e not gone too far. Doubt 'e find water though … hard to see. Need to know jus' where to look to find 'im,' Warri stated unemotionally.

'He was only tryin' to do us a favour, uncle Warri, he didn't mean any harm by goin' off.'

'That true, Jack. Harry good fella and tink 'e do right but do stupid ting. All's we can do is wait.' Warri busied himself with heating what was left of the tea in the billy.

'Can't we do somethin', Reynold?' Jack was worried after what uncle Warri had said.

'No. We do what uncle Warri say, 'e know best.' Reynold walked off to join Warri at the fire.

Reynold and Warri spent time checking the supplies and getting the packhorses ready. Jack noticed that Warri occasionally glanced at the sun then out across the horizon but said nothing. Reynold was equally quiet and sat on his saddle by the fire fondling the ears of his blue heeler cattle dog, one of three that accompanied them on the trip.

As the time neared noon, Jack began to get really anxious and paced about the edge of the camp, his hand raised to shield his eyes from the blistering sun as he searched for some sign of his friend. Warri and Reynold lounged in the shade seemingly unconcerned. 'Jack, yu save energy. Not 'elp if yu wore out by walkin' round 'n round laik blind rabbit,' Warri advised.

Jack didn't understand why they wouldn't start a search and was about to ask when the dogs began to bark, alerting them to movement in the distance. 'Here he comes now,' Jack yelled excitedly, squinting into the distance. His excitement turned to dread when he realised that the horse trotting toward them in the distance was riderless, stirrups flapping empty from the saddle.

'This bad ting, 'e musta fallen off somewhere.' There was concern now in Warri's tone.

'Now we have to go and look for him.' Jack strode determinedly toward Brehardie grabbing the saddle from the ground as he went.

'Jack, yu stay put … Now!' Warri's authoritative command stopped him in his tracks. 'Yu go out now 'n we 'ave two bloke to look for … we wait.'

'But, uncle Warri, Harry might be hurt somewhere and out of water, we have to go.' He was breathing heavily, anger in his voice.

'We wait!' Warri was adamant.

'Wait! Wait for what?' Jack yelled. 'Until he bloody well dies! You're trackers aren't ya, why can't ya track him and find him?'

'Jack.' Reynold walked over to him. 'I know yu worried 'bout Harry, we worried too but we don' know where to look jus' yet. He coulda ridden in lotsa direction and all over.' He swung his arm in a wide arc. 'It'd take long time to track where 'e go. We wait, Jack. Know soon 'nough where to look.'

'How? Where?' Jack was unconvinced, beginning now to get very angry that no effort was being made to find Harry.

Warri got up from under the tree and stood motionless for some time staring around the horizon without speaking. Reynold watched him and Jack wondered what was happening. 'There, Rennol, yu see 'em?'

'Yeah, long ways off. 'Bout two, tree mile I reckon.'

'See what, Reynold?' Jack stared in the direction they pointed to, seeing nothing but the shimmering heat causing dunes in the distance to dance like waves on the ocean.

'We know where Harry is, Jack, we go find 'im now. Grab that waterbag, Rennol and lead Dolly wit' us.' Warri sprung into action throwing the saddle on his horse. Jack only just had time to cinch up the girth strap on his saddle and jump on Brehardie before Reynold left the camp with his uncle.

They were ahead of him but he quickly caught up. *It must be that aboriginal intuition,* he though to himself. *They always seem to know things in a strange way.* When he reached them he asked how they now knew where to look for Harry.

'Can yu see 'em now, Jack?' Reynold pointed skyward ahead of them.

'I can only see a few birds in the distance, Reynold, nothin' else.'

'That's what we waitin' for Jack. Those birds, they tell us where Harry is.'

'What?' Jack was astounded. 'How can the birds tell us where he is?'

'Those birds, they see an animal or somethin' not right out in the bush, they watch. If they think 'e 'urt or somethin', they watch 'n watch then they follow, circle above 'im. Waitin' to see if it safe to go down 'n maybe get a feed. We watch them birds 'n they tell us where Harry is.'

As they closed on the region where the birds were circling Jack could see two eagles, a few smaller hawks and some black crows riding the thermals in the afternoon heat. It was obvious now, even to Jack, that the birds were concentrated on one area not far ahead so he knew it wouldn't be long before they found Harry - but would he be all right or badly hurt or worse still …?' He refused to think beyond *hurt.*

They topped a low rise that fell away to a gully dotted with spindly bush and noticed the marks that Harry had made in the sand as he had stumbled toward the scrub seeking shelter form the sun.

Warri kneed his horse forward in a run toward the spot where he knew Harry had crawled. He was off his horse before it stopped, waterbag gripped in his hand as he fell to his knees beside the still form partly hidden by the bushes.

Jack was immobilised by fear and remained seated on Brehardie as Reynold dismounted and passed Dolly's reins to him before running to where Warri was kneeling.

'Is ... is ... is he still alive, uncle Warri?' Jack could hardly speak, his voice a fearful croak in his throat.

'Rennol, give me a 'and 'ere.' Warri gently turned Harry's inert body over and leaned close to his face 'Not good, need water ... quick!'

Jack reluctantly stepped from the saddle, dropping both sets of reins without thinking, but fortunately the horses stood quietly as they had been trained to do. He walked toward where Warri and Reynold were bent over the motionless figure, fearful of what he would see and was shocked to see Harry's swollen lips and puffy face. Harry's eyes were shut and Jack was sure he was dead.

Warri cradled Harry's head on his lap, holding his hat up to protect his face from the sun. 'Rennol, pour some water slow now in 'is mouth. Only little bit at a time.'

Reynold put the tip of the waterbag close to Harry's mouth and began to pour the life-giving water. It ran down Harry's chin with no response from him.

'Open 'is mouth little bit, easy now, Rennol.'

Imperceptibly at first Harry's lips moved then he opened his cracked lips and sucked at the stream from the waterbag. He coughed and his head rolled aside. Warri held his head gently, telling Reynold to try again. Harry responded better the second time and swallowed as the water trickled into his mouth. He took a few mouthfuls of water and his eyes opened slowly but he was unable to focus. He tried to speak but his voice was just a croak and no words came.

'Shhh, Harry, no need yu talk, mate, jus' lie there 'n 'ave some more water, eh?' Warri's voice was soothing.

'Is he gonna to be all right, uncle Warri?'

'Soon 'nough, Jack. Harry 'e all dry out from the sun, very lucky we get to 'im when we do, 'e not last long if we didn't.'

The three of them sat on the hot sand beside Harry and coaxed more trickles of water through his cracked lips shading him from the lowering sun with their bodies. After some time Harry started to come around but was disoriented and mumbled unintelligibly.

When Warri thought it was safe to do so he put his arms under Harry's legs and around his shoulders lifting him up to carry him to where the horses were patiently standing. 'Harry too crook to ride, Rennol, 'elp me git 'im up on me 'orse. I ride him back to camp. Yu lead Dolly, Jack.'

Reynold helped put Harry astride Warri's horse and then Warri leapt easily into the saddle holding Harry's slumped form against his chest as he kneed his mount forward toward the distant camp. Reynold followed with Jack bringing up the rear, Dolly trailing behind on a long rein.

Back at camp Warri laid Harry on the swag, placing a blanket over him as the evening was beginning to chill as it often did in the desert, even though the days were unbearably hot. 'Open that tinned stew there, Jack, and Rennol … mix it wit' some water to make little soup on the fire for Harry.'

Warri left Harry lying on the swag and walked off into the bush. Jack wondered where he was going as it was dark but knew better than to ask. When Warri returned he was carrying a small leafy bush that he had obviously pulled completely from the ground as it still had roots and dirt hanging from it. Warri stripped a handful of leaves from the bush and, crushing them in his hand, threw them into the bubbling pot of soup.

'What's that stuff, uncle Warri?' Jack was mystified.

'Jus' some medicine to make 'im well.' He didn't explain so when he pulled some roots from the bush and put them in his mouth Jack again asked what it was he was doing.

'Yu too young to learn 'bout this, Jack. Anyway, only ol' blackfella know these tricks.' He chewed the roots into a paste that he spat into his hand before walking over to where Harry lay on the swag. Pulling back the blanket he rolled Harry's shirtsleeve up and Jack noticed for the first time the large deep graze on his forearm. It was red, swollen and angry looking. Warri patted the chewed fibrous mass over the wound and bound it with a strip of cloth.

'That stop it goin' bad, be good as new coupla' days.' Warri inspected his handiwork and stood up. 'Now for the soup. It do Harry real good wit' them leaf in it. Harry shake little bit tonight but in the mornin' … no fever 'n 'e be OK. Bit weak maybe 'n we prob'ly stay camp 'ere 'nother day or so but 'e be fine, Jack. Yu don' worry no more, OK?'

Jack stood awkwardly by as Warri fed Harry the soup slowly from a spoon. At first Harry shook his head but Warri persisted until he finally took a little of the thick beverage. Soon he had eaten most of what was in the pot so Warri then gave him a little more water. He shivered under the blanket but Warri said that was natural and that he'd be all right in the morning. Jack was still concerned for his mate but reassured by Warri's positive statement that left no room for doubt.

Chapter Seventeen

Jack didn't sleep much through the night. Harry moaned and rolled around a lot and, although Jack catnapped, concerns for his friend close by on the swag consumed him, making sleep almost impossible.

Sometime just before dawn Jack realised that Harry was still and not groaning as before so he crawled over to listen. Relieved to know he was breathing deeply he went to the fire and stirred it into flames. Pouring the last of the water into the billy he placed it on the coals when the flames subsided. He sat cross-legged on the ground, waiting for the water to boil, wondering if the decision to come out this far was a wise one realising there was no professional medical help within miles. He doubted that Warri or Reynold would return to Mt Margaret so they could get Harry help in Laverton and the prospect of travelling back without them with Harry so sick alarmed him.

Warri and Reynold joined him at the fire as the sun crept toward the day, light wispy clouds resembling reddish pink brush strokes on the pale morning sky. 'Mornin', young Jack,' Warri greeted him. 'Guess yu not sleep too much last night, eh? Harry 'e toss 'n turn a lot.' He checked the billy and grunted approval when he noticed it was near to boiling.

'Yeah, uncle Warri, he groaned and moaned most of the night but quietened down early this morning. Should we wake him, see how he is?'

'Nah, let 'im sleep, do 'im good, 'e wake up when 'e ready. Yu see, Jack, 'e be much better then. Rennol 'n I we go out to the waterhole, fill up for the trip. Yu stay 'ere to be with Harry and when he wake up ...' He crushed some more leaves and tossed them in the tea, after they had filled their own mugs. '... Give 'im a mug of this after it brew little bit. Put plenty sugar wit' 'im, Jack, 'cause 'e not taste too good in tea but it do 'im good.'

Saddling their horses Warri and Reynold slung empty waterbags over one of the packhorses then headed out of camp toward some low hills in the distance. Jack noted it was in the opposite direction to where Harry had been found.

They had been gone for about an hour when he heard Harry calling him. 'Jack! Are you there? ... Jack?' His voice was a little husky but strong.

'I'm here, Harry, comin'.' Jack splashed the brewed tea and leaves into a pannikin, stirred some sugar in then took it to Harry who was now sitting up. 'How you feelin', mate?' He handed him the mug.

'Bit stiff.' He arched his back. 'Me head feels a bit funny but not too bad.' He looked around, confusion in his expression. 'How did I get back here, Jack?'

'Drink up the tea, Harry, it's got some special medicine in it to get you better.' He urged after Harry took a sip and frowned, peering into the mug. 'We went out and looked, mate. Uncle Warri found ya. Waited until the birds told us where ya were.'

'What birds? How did the birds tell ya where I was?'

'Never mind, I'll explain later. The main thing is that you're OK. I was worried about you and then *really* worried when we found ya. You were as crook as a dog and couldn't speak or move. Just lyin' there in the hot sun under a bush. I thought you were dead, mate … honest! What happened?'

'It's all a bit fuzzy, can't remember anythin' about bein' under a bush or you blokes findin' me.' He finished the tea and shuddered. 'Tastes pretty horrible that; what's in it?'

Jack explained briefly about the leaves but didn't elaborate how Warri had chewed the roots to put on the cut on his arm when Harry noticed the rough bandage and asked what it was.

'I got pretty scared out there, Jack, when I came off Dolly. I musta been knocked out or somethin' 'cause the first thing I knew I was lyin' in the sand with the sun beatin' down on me and no horse in sight. I thought I knew where the camp was but I musta just wandered around in circles because I can remember crossin' over me own tracks once or twice. Hard to get yer bearin' out there.'

'We've both learned a big lesson from this, Harry. How did ya come off Dolly? You were ridin' real good.'

'Snake,' Harry said. 'I was ridin' along and saw a bit of a gully with a few mulga trees and thought it could be the water hole. I went down the slope past a fallen log when this bloody great snake …' he held his arms outstretched. '… Musta been six feet long easy, whipped out from the log right beside us. Before I had time to think, Dolly shied, reared up and turned at the same time. I wasn't ready for it and just fell off. Musta hit me head on the log.'

'Gee, Harry, probably a king brown, eh?'

'Dunno, Jack, but he sure was a biggun. I was worried at first that the snake might have got me or that he was there somewhere but I didn't see him, just his track in the sand headin' outta the gully.'

'Sure you're OK now?'

'Yeah, as I said though, a bit stiff and me throat feels really dry. Me tongue's real furry too. Got some water?'

'Afraid not, mate. Uncle Warri and Reynold should be back with it soon. There's more tea though.'

'No thanks,' Harry said. 'Yuk.'

It was nearing eleven o'clock when the two horsemen returned leading the packhorse loaded with bulging bags of water. Harry was still on the swag but had been up once to walk unsteadily to the edge of the camp to relieve himself before wobbling back to lie down again. He sat up when Warri and Reynold rode in.

'Hey, Harry,' Reynold called to him. 'Yu still wit' us, mate.'

The two dismounted, unloaded the bags and brought one over to where Harry was resting. 'Thought yu might laik a bit of this, young Harry.' Warri poured a mug of water and handed it to Harry who gulped it down thirstily. 'Yu feelin' OK?' Warri asked.

Harry told them he was a bit groggy and that his mouth was dry. Warri explained that it was probably from getting too much sun as well as having nothing to drink. 'Moisture 'e all gone from yer body. Yu be OK in a day or so, Harry. That medicine I give yu 'e work pretty good.'

Harry sheepishly apologised, going on to explain what had happened but before he could finish Warri said 'No need for sorry, Harry, yu learn good lesson though, eh? I bet yu never go out alone again not knowin' where to ride. Bet, too, yu be more careful on Dolly.'

'You're not angry at me, uncle Warri?' Harry had expected a tongue-lashing for his stupidity.

'Angry at *me* for not warnin' yu boys 'nuff 'bout the danger out there. Not angry wit' *yu*, Harry, for doin' it. Warri jus' 'appy yu OK now. We rest up 'ere for 'nother night then get on the road first light tomorra. People spectin' us at Docker.'

'I'm OK, uncle Warri, we can leave now if you like.' Harry went to stand but Reynold put his hand on his shoulder.

'Yu sit back down, Harry, it too late to 'ead out now. Yu 'ave trouble ridin' Dolly laik this anyhow 'n tomorra yu be good laik new, eh?

Warri took a rifle from his pack then walked out from the camp around sundown and they heard two gunshots echo across the desert. He strolled back a short time later carrying two rabbits. Reynold stirred the fire up and when he was satisfied that it was the right temperature he chucked both rabbits into the coals.

'Aren't ya gonna skin 'em, Reynold?' Jack was surprised that they went on fur and all. They hadn't even been gutted.

'No need, Jack, they taste real sweet laik this. Best meat yu ever taste, except for maybe bungarra, 'e real good tucker. Anyhow, why waste time skinnin' 'em when there's no need. Keep all the juice in this way too, make 'im real tender.'

The rabbits were delicious and a welcome change from the canned meat and damper they had had the previous nights. Jack had tasted rabbit before but his mum usually either baked them in the oven like chickens or made rabbit stew. To have them cooked in the coals with the subtle taste of wood smoke on the meat was better than he had experienced before. They ate them with their hands, tearing bits off the carcasses. The boys thought how much life had changed for them in just over a week and a half.

'This is better than me dad's barbecued snags, Harry.'

'Sure is, Jack. He burns them snags more than these bunnies too'

'Yeah and he doesn't skin *them* before he chucks 'em on either.'

Both boys laughed, flicking bones to the dogs waiting patiently at the edge of the firelight and licking their fingers noisily. It did not dawn on them that this was the first time since they had left the safety and routine of their well ordered lives in Perth that they had made mention of 'home' without it emotionally disturbing them.

Harry was indeed 'good laik new' the next morning as Warri had predicted and Jack could not believe the rapid change in his condition. He determined to find out more about the bush medicine Warri had used but when he asked him again about it the old aboriginal just shook his head saying it was 'blackfella medicine.'

♦♦♦♦♦♦♦♦♦♦♦

Harry needed a bit of a leg up to help him mount Dolly the next morning and was obviously nervous to be back on horseback. Warri suggested that he ride the pony around a bit while they cleared camp so he could restore his confidence before heading off. Reynold explained to Jack how the best thing to do when you fall or get thrown from a horse was to get back on straight away so fear didn't set in. With Harry unconscious it wasn't possible but uncle Warri said that it would only take a couple of hours for him to get used to it again. It wasn't so much the fall from the horse he commented but the fear of being lost again in the desert that was on Harry's mind; something he was sure Harry would avoid ever doing again.

Progress was slow that day as Warri was aware that Harry needed plenty of rest spells. In the middle of the afternoon they had been following a dry creek bed when they came to a waterhole that magically materialised before them like an oasis. Tall, white-trunked gums surrounded it and there was a tranquillity that affected the four of them, so there was little talk as they soaked up the atmosphere and its beauty. The crystal clear water was inviting with a sandy bottom so the three boys stripped and jumped in to cool off.

They splashed each other laughing and ducking their heads under while Warri watched from the bank where he squatted in the shade, a cigarette dangling from his lips, smoke lazily wafting around his head in the still air.

'I tink we camp 'ere tonight, boys, good place.' Warri decided when they came out to dry off in the sun. 'Tomorra we be in Docker River.'

Although reluctant to leave the waterhole the next morning to ride again through the desert heat, the prospect of being in Docker River at the end of the day beckoned. Mounting up they rode out into the rising sun, the early morning light painting the distant Rawlinson Range to their left varying shades of purple.

Jack and Harry were awed by the changing vibrant hues of the desert hills as the sun travelled through the sky on its journey from morning to night. What they had once believed was a drab featureless landscape became for them now a kaleidoscope of shifting colour.

'Those hills they called the Petermann Range.' Reynold pointed ahead of them. 'Not long now 'n we in the Territory. Docker not far over the border.'

Jack looked at Harry riding beside him and there was unspoken communication between them as their eyes met. Not only had they left Perth and the familiarity of home but they were now also leaving Western Australia: the creek, Ashmorton, school, Billy Munse, the bike and their families a lifetime behind them.

Chapter Eighteen

Jack Ferguson parked the Holden outside the Elder Smith building in Kalgoorlie. He and Claude Turner went into the office where the receptionist, a blonde woman in her mid twenties with bobbed hair, greeted Jack. He introduced Claude to her as a man dressed in white moleskin trousers and a pale blue checked shirt matched with a brown woollen tie emerged from a side office. He invited them warmly to join him.

Introductions completed, Jack said, 'thanks, Alan, for taking time to see us, mate.'

'No problem, Jack … have you heard any news of the boys?'

'Afraid not other than the letters they sent. They're here, or at least around the district somewhere, but we don't know where.'

'I've had a few of the boys keeping an eye out, Jack, and I've also asked around but nobody seems to have spotted them. Strange you know, as even though Kal's a pretty big place, a couple of kids around the streets would be sure to be noticed. What have the police come up with?'

'Nothing, Alan,' Claude answered. 'The boys have been taken off the missing persons' list and there's no warrant out for them so officially the police haven't been too active. We called in at the station before we came here.'

'The police here have been talking with the sergeant from home but as they can't do anything officially it's just a matter of them being alert as they go about their normal work,' Jack added.

'What are your plans then, Jack?' Alan leaned back in his chair. 'Can I do anything for you?'

'No, not really. I appreciate you booking the accommodation for us at the pub and if we can use the office here as a base, you know … use the telephone from time to time, it'd be a great help.'

'Just treat the place as home, Jack. You too, Claude. Must be a bugger not knowing where they are but I'm sure they're OK and they'll turn up sooner or later.'

They thanked Alan for his assistance and left the office, not sure where to start. They agreed to walk the main street at least and check out some of the clothing stores. The boys had mentioned in their letters that they had purchased work gear so one of the store people might have remembered them buying clothes and hats and possibly the boys had given some clue as to what their plans were.

Driving back to Hannan Street they parked the car and split up, deciding to cover one side of the street each to save time, and to meet back at the car in an hour. Their efforts produced no results. Store people just shook their heads sympathetically but could give no positive leads and the photos that they showed drew blank responses. Meeting up back at the car they were discouraged so thought they might as well drive to the hotel that they had been booked into, have a beer then plan their next move.

They backed out carefully from the kerb, unfamiliar with the 'nose in' parking in Kalgoorlie and turned off the main street, heading for the hotel that Jack knew from previous visits was situated down one of the adjacent streets. Approaching an intersection they came up behind an old battered black Chevrolet sedan stopped before the corner, its bonnet up with a darkly clad figure bent over the motor.

Drawing to a stop alongside the vehicle Claude wound the window down and spoke to the person stooped under the bonnet. 'G'day, anything we can do to help, mate?'

They were both surprised, when the man withdrew his head from the front of the car and turned to face them to see that he was dressed in clerical garb.

'Arhh, thank you, gents, but she's a cantankerous old girl she is. Not sure what the problem is you know. Goes well one minute and then decides to stop for no reason. She's a mind of her own and that's for sure.' The priest patted the hood affectionately.

Jack smiled at the priest's obvious fondness for the old vehicle. 'Can we give you a lift somewhere, Father?'

'No, but thank you for your kindness. I'm sure with a little patience …' He glanced skyward '… and a little assistance from above, that she'll be taking me home soon enough. She does this now and then.'

'You sure we can't help, Father?' Claude persisted. 'No trouble you know.'

'Well maybe if you could be helping me to push her off to the side of the road so I don't block the traffic I'd be appreciating it.'

Jack backed up and parked the Holden. He and Claude stepped from their vehicle and walked up to the Chev. 'Hop in, Father, we'll give you a push. Maybe that'll get her going for you, never know.'

'Worth a try I suppose. I've worn the battery down a bit trying to get her started. If I can just get her home I can fiddle with the carburetor; that seems to be the main problem.' The priest looked at the two men and a slight frown creased his face as he examined them closely.

'Do I know you gents at all; are you from around here?'

'No, Father, we're from Perth, just arrived today,' Jack replied. 'I've only been through here a couple of times and it's Claude's first time in Kalgoorlie so I'm sure we haven't met.'

'Oh well … it must be that I'm getting old like me dear car here.' He jumped behind the wheel, slamming the door shut. 'I'll put her in second gear, see if she starts.'

'OK, Father, don't stop if she starts, just keep going, eh'? Claude suggested.

'I won't, gents, thanks for your help and God bless you for your kindness.'

They pushed the heavy vehicle forward, thankful that there was a slight downhill slope in the road. 'OK, Father … give her a go!' Jack yelled breathlessly when they gained some speed.

The priest let the clutch out and the old motor coughed, backfired twice but then sprang into life, a cloud of blue smoke enveloping Jack and Claude. The priest waved enthusiastically from the window as the black car frog-hopped down the road a couple of times before turning left at the corner to disappear from view, a pall of smoke left hanging in the air.

Father O'Malley drew up in front of the corrugated iron garage at the rear of the presbytery, thankful that his vehicle had made it home, and decided he must ring the garage to book the old girl in for a service.

He stepped from the driver's seat, closed the door and stood for a minute beside the car, his face creased in concentration. *There was something vaguely familiar about those men,* he thought. *Oh well, you must be getting senile, Timothy.* He shook his head and walked off toward the presbytery without giving another thought to the two men who were at that time sitting in the bar of the Criterion Hotel, planning the next move they would make in their efforts to track down Jack and Harry

♦♦♦♦♦♦♦♦♦♦♦♦

There was a message waiting for Warri when they arrived in Docker River. It seemed that plans had changed and he was not to meet up with the herd coming down from Katherine but was to head south, to Angas Downs Station, where there was a mob that needed taking over the border into South Australia.

The note instructed Warri to bring a crew of three or four young stockmen with him plus a couple of good spare horses and make contact with Tom Cooper, the boss of the drove. It didn't take Warri more than an hour to round up three young aboriginal stockmen to join him and Reynold.

Jack and Harry felt a little left out and somewhat intimidated by the addition of three young, but obviously competent, stockmen but uncle Warri told them they would still be a part of the drive anyhow. He also told them that it was the first time the new boys had been on a drove although they were good with horses and were experienced with cattle, having helped out on some musters. He further allayed their fears by telling them that it was agreed that they be a part of the team.

'I make a promise wit' Rennol that I 'elp yu get as close to Kupa Piti as I can. Warri good to 'is word. Still, no wage for yu fellas, jus' yer keep. Tom Cooper 'e not pay for green blokes on a drive. That OK?'

'Thanks, uncle Warri,' Harry spoke for both of them. 'We promise not to cause any more problems'

'Yu fellas stay wit' us, me 'n Rennol. Yu good 'nuff now to 'elp out. Besides, what would we tell Brehardie 'n Dolly, they laik yu boys.'

The boys were elated to be included and they had never expected to be paid. They in fact thought the trip would cost them money but they still had the balance of their winnings tucked safely away in their blueys as they knew the time would come when the money would come in handy.

Reynold accompanied Warri to the store to top up on a few supplies while the two boys stayed to keep watch over the camp. The three new drovers kept to themselves, setting up camp on the edge of Warri's site although they would all share the same campfire and they busied themselves checking bridles and saddles, effecting repairs where necessary. Jack and Harry weren't sure if the new lads didn't approve of them being there or that they were just shy not knowing what to say. One of them, who seemed to be only about a year older than themselves, sat plaiting a stockwhip from strips of leather hide.

Jack and Harry slowly ambled closer and stood watching him work fascinated by his skill as they observed the whip materialise. He looked up, flashed a brief smile then continued, totally absorbed in his work.

'I'm Jack and this is me mate, Harry.'

'Wandoo.' He stated his name but didn't look up.

'That's really great work, Wandoo,' Harry commented. 'I couldn't do anythin' like that.'

'Bin doin' it since I was little fella; me grandfather 'e learn me. Make bridles too.' Wandoo reached down and picked up a bridle at his side holding it up for them to see.

'Gee that's a beauty.' Jack took the outstretched bridle examining it closely even though he knew nothing about saddlery.

Wandoo continued to plait the whip without acknowledging the compliments but they noticed a slight smile etch his face. They stood there feeling awkward so turned to walk away. It was then that Wandoo spoke. 'Uncle Warri 'e tell us yu fellas come all way from Perth, never bin there ... to Perth. Only ever bin to Laverton all me life. It big place, this Perth?'

Realising they had broken through a barrier they turned back to Wandoo 'Yeah, it's big all right but too many people and noisy, eh? Not like out here where you blokes live.' Jack had the presence of mind not to brag about the city and its comforts or tell about his home and the easy life they had compared to the life the aboriginal people endured in this arid, desolate country.

He was not aware at that time that the boy sitting before them and most like him would not want to trade their lifestyle and freedom for the restrictions of living in a large town or city. Although Jack and Harry didn't know it then, and it would take some time for it to develop, they too would one day feel exactly like Wandoo and his people.

'Uncle Warri 'e say yu fellas never rid a 'orse before 'e 'n Rennol learn you 'bout a week ago, that right?'

'Yes, that's right.' Harry was embarrassed to admit they were novices.

'Yu do pretty good. Us boys we watch yu come inta Docker wit' uncle Warri.' Wandoo concentrated on his whip.

'Thanks. We've got a lot still to learn though.'

Wandoo grunted, nodding his head. 'Yeah, it take long time to ride good but yu boys get the 'ang of 'im pretty quick I tink.'

Not knowing what else to say, they were relieved to hear the dogs announce the return of Warri and Reynold from their ride and they walked off to meet them. There was a spring in their steps though at Wandoo's observations of their ability to ride. They were glad though that they had come into Docker at a walk and not at a trot because they still hadn't got the hang of that.

'He seems to be OK, Harry, just a bit shy I reckon.'

'Hope that's what it is, Jack. I feel a bit of a drip around those blokes though.'

'Know what you mean, Harry, but after a few more weeks in the saddle we'll be darn near as good as they are on a horse, eh?' He slapped Harry on the back as they walked.

Harry playfully knocked Jack's hat off his head. 'We need to get these hats a bit worn in, Jack, they look so bloody new compared to everyone else's.'

The clothes they had bought in Kalgoorlie were now creased and patchy with sweat, the newness camouflaged with red dust, grime from riding and ash from the fires. Their hats however, although dusty, still looked store-bought. When Jack picked his hat up from where it had landed after Harry had flicked it from his head, he crunched it in his hands then punched inside the crown.

'You're right, mate,' he said. 'We'll have to work on these.' He punched the hat harder before putting back on his head and pulling the brim low over his eyes.

They greeted Warri and Reynold as they slid from the saddles and were astonished when Reynold pulled two chocolate peanut bars from his shirt. They had forgotten about the chocolate that Harry had bought and given to Reynold way back in Menzies the first day of the trip to Mt Margaret.

'I et mine on the way back.' Reynold grinned as he handed them the chocolates.

'Get an early night, boys,' Warri said as he finished his now customary after-tea smoke. 'We gotta long hard ride tomorra. Not laik the trip over, we need to get to meet up with Tom Cooper 'n 'is boys as soon as we can. They'll 'ave started wit'out us 'n we 'ave to catch them blokes up. Mob too big for jus' them fellas,' Warri grinned. 'They need us fer sure.'

Chapter Nineteen

They hit the track just before sun up riding in tandem with Reynold and Warri leading. Jack and Harry felt important when Warri said they were second in the line and that the new boys could bring up the rear leading the packhorses. Warri set a fast pace and the lunch break was brief with the horses left saddled. There was just time to set a fire, boil the billy, wash down a slice of cold damper and then it was back in the saddle and on the trail again.

Passing through a varying landscape fringed with hills and high bluffs they crossed red sandy ridges dotted with spiky spinifex and saltbush. They saw huge rounded monoliths and jagged sentinels of weathered rock rising up beside the track and they rode through deep steep walled gorges of sheer rock peppered with numerous caves, coming across a number of crystal clear waterholes flanked by ancient gnarled gum trees.

Jack and Harry talked animatedly about the vastness and beauty of the scenery, continually surprised by the number of animals and reptiles they saw. Often, however, they were silenced by the primeval atmosphere of the prehistoric land they were privileged to witness, awed by the fact that few white men had ever set foot through this majestic landscape.

The first night out they camped on the sandy banks of a billabong nestled at the base of rugged red cliffs. It was tranquil beside the still water and in the peaceful silence they all spoke with hushed voices. Even the animals appeared to sense the atmosphere being unusually quiet, particularly the dogs that usually squabbled over food scraps or snapped at each other for dominance of the pack.

On the afternoon of the third day out from Docker River Warri pointed to some distant ranges washed a faded magenta by the afternoon sun. 'See them 'ills there, that's where Lasseter camped in a cave when 'e got sick.'

'Lasseter?' Harry asked. 'Who's he?'

'Yu not heard of Harry Lasseter? I thought ev'rybody know 'bout 'im. Lasseter 'n 'is gold that nobody ever find.'

'Tell us about it, uncle Warri.' The mention of gold sparked Jack's interest

'Well, Lasseter was prospectin' out in this country when 'e got real crook 'n wandered about for days until 'e found a cave over there.' Warri pointed again in the direction of the range with peaks a hazy silhouette against the cobalt blue sky. 'Some of our people find 'im 'n take care of 'im for a bit until some white fellas come across 'em 'n take Lasseter wit' 'em.'

'What happened then, uncle Warri?' Jack was intrigued.

'No white fella ever see where 'e found that gold though they look 'n look for years. 'Bout twenty or so I reckon they look.'

'He found gold then did he?'

'He got lotta nugget on 'im when 'e found 'n 'e plan to go back 'n get rich when 'e better. He pegged a claim out but nobody know where.'

'Why didn't he go back then, uncle Warri?' Harry was now caught up in the enchantment of the story.

'When those white fellas take Lasseter 'e get crooker 'n later 'e die never tellin' anyone where the gold is.'

'Do you know where it is, uncle Warri?'

'Me? Nahh! Yu tink I keep drovin' if I know where all that gold is?' he laughed.

'Do your people out here know where it is then?' Jack persisted.

Warri was quiet for a few seconds before he answered. 'Maybe, Jack, maybe.'

'If they know where it is then, why haven't they told anyone or mined it themselves?'

'If our people tell, it not long before white fellas come in 'n take over. This land then be torn up laik other places. Lotta places out 'ere sacred to us people.'

'You could be rich though ... if you found it.'

'Rich? I got all I need now boys, good 'orses, plenty tucker, this land all 'bout.' He shrugged his shoulders waving his arm in a wide arc about him.

Though the boys tried to encourage him to continue telling them more about Lasseter and the gold Warri declined to talk further about it, dismissing them by changing the subject and diverting their attention.

'Not too far ahead's a waterhole. Yu boys reckon yu can spot 'im? Yu boys ride through 'ere some time yu need to know 'bout tings laik that more than 'bout gold. Yu got plenty gold 'n no got water you die quick out 'ere.'

◆◆◆◆◆◆◆◆◆◆◆◆

Angas Downs station came into view late on the morning of the fourth day's ride, the iron roofs of the outbuildings and homestead glinting in the sun. Jack and Harry wondered if they would get the chance to have a decent bath or maybe get to sleep in a proper bed for a change but their daydreams were short lived.

Reining to a stop beside the vast cattle yards some distance from the homestead they were met by a huge bear of a man with a grizzled grey beard riding a bay horse. He greeted Warri warmly, nodding to Jack and Harry, surprise at the presence of two young white boys clearly evident in his expression although he didn't mention it or address them.

'Mob's got a two-day start on ya, Warri, but I'm sure you'll catch up with 'em tomorrow if ya keep ridin' on. Have a spell though, water the horses.' He indicated a concrete trough near the yards fed by a pipe running from a tall windmill nearby pumping water from a bore.

'I saw ya comin' a ways off and boiled the billy. Also got cook to make a stew up. It's on the stove in the hut over there. It's a big pot so I'm sure there's enough for all of ya. Left a coupla loaves of home-made bread in the flywire safe too.' The big man didn't dismount. 'Have a feed and good luck on the drove. Tom'll be waitin' for you blokes. He's a bit short handed but wanted to get crackin' with the mob rather than just sit around and wait. Good luck!' He waved a hand in parting and was about to leave when Jack kneed his horse forward.

'Sir?' The man was taken aback by Jack's approach. 'Could you post a letter somehow for me and me mate?'

'A letter, young man? Yeah I suppose I could put it with the station's outgoing mail. Where's it goin' to?'

'Kalgoorlie,' Jack replied, holding the rumpled envelope out to the big man. 'I haven't got any stamps though but I can give you some money … how much is a stamp?'

The man examined the address scrawled in pencil. 'Father O'Malley, Catholic Church, Kalgoorlie,' he said half to himself. 'I'm sure the station can stand the cost of a stamp for ya, young man. You and yer mate part of Warri's team?'

'We're travellin' with him and Reynold over there.' Jack pointed to their friend lounging in the saddle next to Warri and hesitated before continuing. 'Harry and me are on our way to Coober Pedy.'

'Coober Pedy! Where are you two blokes from then?' When Jack answered 'Perth', the man peered at him strangely.

'Perth eh? Bit out of yer way up here if ya on yer way from Perth to Coober Pedy aren't ya?'

Jack didn't reply but Warri joined the conversation. 'Boys they good mates wit' Rennol 'ere, know 'im from Kalgoorlie. They comin' on a ride 'n learnin' drovin' from me 'n Rennol on the way to Kupa. Doin' good too, be old 'ands at 'im soon.'

'No business of mine, Warri, just curious is all. I'll get the letter in the mail, son. Good luck on the trip and if ya find a big opal, remember I did ya a favour.' The big man laughed, wheeled the bay around and rode off at a fast canter toward the homestead.

'Does he own the place, uncle Warri?' Jack asked.

'No, 'e jus' leadin' hand. Stan bin 'ere many years though. Probably knows more about this place than the boss I reckon. OK then, let's get some tucker and keep goin'. That Tom Cooper 'e'll lose 'alf the mob lessen we get there to 'elp 'im out. Tom Cooper 'e darn good drover but 'e not as good as Warri.'

They caught up with Tom Cooper and the mob, some two thousand head, as Stan, at Angus Downs, had predicted, around one o'clock on the second day's ride. They saw the dust cloud first and the aboriginal boys became excited, urging their horses into a fast canter, then, as they topped a sandy rise, there about a mile away they saw the herd spread out before them.

Nervous anticipation coursed through Jack's mind as they closed on the cattle strung out ahead with the crew of stockmen herding them from the rear and outriders keeping stragglers splitting from the mob.

Harry was amazed by the noise, a hubbub of cattle bawling, dogs barking, whips cracking and men whistling as they urged dawdling beasts to keep up with the body of the herd. After many days of riding through bush solitude with only the creak of saddle leather, the occasional shrill cry of a hawk or screeching of sulphur-crested cockatoos near a waterhole, the sound, although not loud, was constant and intrusive.

Nearing the mob it was evident that Wandoo and his two mates were anxious to be in the thick of the action so Reynold took the packhorse leads and handed them to Jack and Harry. Then after a nod of approval from Warri the four of them spurred their mounts into a gallop and, with hats waving as they raced toward the mob hooting greetings, they were met by equally enthusiastic riders.

One horseman rode out to meet Warri and the boys. 'This is Tom Cooper comin'.' Warri recognised the rider.

There were brief greetings and some friendly jibing between Warri and the 'Boss Drover' Tom Cooper.

'Where have you been, Warri, you old scoundrel? Getting too old to ride fast now I suppose. You been laying down in the shade of an old ghost gum somewhere I suppose, dreaming about when you were a good fella drover.'

'Only left Angas last night,' Warri lied, a grin on his stubbled face, 'I knew you'd 'ave trouble tryin' to run this mob by youself, Tom. Yu lose many cattle so far?'

'Lost any cattle? Nahh, I think we've *gained* a few.' Both men laughed, obviously well at ease in each other's company, then Tom Cooper nodded toward where the boys were a few yards away, grins on their faces and his tone became serious. 'Who are these blokes Warri? I didn't expect you to have a couple of white lads with you and anyhow, you've brought more hands than I need or can afford.' He turned to Jack and Harry, their grins now gone. 'No offence, lads.'

'Tom, boys they don' want no pay 'n pretty good 'elp too. They bin wit' me 'n Rennol since Warburton. They laik family now.' He smiled over at the boys and winked.

'How come they don't want to get paid for working, Warri? Sounds a bit funny to me.' He was unconvinced.

Jack kneed his mount forward to where the two men were talking leaving Harry with the packhorses. 'Sir, I'm Jack Ferguson and that's me mate, Harry Turner, back there.' Jack nodded over his shoulder at Harry holding the packhorses. 'We just need to get to Coober Pedy, sir. We don't want any pay just the chance to travel with you rather than go it alone and I'm sure we can pitch in somewhere to give a hand for our keep.' He held the man's gaze, taking in his lined weathered face and stubbled chin.

Cooper was surprised by Jack's self-assured approach and stunned to be called 'sir.' He couldn't remember ever being addressed that way except maybe once by a female teller when he had opened a bank account in Alice Springs some years ago. 'Coober Pedy eh? That's a fair ride south and we're not going there anyhow. You and yer mate ever done any droving, lad?'

Jack avoided answering the question directly. 'We can both ride pretty good and use a stockwhip. Know how to look after our horses too. Warri taught us a lot over the past coupla weeks …we won't get in anybody's way.'

Cooper thought for a time, glancing at Harry holding the horses then back at Jack. 'Warri … you vouch for these lads then?'

'I learn 'em lot, Tom, they do good real quick'

'OK Jack, you and your mate can tag along but keep out of the way for a while until I see how you go and seeing as you're coming with us me name's Mr Cooper, or you can call me *boss*.' He turned to Warri. 'Warri, you can take these lads and catch up with Toffy. He's ahead somewhere and you blokes can help set up camp for the night. I'll have a think and see where I can fit 'em in.' He inclined his head in the direction of the boys.' I'll have a yarn with you about it tonight, Warri.' Tom Cooper wheeled his horse around and sprinted back to the mob.

'He doesn't seem too keen to have us along, Jack, does he?' Harry walked the horses forward.

'Hmm, not sure. I think he was a bit surprised at us bein' here that's all. What do you think, uncle Warri?'

'Tom Cooper 'e alright. When 'e see 'ow good I learn yu bloke 'e'll say to me, 'Warri, yu got any more fellas good like these blokes?''

Both boys smiled at how Warri always seemed to be able to answer most questions by including biased self-praise and they had learned to expect this quite endearing habit.

'Why's the wagon up ahead, uncle Warri, and not travellin' with the mob?'

"That's 'nother thing to learn, Harry. Wagon 'e usually always go up front, pick a good place to camp nearby some water, get a fire started 'n set up tucker for the team. Drovers they pretty 'ungry by tea time. Better get started.'

They skirted around the mob to ride on ahead leaving the dusty din of the herd and after an hour or so caught sight of the wagon drawn by a pair of carthorses labouring under the heavy load. The wagon was actually a dray with large wooden spoked wheels. It was a relic of an earlier era with a hooped iron structure supporting a faded green canvas stretched over it to protect the supplies from the sun and dust.

Pots and pans secured on wire hooks along each side of the dray clanged noisily together as the wheels bounced over the uneven terrain. A large tawny-coated dog ambling behind it sensed their presence and began yapping as they approached.

'Whoa there!' The driver seated on a wooden bench reined the horses to a halt as they rode up beside him. 'Well, if it ain't Warri! G'day, ol' mate.' There was a slight twang to his accent that reminded the boys a little of Paddy O'Brien. 'Who's this you have with you then, Warri?'

'G'day, Toffy, yu still cookin' I sees. This 'e's Jack 'this one 'called Harry.' He pointed to them in turn. 'This is Mick Duffy but we all calls 'im, Toffy.'

Toffy had a round cleanly shaven chubby face, a ruddy complexion and small wire-ramed glasses perched on a button nose. They could see reddish grey hair escaping from under his battered hat and he was wearing a longsleeved check shirt but the thing that astounded the boys was that the man wore a large green bow tie. It looked so incongruous with the rest of his drover's attire that they couldn't understand why anyone would wear something so impractical out in the bush where the heat was so intense.

'G'day to ya, lads,' Toffy geeted them. 'There's a waterhole up a bit yonder, Warri. You blokes ride on ahead and get a fire started so we can have a cuppa before we set up camp, eh?'

Leaving the wagon they rode on ahead. 'Why's he called Toffy if his name's Mick, uncle Warri?'

'Don' yu see, Harry?' Warri chuckled. 'When 'e first come out lotta year ago, 'e dressed laik a gen'leman 'n everyone tink 'e some kinda lord or somethin' from Inglan' but 'e jus' normal bloke that look funny. Not long 'n everyone call 'im *The Toff*. Then it get short to jus' *Toffy*. Don' dress funny no more ceptin' 'e still wear that bow tie. Toffy 'e good fella … good cook too.'

'Bet he's not as good a cook as you are though, uncle Warri?' Jack winked at Harry.

Warri didn't reply immediately but looked at him for a few seconds then grinned. 'Yu learn pretty quick, Jack. Yu keep learnin' new ting each day then by time you ol' laik me you almos' know as much as Warri.' He kicked his horse into a canter with a laugh. 'Come on, yu bloke … keep up.'

They found the waterhole that Toffy had mentioned where Warri settled under a shade tree while the two boys collected a stack of wood to set a fire. 'Make 'im a biggun, lotta fella sit 'round 'im tonight. Toffy need to cook on 'im too.' Warri instructed.

When they had the fire set Warri took his rifle, a battered but well oiled five-shot Lithgow .22 repeater from the leather scabbard strapped on his saddle. 'Yu boys ever shoot a gun?'

'No,' Jack answered.

'I shot a few times at the show in Perth once at the shootin' gallery,' Harry said.

'What's a shootin' gall'rey, Harry?' Warri was mystified.

'Well, you pay for say ten shots at these little tin ducks that travel along on a belt. Not with a gun like yours though but with a Daisy air rifle.

'Tin duck eh? Bet 'e don' taste too good this tin duck.'

'You don't eat 'em, uncle Warri, you shoot at 'em to win a prize like a furry monkey on a string or somethin'. It's real good fun.' Harry explained

'Warri only shoot for tucker or maybe kill a snake now 'n then. Besides it's wastin' bullets jus' to shoot for fun. Yu ever win this monkey prize, Harry?'

'Err ... no! Got close though.'

'Bout time yu bloke learn to shoot wit' a proper gun. We gotta bit a time till Toffy gets 'ere.' Warri walked off along the billabong holding the .22 in the crook of his arm, the barrel pointed down at the ground. 'We find good target 'n I learn you 'bout guns. Good thing to know in the bush.'

Warri searched around in a clump of dry grass knowing from previous trips that there was a rubbish tip where drovers had thrown litter. Retrieving three rusty tins from the pile half-covered with sand, he walked about thirty paces to a fallen log where he lined the tins up in a row then returned to where Jack and Harry were waiting.

'Now, yu gotta learn respect for this fella.' He held the gun out. 'A rifle 'e a good friend in the bush but 'e also a bad friend if 'e not handle right. Never walk wit' no bullet in 'im 'n never get on a 'orse wit' a loaded gun in your 'and, too dangerous. If yu get shot out 'ere 'n the bullet don' kill ya, lead poisonin' will. Warri learn you more 'bout handlin' gun in a little bit, first thing though is 'ow to shoot 'im.'

Warri explained about lining up the target with the front sight that looked like a little upside down 'exclamation' mark at the tip of the barrel, with the 'vee' of the back sight. He showed them how to hold the gun steady and fire. 'Don' jerk 'im now, jus' squeeze,' he instructed.

The crack of the rifle reverberated through the trees echoing back from the distant hills as a flock of cockatoos screeched in raucous fear from the trees to circle in terrified wheels of white above their heads. One tin flew from the log with a dull metallic thud. 'Who gonna go first?' Warri held the gun out, its barrel pointed away toward the target area.

Harry volunteered. Sighting along the barrel he fired but the tins didn't move. Trying a second shot, a chip of bark flicked from the log about two inches to the right of the target.

'I know now why yu never win no monkey prize, Harry. Yu close yer eyes when yu pull 'im trigger. Yu only close *one* eye though, not two! Try again, then it Jack turn.'

Harry's third shot never even hit the log but raised a puff of dust some distance past the target. 'That OK, Harry, it take lotta practice to get good. Let Jack 'ave a go then yu take 'nother turn.' Warri reloaded the magazine and clipped it back in place. He gave Jack some basic instruction on how to hold the weapon.

Jack's first shot chipped bark from the log just beneath the target. His second shot clipped the edge of a jam tin toppling it sideways from the log.

Warri was obviously pleased and told him to 'Knock that other one flyin', Jack … take yer time now … steady.'

Jack was elated when his third shot hit the can dead centre exploding it backward from the log. 'Wow!' he said, 'Did I do all right, uncle Warri?'

'Not bad, Jack, but yu miss with that first shot 'n them can they pretty close. Harry yu try 'im again.' Warri took the rifle and slid more bullets in the clip.

Harry's next shot was closer, thudding into the wood just below the target. His second missed completely but the third try, after careful sighting and with his breath held, took the can cleanly from the log.

Harry replaced the tins in a row while Warri showed Jack how to reload the magazine and when he had his second round of shots he took two out of three cans from the log. Warri said that that was enough and that they would do it again the next day. Harry was obviously disappointed with his effort particularly in light of Jack's success.

Warri sensed Harry's frustration. 'Funny eh?' He said. Some fellas good at one ting, others good at 'nother. Jack 'e good shot wit' that rifle. Bit more practice 'n 'e nearly as good as Warri,' he laughed. Yu, Harry, I bin watchin' yu on Dolly 'n yu a natural on a 'orse. Yu sure you not learn ridin' before?'

The flock of birds cautiously returned to the trees as they walked back to where the fire was set. They could see Toffy's wagon approaching the campsite with him no doubt wondering what all the gunfire was about.

Chapter Twenty

For tea that night Toffy served beef stew with potatoes in thick gravy from a large steaming iron pot. After basic food on the ride over, Jack and Harry devoured the meal quickly, smacking their lips and saying …'hhmm, this is good,' between mouthfuls. Toffy was pleased at the compliments, something that was rare from men on a drove and offered them seconds that they devoured with equal relish. There was fresh damper to soak up the gravy and Toffy also had a doughy cake with raisins that they could only manage one slice of each, washed down with the inevitable mug of sweet black tea.

His meal finished, Warri rolled a smoke and moved off to the side with Tom Cooper where they sat and talked privately for some time.

When he returned, Warri called the boys aside. 'Now I bin talkin' wit' Tom Cooper 'n 'e say yu bloke gotta work on the trip. I tell 'im yu work good 'n 'e say, OK.' We talk for a bit more 'bout yu bloke 'n it decided that yu, Harry, will work 'longside Wandoo as yu ride pretty good already 'n you crack a whip good too.' Harry was elated at the praise and the chance to work with the mob.

'Jack, yu ride OK but not good laik Harry so yu ride wit' me mos' of the day 'n I learn yu more 'bout shootin' 'n other stuff. Then in the afternoon yu go 'head 'n 'elp Toffy set up camp laik we do tonight. That OK, Jack?'

'Whatever you reckon is best, uncle Warri.' He was somewhat deflated.

'I tell Tom Cooper yu good shot 'n 'e say yu can 'elp out by huntin' some roo 'n rabbit for the pot. Now I gotta learn yu 'ow to skin ''im, 'n a bit more ''bout that old rifle but I learn yu quick 'n when yu right wit' that rifle I let yu keep 'im to look after, but treat 'im good, Jack.' Jack sparked up at the prospect of learning more about shooting and wondered what Warri meant by 'other stuff.'

Both boys turned in that night exhausted from the day's activities, full from too much stew and looking forward to what lay in store for them tomorrow as they embarked on more adventure, Harry droving stock and Jack learning to hunt. They were soon asleep, not moving until they heard Toffy clanging the cowbell announcing it was time to be up, breakfasted and on the job. They noticed the stars were still very visible as they climbed from the swags but didn't bother to check the time on their watches. It was cold in the morning darkness so they went quickly to the fire to let the flames warm stiffness from their bones, wrapping their hands around the mug of welcome tea that not only heated them inside but also thawed the chill from their fingers.

Over the next week they soaked up instruction like dry sponges, remembering Paddy's advice way back on the train. Jack became very proficient with the rifle, hardly missing a shot, while Harry shone on horseback. Even Tom Cooper was impressed by his ability as Wandoo stretched him by leading him out to round up strays, particularly one big, wickedly horned steer with wild eyes that broke from the mob at every chance.

'Trouble, that steer.' Wandoo told Harry after they had headed off one of his wild escape bids. 'Gotta watch 'im, 'e bad fella, tell by 'is eye.'

One evening, after they had eaten, Tom Cooper said to Warri that Harry needed a better horse under him. 'Not that Dolly isn't a good horse, Warri,' he added quickly noticing the old man's expression. 'But she's getting on now, like us, and that Harry's showing good promise. If he's gonna keep up with Wandoo he needs a younger more spirited horse.'

'S'pose 'e could 'andle somethin' more lively than ol' Dolly. Rennol learn that Harry to ride, did good job, eh?'

'I suppose you taught Reynold all he knows about riding and droving, Warri?' He kept a straight face.

'Rennol 'e me sister's boy, I raise 'im from little fella. I learn 'im good that Rennol.' Warri failed to notice that Tom Cooper was baiting him good-naturedly. 'Yu got any 'orse in mind ,Tom?'

'Has to be one of the spares, Warri. I was thinking about that young colt, looks good stock to me.'

'Where yu get 'im, Tom?'

'We were bored waiting for you to arrive, old timer, so went out and rounded up a few brumbies.' Tom couldn't help the jibe. 'He was the pick of 'em though.'

'Bin broke in?' Warri didn't rise to the bait.

'Not by us but he's certainly been handled before. Could've been broken in too. Won't know till we throw a saddle on him. My bet is he was broken in then got away somehow, went back to the mob.'

'If 'e bin broke before it only take little bit to bring 'im in line 'gain.'

'You're too bloody old to do it, Warri. Couldn't have you all busted up. Got anyone in mind?'

'I could ride 'im, Tom, no worry 'bout that but maybe I let one a them young bloke 'ave a go, eh? That Rennol, 'e can do it.'

'Think he could handle him, Warri?' Tom asked, already knowing Warri's response.

'I learn that Rennol to ride, Tom, 'course 'e can 'andle 'im.'

♦ ♦ ♦ ♦ ♦ ♦ ♦ ♦ ♦ ♦ ♦

Father O'Malley finished morning mass and after changing out of his vestments went to the office where the day's mail had been placed on his desk. Leafing through the envelopes there were the usual bills, a letter from the Bishop and some personal mail, one postmarked Ireland that would be from his sister but the one that caught his attention was a thick, somewhat grimy envelope with his name scrawled in pencil on the face.

He opened the envelope and withdrew a single sheet of paper, two folded envelopes and a ten shilling note. He noticed there was no date or return address on the note.

Dear Father,'

'We are well and enjoying our trip although Harry got lost in the desert for a day and almost died from no water but he's OK now. It's real exciting and we are learning lots about horses and the bush and stuff. Harry and me want to thank you for looking after us and taking us to Mt Margaret. We are camped one day out from Angas Downs station in the Northern Territory and we hope to get this mailed to you from there. We are on our way to meet up with a big mob of cattle and drive them down into South Australia. We are not sure where the mob is headed but wherever it is we are getting closer to Coober Pedy.'

Could you please post the letters for Harry and me and don't forget the promise you made about not telling where we are. We'll keep writing if you can mail them on. Say hello to Paddy if you see him. We have put ten bob in to pay for the stamps. .

It had two signatures at the bottom and a *'PS'* added below it. 'Reynold is well.'

The priest leaned back in his chair and concentrated on lighting a pipe, his eyes squinted to avoid the clouds of smoke. His thoughts centred on Jack and Harry who, only weeks before, were frightened and confused little boys, but who now seemed, from the tone of the letter, to be more confident and somehow more like young men. He couldn't imagine what it must have been like for Harry lost without water and felt the good Lord must have had an eye on him as he was slightly built and had appeared somewhat fragile to the priest. Jack on the other hand was a strapping lad already showing the promise of being a solidly muscled young man. He smiled to himself at the simple phrase in the sentence saying that Harry nearly died, 'but he's OK now.'

There was conflict in the priest's mind. His head told him he should alert the parents to the whereabouts of the boys and where they were headed but his heart argued that these two young lads would be fine. He believed they would grow into two responsible, independent, young men in a very short time. There was also the matter of the promise he had made to them. They had agreed that they would continue to write to their parents using him as a go between while he in turn would not divulge their plans. The boys were keeping their end of the bargain so Father O'Malley felt morally obliged to keep his commitment to them.

His thoughts wandered to where they might be now as it would have taken many days for the letter to get to him from the remote station in the Territory. What an adventure they must be experiencing, out there in the remote outback with a droving team made up primarily of aboriginal stockmen!

He thought to himself how he must tell Paddy next time he turned up at the presbytery that he had heard from them. Paddy was a frequent, if not regular, visitor for a meal, a bed and of course a 'drop of the doins.' He was constantly asking if the boys had been in touch. 'Have ye heard from me boys, Timothy?' was the first thing Paddy always asked. Mrs Lacey also enquired now and then while pretending to show little interest. Each time Father O'Malley said that he hadn't heard from them she would busy herself in the kitchen. 'That'd be right,' she would say, 'we'll never hear from those two again, I'll wager.' She always asked again though.

He read the note a second time, placed the two envelopes in the 'out tray' for posting after he stamped them and opened the top drawer of his desk taking out a large brown folder across which was written 'Jack and Harry'. Intuition told him this folder would one day be bulging though all it contained at this time was a newspaper clipping from the *West Australian* newspaper and now this one page letter. He also slipped the ten shilling note into the envelope before he placed it back in the desk drawer. He relit the pipe and said a little prayer asking God to look after the boys wherever they were. *Forgive me if I've made the wrong decision in helping them.*

♦♦♦♦♦♦♦♦♦♦♦

At the time the priest sat in his comfortable chair surrounded by leather-bound books and tobacco smoke there was much excitement around the Cooper campsite in the Territory. The 'boss' had announced to all the crew after breakfast that they were going to rest up for the day. It was a good waterhole they were camped at with plenty of feed for the herd, he told them, and they were making good time so deserved a rest day. They would only have to run a couple of riders out to ensure no cattle strayed too far, so they could take it in turn, by pairs, to check the mob.

He also stated that Reynold was going to provide some entertainment by riding the black colt. This was greeted by lots of loud hoots and handclaps but when Tom went on to say they would also use the day to kill a beast for the camp larder it was received by wild cheers. The last statement meant the traditional beef ribs roasted on the coals that night and choice steaks for tea the next night. Although roo or rabbit, now Jack's role to provide, was often on the menu to supplement the staple diet of salted meat, the change to fresh beef, even if for only a couple of meals, was a luxury.

◆◆◆◆◆◆◆◆◆◆◆

Anyone with knowledge of horseflesh could recognise the breeding in the colt's confirmation and stance. He tossed his head defiantly, black mane flying when he was led to a clearing Warri had selected a short way from the campsite, rearing on his hind legs and pawing the air in challenge as Reynold walked to him. The colt had been docile enough on the journey, content to be led but he sensed this was different, responding with spirited boldness.

Tom Cooper had noticed when the colt was captured that he was different from the usual brumby. This horse was taller, over fifteen hands at the shoulder, and he walked with his head held high, tail flowing regally. This black stallion had thoroughbred blood and it showed. Tom wondered what his breeding was and how he managed to be running with the brumby herd. Tom Cooper had seen many brumbies over the years and had a great respect for them. Not native to Australia these horses, like the donkeys and camels that roamed across the outback, were introduced. The horse was the only early means of transport prior to the camel being imported to the continent but, as people let them go when they were replaced with camels for haulage or they escaped, they became feral. Although not as suited to the harsh arid environment as the camel, the horse adapted and bred rapidly. Hundreds of them roamed the outback regions providing ready mounts for the drovers.

All the hands, including Toffey with his green bow tie, were gathered to watch the event. Warri called Reynold aside and spoke with him for some minutes, Reynold nodding his head as Warri passed advice to him. Harry sat beside Wandoo with Jack and they fidgeted in anticipation. The babble of conversation ceased and a hush descended over the assembled stockmen as Reynold took the rope halter lead and stood facing the colt. Both Jack and Harry sucked in a breath of alarm as the stallion reared again, eyes flashing as he pawed the air, hooves flashing only inches from Reynold's head. They were astounded that Reynold stood his ground without flinching as the horse repeated the show of defiance, nostrils flaring. They breathed in relief when the horse finally stood, flanks trembling, obviously recognising that the aggressive bluff did not faze the young lad standing before him, his hand held gently out, palm upward, and speaking soft words of encouragement.

Chapter Twenty One

Life had still not returned to normal at the Ferguson or Turner households in Perth.

After receiving the letter from Jack and responding to her husband's positive comments about finding the boys and their returning within a short time, Alice Ferguson was shattered when he returned from searching Kalgoorlie, his efforts fruitless. He told her they had scoured the town, checked out clothing stores, met with the local police and contacted many mining companies in the area to see if the boys had applied for work. It was his opinion that they had maybe gone prospecting or fossicking on their own so could be anywhere in the district trying their luck at one of the abandoned mines or simply sifting through old mullock heaps in the hope of finding a few small overlooked nuggets. Claude had been to see some of the more recognised gold buyers in town leaving contact numbers and addresses in the hope that if they did make a small find they might try to sell it.

Jack endeavoured to display a positive attitude around the house for Alice's sake, maintaining a semblance of normality and routine at home but, when he was alone, he too became dejected, worry eating at him. He and Claude developed a closer relationship than they had previously had, united in a common goal, meeting regularly to discuss options for further searching while sharing the burden of their families' concerns.

These meetings were usually held in the saloon bar of the Exchange Hotel where they shared a few beers and talked through possibilities without involving their wives who for obvious reasons were emotionally fragile.

'I can't understand it, Claude.' Jack sipped his beer. 'It's like they just vanished into thin air. You'd think someone would have seen them somewhere, buying supplies … something.'

'I have to believe they're doing OK, Jack, as it's the only way I can hang in there. I'm having terrible trouble with Jean. She keeps saying that they're gone forever and cries at the drop of a hat.'

'Alice isn't all that stable either, Claude. She's like a robot around the house. Does the cleaning, cooking, looking after the kids and such but it's as if she's in a dream.' He drained his glass. 'Another one, Claude?'

'Why not?' He handed Jack his empty glass. 'What do you think about us going back out to Kalgoorlie and having another scout around?' he asked as Jack returned from the bar with the two beers.

'Have to do something I guess. We can't just sit here and wait. I'm not sure what Christmas is going to be like this year with Jack not home, don't feel much like it.'

'Not that far away either, Jack. Jean says she wants to have a tree with all the trimmings though and she wants to set a place at the table for Harry. Hoping against hope I suppose that he'll just walk in the door.'

'Jack,' the barman called to him from behind the counter. When he looked up the man said, 'phone call, mate.' He held the receiver in his hand.

'Who is it?' Jack mouthed silently to the barman as he reached for the phone.

'Not sure … it's a woman though.' He had his hand over the mouthpiece and winked.

'Hello, yes.'

'Oh, Jack. Come home quickly.' It was Alice's voice.

'What is it, Alice, news of Jack?' His heart almost stopped, fearing the worst as her tone was strained.

'It's another letter, Jack! Another letter.' She started sobbing. 'Come home, Jack, I'm not game to open it alone,' she said through her tears.

'A letter! Now?' Jack glanced at his watch aware that the mail came in the mornings. Alice waited religiously for Tom the postie every day. There had been nothing that morning.

'Tom was sorting the mail for the next day's delivery and noticed Jack's handwriting. He thought he'd bring the letter around this afternoon rather than wait for tomorrow's delivery. Please hurry, Jack.'

'On my way!' He slammed the receiver down. 'Claude, come on. There's a letter from Jack so good chance you've got one from Harry too.' He grabbed his hat from the table and they sprinted out the door leaving the bewildered barman staring after them.

◆◆◆◆◆◆◆◆◆◆◆◆

Dear mum and dad,'

'This is the first chance I've had to write again. We have been very busy and learning heaps. Want you to know that I miss you both and the kids. I love you lots too.'

Don't worry about us, we are well and getting really brown working out in the sun all day. We have a good bunch of mates around us and are being well looked after although I miss your cooking mum.

Alice dissolved into tears as Jack continued to read.

I promise to write regular and let you know how I am. Harry promises too. I hope you understand why we can't come home. One day when we make our fortune we will come and see you but you have to keep it a secret when we do as we don't want to go to jail. It won't be for a while yet though.

We are having a good time but it makes me real sad not to be able to see you. One day that Billy Munse might own up that we didn't pinch his bloody bike and then we can come home free and you won't be ashamed of me. But not until we are rich.

Jack smiled despite the lump in his throat at his sons use of a swear word.

Please don't worry too much mum and hope your work is going good dad.

I'll write again before Christmas. Miss you.

Your loving son,
Jack.

They both sat at the kitchen table unable to speak. Alice was quietly sobbing, a balled-up handkerchief to her mouth. Jack didn't trust himself to speak because he knew if he did he would probably cry as well and someone had to be strong for the family's sake.

The telephone jangled into their thoughts. It was Claude to say that they had a letter from Harry. He read the letter over the telephone to Jack then Jack read his son's note back to Claude. The letters were again very similar both parents being aware that the boys had obviously sat and composed them together.

The envelopes were again postmarked Kalgoorlie. This fact frustrated Claude and Jack so they decided they would travel up there the next weekend to scout around again.

'Maybe …' Claude suggested as an idea hit him. '… Maybe we should check at the Post Office. They must have bought the stamps there and could have talked to someone about where they were or what they were doing.'

'Bloody great idea, Claude! Why didn't we think of that before, damn it.' Jack was angry with himself for the obvious oversight. 'Can you get tomorrow off, Claude? I think we should drive up there straight away.'

'I'm with you, Jack. Give me time to have a bite to eat and pick me up. Jean can call the boss tomorrow to let him know.'

'We'll track the little blighters this time, Claude. They're still in Kalgoorlie and we'll find them for sure now.'

♦ ♦ ♦ ♦ ♦ ♦ ♦ ♦ ♦ ♦ ♦

Harry watched in awe as Reynold stepped close to the quivering black colt, reaching his hand out slowly to stroke its neck and whispering to the horse continually. The stallion pulled back from the unfamiliar contact but didn't rear or react badly, just snorted and stamped one front leg a couple of times.

Reynold reached down, picked up a small blanket used as a saddlecloth and held it out for the horse to see then let the colt sniff it. Slowly he moved the cloth up, gently rubbing the stallion's head then moving it upward over its ears. The horse took a step backwards and Reynold followed, moving the cloth downward along the neck toward the withers. There was silence from the gathered men as he slipped the blanket in place on the horse's back. Reynold then walked the colt around in a circle. The colt tossed its head, snorted, arched its back once but then settled as Reynold continued walking with the horse now obediently following.

Harry realised he wasn't breathing as he followed every move Reynold made. He watched spellbound when Reynold stopped beside the breaking saddle then reaching down picked it up and swung it deftly into place. The horse sidestepped away ears back and pigrooted but Reynold stayed with it, soothing the animal with gentle words until it settled, then, with Wandoo's help, carefully buckled the girth to secure the saddle. There were murmurs of appreciation from the experienced stockmen and a huge smile on Warri's face.

'Rennol 'e ride 'im now, no worry. That 'orse 'e know who boss,' he whispered to Tom Cooper

'Maybe, Warri. Let's wait and see, he's a spirited nag that one.'

A wild cheer went up as Reynold sprang into the saddle in one liquid movement without using a stirrup. The colt, taken by surprise, danced a few steps then, realising that there was a rider on his back, put his head down and bucked. The men cheered and whistled as Reynold, bareheaded now, his hat jerked from his head, sat the twisting horse. Red dust kicked up by the flashing hooves filled the air as the stallion corkscrewed in giant bounds through the dunes. The men whooping with enjoyment, waved their hats above their heads as Reynold gripped like glue to the saddle. Harry wondered how his neck didn't break, so violent were the colt's leaping twists and turns.

After what seemed like an eternity to Harry, but was in reality only about half a minute, the intensity of the stallion's efforts to dislodge its rider waned. The bucks became spasmodic until they developed into half hearted pigroots before ceasing completely. It was then that Reynold dug his heels in and forced the horse to gallop out into the open for a few hundred yards before reining him to a halt, turning him and galloping back, where he pulled the horse to a slithering stop in front of the crowd. The colt stood, flanks covered in a white froth of sweat, sides heaving from its tough battle with Reynold.

'Hey, Rennol?' Warri was more excited than Jack had ever seen him. 'I learn yu good 'ow to sit a buckin' 'orse. Yu 'andle 'im real good, bloke.' Warri did a little jig in the dust.

Reynold smiled shyly as he slid from the saddle. Walking to the horse's head he reached up to gently stroke its forehead, then taking a lump of sugar from his pocket he held it to the colt's muzzle, mouthing soft words close to its ear.

'Good 'orse.' Was all he said as he handed Wandoo the reins and walked away.

The next morning Reynold saddled the colt to ride for the day. The stallion humped his back a couple of times when Reynold hauled himself into the saddle but soon settled down and by sundown was docile and obedient to the rider's commands.

Unsaddling the colt that night, Reynold turned to Harry who was standing close by with Dolly. 'Yu ride 'im tomorra, Harry. Uncle Warri tell me 'e gonna be your 'orse.'

'*My* horse!' Harry was stunned. 'What about Dolly, she's my horse?'

'Dolly she good fella all right but gettin' ol' now. Yu need a better 'orse, Harry. Warri, me 'n Mista Cooper we bin watchin' yu work out there wit' Wandoo. Mista Cooper tell me to ride this fella 'n quiet 'im for yu. Yu gotta name for 'im, Harry?'

'Don't you think it's a bit soon for me to ride him, Reynold? You know what you're doin', mate, but I'm just new at this game.' He was nervous at the prospect that if the horse decided to dislodge him there would be no contest.

'Tomorra I 'elp you saddle up 'n I let 'im meet you. Yu 'ave a little talk wit' 'im.' He patted the horse affectionately. 'This fella be a good 'orse for yu. Wandoo 'e tell me yu go good so yu be OK. After all I learn yu to ride.'

Harry smiled noticing that Reynolds reply had a hint of Warri about it. 'Thanks, mate, I'll try me best.'

He did. The next morning just before sun-up Harry went with Reynold to saddle the colt together. Harry did what Reynold told him, speaking to the horse gently while rubbing its forelock. The stallion fidgeted a bit but Harry, following Reynold's advice, did not flinch.

'You 'ave to let 'im know yu not scared, Harry,' Reynold said. 'Even if you *are* scared, don' let *'im* know it 'cause 'e can smell it if yu scared.'

Nobody appeared to pay any attention to Harry as he joined Wandoo that morning to ride on the wing of the herd. Warri and Tom Cooper didn't miss a thing however and nodded in silent approval to each other as Harry confidently kneed the colt into a canter alongside Wandoo's mount as they rode out into the rising sun.

By the end of the day Harry felt in harmony with the stallion. Not once did the horse display any rebellious behaviour, responding quickly to every command. He had a soft mouth that needed very little rein control for direction so Harry found it hard to imagine that, only two days before, this horse had been a wild-eyed buckjumper. It was obvious, even to Harry, that the horse had been well broken previously and handled with expert care.

He leaned down over the horse's withers to pat his neck. 'You're a beautiful big fella you are. Hard to think you were runnin' with a brumby herd not long ago. You were just a big, black brumby, that's what you were.' It was then that Harry decided on a name.

'It might not be a thoroughbred name but I reckon it's a noble one anyhow big fella. I'm gonna call you 'Brumby'.' He leaned over the horse's neck again. 'You like that name? It's a good strong name, 'Brumby'.' The horse whinnied softly and Harry smiled, sure that the horse understood every word he had said.

Chapter Twenty Two

The drove progressed steadily with Harry improving his horsemanship with each hard day's work in the saddle and Jack becoming what Warri said was 'a crack shot'. There was rarely a time he missed with the rifle, ensuring he didn't fire unless he was certain, barring unforeseen circumstances, that he could hit the target. Warri instilled in him that the animals were a fundamental part of the bush; there for food and not for sport. He only ever shot what was required for the camp and, even though tempted to dispatch the odd snake or two, he resisted, knowing they were no threat and were an integral element of the outback. 'Don' ever let an animal suffer, Jack,' Warri advised. 'If 'e 'urt yu finish 'im off quick.'

Jack now provided all the wild game for the larder riding out alone into the scrub on Brehardie leading a packhorse, confident that Warri's tutoring over many days had equipped him for these solo journeys into the bush, something he would never have attempted without the old Aboriginals teaching. He learned how to read signs to track animals and Warri had patiently shown him basic bushcraft. He now knew how to spot markers indicating waterholes and the skill of picking landmarks to avoid getting lost.

On one excursion Warri led him into a narrow high-walled gorge. They followed a winding creek bed to a waterhole of emerald transparent water where Warri dismounted and indicated to Jack that he follow.

Warri guided him along a narrow ledge that wound upward from the floor of the gorge opening onto a broad, flat expanse of bare rock half way up the cliff that was invisible from the ground. At the far end of the rocky platform was a cave, its entrance almost a perfect arch leading to a high-roofed grotto. Jack sensed the awesomeness of the place even before Warri spoke.

'Jack, this is special place I show yu. No white fella ever bin 'ere before. Maybe, but don' tink so. It's not sacred laik it wrong yu be 'ere or nothin' but special to my people for a thousand years or more.'

Jack then noticed as they walked to the cave mouth that the entrance wall was covered with ancient weathered carvings. Inside, the cave walls and even the roof had carvings and paintings of many kinds, some indistinct from age, others clear with colours highlighting the designs etched in the rock. Jack figured there must have been hundreds of shapes and designs. He stood spellbound, his eyes roaming the primeval art in the natural gallery as Warri spoke softly.

'Look, Jack. That fella, kangaroo, 'im emu, other one there 'e bungarra.' Warri reverently traced the drawings of animal footprints with an outstretched finger. 'These paintin's very ol' Jack. Tell the 'istory of our people, animals ... stories of our Dreamtime ...' His voice trailed off his mind imagining the people chiselling designs with pointed stones, then using natural earthy materials, rocks or clays of different colours ground to powder and mixed with water or spittle to produce paints.

When they returned to the floor of the gorge beside the waterhole Jack looked up to where they had been but all he could see was a sheer rock wall, so well concealed was the cave and its treasures.

'Thanks, uncle Warri.' Jack felt he should say more for the privilege that had just been extended to him but no expressive words came to him.

'Yu good fella, Jack. Yu learn quick 'n Warri know yu 'ave respect for our people "n our ways. We keep this secret little bit, eh?'

'I won't tell anyone about it, uncle Warri, not even Harry.'

'It all right if yu tell Harry 'bout it but not 'ow to find 'im. Now Warri better learn yu more 'bout huntin' or else we go 'ungry. Yu think yu can track some roo for tea?'

Jack knew the subject of the cave with its ancient paintings was closed and would not be spoken of again. He also decided that he wouldn't tell Harry out of respect for Warri and the people who, from the dawn of time, had recorded their history and left it concealed in a cave deep in the heart of central Australia.

♦♦♦♦♦♦♦♦♦♦♦

'Hard to imagine what we used to be like back in Perth isn't it, Harry?' Jack said one night after they had eaten their fill. They were seated on a tree stump away from the body of the camp with a mug of tea.

'Yeah, Jack. Seems like it was years ago.'

'Do you miss it … home?'

'No … I don't think so,' He said thoughtfully. 'I miss mum and dad but, and the family … not the place though. I certainly don't miss school,' he added with a grin.

'Me neither,' Jack agreed, 'life has certainly changed for us, Harry.'

'Wouldn't mind a chocolate bar now and then though or some fish 'n chips.'

'Too right! How about icecream with strawberry sauce?'

'Yeah, or caramel, eh?' Harry smacked his lips. 'Be good to go to the pictures sometime as well.'

'We're sort of livin' a picture aren't we, Harry? The life we have now seems to have more adventure than any of the pictures I ever seen back home.'

They were silent for a time listening to the night sounds, the herd settling for the night with only an occasional bellow, horses hobbled nearby softly whinnying to each other and snorting as they fed, and the hollow tinkling of bells around their necks. The odd coughs and murmur of voices from the men around the campfire and a dog barking drifted to them in the evening air. Sometimes the call of a night bird hunting on the wing for small rodents, or a dingo howling in the distance, could be heard but generally, though, there was just the desert silence with a gentle whisper of wind through the mulga.

Jack noticed one morning and commented to Harry that the young aboriginal boys, normally vibrant and laughing were unusually sober. 'They say anything to you, Harry?' He asked.

'No. Come to think of it though they weren't as noisy around the fire last night either.'

Wandoo was also unusually quiet as he rode with Harry carrying out their normal duties on the wing but when Harry asked if anything was wrong, Wandoo just shrugged his shoulders without replying.

Jack returned late in the afternoon with a kangaroo slung over the packhorse and three pair of rabbits tied to his saddle. Dumping the carcases near the wagon where Toffy was setting up the fire ready to prepare tea he walked up to him. 'Why's everyone so quiet, Toffy?'

'You noticed did you, lad?'

'Can't help it! There's hardly been a 'whoop' or a laugh all day. Those blokes are normally full of life. What's goin' on?'

'Tonight's a special night for them boys, Jack. Happens on every trip when we have a bunch of young bucks with us.' He went about his tasks without commenting further.

'What sort of special night, Toffy?' Jack persisted, his curiosity aroused.

'Well, I don't know the ins and outs of it, Jack, as I never really worried much about it but there comes a time when the young blokes go through an initiation to become men. They head off into the scrub to some sacred spot where the elders perform a ritual on them. They go out boys and come back men, according the aboriginals anyhow.'

'What's the ritual, Toffy?'

'Don't know for sure, never seen one. You'd have to ask Warri or maybe Reynold as he went up last time we were on a drove. Don't think they'll tell you much though. It's very secret.'

Jack waited impatiently for the day to end, skinning the roo before slicing steaks off it for Toffy, then filling in time by running a cleaning rag through the rifle. When he saw the riders coming into camp he went to meet them. Singling Harry out he asked him if he knew what was going on or if Wandoo had talked at all.

'No, Jack, he was very quiet, all day.'

Jack repeated what Toffy had told him so they decided to speak with Reynold and when they got a chance they drew him aside.

'Reynold, the boys have been real quiet today, what's goin' on?'

'Not much, why?' Reynold seemed evasive.

'Toffy says there's an initiation or somethin' on tonight somewhere. We were wonderin' about it that's all.'

'It blackfella stuff, Harry,' he said, as if that concluded the conversation.

'Reynold,' Jack joined in, 'if you don't want to talk about it that's all right, mate, we were just wonderin' that's all. Everyone seems on edge.'

Reynold looked about him to make sure they were some distance from anyone else before speaking. 'It jus' for blackfella, Jack, not for white men to know.'

'We just want to know what it's about,' he persisted. 'Toffy told us it's some sort of initiation where the young blokes become men.'

'Us boys come to a age where we go 'long to special place up there.' He waved his arm vaguely toward the distant purple-clad hills. 'Elders they get sacred stones out 'n talk wit' the spirits then 'ave ceremony so we no longer boys but men.'

'What sort of ceremony, Reynold?' Jack was fascinated.

'Can't say, Jack, it secret stuff.' Reynold glanced uneasily around him making sure they were out of earshot of the other men. 'We aboriginal people 'ave many ceremony. They very special for us. All 'cross this land where aboriginal people live we 'ave special ceremony for blackfella only. Womens don' even get to go to most of 'em, only men. Old grandfathers they tell me that some ceremony bit diff'rent place to place but mos'ly they same. Can't tell you no more now.'

'Can we come up too … to this ceremony?' Harry asked

'No!' He was emphatic. 'I tell you already. It fer blackfella only, no whites.' He eyes narrowed. 'Don' ask no more question, eh? I can't tell you 'bout it.' He started to walk away when Jack called him back.

'Reynold, we're sorry, mate. We didn't mean to get you angry … honest.'

'OK, Jack.' He relaxed a little, a tentative smile etching his lips. 'We's mates for sure 'n I'd tell yu if I could. Do yu bloke 'ave initiation where you come from?' Reynold made an attempt to show he wasn't too offended by their questions.

'No, Reynold, not really,' Jack replied.

'Some churches have what they call 'confirmation',' Harry added

'Confirmation 'e lot diff'rent, eh? We ave 'im too … at the mission.' Reynold left them, walking over to where the aboriginal boys and stockmen were grouped around Warri.

Around dusk all the aboriginal men and boys rode out toward the hills in a group with Warri leading.

'Save on tucker tonight,' Toffy said with a grin.

Tom Cooper noticed that Jack and Harry were subdued that evening around the campfire so he moved close to them, the almost mandatory mug of tea in his hand, half-smoked cigarette drooping from his lips. He squatted beside the boys and stared into the coals, his eyes squinted from the cigarette smoke curling from the butt in his mouth.

'Funny thing this initiation ritual,' Tom spoke to no-one in particular. 'Doesn't mean much to us blokes but to them it's very important.' He flicked the butt into the ashes. 'The young fellas are considered boys regardless of what they can do, how well they ride or how good they hunt until they go through some special ceremony'

The two boys looked at him but didn't speak

'Not the same as us, where a man is judged on what he can do, what sort of bloke he is … regardless of his age.'

'What happens, Mister Cooper?' Jack asked, 'what do they do that makes them men?'

'It's not what they *do* Jack it's what's done *to* them.' He took the makings from his shirt pocket, stuck the corner of a cigarette paper in his lips and began to roll a small ball of tobacco in his palms. 'Lots of cultures have rites and customs. The Jewish people, for instance, have circumcision of boys at around the same age as these fellas.' He pointed into the darkness at the direction the riders had gone, 'that's a sign to them that the boys are now of age. Same sort of thing goes on with the aboriginal people. I understand there are lots of stages the boys go through before initiation as men.'

'You ever seen an initiation, Mister Cooper?' Harry queried.

'Me?' Cooper shook his head and licked the rolled cigarette. 'No. I don't know of any white bloke that's actually seen one. It's a very secret ceremony, been going on for thousands of years. Sometimes they circumcise the boys or knock a tooth out with a rock or stick, or give 'em tribal markings where they make cuts on their arms or chests and rub ashes into them. Pretty painful I'd reckon, but it doesn't seem to affect 'em too much. Just goes to show how tough these young fellas are.'

'Gee!' Harry shuddered. 'Sounds awful. Glad I don't have to get initiated.'

'In a way you do, Harry … get initiated that is.' Copper stood up and stretched. 'We don't knock a tooth out or nothing like that,' he laughed, 'but you're initiated by being watched to see how you handle the things you're expected to do.' He swigged the last of his tea from the mug then tossed the dregs into the fire.

'Reckon by watching you two blokes over the past coupla weeks you've tackled everything like two men anyhow. As far as we're concerned, me and Toffy, you fellas are initiated.' He walked off into the darkness.

◆◆◆◆◆◆◆◆◆◆◆◆

Tom Cooper was usually first in the saddle each morning, up well before dawn and inspecting the herd as the first rays of sun crept over the horizon. The herd was big so he obviously didn't know every beast individually but he had the drover's uncanny ability of being able to know if any were missing.

Casting his eyes over the cattle one morning he knew intuitively that something was wrong. The big, wide-horned steer, that led Wandoo and Harry on many a wild dash through the scrub with his bids for freedom, was gone. Standing in the stirrups he searched the bush but could see no sign of him. He did find tracks in the sand leading away from the mob and guessed there were about fifteen head of stock that had made a break with the steer. If it had just been the steer alone he might have let him go, as he was a troublemaker, but fifteen or so head had to be found. He did decide, though, that the big red steer would end up as ribs on the fire the next time they needed meat.

On his way back to camp he met Harry riding with Wandoo.

He told them of his discovery. 'Better get cracking and round 'em up before they get too far.' He pointed in the direction the tracks led. 'You can track 'em easy but they've got a bit of a head start, not sure what time last night they bolted'

'OK, boss,' Harry said, 'Wandoo and me'll find 'em.' He nudged Brumby into action.

Tom Cooper was confident they would find the rogue steer as he watched Harry and Wandoo spur their horses across the dunes into the desert. *Could be a while though,* he thought to himself. *Those cattle could be a long way off by now.*

They were. The tracks were easy to follow most of the time but they had to slow up occasionally when they crossed hard stony ground, the tracks almost invisible to Harry but not to Wandoo. Wandoo knew the small mob was heading for water and they found them around nine o'clock in the morning camped beside a small waterhole. Splitting up, the two riders circled around coming in from ahead of the herd, hoping that if they broke away it would be in the direction they had come from rather than further out into the desert.

When the rogue steer saw the riders he raised his head in surprise, flicked his tail a few times, then made a run for it. The rest of the cattle just moved off from the waterhole a hundred yards or so, watching Harry and Wandoo take off after the breakaway

Wandoo yelled out a 'yehaah' and kicked his horse into a gallop, intent on heading the beast off to turn him back to the waterhole, with Harry on Brumby riding neck and neck beside him. They closed on the steer and Harry eased back to let Wandoo take the lead. They had played this game with the same rogue beast many times before, taking it in turns to be the one to head him off.

Wandoo, feet straight in the stirrups, was stretched over his mount's neck as he drew alongside the steer. The beast tried to turn right but Wandoo leaned his horse against it, shouldering the beast back. Anticipating the next move, he reined back slightly, crossed behind the steer then spurred his mount up to the left of it, leaning in again. The steer propped suddenly and Wandoo shot past, but wheeled his mount and at full gallop quickly caught up again.

Without warning, Wandoo's horse fell, catapulting tail over head, dust and sand flying while the steer continued its flight for freedom. Harry watched in horror as Wandoo hurtled like a rag doll through the air landing with a sickening thud where he lay motionless in the sand.

Reining Brumby to a halt, Harry leapt from the saddle and ran to where his friend lay, fearful of what he would find. Wandoo was face down in the sand so Harry carefully turned him on his back and wiped the dirt from his mouth and nose. Wandoo didn't move so Harry pressed his ear to Wandoo's nose but could hear no breathing so was convinced he was dead.

In a shocked panic he stood and looked around unsure of what to do. The steer was nowhere to be seen and Wandoo's horse lay close by. It tried to stand but whinnying in pain it stopped struggling and collapsed back on the sand. Harry knew then that its leg was broken. It must have stepped in a hole, possibly a rabbit burrow, which had caused the fall and snapped the mare's front leg.

Then he remembered to check Wandoo's pulse as he had seen his mother do when he or his father had been sick. He pressed Wandoo's wrist with his fingers feeling nothing at first but then when he moved his fingers slightly there was a small flutter beneath his touch. Pressing at various points on the wrist he located the artery, reassured to find that there was a regular beat. Wandoo was just unconscious but what injuries he had suffered he didn't want to think about.

Harry knew he had to get Wandoo to shelter somehow as the sun, already a fireball, was climbing the cloudless sky. Harry put his hands under Wandoo's arms and began to drag him to a nearby clump of stunted mulga conscious that he might be damaging his friend further but aware he would surely die if left in the intense heat on the sand.

♦♦♦♦♦♦♦♦♦♦♦♦

Jack saddled Brehardie just after lunchtime, slipped the rifle into the scabbard and, leading Dolly, rode out to see what game he could bag for the pot. He had been out an hour scouting through the hills when he noticed hawks in the distance circling on the thermals like leaves in a willy-willy, tiny dots in the sky. Paying no particular attention to them he continued to look for signs of kangaroos or emus but the circling birds niggled at the edge of his mind so he decided, curiosity aroused, to investigate.

Led by the birds he rode toward low hills backed by distant peaks. A cairn of stones he passed indicated that a waterhole was ahead and he wondered what was sick or already dead that had drawn the birds.

Coming on the waterhole he saw a number of cattle but the birds circled some distance beyond it. He saw the two horses first, Brumby close to a clump of mulga and Wandoo's bay mare on its side in the sand. Jack spurred Brehardie forward, noticing slight movement below the trees. As he neared the trees Harry ran from the shade calling out to him, his arms waving frantically to attract attention.

'What happened, Harry?' He jumped from the saddle letting the reins drop and ran to his friend. 'You OK?'

'Yeah, Jack. Thank God you found us, mate. It's Wandoo. His horse fell ... broke its leg I think.' He pointed to the bay mare. 'Wandoo's out to it and I can't get any sign of life from him.' There were tears of concern in his eyes and fear in his voice. 'What're we gonna do, Jack?'

'Gee, Harry, you sure he's not dead?' Jack looked at Wandoo's still form then glanced at Harry, remembering the time when he thought *he* was dead.

'He's got a pulse, I checked,' Harry assured Jack. 'I dragged him over here into the shade and I've been sprinklin' water on his face to keep him cool.'

'We gotta get him back to camp somehow, Harry.' Jack stood deep in thought, his brow furrowed in concentration. 'We got Dolly, if we can get him on her we can lead him back.'

'Guess so, Jack.' Harry was reluctant to move Wandoo, frightened that any movement might injure him further or even kill him, but knew there was no alternative. He had to be taken back to camp.

'What about her?' Harry pointed to the bay mare that was now sitting up on its haunches but unable to stand.

'Gotta shoot her, Harry. Horse's no good with a broken leg.' Jack sounded like a seasoned bushman, well beyond his years. He walked to Brehardie then taking the rifle from his saddle he slowly moved to the injured animal.

Harry turned away as Jack placed the barrel close to the mare's head. When the sound of the shot had faded and Jack returned they didn't speak for some time until Harry asked, 'do you know where the camp is, Jack? I've got a general idea but was relyin' on Wandoo to lead us back.'

'Not exactly, as they would've moved on through the day. I do know where we were camped last night though so that'd put 'em about twenty mile or more due east of there. We'll have to wait till its cooler though ... let the sun get down a bit.' He glanced up at the blistering orb, checking his pocket watch.

'How we gonna find the camp in the dark, Jack?'

'By the time the sun goes down completely we'll be a lot closer and we'll see the campfire from miles away out here.

'How do you know all this stuff, Jack?'

'Uncle Warri, he 'learned me good'. Jack imitated Warri and laughed slightly, easing Harry's anxiety.

Chapter Twenty Three

Warri became uneasy when Jack had not returned by late afternoon. He sought out Tom Cooper, expressing his concern.

'Young Harry and Wandoo haven't showed up yet either, Warri, but I expected them to be a while. If those cattle had wandered a long way off it's possible they may not be back till the morning. Maybe camped up somewhere for the night. I'm not too concerned, they're both good horsemen and Wandoo knows his way around, no worries.'

'Yu right, Tom. Maybe Jack 'e come 'cross 'em 'n is givin' 'em a 'and, eh?'

'More than likely, Warri,' Cooper reassured his friend. 'If they're not here by the morning we'll worry about it then. Can't do much now … it'll be dark soon.'

After tea that night, as the men settled into their swags and blankets, Toffy piled the fire high with wood. He wasn't as relaxed about the lads not returning as Tom Cooper seemed to be. He understood about Harry and Wandoo being slowed down by the cattle but Jack not being back made him uneasy so he decided he would tend the fire for the night, loading it with wood to keep it blazing as a beacon.

◆◆◆◆◆◆◆◆◆◆◆◆

When the heat of the day lost its intensity Jack led Dolly close to where Wandoo lay and they both lifted him as gently as they could onto the horse's back. Roping him securely in place his arms on each side of Dolly's neck, head resting on her mane, they mounted up then began the trek back in the direction of the main herd, Wandoo on Dolly between them.

Neither of them looked at the body of the mare as they left, its belly already beginning to swell in the heat. Jack knew the birds that had scattered in terror at the gunshot would soon return for their grizzly feast.

They stopped frequently to check Wandoo was breathing and make sure the ropes were secure. As the sun sank and twilight descended Jack set a bearing on a star low in the sky before them, as Warri had taught him. He was apprehensive about it though, as previously there were no serious consequences if he made a mistake. This time it was life or death.

The star Jack watched climbed steadily through the velvet night sky to become just one of millions of sparkling pinpricks of light, making it difficult recognise. Sometime after midnight he lost sight of it, completely unable to differentiate between it and the other trillion stars. Not mentioning this fact to Harry, Jack kept riding at a steady walk in the direction that he hoped was right, doubt niggling at him.

◆◆◆◆◆◆◆◆◆◆◆

Toffy woke with a start. Cursing under his breath he looked at the fire that was now just a mass of glowing coals and ash. He rapidly threw small twigs on to the embers and when they caught fire he fed larger branches into the flames. Before long it was crackling, tongues of fire, licking the night, and he settled back on his swag, determined to stay awake. He was thankful when Warri materialised out of the darkness beside him.

'Bit big for a billy.' He pointed at the fire. 'Couldn't sleep much. It OK I sit wit' yu little bit, Toffy?'

'I'd welcome the company, Warri.'

The two men sat without speaking, watching the flames devour the branches, sparks whirling above it, and waited.

♦ ♦ ♦ ♦ ♦ ♦ ♦ ♦ ♦ ♦ ♦

'Look, Jack!' Harry's voice in the silence startled him.

'What, Harry?'

'Over there, Jack, to our left. That glow …what is it?'

'It's a fire, Harry!' Jack said a silent prayer of thanks 'Long way off but it's got to be the camp for sure.'

'How come we didn't see it earlier?'

'Dunno, must have just thrown more wood on it.' They turned in the direction of the glow and Jack mumbled another prayer of thanks that he hadn't led them too far off track and missed the beacon that had obviously been fuelled through the night.

♦ ♦ ♦ ♦ ♦ ♦ ♦ ♦ ♦ ♦ ♦

The dogs announced their arrival as they rode into camp just before dawn. Tom Cooper was standing with Warri and Toffy beside the fire and they quickly summed up the situation. Lifting Wandoo down from Dolly they carried him to the wagon to check the extent of his injuries by lantern light. No one asked what had happened until they came back to the fire. Toffy stayed with Wandoo.

'No broken bones at least,' Tom Cooper said. 'Just concussed I'd say. Pretty bad, that's for sure, but now he's back Toffy will watch him. Can't do much else out here. Did you find the cattle?'

'Yeah we did,' Harry answered. 'They're still out there.'

'You wanna tell us what happened?' Tom Cooper took his tobacco pouch from his shirt pocket and started to roll a smoke. Warri squatted next to the fire.

Harry explained how they had found the cattle beside the waterhole, describing their chase after the steer when he broke away and about Wandoo's horse falling.

'How did *you* find them, Jack?' Cooper asked.

'I saw a bunch of hawks circlin' way out and went to find out what was goin' on. Found Harry with Wandoo where he'd dragged him to some shade.'

Warri looked at Jack, nodding his head knowingly.

'And you backtracked in the dark to find us?' Tom Cooper said but it was more a statement than a question so Jack didn't comment.

'What about Wandoo's horse? Where's she?'

'Out there,' Harry answered. 'Broke a leg in the fall.'

'Broke a leg?' Cooper looked at Warri. 'We'll have to go out and shoot her. Can't leave her to die like that.

'It's done!' Jack said quietly, not wanting to elaborate.

'Fair enough.' Tom Cooper knew not to press the subject. He was astounded at how these two young lads, just kids from the city, had coped so well with a major disaster. He noticed Jack staring blankly into the flames and understood the emotion that would be flooding his young mind after such a traumatic experience. 'Here, Jack.' He passed over his tobacco pouch. 'Feel like a smoke, mate?'

'Yu know where them cattle is?' Warri spoke for the first time

'They'll have stuck close to the water I guess,' Jack answered.

'Can you find this waterhole again, Jack?' Cooper asked.

'Sure 'e can,' Warri answered for him.

'We'll stay here a day or so.' Tom Cooper made a decision after weighing up the situation. 'Go back and bring those cattle in, get Wandoo's saddle and stuff. It'll also give Wandoo a chance to recover without rattling around in the wagon straight away. Just hope to God he'll be OK. You did real well, lads, real well.' He walked off to advise the rest of the crew about his decision, leaving the boys with Warri at the fire.

'Yu bloke wanna cuppa?' Warri surprised them by moving to the billy at the edge of the fire and pouring two mugs of tea that he handed to them, something that he had never done before.

'Yu men rest up today, yu had a long night.' The boys didn't miss Warri's use of the term 'men' as he had always called them either boys, lads, fellas or blokes ... never 'men' before.

Warri sat staring into the fire. 'Take a man to do what yu bloke did. Yu no longer boys, eh? Brehardie 'e your 'orse now, Jack.' He held his hand up to silence Jack's protest. 'Tom Cooper say Brumby 'n yu good team too Harry so Brumby 'e your colt now and Dolly ... that fella she make good pack horse for yu two fellas.'
He turned on his heel and faded into the breaking dawn.

Wandoo gained consciousness towards the end of the day, opening his eyes and staring blankly around him at first but then, after a couple of hours or so, was more awake and able to mumble a few words in answer to Toffy's questions about how he felt.

Jack led Tom Cooper and Warri out to the waterhole the next morning leaving Harry to ride the herd. Jack was amazed at the speed of Wandoo's recovery as he was now sitting up having taken a small bowl of beef broth that Toffy had made. He was weak and dazed but Warri had again woven his magic with secret bush remedies plucked from the desert, saying that in a day or so Wandoo would be back on one of the spare horses and a part of the team again. Tom Cooper said that, in the meantime, Wandoo would travel in the wagon.

They found the cattle not far from the waterhole but there was no sign of the rogue steer that had obviously escaped into the wilderness. The men cut the saddle from the dead horse after chasing scavenging birds into the nearby mulga where the black crows insolently cawed in protest at the interruption. The hawks circled far above waiting to return when it was safe. Tom Cooper spared Jack the trauma of being involved with the macabre task, sending him instead to start heading the cattle back to the main herd.

♦♦♦♦♦♦♦♦♦♦♦♦

The trek progressed without further incident, following the established stock route forged over many years by drovers like Tom Cooper and those that had gone before him, seeking out waterholes and best feed areas for their mobs.

They came to the Finke River, a brown sluggish stream with the odd deeper waterhole on a few of the bends, and following the river for some miles they eventually crossed the border into South Australia heading for Oodnadatta.

♦♦♦♦♦♦♦♦♦♦♦♦

'Dear Father.'

The priest began reading the latest letter that had arrived that morning.

> By the time you get this we will be getting close to Anna Creek Station and nearer to Coober Pedy. It has been an exciting journey and we have learned so much in the past weeks.

> It's hard to think of what life was like now that we have come so far and seen so much and we can't wait to get to the opal fields and make our fortune. We don't know how we will get there as the mob goes on down to Marree so we will probably leave them at the station. We can maybe ride over, as it's not far, only about 90 miles.

Father O'Malley sucked in a sharp breath. 'Dear Mother of God!' He said aloud. 'Only ninety miles! Are they mad?' He continued reading.

> We have put letters in for you to post on to our mums and dads if you would. We hope they get them before Christmas. Mr Cooper (he's the boss) says we will have Christmas at the station and that it will be a bang up do. It will be hard saying goodbye to our mates especially Reynold and uncle Warri. We will miss not being at home for Christmas too so hope the station will have plum pudding with sixpences in it.

> Jack and Harry

> P.S. have a happy Christmas and say hello to Paddy.

Father O'Malley placed the letter on his desk and sat deep in thought, staring at it.

He wondered what things had happened to them on the trip that made them think nothing of riding ninety miles alone over the arid desert. Were they really experienced enough in such a short time to attempt what, to him, seemed a colossal trip or were they just being foolish and overestimating their abilities?

He found little comfort in the fact that the boys had travelled hundreds of miles already, as that was under the watchful eye of experienced bushmen. He thought they had probably just ridden at the tail of the mob and collected wood for the fire, doing small tasks that they could handle with their limited skills and were now overconfident. He hoped that Warri, or at least this Tom Cooper, would step in and stop any madness about riding *ninety* miles.

He picked up the two envelopes addressed by the boys and considered if he should write to their parents or maybe telephone to let them know their sons' whereabouts. He felt responsible for them being where they were and knew he would hold himself accountable for contributing to any harm that may befall them. He decided he just couldn't carry the subterfuge on any longer and reached for the telephone.

Turning the handle he asked the operator to find the number for a 'John Ferguson' in Perth. He read the address to her and waited with the receiver to his ear when his eyes noticed a faint pencil line in the right hand bottom of the letter. Picking the note up, he examined it closer realising that the pencil mark was in fact an arrow pointing to the right indicating that there was more over the page.

> We were a bit worried at first that we told you our plans but now we know you are our friend just like uncle Warri and Reynold. Paddy said we could trust you. Thanks for helping us.
>
> Yours truly,
> Jack and Harry.

The operator said, 'I have the number for you sir it's ....' The priest replaced the receiver in its cradle.

◆ ◆ ◆ ◆ ◆ ◆ ◆ ◆ ◆ ◆ ◆

Anna Creek was more like a small town than a station. There were numerous outbuildings, their iron roofs shimmering in the summer sun. Tom Cooper had told them that this was the biggest cattle station in the world, not just Australia, and they couldn't believe the size of it.

'This place,' he told them one night when they were camped on the property but still two days journey from the homestead '... covers six million acres. In America they reckon they've got big ranches but Anna Creek is about six times bigger than any ranch in the States,' he said proudly.

'Six *Million* acres!' Jack was stunned. 'That's huge.'

'Yeah. You could fit England into it and still have a lotta land to spare. They run about twenty thousand head of cattle give or take a few and it takes the stockmen months to muster then drove 'em down to the railhead for market.'

'Must be a lot of blokes workin' here then,' Harry said.

'Not sure how many exactly but probably fifty or sixty.'

The homestead itself, set among the red sand dunes dotted with spinifex and clumps of mulga, was rambling with a high roof. Wide verandahs ran on all sides and tall trees surrounded the building. There were a number of grassed areas with neatly raked gravel paths that linked the main house to servants' quarters, a bakery, killing pens and sheds. A small warehouse stocked station supplies and a large corrugated-iron clad shed housed a diesel motor with racks of batteries that provided 32-volt power for the whole complex. There was also a schoolhouse, near the tennis court, where a privately employed teacher educated the station children and a windsock hanging limply in the desert heat, signposted a private airfield.

Water was pumped from bores then reticulated through the flower gardens as well as to a securely fenced area where the station fruit trees and vegetables grew. Cottages accommodating married station hands were situated close to the cattle yards and machinery and tack sheds were close by. Rows of single rooms under a roofed area provided accommodation for the single men where a cook provided meals for station hands and ringers.

Tom Cooper's team reached the station homestead on Christmas Eve. The cattle were herded into a large holding paddock beside the cattle yards so for the first time in many weeks the drovers could relax knowing the herd was secure. The horses were let loose in the yards where they could run unsaddled in relative freedom without hobbles on their feet or bells around their necks.

A quiet excitement was evident among the drovers at the prospect of Christmas at the station. Even Toffy could have a break, as the station cook would be providing meals for the station hands and Cooper's crew while they were there.

Tom Cooper left the men to settle the herd and horses in as the manager had invited him to the homestead. He didn't return until late in the night, his gait a little unsteady.

Christmas morning dawned hot and dry, guaranteeing another scorching outback day with the temperature expected to reach well over 110 degrees. Jack woke early to find Harry already out of his swag, sitting on a fence rail at the horse yards, so he ambled over and climbed up on the fence to join him.

'Mornin' Harry, Happy Christmas.'

'Yeah … Happy Christmas.' Harry's response was subdued.

'What's the matter, mate?' Jack asked, sensing his friend's gloominess. 'You missin' home?'

'I guess so, Jack. Just wonder how mum and dad and the kids are that's all.'

'Me too.'

They were silent for a time lost in thought, picturing what Christmas morning would be like at home. Their families, up early, would be gathered around the Christmas tree decorated with streamers and tinsel, a star at the very top. There would be excited laughter as presents were passed around, the living room a mass of discarded wrapping paper. Cards from family and friends would be strung around the walls and over the fireplace, with the aroma of stuffed roast turkey already wafting through the house.

Their imaginings failed to recognise the fact that with them not present and their whereabouts unknown the Christmas day festivities would be dampened in Ashmorton. There were certainly decorations, presents and turkey roasting but the atmosphere was heavy at the Ferguson and Turner households with only the younger kids boisterously excited, unable to grasp the significance of how their parents were feeling.

'Come on, Harry, we made a promise we wouldn't get homesick, remember?'

'Yeah, I remember. When we got on the train at Northam,'

'Well a pact is a pact isn't it?'

'You're right, Jack, but I can't help missin' everyone, especially as its Christmas and all.'

'I know, mate. I feel the same, but we can't do nothin' about it.'

'First Christmas I never had any presents, Jack.'

They continued to sit on the rail watching the horses. 'You wouldn't have Brumby if we were still at home and I wouldn't have that old Brehardie.'

'He might be old but he's a good horse just the same, Jack.'

'Knows more about drovin' than I do that's for sure.'

'I guess we're just a couple of ungrateful buggers, Jack. Best I could hope for at home would be a bike for Christmas and look ...' Harry pointed to the black stallion. '... He's better than any bike.'

'Yeah, if we had bikes some rotten kid'd probably pinch 'em anyway!' He nudged Harry in the ribs. Laughing they lost their balance almost falling from the rails.

'Hey, you blokes.' It was Tom Cooper 'Get over here.'

They climbed down, wondering what might be wrong, as they walked to where Tom Cooper was standing, a stern expression on his face.

'What is it, boss?'

'Never mind, just follow me.' He strode purposefully toward the wagon.

'You there, Warri?' Cooper called. Their old friend stepped into view from behind the wagon. Both boys were mystified and concerned.

'Now,' Cooper said with gravity when they reached Warri. 'This bloke's got a bit of white stubble on his chin but I reckon he looks nothing like Santa Claus but ...' He paused for effect '... show 'em, Warri.'

The old aboriginal had a wide grin on his face as he reached into the back of the wagon. Taking out a long brown paper wrapped parcel he handed it to Jack. 'Open 'im, Jack.'

Jack tore the roughly wrapped paper away and stunned, stood with his mouth open.

'You laik 'im, Jack?'

Unable to speak at first he just nodded dumbly, tears filling his eyes but then he managed a mumble, 'Is this for me?'

Cooper and Warri only nodded because Jack's response affected them to the point where they were afraid to speak in case of showing too much emotion, something that drovers didn't do.

'Wow, Jack, what a beauty, can I see it?

Jack handed the rifle to Harry. It was a .22 Winchester lever action repeating rifle. The gun was light and beautifully balanced.

'Wh … where did you get it?' Jack stammered.

'Tom 'e get 'im from the station manager.' Warri's face was beaming.

'What? … I … I don't understand.'

'The station usually keeps spares on hand so we decided to ask if there was one we could have. The manager let us have this one.' Tom Cooper explained. 'Happy Christmas, Jack.'

'Sorry we don't have a gun for you, Harry.' Cooper said, aware from Harry's expression that, although pleased for Jack, he was crestfallen.

'Don't need a gun, Mister Cooper. Jack's the shooter and I already have Brumby.'

'Yeah well, as you seem to be the stockman, Harry, Warri thought you might need this.' He nodded to Warri who again fumbled under the canvas of the wagon with his back to Harry.

When Warri turned to face him Harry couldn't believe his eyes. Cradled in the old man's arms was a blue cattle-dog pup. Warri handed the squirming bundle to Harry and it licked his face, tail wagging furiously as he cuddled it.

Tears welled in his eyes as he looked at the two men. 'A cattle dog! How did you know I wanted a cattle dog?'

'I seen 'ow you laik them others on the drove, yu good wit' animals, Harry. This fella she bred well. She be top dog yu treat 'im right.' Warri reached out to tickle the pup's ears.

'It's a girl dog then?' Harry turned the pup upside down to check.

The manager's bitch had a litter a few weeks ago. That's the only one left but it's good that it's a bitch,' Tom Cooper said. 'Bitches are very loyal 'cause they don't run off looking for company like a dog will. Besides, you can breed from her. You just have to make sure when she's on heat that no dingo gets to her though. Bad mix, a domestic dog and a dingo.'

'I don't know what to say, boss.' Jack cradled his rifle. 'Thanks, uncle Warri, it's a beaut gun.'

'Best Christmas present ever, uncle Warri, boss … thanks.' Harry lifted the wriggling fur ball up to look at her. 'I'm gonna name her Anna,' he said, 'after the station.'

The two men were embarrassed. Unsure of how to respond to the boys' expressions of gratitude they stood awkwardly in the dust beside the wagon. 'Yeah, OK then.' Tom Cooper reverted to his normally gruff manner. 'You blokes better get washed up. Get ready for some tucker. Come on, Warri, let's leave these two to get ready.' They turned and walked toward the ringers' quarters.

Chapter Twenty Four

Tom Cooper as the *Boss Drover* was asked to the homestead for Christmas Dinner but politely declined the invitation telling the manager that he wanted to be with his men. Jack and Harry didn't know what was on the table up at the main house but figured it couldn't be any better than what was served to them and the men from the quarter's kitchen.

There were too many people to fit inside so the meal was served under a big canvas marquee erected for the day. The sides were rolled up to let some air in and trestles with bench seats were set up in rows. The aboriginal drovers and ringers congregated at one end while Tom Cooper, Toffy, Jack, Harry and the rest of the men sat at the other. There was a lot of merriment and many 'oohs' and 'aahs' of appreciation as each course was served.

There was crisp-skinned turkey with cranberry sauce, roast beef and pork. Platters of roast potatoes and onions were set out with big bowls of green peas. Pitchers of rich, brown gravy were also placed on the tables alongside bottles of ice-cold beer and lots of soft drink, plus jugs of cordial. Also spread around the tables were little bowls of nuts, sugared ginger, liquorice allsorts and raisins. When everyone thought they couldn't eat another crumb the cook served bowls of steaming plum pudding with lashings of cream and custard. There were no sixpences but the boys didn't worry.

Dinner lasted to well into the afternoon when nearly everyone, fully satisfied, drifted off to find a quiet place to doze. Jack and Harry noticed that Warri had left the gathering early appearing a little unsteady on his feet as they watched him walk off. They knew he hadn't been drinking alcohol so wondered if he was all right but soon forgot about him as they became engrossed in the feast set before them.

It was Reynold who raised the alarm. Jack and Harry had just left the covered area when he ran breathlessly up to them. 'Where Tom Cooper? Where boss?' He was obviously agitated.

'What's up, Reynold?' Harry asked.

'Uncle Warri 'e crook, eh? Real crook! Yu seen Tom Cooper?'

Jack told Reynold that Tom was still finishing off dinner with a cup of tea back at the shelter. 'Where's uncle Warri?' he called as Reynold ran off.

'Back there.' He pointed over his shoulder to the wagon.

They found Warri in the shade leaning with his back against the rear wheel of the wagon, breathing shallowly with his eyes closed.

'Uncle Warri.' Jack touched the old man's shoulder shaking him gently. 'You all right, uncle Warri?'

Opening his eyes slowly he looked at them. His voice was a whisper when he spoke. 'Warri, 'e not too good. Big pain … 'ere.' He indicated his chest.

Reynold came running with Tom Cooper behind him. 'What's up, old mate?' Tom said, kneeling beside Warri.

Warri told him briefly as perspiration streamed in rivulets down his weathered face.

'Just rest there, Warri, I'll be back in a minute. Get him some water, Reynold. You blokes stay here.' He leapt to his feet running to the quarters where he went inside only to reappear a minute later with one of the ringers. They went quickly to a station vehicle parked close by. They drove off, wheels spinning, in the direction of the homestead.

Tom Cooper returned to the wagon with the station manager. They checked Warri then lifted him into the back of the vehicle onto a mattress. Reynold jumped up beside him holding a hat to shield Warri's face from the sun as the vehicle drove off, leaving Jack and Harry standing in the dust.

The afternoon dragged on with the men standing around in small groups talking quietly, glancing now and then in the direction of the homestead. Near dusk, Tom Cooper returned driving the car with Reynold sitting in the back. He parked it and walked over to Jack and Harry.

'Seems like Warri's had some sort of turn. Dunno what but the manager's wife is taking care of him for now. They've contacted the doctor by pedal wireless and he's given them some instruction on what to do.'

'How is he?'

'Not too good, Harry. He'll have to stay here. They'll watch him and if he gets worse then they'll put him in the plane and fly him out to get some proper medical help. We'll have to see how he is in the morning. No sense worrying as we can't change it but I need to speak to you blokes about something.'

'What about, boss?'

'Well, Jack, you were going to leave us here and head off to Coober weren't you? That was the plan?'

'We thought we would, yes. This is the closest point to Coober Pedy and one of the ringers told us there's a rough track across from here that we can follow.'

'Coober is only about eighty or so miles from here that's true. Rough country but I think you blokes have proved that you can make it as long as you keep your wits about ya.'

'What did you want to talk to us about, boss?' Jack sensed their plans were about to be shot down.

'I'll put it straight, lads.' Cooper looked them firmly in the eyes. 'With Warri crook, Reynold isn't going to be much help on the ride down to Marree. Wandoo's coming good but he's not as sharp as he was so I'm gonna to be a bit short-handed for the trip. I asked the manager here if he could lend me a coupla blokes but he has a lot on and can't spare anyone.'

'So you want us to stay on then to give ya a hand?' Jack guessed the question that was coming

'It'd be a favour, Jack, yes. I have to get this mob there on time as there's a bloke coming up from Adelaide for an inspection and to make offer on them. If the bid's good enough the owner will take it rather than have to ship them down to market and run the risk of getting a lower price and still have the rail costs on top.' He pushed his hat back scratching his matted hair. 'Have a think about it … let me know in the morning.'

Jack looked at Harry and saw him nod his head slightly. 'Boss,' he said, 'we'll stick with ya to Marree. We wouldn't be here if it weren't for you.'

'You sure?' Cooper looked at Harry.

'We won't let you down, boss.'

'Thanks. We head off at first light.'

The news of Warri the next morning was not encouraging. Tom Cooper reported that if anything he seemed to be a bit worse. The pain had stopped but he was very weak from not having eaten anything or taken any liquid. He really didn't seem to know Tom was with him, sleeping most of the time.

'Best thing for him though, to stay here. Gotta be thankful it didn't happen on the track. OK, let's get this mob on the move.' Cooper kicked his horse into action.

Reynold was very quiet after they left Anna creek heading to Marree, not communicating and only speaking in monosyllables when asked a question. The last night before they were due to arrive at the railhead town however, he edged up to Jack at the campfire. 'Yu goin' to Kupa when we git to Marree eh?'

'We hope to, Reynold, yes.'

Reynold looked at the ground, hands stuck deeply in his pockets. 'Uncle Warri 'e maybe finish eh?'

'Nah, Reynold, he's tough.' Jack looked over at Harry for support.

'You bet, mate.' Harry took the cue 'He'll be OK. He just needs to rest up for a bit. Too much plum puddin' I reckon.'

Reynold didn't respond to Harry's attempt to lighten the situation. 'Maybe, Harry, but I tink 'is drovin' days over for long time.'

'What are you gonna do then, Reynold?'

'Dunno. Stay wit' Mista Cooper or maybe look for 'nother mob goin' somewhere.' He sounded miserable and confused.

'Would you like to come with us, Reynold?'

'Wit' yu, Jack? To Kupa Piti?'

'Why not? That'd be good wouldn't it, Harry?'

'Yeah, for sure.'

'Know nothin' 'bout opal minin', Rennol 'e jus' a drover, Harry.'

'We don't know anythin' about it either, mate, so we can all learn together. You gonna come?'

'Not sure. Maybe … maybe not.'

Jack felt Reynold didn't want to impose but knew that he wouldn't have brought the subject up if he didn't want to go with them.

'Reynold, Harry and me would really like you to come with us. You're our mate and we've been together a long time now so we'd miss ya if you didn't come.'

'Too right, Reynold,' Harry encouraged, 'it'd be just like when we started out from Kalgoorlie, mate … just the three of us. Go on, what do ya say?'

Reynold thought for a few seconds. 'OK. If yu need me then I come wit' yu' His face lit up in a broad smile. 'Yu right … we all laik brothers now 'cause we got same uncle eh?'

◆◆◆◆◆◆◆◆◆◆◆◆

Marree, set on a barren red treeless plain was dusty with the hot wind blowing sand in from the surrounding desert. A small number of low weatherboard dwellings clung to the outskirts of town and a few more substantial buildings with broad, wide verandahs were scattered to form the main street. The most impressive building was the Marree Hotel, a two-storey square brick building with a second storey balcony.

The cattle were yarded. It was the end of the drove so a melancholy descended on the drovers who as one, both black and white, had for many weeks urged, coaxed and cursed the cattle through the outback wilderness. Together they had crossed desert sand, gibber stone plains, rivers and mountain ranges.

It was also pay day and Tom Cooper had been to the bank with Toffy. Returning with the cash they set up a table near the wagon where the boss called each of the drovers by name to collect their money.

Jack and Harry busied themselves checking their gear while the men collected their hard-earned cash. They were occupied so didn't hear their names at first until Tom Cooper bellowed, 'Ferguson, Turner.' Surprised, knowing the deal was their keep only in exchange for being able to join the drove, they walked over to where he sat at the table with Toffy.

'Yes, boss?'

'Sign here.' Cooper held out a pen and pushed the cashbook in front of them.

'What for?' Jack was puzzled.

'Can't pay anyone unless they sign for it.' He held the pen further out towards them.

'We can't do that, boss,' Harry said.

'What?' Cooper asked in mock surprise. 'Don't tell me you blokes can't write.' He turned to Toffy beside him. 'Don't teach 'em anything at school in Perth these days it seems, Toffy.'

'We didn't expect to get any money, boss. We've had a lot from you already. You got us here, put up with us learnin' and all. You also gave me that colt.'

Yeah,' Jack joined in. 'What about the Christmas presents too?'

'You fellas have earned your pay as much as anyone on the trip. It's not a lot and besides, you'll need to bankroll your prospecting to buy some mining equipment. Now ... don't bloody argue just sign here.' Tom Cooper tapped the wages book where he had written their names.

The boys could not believe their fortune. Their bankroll was now replenished, they had three horses, a new rifle and Anna, Harry's blue heeler dog. Now all they had to do was get to Coober Pedy. How, they didn't know.

This question was answered when Tom Cooper stood up from the table. 'Now, I noticed when we came into town that there was a camel train near the railhead. If I'm not mistaken it belongs to an old Afghan teamster who's been in this area for many years. There used to be lots of 'em once but there's only a couple left now. If I'm right, the one I saw still takes a camel team of supplies from the train to outlying stations and often goes to Coober Pedy. If you like I'll take you down there in the morning to see if he's heading your way. We'll ask if you can travel with him.'

'That'd be great if you can do that, boss ... thanks.' Harry was curious. 'I didn't know there were camel trains working out here.'

'Been here for years. Not as many now as there used to be though. Marree was once the main centre for them in this area. Years ago a lot of Afghans or 'Ghans' as we call 'em, were brought to Australia to run the camels. Funny lot though, never fitted in too much with us and were never accepted. They still speak very little English and have their own religion that doesn't allow them to eat certain things so they set up a small community on the edge of town. Hard workers though and keep to themselves. Don't drink either,' Tom added, 'which is a plus out here. Work has dropped off for them now as roads have opened up and the rail lines have spread across the country. We'll check it out tomorrow.' He then changed the subject completely. 'Time now to celebrate the end of the drove and a job well done.'

'What sort of celebration, boss?'

'The only sort. Go down to the pub for a few beers to wash the dust out of the system,' he laughed as he packed the books and cash tin away in the wagon. 'Reynold and Wandoo will probably meet up with their mates and some of the other local aboriginal people, as they aren't allowed in the pub of course. More than likely have a feast out on the reserve somewhere but Toffy and me will go with the other blokes to hit the high life in town. We'll meet up with a few old mates, have a laugh … tell a lotta lies.' He was in a jovial mood.

Cooper noticed though that the two boys were unsure about what they would do and realised they couldn't celebrate, as they didn't know anyone. 'How about you two blokes come with us?'

'To the pub?' Harry was shocked.

'We're too young to go to the pub, boss,' Jack said.

'You won't be able to get on the turps with us that's for sure but you can sit out in the lounge. Have a feed, a couple of lemonades or something and at least feel a part of what's going on. You're part of the team so you gotta celebrate as well.'

'They wouldn't let us in, boss.'

'You're with me, boys, they'll let you in all right! Wanna come?'

'You bet,' Jack said.

♦♦♦♦♦♦♦♦♦♦♦♦

Jack Ferguson Senior was in Adelaide with the main cattle buyer for South Australia, a man named Bill Martin. Bill knew the market well and Jack had worked with him before. Jack was staying in a hotel in the city, having travelled over from Perth, as his company had a client that was looking for quality beef to build up the herd on his property.

Jack was not happy leaving Alice particularly so soon after Christmas. The day had been a traumatic time for them all with their son still missing, even though he had contacted them. Another letter had arrived from Jack just prior to Christmas saying he was well and for them not to worry but it did not ease their concern of not knowing exactly where he was, or lift the sadness at not having him home. Jack also had an uneasy feeling about leaving Western Australia believing that his son and Harry were still in the state, somewhere in the goldfields. It was an irrational thought, he knew, but he felt he was letting his son down by leaving the state as it just put him further away from where he was. He nonetheless welcomed the chance to be involved in a buying trip as at least he could concentrate on something other than finding his son.

Bill Martin joined him for drinks then they went for dinner in the hotel dining room. Martin knew nothing about his son's disappearance so Jack decided not to mention the subject as it only disturbed him, and the buyer would not be able to help here in South Australia anyhow.

'What time we leaving in the morning, Bill?' Jack pressed the serviette to his lips, folded it and placed on the table.

'Need to get away early, Jack, got a long drive up to Marree.' Martin looked at his watch. 'Saying that, I better make a move.' He stood up from the table. 'Let me get this, Jack.' He reached for the bill.

'No, mate, I'll just put it on my room account. Charge it to the company.' Jack signed the docket and then walked through the lobby to the hotel entrance to see his guest off.

'You sure these cattle are there, Bill? We don't want to drive all the way up there to find they're still on the road somewhere.'

'Talked to Marree this afternoon, Jack. They arrived today and are yarded. The drover in charge is a bloke called Tom Cooper. He's very reliable … always gets his mob in on time. You'll meet him tomorrow as he also acts on behalf of the owner. See you in the morning, Jack. I'll pick you up early.'

'See ya, Bill.' Jack walked to the lift to go to his room.

◆◆◆◆◆◆◆◆◆◆◆◆

Wide-eyed with fascination the two boys sat in the lounge captivated by the atmosphere of the pub. There were two couples at one table in the lounge, their voices raised to be heard over the din coming from the front public bar where Tom Cooper and Toffy stood leaning on the counter engrossed in animated conversation with a dozen or so other men. As the bar serviced both areas they could see everything that was going on so felt they were definitely a part of the celebrations. On more than one occasion Tom Cooper or Toffy would look in their direction to give them a wave and the barmaid, a large woman with yellow blonde hair piled on her head, large gold earrings and red painted lips kept filling their lemonade glasses and smiling at them. 'You're part of Tom Cooper's team, lads, and that's good enough for me,' she said as she topped their glasses up again.

The front bar was packed with men of all ages. There were drovers, ringers, railway workers and a smattering of town folk distinguishable by their dress. A group was playing darts at one end of the bar and a pool table was fully occupied at the other. The room was filled with laughter, loud voices and a haze of blue tobacco smoke.

Nobody knew, or really cared for that matter, how the fight started.

There was a sudden commotion as two men struggled with each other before one let fly with a right hook that sent his opponent flying into the mass of drinkers at the bar. Tom Cooper was shoved against the counter, his beer spilling over his shirt. Placing the empty glass carefully on the polished bar top he made a show of wiping the beer from his dusty shirt then turned around slowly. Grabbing the offender by the collar with his left hand he hit him hard on the chin with his right fist. The poor bloke, having taken two solid punches, collapsed in a heap at Tom's feet.

As if that was a signal, the whole bar erupted in curses and wild swinging punches. The barmaid screamed for them to stop, ducking to avoid a bar stool that narrowly missed her head and smashed into the bottle display on the back wall with a crash of shattered glass. She continued screaming abuse at the men as she ran up and down behind the counter yelling and waving her fists. At one stage she leaned across the bar and grabbed a man by the hair, yanking his head back, fortunately just in time to miss the punch aimed at his nose.

Tom Cooper was right in the middle of the heaving mass of men towering about six inches over them. He was bareheaded now, his hat somewhere trodden underfoot on the beer-swamped lino, swinging punches with devastating effect at anyone unlucky enough to be in range. Toffy, to the boys' amazement, ignored the brawl and just went on calmly drinking his beer, seemingly oblivious to the mayhem around him.

The publican appeared suddenly from behind the boys and pushed through the counter door into the bar servery. He was not a big man and was dressed in a collarless shirt and waistcoat and wore silver armbands to keep his shirt cuffs from swallowing his hands. He yelled loudly for the fighting to stop but was ignored completely. He stood for a moment surveying the damage to his hotel. There were broken glasses, smashed chairs, a front window shattered, tables overturned and a sea of spilt drink sloshing on the floor.

Jack and Harry sat transfixed watching the fight, unable to believe what they were seeing. They yelled in shock and jumped from their stools however when the gunshot exploded. The men fighting stopped in mid-punch and stood frozen in action like comical statues, staring at the publican.

The little man stood behind the bar, the still smoking twelve-gauge double-barrelled shotgun in his hands, this time pointed across the counter. Nothing was said for what seemed like minutes then Tom Cooper spoke. 'Bloody hell, Bert … you've blown a dirty big hole in yer own ceiling.'

All the men looked up to see where the shotgun pellets had hit the ceiling leaving plaster hanging in straggly threads from the gaping hole. Laughter, just a ripple at first, turned to great gales that swept through the bar. Men had tears in their eyes, holding their sides while rolling around bumping into each other. Men who just minutes before were attempting to murder each other were now slapping the very same people on the back like great mates, laughing and pointing at the damaged ceiling.

♦♦♦♦♦♦♦♦♦♦♦♦

'You blokes have a good time?' Cooper asked as they walked with him and Totty back to the camp.

'Geez, boss,' Jack said, 'that was some fight! Never seen nothin' like that before.'

'Yeah, wasn't too bad,' Tom said as if he was discussing the meal. 'Said we always celebrated at the end of a drove didn't I?'

♦♦♦♦♦♦♦♦♦♦♦♦

The cameleer was a tall beared man with a hooked nose separating dark wary eyes under hooded brows, his height accentuated by the long striped shirtlike garment he wore down to his ankles. The boys could see he wore boots, weathered and scuffed, that seemed out of place with his garb. He didn't have a hat on but wore a cloth over his head secured with a woven band of cord so only his face was visible. Jack started to giggle furtively because the man reminded him of the costume the teacher had made him wear in a Christmas nativity play a couple of years ago. Jack whispered to Harry that he thought the play costume looked more authentic than what the cameleer wore.

Tom Cooper and the man were obviously aquainted. After greeting each other they talked for some minutes glancing in the boys' direction several times. A number of tawny coloured camels were in a nearby post-and-rail yard, their flat elongated heads swivelling on long necks. They had haughty expressions on their faces as if they were superior to everything about them, and made half-grunting coughing sounds while they snapped viciously at each other.

'They look pretty bad-tempered those camels, Harry.'

'Too right, Jack. Glad we've got horses. I wouldn't like to get too close to them.'

Tom Cooper signalled for the boys to join him with the camel driver so they dismounted and walked over, leading their horses. Tom Cooper introduced them by their Christian names to the Afghan.

'Ishmael Mohamed Hassan, at your service.' The man flashed a smile, bowing his head slightly to them but not extending his hand, so the boys just nodded awkwardly in response.

'Call him Ishmo, lads; everyone else does,' Tom smiled. 'He acts a little strange at times, doesn't speak much English and in fact, saying his name is about the longest sentence he says.' Tom laughed at his own joke. 'He's all right though, aren't you, Ishmo?'

'You go to Coober Pedy with me?' The tall man asked.

They both nodded, unsure of what to say in the presence of this comical-looking character.

'You may be joining me then. This afternoon we are leaving.'

On the way back to the wagon to pick up their belongings they were concerned about whether they were doing the right thing. Travelling with bad-tempered, biting camels and heading off into the desert with a cartoon character was not what they imagined would be part of their journey to Coober Pedy.

'Ishmo's all right, lads, no need to worry,' Tom said when they expressed their concerns. 'He's well respected for his bushcraft and he's never been in an ounce of trouble all his life out here. People are a bit suspicious of the Afghans but Ishmo is as honest as the day is long. I wouldn't let you go with a no-hoper, you know that. Just takes a bit of getting used to is all.'

'OK. We believe you, boss, don't we, Harry?'

'Yeah, guess so. Thanks, boss, for arranging it for us.'

'Right you are. There's one other thing though.' He paused waiting for their attention. 'I'm not your boss any more and I'm sure we'll run into each other again. It may be a big country but life has a habit of bringing friends together out here. Next time we meet I'm not *boss* or *Mr Cooper* ... you call me Tom, OK?'

♦ ♦ ♦ ♦ ♦ ♦ ♦ ♦ ♦ ♦ ♦ ♦

They loaded their gear carefully on Dolly, lashed their blueys to the saddles and checked their saddlebags. Reynold was waiting as they worked, with his meagre belongings tied in a sugarbag to his stock saddle.

Toffy stood by the wagon, watching the boys prepare for the next leg of their journey, knowing he was going to miss these two young lads. He had been on a drove before with Reynold and liked his company also but there was something special about these blokes. They were determined, willing and caught on quick. He had no doubts they would find opal, probably lots of it.

Tom Cooper rode in as they were about to mount up. He told them he had received a message to say that Warri had been airlifted to hospital in Adelaide and was responding well to treatment. This news buoyed their spirits particularly Reynold who was beaming.

'Yu 'ear that news? I tol' yu uncle Warri 'e gonna be all right, eh?'

They said goodbye to the team drovers but couldn't see Wandoo. Shaking hands with Toffy and Tom Cooper they climbed into the saddles but found it hard to just ride out, as it seemed so final. Toffy had disappeared somewhere behind the wagon and Tom Cooper walked to his horse.

'Gotta go,' he said. 'There's a buyer due shortly from Adelaide. Have a good trip and keep in touch when you can. See ya.' He touched his hand to the brim of his hat in a friendly salute then kicked his horse into a canter toward town without looking back.

The three young riders had only gone some yards when a 'whooping' figure on a galloping horse came up fast from out of the dunes. Pulling the horse to a slithering stop in front of them, Wandoo said breathlessly, 'nearly miss yu blokes, eh?'

'We looked for you, mate, but couldn't find ya. Glad ya turned up.'

'I bin out on reserve camp, Jack. Got somethin' for yu though.'

Wandoo took two beautifully crafted leather stockwhips from the pommel of his saddle. He handed one each to Jack and Harry. 'Jus' to say thanks.'

Before they could respond, Wandoo wheeled his horse without another word and returned over the dunes swallowed by the dust, leaving the boys to just stare in wonder at this gift of friendship.

'Makes ya stop and think doesn't it, Harry? We've lived all our lives in the city and been out here only a coupla months and made more friends, good ones at that, than we ever had back there.'

◆ ◆ ◆ ◆ ◆ ◆ ◆ ◆ ◆ ◆ ◆

Jack Ferguson slumped back in the comfortable leather seat of Bill Martin's Ford watching the desert blur past the window as they neared Marree. 'Not all that different out here to much of the other outback country is it, Bill?'

'There are certainly similarities. There's not much in the way of trees and plenty of red dust and spinifex out here but that's like a lot of Western Australia country too. We've maybe got more salt lakes though.'

'Yeah, and there are pockets in Queensland and the back country of New South Wales much the same, the Territory too.'

'Not far away now. We'll inspect these cattle first then have a couple of beers in the pub and make our offer in the morning if the stock is as good as I'm told they are.' Bill Martin looked at his watch, 'Made good time, Jack.'

'At this speed we could go back tonight,' he joked.

'Marree dead ahead.' Martin nodded through the windshield at the shimmering buildings materialising out of the desert in front of the bonnet. 'Look at that!' He slowed the Ford to point through the window, 'Don't see that too much these days.'

'A camel train!' Jack spotted the line of animals strung out and silhouetted against the sky some distance to the left heading west into the sun. 'Don't often see riders on horseback with them either,' he said, noticing the three horsemen trailing the camels, leading a pack animal.

'That's true. Wonder who they are?'

'Just some silly buggers heading out into the heat.' Jack wiped sweat from his brow. 'Give me a comfy bed with a couple of coldies anytime, Bill. Don't fancy camping in the open like those blokes have to.'

An image flashed briefly into his mind as he spoke, of his son Jack and young Harry Turner, camped on the ground near some old abandoned mine shaft out of Kalgoorlie or Coolgardie or wherever the hell they were, with not enough to eat and in rags. He quickly dismissed the thought, as blocking these images out when they came was the only way he had learned to survive. Otherwise he would be a mental wreck and no good to anyone, his son included.

'Let's find this Tom Cooper and check the mob out before the light fails.' Bill Martin swung the big Ford into a park at the front of the hotel. They both noticed one of the front plate-glass windows was boarded up.

Chapter Twenty Five

The boys soon learned that their first impressions of Ishmo were very wrong. He certainly looked strange and talked differently from anybody they had ever met but he proved to be a wealth of knowledge about many things and two in particular ... camels and opal mining. The information on camels didn't interest them too much as they couldn't see how anyone could love these long-legged, awkward-looking animals like Ishmo seemed to do. They had to admit though as the trip progressed that they weren't as bad tempered as they first appeared and when they were on the trek, roped together, were docile and gentle. The animals protested loudly though every morning as they were being harnessed.

The pace was slow. Ishmo explained one night that to force camels to walk fast was a mistake, as the animals would cover more ground if allowed to set their own rhythmical speed of around three miles an hour. They could walk all day, heavily loaded, without stopping at this pace he said.

'And they don't need to drink because they store water in that big hump don't they, Ishmo?' Harry sounded knowledgeable.

'Oh, no, no, no!' Ishmo waved his hands emphasising his dismay. 'Not in the hump, goodness no. Hump is food.'

'Food?' Harry was amazed.

'Not food but ... how you say it? Yes, yes ... fat.' He bobbed his head several times, white teeth flashing from his dark bearded face as he smiled. 'Camel not drink much all time, no. Camel not wanting much water.'

'Think I'll stick with horses, Ishmo,' Harry said.

'Horse good yes ... but to ride the camel ...' Ishmo shrugged his shoulders without explaining as if words could not describe the experience.

'Could I have a ride sometime, Ishmo?' Jack asked

He nodded to Jack then looked at Harry and Reynold. 'You like ride the camel?'

Harry wasn't too excited about the prospect but Jack urged him on 'Go on, Harry, it'd be fun. Bet I can ride better than you,' He goaded.

'You're on, then.' Harry turned to Reynold. 'Reynold, you in are you?'

'Yu bloke mad. Rennol 'e not ridin' no camel. That final!' He walked purposefully away from the fire leaving no room for argument. Jack realised then that, although competent on horseback and fearless in the saddle, he was terrified of the camels.

They learned from Ishmo through sign language, broken English and a lot of laughter more about camels than they really needed to know. That their eyes had lashes with brows that kept the sand and sun out and that their noses were just slits with muscles inside so flies or dust couldn't get in. They learned that a camel's two-toed feet were wide and a bit like snowshoes for walking on the sand and had thick pads to walk over stones without damage on uneven ground.

The coats were short now in summer but in colder weather, Ishmo said, grew some inches long which was highly valued and that they had incredible eyesight able to see for miles. A camel could survive in 100-degree heat they learned, for more than two weeks without water.

Averaging around thirty to forty miles a day the boys' excitement grew with each sunrise. Coober Pedy, their goal when they left Perth, was now only days away. The route Ishmo followed travelled back over much of the country they had covered coming down from Anna Creek to Marree and although they eventually were on station property they passed many miles south west of the actual homestead.

Ishmo's other favourite subject was opal mining. He explained to them that he wanted to look for opal but couldn't leave his beloved camels that had been his life since arriving as a boy with a load of them many years before. The boys couldn't determine his age but figured he must be well over seventy. He hadn't needed any papers to come to Australia when he did as he was considered just part of the package when the camels were shipped. Ishmo had never married as there were no Afghan brides to be found and he had lived an almost hermit-like existence, shunned by all except a few whites and his fellow cameleers.

'You know a lot about opal mining then, Ishmo?' Harry asked.

Shrugging his shoulders, an expression he had perfected to aid his limited command of the language, he said, 'No, no. Little bit, yes.' The boys knew this meant practically all there was to know.

'How did you learn, Ishmo?'

'Come Coober Pedy many trip. I watch, I listen.'

'Have you ever found opal then?' Jack asked.

'Small chip, off ground.' He acted a charade, walking around eyes searching the sand then stooping to pick up an imaginary stone and examining it. 'Ahhh good, yes.' His theatrics almost had the boys believing he had actually *found* a stone there in the dunes.

'So you've never been mining, you know, digging for opal?' Jack was suddenly embarrassed when he found himself imitating digging with a shovel.

'No, no, no mine. Well yes, yes, small mine.' He looked confused unable to explain clearly then became agitated. Ishmo could understand English but command of the spoken word had eluded him all his life frustrating him incredibly. It was at this point that people usually thought he was an imbecile and walked away so he was surprised when Jack continued patiently.

'Go on, Ishmo, you haven't done any digging for opal you say.'

'Yes, no digging.'

'What about the *small mine* you mentioned? Harry asked.

'Small mine? No, no digging.' He shook his head in frustration breaking out in his native tongue.

'Well, Ishmo, you've done better than us,' Jack said. 'You can understand and speak our language but we can't speak or understand yours at all.'

Overwhelmed by the wisdom of this young Australian boy and his acceptance of Ishmo's speech difficulties without ridicule quite humbled the Afghan. 'We stop now. Tomorrow I talk better.'

The following night sitting around the small fire with mugs of tea Ishmo put the pannikin down on the sand and went to his bedroll returning with a worn chamois leather pouch secured with a thong. Untying the knot he withdrew some dog-eared pieces of paper and leafed through them.

257

Squinting in the dull flickering firelight he selected one page that he handed to Jack, nodding for him to read it.

Jack examined the document for a minute without understanding but then it dawned on him what it was. 'This is a claim on a mine at Coober Pedy,' he said, looking up at the Afghan.

'Yes, yes!' He bobbed his head smiling. 'Yes, small mine, no digging.'

'You have a claim on a small mine?' Jack spoke slowly as he thought it through. 'But you haven't mined it yet. Is that what you mean, Ishmo?'

'Yes, no mining yet.'

Communicating was difficult so there were a number of times when the boys misunderstood Ishmo's explanations and collapsed in fits of laughter but Ishmo didn't get upset at these times and instead he laughed with them. *You have not laughed like this in many years, Ishmael,* he said to himself. *This is good.*

Before they turned in for the night they had established that, some years ago, Ishmo had done some prospecting after learning all he could about the opal fields over many trips to the area. Fossicking around he had found chips and 'floaters', faded surface opal that indicated stones were present. He had filed a claim but never mined it for many reasons, least of which was the racist attitude he knew he would encounter. The claim was still legally his though and he had the document to prove it.

They talked every night about opal mining, Ishmo animated and interspersing his explanations with many charades and shrugging of shoulders.

On the last night before reaching Coober Pedy they sat cross-legged around the fire, a million stars suspended in the heavens above them, listening to the crackle and hiss of the fire and feeling the cold desert wind on their backs. There was little conversation, each one of them reliving the trip and the boys wondering what the new day would bring.

Jack stretched and yawned and got to his feet but Ishmo held up a hand to indicate that he should sit again. Jack squatted between Harry and Reynold and the three of them looked intently at Ishmo waiting for him to speak.

'Jack. Harry.' He nodded to them as he spoke. 'I think much. Mine no good you no dig. You dig yes?'

'I don't quite understand, Ishmo, we want to dig, yes.' Jack was unsure of what the old Afghan was trying to say.

'No, no! You dig little mine.' Ishmo pulled the mining lease from the folds of his shirt. 'You, Jack, you, Harry, you dig Ishmael mine.' He tapped the mining lease with a grimy finger.

The significance of Ishmo's statement rocked Jack. 'We can't take over your mine, Ishmo, it belongs to you?'

'Yes, yes, me. But you dig and we share, yes? Ishmael not dig, too old now.'

'How would you know if we found any opal? When would we see you?'

'Yeah. How would we pay you your share?' Harry asked.

'Dig first, share later. Ishmael much happy you dig.' He looked to Reynold who sat silently staring at the fire. 'Your friend dig too. He work with you, you pay?'

'Yes, Ishmo, Reynold's our mate and he'll certainly get some pay if we find opal.'

'Not *if,* you find opal,' He stated with confidence. 'Then it … how you say? Deal, yes?'

'A deal.' Jack and Harry said in unison and looked at Reynold who nodded enthusiastically, a huge grin on his face.

◆◆◆◆◆◆◆◆◆◆◆◆

Having left the civilisation of comfortable Perth living to travel through some of the remotest country on earth Jack and Harry had experienced first-hand the barrenness that the Australian outback can present. Its wide gibber stone flats, the endless shifting red sands, vast salt claypans devoid of vegetation and deserts where the shimmering horizon was indistinguishable from the sky were beautiful yet daunting, but nothing prepared them for the desolation of Coober Pedy.

It wasn't that the natural geography of the place was so foreign to them as they had crossed similar country before. Here, however, in the centre of the treeless Gibson Desert, with its endless undulating plains broken now and then by twisted dry creek beds lined with dead, spindly mulga, the terrain looked like it had been attacked by swarms of giant ants.

The hot wind unceasingly clogged the air with dust, whipped from the blowers and hundreds of white mullock heaps where miners had sweated and cursed to sink their shafts as they burrowed drives into the stony earth in search of the precious gemstones. As they approached the town along a rutted red ribbon of track flanked by flat-topped sandstone ridges, they passed many diggings where roughly built sheds and corrugated-iron shelters sat forlornly in the intense heat beside a warren of gaping shafts.

Whatever Coober Pedy was imagined to be in the boys' minds over the past weeks as they progressed towards their magical dream, this was not it! This looked more like some devilish nightmare that you wake from' shaking and sweating.

◆◆◆◆◆◆◆◆◆◆◆◆

Dear Father,

Got to Coober Pedy yesterday. Water is scarce and the dust blows all the time from the wind. We got here with a camel team. Ishmo, the Afghan camel driver has a claim he said we could mine on. We saw it this morning and it's just a piece of dirt with a tin shed on it so we have to start from scratch by digging a shaft.

Ishmo knows a bloke here who has a mine and we met him too. He's going to give us a few tips to get started. It will mean a lot of hard work but Reynold is with us so the three of us will dig. Uncle Warri got real crook and we had to leave him at Anna Creek station.

It's really exciting here with mines everywhere. There are a lot of people but they seem a bit strange. There are shops and everything so we will buy some tools and stuff. We got paid by Mr Cooper, the drover, so have a bit of money to go on with till we find opal.

We had a beaut Christmas even though we missed our families. I got a new rifle as a present and Harry was given a cattle dog pup called Anna. We also got the three horses we were given along the way.

Will write again soon. Say hello to Paddy when you see him.

Thanks for sending our letters on.

The priest read the letter for a third time. *A rifle for goodness sake! What sort of person gives a kid a rifle for Christmas?* He shook his head in disbelief. Taking the folder from his desk drawer he placed the note inside, reading again the newspaper clipping. *One day they must see this,* he thought to himself then put the folder back. Standing up from his desk he left the office, the two envelopes addressed to the boys' parents in his pocket, and walked to the shed to get his car started for the drive to the post office.

◆◆◆◆◆◆◆◆◆◆◆◆

'We've got them this time Alice!' Jack tapped the letter on the table with his index finger.

'What do you mean, dear?' Alice wiped her eyes after reading the letter. She still burst into tears every time she saw Jack's simple handwriting but had begun to accept the fact that her son was all right or surviving at least. This acceptance didn't alleviate the pain of not seeing or talking with him face to face. There was an ache in her heart she knew would not go until she could hold her little boy in her arms once more.

'This bit here where he says they are on the way to making their fortune.' Jack picked up the letter and read. 'We bought some mining gear and are working a claim that belongs to a mate of ours.' He held the page up flicking it with the back of his hand. 'By God Alice, I'll find them this time.'

Alice, in her haste to devour every word of the letter, had missed what Jack had picked up. The letter received that morning was much the same as the others, giving no clue to their whereabouts only telling them not to worry and that they were both well, but there seemed to be a buoyancy in this one that had not been evident in the others. There was no mention of Billy Munse or the bike and, seemed more positive, a confidence apparent in the writing.

'The Goldfields cover a very big area, Jack; how can you narrow it down?'

'They're working their own mine somewhere on the fields so that eliminates checking the big operations out. That still leaves a lot of areas to cover, Alice, I know, but the miners are a close knit group so someone is sure to know of two young kids working a claim.'

Neither of them was to know that the *claim* their son was referring to was many hundreds of miles from Kalgoorlie in the heart of the desolate South Australian desert.

Chapter Twenty Six

The parcel of land where Ishmo had pegged and registered his claim was roughly nine miles west of the town in an area that was known as either Larkin's Folly or the Nine-Mile. Ishmo had pegged a claim there about four years previously after good quality opal was found in the region, just past Geraghty Hill, but had never worked it. He only had one friend in the area, a swarthy, solidly built Italian man with broad shoulders and bulging biceps developed from hours on the end of a pick and winding buckets of rock and clay from the bowels of the earth with a hand windlass.

His name was Bruno and the boys wondered how these two unlikely characters, one a tall wiry bearded Afghan, the other a short thickset Italian would ever have become friends. They learned that one day when Ishmo had been prospecting the areas around Coober Pedy he came across Bruno in the middle of a rough stony track cursing loudly and kicking a lopsided, heavily loaded wheelbarrow stacked with mining equipment and supplies. The axle had snapped on the barrow and Bruno was furious with it, his only means of transport now useless.

Ishmo, to the Italian's surprise, had stopped to offer assistance. Suspicious at first Bruno waved the Afghan away, stubbornly refusing help but common sense eventually prevailed and the load was transferred to Ishmo's camel and carted to where Bruno had his small mine. In return for this favour Bruno had helped Ishmo register his claim with the Department Of Mines.

Each time Ishmo transported a camel train of goods from the railhead at Marree to Coober Pedy, he would visit Bruno. How they communicated was a mystery to the boys as Bruno's English was as broken as Ishmo's was but somehow they managed it. The day Ishmo took the boys to meet Bruno the two of them moved off some distance, leaving the three boys by the open shaft beside the mullock heap, and with much waving of arms, charades and loud voices they struck a deal. The boys would help Bruno work his mine three days a week in return for Bruno teaching them the basics of opal mining.

The boys decided that it was important that one of them stay at the Eight Mile to look after the gear, make the shed more secure and start digging the shaft. Bruno also said his underground drives were low with limited room to work so Reynold readily volunteered to stay at the nine-mile claim, happy to be alone for three days of each week and not have to go underground, the prospect of which unnerved him.

'You laik rabbit diggin' burrow, eh? Rennol 'e work on top. No laik goin' inta ground.'

'What about diggin' our shaft, Reynold?' Harry asked

'Rennol dig 'im up to 'ere?' He held a hand up to the top of his head. 'Then Rennol 'e wind handle for you bloke,' he said, meaning the windlass.

'Righto, Reynold.'

Ishmo stayed for one night with them beside the tin shed that was to become their home until something more suitable could be established. It was very basic, constructed of rusty corrugated iron nailed over an assortment of timbers scrounged from dumps.

It had a dirt floor and one window that was just a square of tin that swung outward, propped open with a stick. The door was made from discarded packing crates but was solid enough and secured with a heavy padlocked chain. There were numerous rips and old nail holes in the iron but that was of no concern as rainfall was minimal, but it did let the white powdery dust in.

The only item that could be described as 'furniture' was a rickety table roughly nailed together from planks, also scavenged from old abandoned diggings. It was unsteady, leaned to one side and had wide gaps between the planks but to the boys it was a luxury. Apart from the Christmas dinner at Anna Creek station, there had been no table on the drove and everyone ate their meals from tin plates resting on their knees. The only other items in the shed were a shovel, two picks, a sieve and an old, wooden-wheeled barrow, equipment that Ishmo had collected over the years for his mining venture.

The boys decided after Ishmo left, saying he would be back 'Sometime, yes,' to use the shed for storage only, opting to set up camp outside and sleep as they had done on the drove, under the stars. They felt a sense of permanency, though, able to unpack their blueys and hang spare clothes on nails driven into the shed frame. They also hung the swags inside each day, as the area was inhabited by poisonous scorpions and spiders that would slip into bedrolls, boots or clothes and were known to inflict painful, possibly life-threatening, stings on the unwary. There were also deadly snakes that hunted in the cool of the night.

The first day they went to Bruno's claim to begin their opal education they were excited yet apprehensive, unnerved by the prospect of going underground and not knowing what to expect. They had heard of cave-ins where unstable earth had collapsed, entombing miners beneath tons of rock and rubble, of snakes lurking in dark crevices poised to strike an unsuspecting hand and of stale, suffocating air.

Bruno was waiting for them, welcoming them with a broad smile and leading them to the shaft that was framed by a flat, timber headwork with a windlass that had a rope attached that descended into the blackness.

'I go downa first. When I calla you name, you come.' Bruno expertly swung his thick legs over the edge of the shaft onto the rope ladder and disappeared into the gloom.

Neither boy spoke as they waited for Bruno's call and when they heard his faint muffled voice Harry nodded and Jack stepped up to the shaft. Imitating Bruno he swung over the edge, his feet finding the rope rungs, and he began to shakily descend the ladder, swaying from side to side. The shaft was quite narrow and he didn't look down as he climbed, darkness rising to meet him. He glanced upwards and could see Harry's head diminishing in size as, holding his breath, he lowered himself down the ladder.

When his feet finally touched ground he realised he had had his eyes shut for the last few feet and, when he opened them, to his surprise he was standing in what was a large, circular shaped, high roofed cavern. There was a lit lantern hanging from a divot driven into the wall and as his eyes adjusted to the gloom he could make out four cave-like tunnels or 'drives' as they were called. They ran off like wheel spokes from the central hub of the bowl-shaped dugout at the bottom of the shaft.

Harry came next in much the same awkward swaying manner that Jack had. He was breathing fast and his eyes had a fearful look when he reached the bottom but he soon recovered, fascinated by the cavern and the beckoning dark mouths of the drives.

Bruno took two candles from a shelf carved into the wall and, lighting them from the lantern, he handed one each to the boys. Taking two small picks he beckoned them to follow as he stooped and entered one of the drives. It was some twenty feet long and came to an abrupt end, a wall of clay facing them.

Bruno reached up and tapped the roof with his pick, 'Good solida roof,' he said, 'sandastone.' He explained that opal-bearing dirt was usually beneath the layer of sandstone and that when they dug their own shaft at their claim and broke through the layer they should then start a drive off from the base of the shaft.

They spent the day digging and wheeling loads of rubble and clay in a barrow to a pile at the shaft base then shovelling it into the windlass bucket. They took it in turns to climb up the ladder and wind the heavy handle to haul the bucket from the depths. Bruno told them to always stand clear when the bucket was going up or down; a snapped rope he said could send the bucket hurtling to the bottom and was very dangerous.

They found no opal that day and were exhausted by the intense and constant physical labour when they finally ceased work late in the day. There was an added bonus though to being in the drive because the aboveground temperature was many degrees hotter than below the surface. This was why most of the permanent dwellings in Coober Pedy were underground, protected from the heat by the natural insulation of tons of earth.

'You start digga you shaft yet?' Bruno asked at the end of the day.

'Not yet. We're not sure where to start, Bruno,' Harry answered, brushing flies from his face.

'I come looka for you. Show you where besta to dig. You can wait coupla days?'

'That'd be great, Bruno. We'll tell Reynold to hold off till then.'

They worked with the Italian for two more days, digging, hauling, sweating and learning, then on the morning of the third day Bruno came to their claim just on sun-up.

Surveying the terrain Bruno shook his head. 'No digga da shaft.'

'What?' Jack was shaken.

'You mean there's no opal here?' Harry said, similarly stunned.

'No can tell ifa opla not here. You need to digga to find out.' He looked around picking up some stones and examining them. 'Good though.'

'But you said not to dig.' Harry was confused.

'No. I say don'ta dig *shaft*, not don'ta dig.'

The three boys looked at each other completely bewildered. They had trouble interpreting Bruno's broken English and were also amused that he called opal 'opla'.

There was a low sandstone ridge running through the claim that rose to a flat peak near the centre and it was to this that Bruno walked. The ridge was around a hundred and fifty yards wide where the peak rose, presenting a sandstone face around thirty feet high that sloped slightly backward from where he was standing.

Bruno motioned for the boys to join him at the foot of the rock face. 'Youa very lucky, you no need to dig shaft downa like dis,' he made shovelling motions at his feet, '… but you dig inna like dis.' He repeated the shovelling motion but this time at chest level straight at the rock face.

'You slopa you shaft down little bit, go right in under da sandastone.' He was beaming from ear to ear. 'Maybe I swoppa you eh? You digga my mine and I taka dis one … itsa easy.'

Reynold was pleased not to have to dig a shaft straight down and for some reason didn't find digging a tunnel straight into the rock face threatening. He took a pick and immediately starting to chip away at the rocky clay.

'You digga da house first.'

'What do you mean, Bruno? Jack asked

Firsta thing you do is make ada place to live. You dig him wide, make ada room, then runna you drive from him. You then have house *anna* da mine.'

As the days passed Jack and Harry absorbed everything they could from Bruno who delighted in their company and in sharing his knowledge with them. They made no big finds with Bruno but small pockets of colour were dug or chipped from the clay below the sandstone. It was hard, repetitive work but they thrived on it, happy to be underground where it was many degrees cooler than on the surface where the angry sun beat ferociously, the wind sandblasted them and the ever present flies explored their mouths, ears and noses.

They developed a pattern of working three days a week with Bruno and three days with Reynold fashioning their dugout. They went to town one day a week for supplies and to cart water, which was non-existent in the diggings.

It was in the third week of this pattern that they arrived back at the nine-mile from a trip to town to find the tunnel abandoned, tools lying idle at the mouth and no sign of Reynold. They checked the shed and called out to him but there was no response.

Drinking the inevitable mug of tea beside the campfire that evening under a twinkling blanket of starlight they discussed what could have happened to Reynold. They had no idea where he could be and why he would leave without some explanation. They stopped talking when Anna padded to the edge of the firelight and started whining, her tail wagging as she stared into the night.

'Who's there?' Jack called.

'That you, Reynold?' Harry shouted into the darkness.

There was no answer and they heard no sound so when a figure materialised out of the blackness beside them they let out a yell and jumped to their feet.

'Reynold! You scared the livin' daylights out of us, mate. Where the hell have ya been? We were worried about ya?' Jack slapped Reynold's shoulder in welcome. 'You had any tucker?'

'No tucker, Jack, not 'ungry. Gotta go, eh?'

'Go! Go where? I don't understand.' Harry held out a mug of hot tea. 'Gotta good brew, mate, here have one.'

'No. Rennol 'e jus' come to say goodbye 'n pick up swag.' He hesitated obviously upset by something. 'I gonna miss yu bloke.' They could see tears glistening in the firelight before he turned his head away.

'Come on, Reynold … you're not gonna leave us, mate. What for?'

'Gotta go, Jack.' He offered no explanation.

'What's the matter, Reynold? You can't just go off without tellin' us why.' Harry walked to him and putting his hands on his shoulders looked him directly in the eye. 'Now what's goin' on, mate?'

'Rennol 'e jus' cause yu problem. Better I go.'

'*What* problem?' Jack was getting frustrated, his voice showing a hint of irritation.

'Those bloke, they tell me to go.'

'Blokes! What blokes?'

Reynold sat on the ground his head in his hands and told them. 'Today, after yu go, these bloke come. Rennol 'e diggin' and don' 'ear 'em straight up. Come out from inside 'ole 'n was blinded little bit by the sun. Then this bloke grab me 'n push me up long the rock. Then he say, 'yu black bloke not welcome 'ere. Opal for white bloke, yu take off 'n don' come back.'

'What'd you say to 'em, Reynold? Did you tell 'em that we all work together on this?' Harry was angry.

'I tell 'em I work this mine wit' me brothers 'n they say, 'yu tell yu brothers to take off too.' Then they push me little bit more 'n say they comin' back nex' day 'n if I still 'ere they gonna beat me bad.' He was trying hard not to let his tears show. 'So I go now 'n save you trouble wit' them fellas. When they see yu is white bloke, I tink they maybe go way.'

'You're not goin' anywhere, Reynold. We're stayin', mate, and so are you. They can't kick us off this claim.'

It took some persuasion but they eventually convinced Reynold to stay, saying they would sort it out if the men turned up again the next day. They then worked out a plan of what they would do if the trespassers did come back.

◆◆◆◆◆◆◆◆◆◆◆◆

'You in there, darkie?' The voice was cocky and mocking. 'You better not be or you're in fer a bashin' for sure.' Two other voices laughed at this threat.

'Go on, Reynold, you know what to say.' Jack nudged him to walk out of the tunnel where the three of them were hidden. 'We won't let 'em touch ya, mate, just say what we told ya to say.'

Reynold walked boldly out into the morning sunshine causing shocked gasps from the men who expected him to have run away in the night.

'Well, well, well. Look at this willya. We got us a little smartie pants here,' the self-appointed leader mocked. 'You got a bloody cheek haven't ya, but you'll be gone in a minute, mate, and with a good kick up the backside to send ya on yer way.'

Reynold spoke his rehearsed line 'Yu need to talk wit' me brothers. They say yu jus' big win'bags, eh?'

The leader was taken aback at this unexpected show of defiance and spluttered 'You what? ... You callin' us names? That'll get ya a bigger hidin' you little ...'

Harry stepped from the tunnel mouth, Anna growling beside him, stopping the man in mid sentence. 'Can *I* help ya, mister?' He was shaking at the knees but didn't let it show, glad of Anna's growling support.

'Who the hell are *you*?' The man turned his attention to Harry, his companions standing behind him with belligerent expressions on their faces.

'No. Who are *you* and what are ya doin' on our claim?'

'I'll show you who *I am,* young fella.' The weedy man with haunted, watery eyes took a step toward Harry who retreated a step. 'You obviously need a thrashin' too, eh?' He turned to his companions 'Come on, men; let's teach these two cheeky young bastards who's who around here.'

The three men moved forward, wary of the dog, but stopped dead in their tracks their mouths slacking open as Jack stepped from the shelter of the tunnel mouth, the Winchester levelled steadily at them.

What the! ... Hey ... put that gun down, young fella!' The weedy man's voice had lost its aggressiveness, his eyes darting from Jack to Harry, then, back to Jack. The two other men with him raised their hands slightly; retreating two or three steps.

'You didn't answer me mate's question. Who are ya?' Jack amazed himself at the confidence he showed but didn't feel.

'We … er … we just thought this young, black bloke here musta jumped yer claim. Only helpin' out, mate, no need to get all shirty. Now just put the gun down before it goes off and hurts someone.'

'Only helpin' out were ya? Then you can help out again by gettin' off our claim as you're trespassin'. We don't need your sorta help, mate, so clear off the lot of ya.' Jack indicated with the rifle barrel the direction for the men to go.

'You can't threaten us, mate.' The watery-eyed man tried to reclaim some authority. 'Bet it isn't even loaded that gun. What do ya reckon, fellas?' He said over his shoulder to his two companions, without taking his eyes from the rifle pointed at him. Jack didn't respond so he continued. 'Yeah, that's it,' he laughed, 'not even loaded. Bet yer don't even know *how* to load it either and I also bet ya don't know how to use it.' He took a tentative step forward and his friends lowered their arms believing that there was now no threat from the kid with the unloaded rifle.

Jack looked past the men to a stunted mulga a hundred and twenty yards behind them where he had hung an empty jam tin the night before. 'Just have to see. Maybe I did forget to load it.' He put the rifle to his shoulder and the men cringed, then, realising the rifle was not pointed directly at them, looked behind to see what Jack was aiming at.

The rifle shot cracked loudly in the still morning air echoing around the nearby sandstone ridges as the tin exploded into the air from the dead branch and, hitting the ground, rolled a couple of times before it stopped. 'Yeah,' Jack said quietly. 'I musta forgotten to load it.' He levered another shell into the breech.

Jack brought the barrel around to point directly at the three men. 'Now get off our claim and don't come back. The next shot won't be aimed at a tin can.'

The three boys collapsed in emotional, relieved laughter after the men scrambled over one another and, running into the surrounding mullock heaps with Anna yapping at their heels, were swallowed up by the sand dunes.

'Do ya think they'll come back, Jack?'

'Hope not, Harry, 'cause I didn't know what to do next if they hadn't of bolted. You know I wouldn't have shot 'em don't ya?'

Reynold and Harry shrugged but didn't reply and Jack had a chilling thought that maybe he *would* have fired if the three intruders had continued to threaten him and his mates.

Chapter Twenty Seven

Jack and Harry related to Bruno what had happened to Reynold the day before and described their confrontation with the three men that morning as an explanation for why they were late at his claim. Bruno listened intently, just grunting occasionally as the boys talked. His face lit up when Harry described how Jack had run them off with the rifle.

'Not from arounda here,' Bruno said. 'The people onna da field would not do that. I ask around, maybe someone seea dese men. I think you shoulda stay at your claim froma now on'. You got lotta work to do and me OK now. You helpa me out big time. When you wanna help you just come aska me and I show you whatta to do.'

They worked Bruno's mine for him that day but Bruno excused himself late in the morning and left them, not saying where he was going. The boys had finished up for the day and were about to leave when Bruno reappeared.

'You notta worry 'bout those men no more,' Bruno said.

Why's that, Bruno?' Harry was curious.

'Never mind, just notta worry, OK? Now, you stay atta your claim tomorrow. I come round later inna day and see watta you do. Give a little advice maybe.'

Bruno didn't explain to the boys that he had been into town to see some miner friends of his and have a couple of vinos and to tell them about the three men that had tried to run the boys off their workings. There was not a lot of discussion about the incident but Bruno's friends decided that these men were not a welcome element in the opal fields and that an eye would be kept out for them.

The boys were not aware that they had already earned a reputation in the area in just a few weeks. All the locals knew of the two young drover lads that had arrived in Coober Pedy and started mining the Afghan's long idle claim with their aboriginal friend. The people learned from Bruno of their honesty and hard working ethics so word quickly spread throughout the close knit mining community that there were two more miners considered 'local'. Reynold was also well respected for his work digging the tunnel into the ridge and for his loyal friendship with Jack and Harry. The news that some claim jumpers with bad attitudes had tried to intimidate the three young lads with violent threats angered the miners who, although they kept to themselves and normally never meddled in other peoples business, could unite in a split second to defend their own kind.

◆◆◆◆◆◆◆◆◆◆◆◆

A battered, rust-coloured Dodge utility caked in dust and spewing smoke pulled into the garage on the main street of Coober Pedy beside the petrol pumps. It was after dark and the driver, an untidily dressed, thin man, paced impatiently beside the vehicle as he waited for the attendant. 'Fill 'er up mate,' he snapped, 'we're in a hurry.' He walked off to the men's room. His two passengers left the vehicle and wandered to the garage entrance where they filled in time looking at the racks of motor oil, tyres and batteries on display.

The garage attendant noticed two things in particular. The back of the ute was piled with camping gear indicating these three men were itinerant or newly arrived in town, and the driver, who pulled cash from his pocket to pay for the petrol, had unusually watery eyes. He watched the men closely until they returned to the Dodge and drove out onto the street before he lifted the telephone receiver, asked for a number then spoke softly and briefly into the mouthpiece.

'Where we goin' now?' One passenger asked the driver.

'I dunno, just drive around a bit I suppose … look for an opportunity.'

'Another opportunity, eh? Well, let us pick the mark next time, Joe. Last time you got us run off by a coupla bloody kids.' The man nudged his fellow passenger and they both laughed.

'Shut up or you can bloody well walk, it's my truck,' The driver snapped angrily.

They drove in silence for some time until the driver said, 'what's this then?' A vehicle with its bonnet up appeared in the headlights on the side of the road just out of town.

The Dodge slowed to a stop alongside the stranded car and the man seated on the passenger's side leaned out of the window. 'Need a hand, mate?'

'Yeah, thanks for stoppin'. The motor just conked out. Know anythin' about cars?'

'You might just be in luck, mate,' the man answered, glancing at his companions. 'Joe here's a mechanic, aren't ya, Joe?'

'I guess we could have a look at her for ya, yeah.' Joe, the driver, summed up the situation, making sure the man was alone, then nodded to his two passengers before picking up a tyre lever from beside the seat and stepping from the Dodge. 'Come on, men,' he whispered, 'opportunity knocks.'

◆◆◆◆◆◆◆◆◆◆◆◆

The monthly finance committee meeting had concluded for the evening and Father O'Malley excused himself from the gathering after spending what he considered to be an acceptable time with them drinking tea and forcing a rather limp tuna and lettuce sandwich down. They were dear loyal parishioners but the priest couldn't wait to escape from the irrelevant chitchat that habitually followed these meetings. Besides, Paddy O'Brien had appeared that morning and was waiting for him.

Sitting in the cane chairs on the presbytery verandah, the evening breeze brought little relief from the heat. Father O'Malley busied himself filling his pipe while Paddy poured two healthy nips of Irish whisky into large tumblers.

'And here's lookin' at ye, Timothy, me mate.' Paddy threw back his head, emptying the tumbler in one gulp, reaching again for the bottle.

'It's no wonder it is that you feel like you do in the mornings, Paddy, you drink far too much, m'lad.' The priest sipped at his glass.

'Arhh, Father it's little I have left to enjoy I'll be tellin' ye. The mornin's I feel the worst are the ones when I *haven't* been havin' a drop of *the doins.'* Paddy laughed

They talked on into the evening, the level of the bottle sinking past the label. 'And tell me, Father, have ye been hearin' from me lads, Jack and Harry?'

'Not for a little while, Paddy but they've reached Coober Pedy by their last letter.'

'To be sure they have. I never doubted they'd make it,' he chuckled. 'Did they say if they've been findin' any of that opal yet?'

'It was early days, Paddy, but I'm sure they'll write again soon. It worries me though, those two young lads out there in the wilds of Coober Pedy.'

'I'm sure there's no need to be worryin', Timothy, they're made of good stock those two.' Paddy poured another healthy nip. 'It wouldn't be surprisin' me none if there was Irish blood in 'em somewhere you know.'

'I've heard some stories that it's a rough place full of hard men and it concerns me that they could walk into trouble easily and not know it.' The priest continued to voice his fears.

'Arhh ya worry too much, Father, they can look after themselves and they'll be makin' friends for themselves in no time at all.'

'Do you think that those hard-working hard-drinking miners would worry about a couple of kids, Paddy?'

'To be sure, to be sure. Not that I'm a bettin' man, Father, but I'd wager that there are good men, hard as they are, that'd be takin' good care of 'em even as we speak.'

'I hope so, Paddy, I certainly hope so. Care for a nightcap?' Father O'Malley started to pour without bothering to wait for an answer from his old friend.

♦ ♦ ♦ ♦ ♦ ♦ ♦ ♦ ♦ ♦ ♦ ♦

The three men advanced slowly on the lone man beside the motionless car, the headlights from the Dodge casting their shadows in long spidery streaks down the roadway.

Joe weighed the tyre lever in his right hand and licked his lips nervously, then, everything went suddenly black as the Dodge's headlights snapped off. Spinning around, the men couldn't see anything but heard the door of their truck slam shut. Confused and concerned they stood together in the dark and were then blinded by the two powerful beams that flashed on from the blackness beyond the stranded car trapping them like rabbits in a hunter's spotlight.

A disembodied voice from the darkness behind the spotlights said, 'you always fix a motor with a tyre lever, mate?'

Joe and his friends knew then they were in trouble but couldn't comprehend why. How could, what seemed to them to be a perfect chance to rob someone, turn out to be a trap set for them? Then they understood.

'You blokes not as confident now that you're not pickin' on kids, eh?' the voice said.

'Hey!' Joe was frightened now. 'That was just a misunderstandin', the kids got it wrong.'

'The only thing the kids got wrong was not puttin' the bullet between yer eyes, mate.'

Joe's two companions began to panic. 'It was all his idea the bloody fool, we didn't do nothin', mate, honest.'

'Birds of a feather flock together I always say. You're as bad as each other. Love the way, too, that ya stick up fer yer mate.' The voice was behind them now and they whirled around but could see nothing.

'What'll we do with 'em? Shoot 'em or hang 'em?'

'Maybe we should do what we do to all moonlighters that rob a bloke's claim at night when he's asleep.' Another voice suggested.

'Good idea … just drop 'em down an old shaft out in the bush. If the fall doesn't kill 'em they'll starve to death or maybe get bitten by a king brown; lots of 'em down those old abandoned shafts.'

The three men in the spotlights were terrified now, shaking and close to tears as they milled around in the powerful beams, spinning from the sound of one voice to the next like cornered animals.

Then a new voice joined the debate. 'I thinka maybe we use da shotagun, just blowa da knees away. Dey can then crawla back down da holes dey comma from, eh?'

'That's the best idea yet … yeah! You bring yer shotgun with ya, Bruno?'

'Of course.' There was silence for a time except for the whimpering sounds from the three men clinging together in the dirt road their hands held up to shield their eyes from the glare of the lights.

'OK then, that's the verdict! Court's over … carry out the sentence.'

The three men distinctly heard the hammers cock on the shotgun seconds before the thunderous blast shattered the night calm.

Screaming, Joe slumped to the ground. One of his companions fell to his knees sobbing and begging for mercy, while the third man just stood, transfixed with fear, his arms over his head.

'Cripes, Bruno, ya missed! I thought ya were a better shot than that.' The first voice said.

Realising he had not been hit Joe was horrified to discover he had soiled his trousers.

Voice number one spat out the next words. 'You blokes jump in that old Dodge and get outta town now. You've got a full tank of petrol, enough to get ya well away from here, and if ya run out in the desert we couldn't care less. Just remember tonight, burn it in yer memories and lay awake thinkin' about it but …' the voice became louder, 'Never forget what I'm about to say next. If ya ever come near our town again as long as ya live or ever touch or threaten one of our people, whether it be here or somewhere else, then you'll wish we *had* shot ya tonight, so help me God.'

The lights flicked off, leaving the three men blinded now by the sudden darkness. In a daze, they heard the stranded car start up, and a powerful engine beyond it in the dunes, burst into life. Within seconds they were alone, shaken and disorientated in the chill desert night.

◆◆◆◆◆◆◆◆◆◆◆◆

Bruno arrived at the nine-mile diggings the next morning just on sun up and the boys noticed he was in a bubbly mood as he greeted them but they didn't ask why and Bruno never offered any explanation. They shared a mug of tea around the campfire and when Bruno asked how they were progressing with the dugout, they told him they were ready to start a drive off it and seriously look for opal.

Bruno nodded his approval as they entered the oval shaped cavern that was now used as a rough dwelling. They had moved the old wooden table into the cave and it took pride of place against one wall where a couple of shelves had been carved into the clay, now housing some tinned goods, cooking pots and other odds and ends. Although Reynold had been responsible for the major part of the excavation, he still opted to sleep outside as he had done most of his life, under the stars. Jack and Harry however, were using the dugout as their main dwelling except for cooking that, for obvious reasons, was done outside the entrance.

Bruno asked where they planned to start their drive. When they pointed to the rock face, he took a small pick and began to scrape away at the area, examining his findings closely as the boys watched with interest, wondering if their selection was right.

'You have picka good spot,' Bruno eventually said. 'Itsa where I would dig. Follow seam down lika dis,' he traced the sandstone with his finger, 'and with a littla luck you maybe finda stone.'

'So you reckon this is where the opal is, Bruno?'

'Harry, the opla is where the opla is.'

'What do ya mean, Bruno?'

'Opla isa where you find her. Dis dirt she looka probable.'

When Bruno came outside he looked at the pile of clay and rubble from the cavern the boys had heaped near the entrance. 'You looka in dis?'

'No we didn't think it was worth it as we hadn't started on the drive yet.' Jack realised they had made a mistake when Bruno arched his brows and rolled his eyes.

'As I said ... opla issa where you find her. Gooda luck, boys. I see you fewa days time.'

'Well I guess we should start here then.' Jack reached down, picked up a golf ball sized rock from the dusty heap of rubble and chucked it toward the dugout entrance.

'Good shot, Jack ... ya hit the shovel dead centre, mate,' Harry said. 'I'll go and get the old sieve from the shed and you grab the two shovels. We'll sift through this lot before we start diggin' the drive.'

'Righto, Harry … ya never know I suppose. Come on, Reynold, let's grab the tools.' They walked off to get the shovels.

◆◆◆◆◆◆◆◆◆◆◆◆

Shaun Logan had been born in Bendigo Victoria. Although proud of his paternal Irish heritage he considered himself Australian to the core. His father, an underground miner on the Bendigo goldfields, had married his mother, a nurse, in 1914. Shaun was born eighteen months later just two months before his father was tragically killed when a roof collapsed, entombing him under tons of crushing rock. Shaun's mother, grief stricken, could not bear to stay in Bendigo, seeing as she did each day, the mine head-works dominating much of the city's skyline, so she accepted an offer from a maiden aunt to move to Adelaide and escape the constant reminders of her husband's death. She was able to work there as a nurse, and her aunt offered rent-free accommodation which meant she could save a little money to ensure her son got an education that would enable him to follow a career, she determined, would not in any way be associated with mining.

His mother was thrilled when Shaun had entered the seminary and was ordained a priest. She accepted, with some misgivings, when he served as a chaplain with the army during the war, but cried for weeks, long buried ghosts of grief haunting her, when he was appointed to the parish of Coober Pedy, the roughest and most remote mining town in Australia.

Father Shaun fitted Coober Pedy like a made-to- measure suit. He was a strongly built man with an outgoing personality, played football, enjoyed a beer, and officiated at the annual race meeting. In a town where religion was accepted as necessary only for the rare wedding or odd funeral, but was otherwise considered by most as superfluous, Father Shaun was the exception, held in high regard for his beliefs and his commitment to the community with its diverse residents.

The priest knew everything that happened in Coober Pedy and was intrigued when the three young drovers had come to town. He laughed when he heard how they had run off the claim jumpers and understood the bush justice that had been metered out to the perpetrators by the locals. It was a surprise therefore, when he opened the letter with the Kalgoorlie postmark and read the letter from Father Timothy O'Malley, to realise that the boys mentioned in it, were the same three young miners.

◆ ◆ ◆ ◆ ◆ ◆ ◆ ◆ ◆ ◆ ◆ ◆

Jack picked up a shovel and turned to walk back to the mullock heap when he heard Reynold draw in a sharp breath. Turning, he saw him bend to pick something up from the ground.

'Crikey, Jack, look at this fella.'

'What is it, Reynold?'

'That stone you threw, Jack.' Reynold held a chip of rock up to the sun. 'When 'e 'it that shovel 'e split up little bit. Look at 'im.'

Jack took the small piece of stone that Reynold handed to him and was shocked to see the pinwheels of vibrant colour flash in the sunlight. 'Wow Reynold … it's … it's…' He couldn't get the words out for excitement.

'Opal, Jack! It's opal.' Reynold fell to his knees, searching in the dirt for more. 'Yahoo!' He yelled and pounced on the other half of the broken stone.

Harry, seeing his mates' excited actions, dropped the sieve and, running to where they were, gasping in awe. 'Is it …? … By heck it *is!*' The three boys linked arms and danced like madmen in the dust.

Chapter Twenty Eight

Bruno was as thrilled for the boys as if he had made a major find himself. After watching them laboriously sift through the heap with their old hand sieve, he suggested that they needed a bigger, more efficient method' to separate the fine clay and dust from the rocks more quickly, so they could then hand sort the stone.

They went with him back to his claim where Bruno searched through a rubbish heap that had gathered over time, and containing some old equipment he had discarded after replacing it with newer items. He dragged from the pile of rusty junk, a metal bed frame with a wire base, and some odd pieces of timber.

Transporting the bits back to the nine-mile in the back of his Land Rover he showed them how to set the bed frame up on end at a 45-degree angle, propped on the old scavenged timbers. Although rickety, this now made a sieve six feet by three feet and they could shovel the mullock onto it. The dirt went through the wire, leaving the stones to fall in a pile at the bottom, for sorting later.

'We said we'd make our fortune, Harry, and we're on our way.' Jack was exuberant.

'You bet, Jack. What d'ya reckon, Reynold ... we gonna be rich or what?'

Reynold was too busy shovelling dirt onto the sieve to answer but nodded vigorously, a broad smile on his dark face that was now covered with white powdery dust.

The boys heard the car approach mid-morning. It stopped at the bottom of the slope so they ceased working and stood watching suspiciously, nervous after the experience with the claim jumpers. Jack kept the loaded rifle near at hand, just inside the dugout entrance, and he moved a few feet closer, ready to grab it at the first sign of trouble.

A man, neatly dressed in dark trousers and white short sleeved open-necked shirt, stepped from the vehicle and plonked a brown wide brimmed hat over his dark wavy hair before walking up the slope to where they were standing. He stopped after a few feet and called to them. 'Is it all right to come on up. Don't want to get shot at!'

'Depends, mate. Who are ya and what do ya want?' Jack glanced to where the rifle was; a little confused by the man's reference to being shot at.

'I'm Shaun Logan.' He made it a practice never to introduce himself as 'Father'. 'I've got a message for a Jack Ferguson and a Harry Turner … am I at the right mine?' He knew, of course, who the boys were but waited for their reply.

'Who's the message from then?' Harry asked with hands placed defiantly on his hips.

Shaun Logan respected that a man's claim was his own territory knowing that it was an accepted thing in the fields that no stranger would just walk on to it without being invited. The priest stood in the sun, impressed by their mature approach to his unannounced arrival.

'I've actually got a letter for both of them.' He watched their surprised reaction. 'I'm the local priest here, can I come on up?'

'A letter? For us?' Jack looked at Harry then back to the man who said he was a priest.

'You don't look like a priest and ya haven't said who the letter's from.'

It was Father Logan's turn to be surprised. He was unaware of the reason they had left Perth as Father O'Malley hadn't revealed this to him in the letter but had purely asked if he knew of them and, if they were in Coober Pedy, could he please make contact and pass his letter on to them. He therefore couldn't fathom their reluctance to let him come onto their digging but put it down to the claim jumping episode that must have spooked them more than he thought it had. Even the dog, a blue heeler, stood with its hackles raised, beside one of the boys.

'Father O'Malley wrote to me and asked me to give you this.' He waved an envelope in the air.

'Father O'Malley? He wrote us a letter? Better come on up then. That alright with you, Harry?'

'Yeah,' the boy with the dog said and reached down and touched its head. 'Sit, Anna … sit.' The dog obeyed instantly, without taking its eyes from the priest.

He walked up to them. 'Which of you is Jack and which one's Harry?' He smiled warmly. 'I guess you must be Reynold.' He held out a hand that Reynold took shyly before moving off a few feet and staring at the ground.

After talking with the man for a few minutes the boys relaxed under his friendly, matter-of-fact manner, the small gold crosses on his collar the only clue to his being a priest. Nearing midday it was fiercely hot in the sun, a time when the boys normally moved underground to work, so they invited the priest to join them in their makeshift abode. Reynold stayed outside shovelling dirt against the sieve.

The boys asked their visitor what Father O'Malley had written in the letter to him. Shaun Logan explained that the letter from Kalgoorlie had surprised him. He told them he knew of their presence on the fields and that, indeed, the whole town knew of them. This statement astonished the boys who just shook their heads in disbelief. 'The note from Father O'Malley,' he said, 'purely asked if I knew of you and if I could pass on the letter.'

They spent some time telling him that Father O'Malley had helped them get to Coober Pedy by taking them to Mt Margaret Mission and some highlights of their trip with Warri and Tom Cooper but they omitted any reference to being wanted by the police in Western Australia.

As he was leaving, the priest told them that they could call on him any time if they needed help or just to have a yarn so they asked him was there any way he could find out how uncle Warri was as they were worried about him.

Reynold stayed digging while Jack and Harry walked with the priest to his car. 'See ya,' he said and drove off down the rutted track. They returned to the dugout anxious to read the letter addressed to them from Father O'Malley. Reynold didn't seem interested so Jack tore the envelope open and began to read aloud.

> My dear Jack and Harry,
>
> It will be by the Grace of God if this gets to you as it is a remote chance sending it via Father Logan but I thought there might be a possibility he has heard of you and can deliver this letter.
>
> If you are reading this I hope you are in good health and keeping out of harm's way. I only know what I have heard about Coober Pedy but knowing the hardships of mining in and around Kalgoorlie and understanding that conditions are far worse where you are, I am most concerned for you both and for Reynold.

'Gee,' Harry said. 'He uses big words. Must be because he's a priest.'

'More likely 'cause he's *old*, Harry.' Jack continued reading.

> Thank you for writing your letters and I have, reluctantly I must admit, kept my promise not to tell your parents where you are but this secret is painful for me and I hope and pray you will let them know soon.
>
> I am most impressed with your achievements to date and with your trip but Paddy says he knew all the time you would get to Coober Pedy and has no doubts that you will make your fortunes!!! He is a man of great optimism if not stability and a dear friend despite his misgivings.

'There he goes again, Jack. I can't understand most of that.'

'Harry!' Jack was getting annoyed at the interruptions as he was finding it hard to read the letter anyway. 'Shut up.' He held it out to Harry. 'Here then ... you bloody read it.'

'Sorry, mate,' Harry giggled. 'Go on.'

> He stopped over last night and sends his regards to you both. He is still the same jovial man without a care in the world but I sense he misses you a lot.
>
> I took the liberty of inquiring about Warrinidding by contacting the manager at Anna Creek station and am pleased to tell you he is well recovered and back at Warburton. Tell Reynold the news.
>
> I am looking forward to receiving more correspondence from you and Mrs Lacey has also asked about you.
>
> Sincerely your friend,
> Timothy O'Malley

The next couple of weeks proved to be a tedious time for the three boys. Because of the intense Coober Pedy heat that baked them, the wind that blew constantly, peppering them with sand and white powdery dust, and the flies that never ceased exploring their eyes, mouths and noses, they decided to work outside from early morning to around eleven o'clock in the morning. After then they retreated to the dugout where they could escape from the heat, wind and dust but unfortunately not from the persistent black bushflies that followed them even underground.

They worked on what they thought was a seam, scraping, chipping and digging clay and rocks that they hauled out to the mullock heap. They then shovelled it through the sieve and found opal but it was worthless 'potch' as it was known on the fields. Bruno had told them when they worked his diggings that finding it, however, was an indication that valuable or even precious opal could be nearby, but they didn't find any.

Working through the dugout rubble in the mornings they did find a little more opal similar to the stone they initially found and decided to take it all to Bruno to see if he could sell it for them. They needed money for supplies and they didn't want to break into their saving, so thought they might be able to get a little for what they had found.

Bruno examined their findings, a number of smallish stones and some chips that Reynold had fossicked around the fields. He pursed his lips a couple of times but made no comment on the quality except to say that it was probably saleable. There was a buyer due in town that week he said and if they trusted him enough he would take it in with his parcel and run it past the buyer. They readily agreed, telling Bruno that of course they trusted him, so he took a small calico bag with a drawstring, the boys commenting that it looked like a bag they kept marbles in at home, and placed their opal in it.

Working back on their drive the next couple of days seemed interminable, waiting for Bruno to appear, but when they saw him driving up in his Land Rover they became nervous. Bruno's expression didn't reveal anything and they knew that their opal was probably worthless or he had it sold for a pittance. At least, they figured, there might be enough to buy some more tinned goods and tea but they were hoping to get timber and nails to upgrade their dugout a little.

Bruno sat down on an upturned kerosene tin in their dugout and placed an envelope on the rough-hewn table. Putting a match to a candle he drew some notes from the envelope and started to count them in the yellow dancing light, placing each note carefully in a pile as he did so.

'Ten a twenty, thirty a forty, fifty a sixty ...' He didn't look up as he counted or he would have seen the expressions on the boy's faces turn from *'pleased'* to *'stunned'* as he went on. 'One a hundred anda ten, anda twenty, thirty anda forty...' He continued counting, the boys numb with shock and when he reached 'Fiva hundred.' He paused taking a deep breath.

'Fi ... fiv ... ah ... five ... hundred quid!' Harry stammered.'

'Shhh ... you breaka da count.' Bruno licked his fingers dramatically and continued. 'Fiva hundred anda ten, anda twenty ...' He stopped at 'Sevena hundred and twenty fiva pound.' The Italian looked up from the pile of notes in front of him, a huge smile breaking out on his face. 'Alla yours!' He patted the pile of notes affectionately.

Jack tried to speak but it sounded like a high croak then coughing, he said hoarsely, 'seven hundred quid!'

'Anda twentya five,' Bruno corrected.

'It's a bloody fortune, Harry, look!' Jack stared at the pile in the centre of the table.

Harry said nothing and just stared blankly at the money, his mouth moving but no sound escaping.

'Bruno, you're a champion, mate.' Without thinking Jack launched himself at the short, heavily-built Italian, throwing his arms around him in a giant bear hug.

Bruno, taken by surprise, stood stock still with his arms stiffly at his sides. It had been many years since another human being had ever expressed gratitude or affection in such a demonstrative way and he was self-conscious of this young man's spontaneity but then he slowly brought one arm up and patted Jack on the back. His other hand surreptitiously wiped tears that had formed in his eyes.

◆◆◆◆◆◆◆◆◆◆◆◆

Paddy O'Brien was in a gleeful mood when he knocked firmly on the presbytery door around ten thirty at night. There was no immediate answer so he persisted until a light flicked on in the hallway. 'Yes, I'm coming,' a voice said irritably. 'Who is it?'

'It's me, Timothy. Your old friend Paddy. Are ye gonna let me in now or do I have to stand out here all the night long.'

Father O'Malley opened the heavy door and a beam of light from the hallway fell on Paddy, his hat placed at the familiar jaunty angle on his head and a smile dancing on his lips. 'Good heavens, Paddy.' The priest looked at the clock in the passageway. 'Do you know what time it is, man?' 'It'd be time for a little bit of the 'doins' that's what time it'd be.' Paddy waved a bottle in front of the priest who rolled his eyes despairingly.

'Come in, Paddy, come in, before you wake the whole neighbourhood.' He stood aside to let his friend enter. 'I won't be joining you in a drink though at this time of night and that's for sure.'

'Ahh, Father ye've got to be celebratin' with me now. It'd be a fine thing if an old friend won't share a man's joy.' Paddy tripped down the hallway toward the kitchen. 'I'll just be gettin' a coupla glasses then.'

'Well, just the one, Paddy, I've got a busy day tomorrow and what is it then that we've got to celebrate now that won't wait until tomorrow?'

'Aahh, lady luck she's been smilin' kindly on Paddy O'Brien tonight, Father. I was borrowin' a coupla quid I was from a good friend of mine, little colleen that I know.' He winked at the priest who tried unsuccessfully to hide his smile. 'And as luck would have it there was a little two-up game on tonight and I managed with me usual skill to be makin' a few quid profit.'

'So you've come here from a two-up game have you, Paddy?'

'Well … I have to be honest, not directly, Father.' Paddy looked coyly at his glass before throwing the contents down in one gulp.

'Don't be telling me you've been around in Hay Street again and turning up here at this hour.' There was a note of annoyance in his tone.

'Father, you know me, I was havin' to return the money I borrowed now wasn't I?'

'You're incorrigible, Paddy, that's what you are. Now how much 'profit' did you make then that'd bring you scurrying round here all lit up like a beacon.' The priest looked at his empty glass, moved to put it on the table then shrugging, poured another nip from the bottle.

'Enough for …' Paddy pulled a wad of money from his coat pocket and peeled a ten-pound note from it and, placing it on the table, said, '… to be able to be makin' an offerin' for the plate.'

'I'd prefer it if you put it in the offering personally during mass on Sunday, Paddy.' The priest fixed his friend with a steely eye. 'A little visit to confession wouldn't be going astray either, y'know.'

'Aahh the good Lord is knowin' me heart, Father and besides …' Paddy poured another healthy slug into his glass, '… how could I be tellin' *you* me secrets, you bein' me mate an' all.'

The priest shook his head in despair. 'It'd do you no harm to go to mass now and again on a Sunday, Paddy.'

'It's all right for you, Timothy, you go every Sunday 'cause you're the praiste an' all. You run the show.'

'No, Paddy. I go every Sunday because I want to and because I'm a Christian, not just because I'm the priest.' He looked closely at his friend. 'Perhaps you should leave some of that cash with me for safekeeping, Paddy, otherwise you'll be spending it all by tomorrow night.'

'No, Father, I've got a plan for this money.'

'And what plan would that be, Paddy?'

'I'm goin' to be buyin' a train ticket tomorra. Time to be movin' on a bit and I thought I'd be tryin' me luck out in Coober Pedy.'

'Coober Pedy, eh? Wouldn't have anything to do with a Jack or a Harry being there would it?'

Paddy smiled and stroked his stubbly chin, head angled to one side. 'Now, why would ye be thinkin' that now?'

♦ ♦ ♦ ♦ ♦ ♦ ♦ ♦ ♦ ♦ ♦

Reynold had busied himself outside while Bruno had counted the money. When Bruno's old Land Rover had clanked off down the track, Harry called him in and showed him the pile of notes. It was beyond Reynold's capacity to comprehend such a large amount of cash so he said nothing, just stared in awe. They had put a portion aside for Ishmo's share and wanted to surprise Reynold by giving him a return for his efforts.

He protested by shaking his head and refusing to take the notes that Harry held out to him telling him it was his share. 'No. Rennol not take no money, eh? Yu bin real good to me, tucker, place to live … you treat Rennol laik 'e one 'n the same laik you. Don' need no money.'

When both boys insisted he take some money he eventually weakened. 'OK, Rennol 'e take ten quid.'

'You've gotta take more than that, Reynold,' Jack pressed.

'You deserve more than ten quid, mate,' Harry said, still holding the notes out to Reynold.

'Tell yu what …' He thought for a moment. 'I take ten quid for Rennol, yu send little bit more 'ome to uncle Warri. Warri 'e maybe need that money now 'e not drovin' for a bit.'

Early the next morning the three boys decided they would walk to Bruno's claim and thank him again for his negotiations with the visiting buyer on their behalf. They also wanted to ask his advice on upgrading the dugout and purchasing some more efficient equipment.

Arriving at the claim they were surprised not to be met by Bruno's mongrel dog, Shaggy, that, regardless of how many times they visited, still ran barking furiously at them to warn Bruno of their presence and to show them he was guarding his master's domain.

There was an unnerving silence about the place and they sensed, rather than knew, something wasn't quite right. Walking to the shaft mouth they saw it was open and that the timber-planked cover that Bruno pulled over it at night to stop snakes or small animals falling in, was cast aside. Bruno was obviously working down his mine but then they noticed Shaggy lying on his belly staring at the open shaft and whimpering. The dog looked up as they approached and wagged its tail half-heartedly but continued to whine.

'Bruno, you there?' Jack called down the shaft. There was no response.

'I'm goin' down,' He said. 'Reynold, you run over to the shed and grab one of Bruno's spare lanterns will ya?'

'I'll come with you, Jack.'

'Righto, Harry, let's wait for the lantern though.' Jack reached down and patted Shaggy until Reynold returned with the lantern They lit the lamp then Jack swung his legs over the edge of the shaft onto the rope ladder. Harry waited until Jack was clear then followed, leaving Reynold peering into the shaft anxiously watching them descend into the blackness.

Stepping from the ladder, Jack held the lantern high to light up the base cavern but it was empty. Harry joined him and they looked around at the drives and seeing the barrow near the entrance to one of them and evidence of recent activity they decided they should investigate that tunnel first. Calling out again but getting no response they looked nervously at each other as they stooped to enter the drive.

Rounding a sharp bend some ten feet in they were shocked when the lantern lit up a wall of fallen rock and rubble blocking the drive that they knew, from previously working there, continued for another thirty or forty feet.

'My God, Jack.' Harry whispered for some reason. 'It's caved in.'

'Bruno, Bruno!' Jack started yelling then put the lantern on the floor and started frantically to pull at the rocks, scraping clay and dirt fruitlessly with his hands. 'Bruno!' he yelled, 'can you hear me?'

'We gotta get help, Jack.'

'Yeah, and some more light and shovels. Hang on, Bruno, we'll be back,' He yelled at the formidable rock wall.

They relayed to Reynold what had happened telling him to go and get help while they started to dig but Reynold shook his head. 'No good me goin'. Blokes take no notice of blackfella. They jus' tink I lyin' or somethin'. Yu go, Harry, 'n Rennol 'e 'elp Jack dig.'

'But you won't go down a shaft Reynold and Jack needs help'

'Rennol 'e go down 'cause Bruno 'e need 'elp quick.'

'He's right, Harry … you go for help.'

Harry ran to Bruno's Land Rover that he had started and moved some short distances a few times before, and pressed the starter. The motor turned over slowly then thankfully fired into life. Harry crunched the gears and letting the clutch out suddenly, headed off in jerky leaps down the track, pressing the horn to gain attention; while Jack and Reynold, now with another lantern, followed the two shovels they dropped down the shaft.

The two boys dug frantically at the rubble. They found the shovels too cumbersome to make much effect so reverted to using their bare hands in a desperate attempt to reach their entombed friend. Dust clogged their eyes and nostrils and it was hard, cramped in the confined space, but they worked ceaselessly, breaking nails and ripping skin from their fingers as they clawed at the rubble.

They two boys, near exhaustion and sweating in the dust laden air, didn't notice the men come down the shaft and move up behind them until a voice broke through their frenzied concentration. 'All right, lads, have a break … we'll take over for a while.'

Climbing the rope ladder to the surface was an incredible effort, their arms and legs feeling like jelly from the strenuous effort to dig Bruno out. When they reached the top they were blinded for some moments by the blazing sun as unseen hands hauled them out. When their eyes adjusted to the glare they were staggered to see the amount of activity on the surface.

There were vehicles parked all over the claim and men ran everywhere. A truck-mounted generator was located beside the shaft, two miners were bolting a steel ladder together and a motorised windlass was also being put in position to speed the removal of rubble from the mine. Trestle tables were erected under a canvass tarpaulin and a fire was burning to boil water for tea.

A stranger led Jack and Reynold to the tarpaulin shelter. Sitting them down he gave them a mug of tea each then brought a bowl of water, soap and towels for them to clean up. Seeing the cuts and abrasions on their hands from tearing at the rocks he walked to his truck and returned with a first aid kit. After they had washed up he applied antiseptic to the injuries that at first appeared serious but were revealed minor after the bloodied dirt was washed away. The two boys were in a daze watching the rescue get into full swing. As they sat there a number of men walked past and nodded to them and two actually came to them where they were sitting. 'Well done, lads,' they said, 'bloody good effort.' Reynold, being naturally shy, was embarrassed by the attention and stared intently into his mug of tea.

Harry joined them under the shelter. They told him they hadn't been able to reach Bruno and the three of them watched the activity as instructions were shouted, curses filled the air and men worked non stop to reach the buried miner.

There was less frantic activity as the rescuers settled into a routine, working in shifts to reach Bruno, but as the hours passed, hope of finding him alive waned and a quiet settled over the workers. Father Shaun Logan arrived and after inspecting the rescue efforts and giving words of encouragement to the volunteers, came to where the boys were waiting.

'You three have done a great job,' he said quietly.

'We couldn't reach him, Father. We couldn't bloody reach him!' There were stinging tears in Jack's eyes.

Chapter Twenty Nine

Father O'Malley drove Paddy to the railway station. He was convinced the night before that it was just the Irish whisky talking but Paddy was up early, his usual cheeky smile and good-natured banter giving no indication of the amount of 'the doins' that had been consumed. The empty bottle in the middle of the kitchen table the only evidence.

Purchasing his ticket, Paddy returned to the car to pick up his meagre belongings and to bid goodbye to his friend. The priest stepped from the car, walked to the boot, opened it and retrieved a brown Gladstone bag that he held out to Paddy.

'What's this then, Timothy?'

'Don't be offended, old friend, but I think your hessian sugar bag has seen better days and I thought this'd come in handy for the trip.' He handed the bag to Paddy. 'There are a couple of things in there that might just come in handy for you too. Some shirts, socks, you know … basic things like that.'

'Timothy, I never expected …'

'Nothing fancy, Paddy.' The priest interrupted him. 'There's something else as well.' Reaching into his coat pocket the priest took a buff coloured envelope out and gave it his friend. 'I'd like you to pass this on to the boys when you run into them.'

'I'll be seein' them and that's for sure, Father. I'll pass it on.'

The two men stood awkwardly facing each other, both aware it could be some considerable time before they saw each other again.

The train whistle blew, signalling its departure, and they welcomed the sound that broke the self-consciousness of the moment.

'Well, Paddy, better get on board then.' The priest held his hand out. 'You be taking good care of yourself now, you hear?'

'You are a dear and treasured friend, Father.' Paddy took the priest's hand, shaking it warmly. He stood for a second looking into his friend's eyes. 'No use wastin' this ticket is there by standin' here then?' he said suddenly with a quick smile and a wink.

Picking up the Gladstone bag he touched his finger to the brim of his hat. 'Keep a glass clean for me, Timothy, I'll be back with a *case* of Irish after I'm makin' me fortune in Coober Pedy. Aahh, I can feel it in me bones. Be seein' ya, Timothy.' Paddy grabbed the handrail and leapt onto the train steps leaving Father O'Malley alone on the platform.

'I'm going to miss you, you Old Rascal.' The little Irishman had already vanished into the carriage and the priest's words were lost in a hiss of steam as the engine pulled away from the platform.

◆◆◆◆◆◆◆◆◆◆◆◆

A blazing sun fried the rescuers at the shaft mouth. Wind whipped sand into their eyes but there was no complaint from them and it didn't halt their grim determination to reach the trapped miner far below the baked surface. Shaun Logan suggested to the boys that they should return to their dugout to escape the heat, as they could do no more than they had already done, but they refused, saying they would wait until Bruno was found.

The day edged toward dusk and the searchers battled on. It seemed like tons of earth and rock had been hauled from the pit as the pile of rubble beside the shaft grew higher. As each shift of workers came to the surface caked in dust and sweat they just shook their heads despairingly. The priest was disturbed that *if* the miner was found, his condition could shock the boys as the chance of him being alive was remote and injuries from tons of rock would be horrific so he determined he would stay to shield them as best he could from any trauma.

As darkness blanketed the scene the generator was started, flooding the area with glaring light that gave a surreal atmosphere to the drama being played out, as if the rescuers were actors on a stage, except this was not a play …this plot was real.

The men were exhausted and robotic in their actions. Reynold had given up watching them to walk back to the nine-mile but Jack and Harry stayed, keeping silent vigil beside Shaun Logan. The man directing the rescue attempt, Jim Leslie, the owner of a large mechanised mine that had supplied most of the equipment, came to where they were sitting. Taking a long swig from a waterbag he wiped his mouth with the back of a hand. 'I don't want to be pessimistic but there's little hope that Bruno will be found alive. Sorry, lads, but we have to be realistic.'

Shaun Logan, glancing at Jack and Harry, protested that there was always hope until the search proved otherwise.

'You're right, Shaun, and we haven't given up hope but …' Leslie looked at the boys, weighing his next words, '… we have to face facts. I'm not gonna hold your hopes up and then have you let down. You blokes …' He spoke directly to Jack and Harry. '… have done a fine job. Without you there would be no rescue effort happening at all and I'm sure you're mature enough, from what I've seen of you, to accept the possibility that he hasn't made it.'

He turned to Logan. 'No use pretending, Shaun, you better get these young men home. We'll call 'round to them as soon as any news breaks.' He walked purposefully back to the shaft.

In a daze, the boys let the priest lead them to where his car was parked. Harry got into the back seat and Jack opened the front passenger door but stood looking back at the scene for some seconds before he moved to enter the car. Slipping onto the front seat he was closing the door when men started running to the shaft head as a shout went up. 'We've got him!'

♦ ♦ ♦ ♦ ♦ ♦ ♦ ♦ ♦ ♦ ♦ ♦

Paddy had a window seat. He stared into the darkness as the train sped toward Pt Augusta and as he had never been to South Australia he was imagining what it must be like in Coober Pedy. He had of course, heard tales of the town and its rough-hewn inhabitants and wondered how Jack and Harry would be faring in such an alien environment. He was looking forward to seeing the two small boys again, finally admitting to himself that part of his decision to leave Kalgoorlie was to see that they came to no harm.

Paddy had had what he termed a 'marginal' childhood. Born in County Corke, Ireland, the fourth son of a struggling village baker, he had left home at the age of twelve, unable to win his father's love or approval for anything he did. Working for a time on the docks he developed a passion for Irish whisky and gambling that had seen him have many highs, but mainly lows, in his life. His mother had been a wisp of a woman and his memories of her were vague, as she seemed to be alternately always weeping or praying … or both.

He knew he looked like his mother, who was small of stature. He had inherited her flaming red hair and blue eyes although Paddy's hair was now streaked with grey and had lost its lustre. The legacy he got from his father was a sense of humour and a 'devil-may-care' attitude to life.

305

Migrating to Australia he had tried a number of ventures, including prospecting around the goldfields where he made a few finds to finance his penchant for gambling but there was a wanderlust in his bones and he could never settle down to anything substantial. He had a number of 'associates' but only one friend, Timothy O'Malley.

When he had met the boys on the train there was something about their naive determination that had reminded him of when he had left the bosom of his family to discover life. He felt he could be of assistance to them in some way and it never occurred to Paddy that it was he who was searching for acceptance and the need to be part of a family.

Opening the Gladstone bag that was beside him he rifled through the contents, humbled that Father O'Malley had taken the time to select some things to make his trip and stay in Coober Pedy more comfortable. The shirts, although not new, were washed and neatly ironed, no doubt by Mrs Lacey, the housekeeper. There was also a pair of grey twill trousers and Paddy wondered how they would fit him as Timothy O'Malley was a much taller man than Paddy but when he held them up, much to the interest of his fellow passengers, he saw they would be almost perfect. He realised that they must have come from Mrs Lacey and speculated for a moment what her husband would say when he discovered a pair of his pants missing. There were socks, three pair of new underpants, and half a dozen handkerchiefs. Then his hand felt something hard at the bottom of the bag. Knowing instinctively what it was he said half aloud, 'Timothy, it's a friend indeed that ye are.' He took the bottle from the bag.

Paddy remembered the envelope he had been given. He took it from his coat pocket, turning it over thoughtfully wondering what was in it. *Probably just a letter for the lads,* he thought and placed it at the bottom of the bag for safekeeping. He uncorked the bottle and, taking a swig from it, he noticed the disdainful look from the woman seated opposite.

'Hello there, m'lovely.' Paddy held the bottle out. 'Would you like to be joinin' me then in a little celebratory drink? ... No? Oh well then ... all the more for Paddy. Cheers!'

The woman turned several shades of red and snapped her head back to the book she had been reading, never looking in Paddy's direction again for the entire trip. Relaxing back in the padded train seat he closed his eyes and, listening to the rhythmic clatter of the wheels, wondered what the two boys were doing at that moment before he drifted off to sleep, the bottle clasped securely on his lap.

◆ ◆ ◆ ◆ ◆ ◆ ◆ ◆ ◆ ◆ ◆

'They've found him!' became the catch cry as men ran to the shaft mouth. Jim Leslie stood beside the windlass. 'Stand back!' He shouted firmly. 'We don't know much yet, other than that they seem to have broken through the rock and reached Bruno.'

Jack burst from the car before the priest could stop him and ran full pelt to the shaft. 'Mister Leslie ... is he all right?'

'Settle down, son.' The man placed a firm restraining hand on Jack's chest. 'Best you wait back by the car.'

Jack was determined to stay and, resisting the man's attempts to turn him back to Harry and the priest who were standing off at a distance, he moved away a few feet so as not to interfere with the men at the shaft mouth. A dust-caked face appeared at the top of the ladder, white in the glare of the spotlights. 'We broke through,' he gasped, 'we found him.'

'How is he?' Jim Leslie placed himself between the man and Jack when he asked the question.

'Blood miracle it is.' The man climbed from the ladder. 'Seems like Bruno was working at the drive face when the roof caved in behind him, cutting him off and leaving him in about four or five feet of tunnel. Not a scratch on him but he'd passed out from lack of air by the time we got to him.' He shook his head in disbelief.

'He's come to, now that air's gettin' to him, but he's mumblin' like a madman. Pretty shook up too.'

'You mean he's not hurt? Not at all?' Leslie was astounded.

'Like I said … not a scratch on him but I think he's lost his mind.' The rescuer shook his head touching the tip of his finger to his temple. 'When he came to he yelled at us to get out of his mine! Can you bloody well believe it?'

'Yes, I can actually,' Leslie replied. 'I think I'd go a bit mad too if I was trapped forty feet underground, believing I was going to die there and just waiting in pitch dark silence for the air to run out.'

'Yeah, suppose so. He's clutchin' a rock or somethin' and won't let anyone see it or touch it. Keeps yellin', *Itsa mine, itsa mine!*'

♦ ♦ ♦ ♦ ♦ ♦ ♦ ♦ ♦ ♦ ♦ ♦

Bruno was brought up from his tomb, the bright lights blinding him. A man on each side held him upright as his legs wouldn't hold him as they half dragged, half carried him to the shelter where a nursing sister was waiting to examine him. Jack and Harry were stunned to see their friend. His eyes were wide open and staring like a frightened animal, his lips moved constantly, mouthing silent words; and his arms were folded tightly against his chest shielding some unseen object.

The men eventually forced him to lie on the stretcher so the nurse could look him over but they couldn't get his arms from his chest. Whenever they tried, Bruno would start writhing and screaming, 'Itsa mine! Itsa mine!' and looking wildly about him without focusing.

The nurse held a needle to the light, squirted a small amount of liquid from the tip, and then plunged it unceremoniously into Bruno's upper arm. He gave no indication that he had felt the needle and continued staring at imagined foes. When the sedative took affect, his muscles relaxed, his head lolled to one side and he closed his eyes. The nurse unfolded his arms and gasped when she saw what Bruno had been protecting.

'Good heavens! Will you look at that?' Jim Leslie reached down and took the rock from Bruno's chest.

It was shaped roughly in the image of Australia, about five inches thick and a foot long and nobody could miss the vibrant colours highlighted by the generator-driven lights. Miners stood staring in reverent awe at the stone that Leslie passed to the priest. 'This is what he almost died for. You better keep it safe for him, Father. I'll leave a couple of my men on guard overnight to make sure no moonlighters decide to go down the shaft to see if there's more opal like Bruno found.'

'Nobody would go down after a cave-in, would they?' Jack asked. 'Not until they knew it was safe?'

Jim Leslie smiled. 'You just never know, son. You can trust the blokes involved in the rescue but when the word's out about what Bruno found, rats will surface and risking their life for a fortune is nothing to them.'

Jack and Harry stood beside the priest, mesmerised by the size of the opal, as the stretcher was lifted onto the back of a utility and Bruno was driven off to the medical centre. They didn't speak, lost for words at the miracle of Bruno being found alive and the opal he had found, as they drove with Shaun Logan from the now almost deserted mine. As the car bounced onto the track leading to town, the generator was switched off and darkness fell over the shaft, the mine, and the two men remaining on guard.

The priest insisted that the two boys come back with him to his place for a bath and a cooked dinner. They didn't realise he was nervous about minding the opal overnight and would welcome their company. They were too exhausted to argue but said they needed to let Reynold know that Bruno had been found. Stopping by their claim they told him the news but he declined the priest's invitation to join them for a meal. Harry carried a calico bag that contained some opal pieces and had their cash bundled safely beneath his shirt and Shaun Logan was comforted when Jack returned to the vehicle carrying his rifle. They trusted Reynold but they knew it made him nervous to be left minding their riches so didn't want him to have the responsibility.

The meal was simple at the priest's house: lamb chops with mashed potatoes and tinned peas, but to the boys it was a sumptuous banquet. Relaxed from a hot bath, something they had not experienced for many months, having to tub up in a bucket, they were drowsy and Shaun Logan suggested they stay the night. 'We can go to the first-aid post in the morning to see how Bruno is.' The boys didn't argue.

♦♦♦♦♦♦♦♦♦♦♦♦

Alice Ferguson performed her now nightly ritual before going to bed. Kneeling beside the bed she placed her elbows on the eiderdown and asked God to protect her boy and bring him home safely. She had never been 'religious' and didn't attend church but had a belief in God and since Jack had gone, she prayed a simple prayer every night. She found some comfort in believing that God knew where her son was and could see him as she prayed which made her feel closer to Jack. 'If only I could hold him,' she prayed softly, not wanting to disturb her husband who didn't believe that a god even existed.

♦♦♦♦♦♦♦♦♦♦♦♦

Even though they were exhausted, when Jack and Harry went to bed in Father Logan's tiny spare bedroom they found it difficult to sleep as the events of the day whirled through their minds. When Jack closed his eyes he could still see the glare of the lights and the frantic rescue efforts. His hands were bruised and sore from tearing at the rocks and his legs ached so he switched on the light. 'You awake, Harry?'

'Yeah, I can't sleep. What a day? Do you think Bruno'll be alright, he seemed a bit crazy?'

'At least he's still alive, Harry. I thought he was a goner, didn't you?'

'Makes ya stop and think, eh? It could have been us down there when that roof caved in ya know.'

'Don't want to think about that, Harry. I'm amazed at Reynold, though; he worked like a demon down there even though he hates bein' underground.'

'He's a good mate. Everyone was surprised when I went for help and said that Reynold was with you back in the drive tryin' to reach Bruno.'

'Didn't take ya long to get help, Harry.'

'The first blokes I told jumped into their truck and raced into town. Before long there was a stream of vehicles and men headin' out. Took and hour or so though.'

Jack was amazed that it had been over an hour that he and Reynold had furiously clawed at the rocks. It had seemed like only minutes. The two boys were quiet for a while each locked in thought.

'Jack ... do ya ever miss home?'

'Of course I do, Harry. I just don't talk about it that's all.'

'Me neither, but I do miss it. Do ya think we'll ever get back there one day?'

'Yeah ... one day I guess.'

'It'd be good to see everyone again wouldn't it, Jack?' He patted the mattress. 'Sleep in a proper bed, eat good tucker.'

'I miss the water, Harry. There's no bloody water around here *or* tall trees. It'd be great to go down the creek, catch a coupla yabbies ... go for a swim.'

'A swim? Wow! How about a day at the beach?'

'There are a few things I miss out here, Harry, apart from the family.'

'Like what?'

'Well ...' Jack propped himself up on an elbow. 'Girls for one. There are no girls out here.'

'Girls?' Harry stared thoughtfully at the ceiling. 'Yeah ... I suppose so. Never really thought about girls much but now that ya mention it I haven't seen any around.'

'Do ya know what I miss the most though, Harry?'

'What's that, Jack?'

'Promise ya won't laugh?'

'Of course I won't, mate. What *do* ya miss the most?'

'Mum's hugs.' He turned out the light.

Chapter Thirty

'You awake, lads?' Shaun Logan pushed the curtain aside and peered into the room to find both beds empty. He was surprised but then realised that they probably woke up before dawn every morning. He found them outside and smiled when he saw they had found his old bat and were playing two-man cricket, using the wall of the dugout for a backstop.

'You blokes play cricket, I see.'

'Haven't for ages,' Harry replied as he bowled a spinner at Jack who returned it expertly. 'We used to play regular at home.'

'There's a couple of teams here you know. We're a bit rough around the edges but enjoy a get-together now and then. Maybe you could join in. We could certainly do with a couple of good hands.'

'Maybe,' Harry said as Jack walked up to them, swinging the bat at imaginary balls.

'That's my spare bat,' the priest said, 'and there are two or three old worn-out balls about the place. Why don't you take 'em back with you and have a hit now and then. You can't just work all day, every day you know.'

'Thanks, we will, eh, Jack?'

'Yeah, be good fun. We could even teach Reynold a few of the finer points.' He laughed thinking how Reynold would take to cricket.

'I suppose you miss kids your own age to mess around with? What made you come out here?' Shaun Logan asked, then saw the closed expressions shadow their eyes and knew he had innocently touched on a sensitive issue. He quickly changed the subject. 'Let's grab a bite of brekky before we head off to see how Bruno is.'

Both boys were quiet while they ate and the priest wondered what it was that had brought these two young boys from Perth to Coober Pedy. He was curious as to how they knew Father O'Malley but refrained from asking any questions, knowing that a man's business was his own, especially out here in the opal fields. Even though the boys were young in years they had proved a maturity many older men had yet to achieve. *When the time is right,* he thought, *they'll tell me.*

They drove in Logan's car toward the medical centre but on the way the priest pulled up at a building that had a sign out the front clearly marked, 'POLICE STATION.' As he parked the car and switched off the motor he noticed the nervous looks on the boys' faces that fuelled his curiosity further but he made no comment.

'I'm going to leave Bruno's opal with the sergeant.' Shaun Logan stepped from the car with the stone wrapped in a small blanket. 'I don't want the responsibility of looking after this. It's too valuable so I'll let the police mind it for Bruno. Won't be a minute.'

The boys shrank down in the seats hoping the policeman wouldn't see them if he came out of the station. The sergeant had been at the rescue the day before but they had avoided any contact with him and he seemed oblivious to their presence, which suited them. There was a sinking feeling in the pit of their stomachs when the sergeant walked from the station with the priest, both heading to the car.

'So!' The policeman walked to the window. 'You're Jack are you?' Jack was mortified but when he held out his hand in greeting he tentatively shook it, avoiding any eye contact. 'I just wanted to say that without you and your mate here ...' He went to Harry's door, '... poor old Bruno wouldn't have made it.'

The policeman took their nervous looks for shyness and he stepped back from the car. 'You blokes need anything at any time, just give me a call.' He told Shaun that he'd look after the opal then walked back into the station.

The nursing sister told them that Bruno was all right physically, but dehydrated. His mental state was a concern, she said, as he had obviously been affected badly by the trauma and isolation of being buried alive. 'You can go in to see him but don't expect any response. He just lies there, staring into space, won't communicate and hasn't eaten anything.' She directed them to Bruno's bed.

The three of them filed into the room where Bruno was. It was strange to see him lying quietly in the bed and cleanly shaven. Normally he was covered in dust, waving his arms about and with three days' stubble on his face.

'Morning, Bruno.' Shaun Logan spoke cheerfully, moving close to the bed while Jack and Harry held back, not quite knowing what to say. 'How are you feeling?' There was no response so the priest indicated with his head for the boys to come forward.

'Er ... g'day, Bruno, it's me, Jack.' There was a flicker of Bruno's eyelids indicating he had heard and recognised the voice but there was no other reaction.

'Hello, Bruno.' Harry moved beside the bed, receiving the same flicker but nothing else.

The silence was awkward so Jack spoke up again. 'That was some opal you found, Bruno.'

The little man blinked rapidly and turned his head toward Jack. 'Itsa mine!' He started to get agitated and tried to sit up but fell back on the pillows.

'It's OK, Bruno.' Shaun Logan put a hand gently on the Italian's shoulder. 'We know it's yours and we have it in a safe place. Nobody will take it.'

'Mine. I finda her ... itsa mine,' he mumbled, his voice trailing off into silence.

They stayed another couple of minutes but Bruno seemed to have fallen asleep so they left, concerned that he had indeed lost his mind. The nursing sister told them he would be kept in for observation for a few days to see how he progressed before any decision was made to transfer him to Adelaide for further treatment.

Shaun Logan asked the boys as they walked to his car if they would act as caretakers of Bruno's claim until he was well enough to make a decision as to what he planned to do with it. It was the priest's opinion that Bruno would never be fit enough mentally to handle going underground again but didn't reveal his thoughts to them, not wanting them to be overly concerned about their friend.

'Do you think it'd be all right with everyone though?' Harry felt there were probably more qualified people to look after it. 'Maybe that Mr Leslie bloke wants to do it. He left a couple of his men to guard it last night.'

'I know Jim Leslie.' The priest got into his car and pressed the starter. 'He's a good man in an emergency but he's a hard-nosed miner with a big operation to run and he won't want to waste time, or men, looking after Bruno's small claim ... particularly as nobody can work it without him being there.'

He moved off into the street without checking for cars, as there was very little traffic in Coober Pedy. 'I'll talk to Leslie and tell the police sergeant you blokes will mind it. That's if you want to?'

'We can keep an eye on it, for sure.' Jack was a little concerned about involving the police but figured that it wouldn't be a problem as the sergeant obviously hadn't been advised that he and Harry were both wanted in Western Australia. Jack was sure the sergeant would have arrested them long before this otherwise, and especially this morning when he talked with them.

'It'd mean that at least one of you would have to stay there overnight. That's when moonlighters would have a go, the gutless buggers.' He spoke vehemently. 'They wait till dark then slip in and pinch another bloke's opal.'

The priest dropped them off at the nine-mile where the car was greeted aggressively by Anna until Harry stepped from the vehicle, when her barks turned to whimpers and furious tail wagging.

Discussing Shaun Logan's suggestion of looking after Bruno's claim the three boys decided between them that, as it was the one most threatened by pilfering, that Reynold would stay at the nine-mile and Jack and Harry would go over before dark each night to the eight-mile diggings at Geraghty Hill.

Working deep in the drive that afternoon they were conscious of how vulnerable they were if there was a cave in. While Reynold and Jack had been clawing at the rocks, digging clay with their bare hands to try and reach Bruno, the danger hadn't occurred to them in the heat of the moment but now, the memory so vivid, they continually glanced at the sandstone ceiling of the drive.

'Let's take a break, Harry.'

'Suits me.' Harry took another glance at the roof and taking the hurricane lantern went ahead of Jack out of the drive.

317

'Find anything, Reynold?' Harry went to where Reynold was sifting through rocks from the sieve on an old sheet of corrugated iron they had set up as a sorting table.

'Nah. Rennol' look 'n look but no colour today, Harry. Yu look at 'im, maybe yu get lucky.'

Harry and Jack joined Reynold, poking at the small rocks, picking the odd one up for closer inspection but discarding them all as just that … rocks.

'Someone 'e come.' Reynold looked up, his head tilted at an angle.

'What d'ya mean, Reynold? I can't hear anythin', you must be imaginin' …'

They then heard the sound of a car approaching and Jack looked at Reynold with a smile. 'You've got great hearin', mate; wonder who it is?' Checking that the rifle was in easy reach, they waited for the vehicle to appear.

'Hope it's not that bloody copper, Jack.'

'No,' Reynold said, 'copper 'e drive one a them Lan' Rovers.' He listened intently again. I think it that priest car 'gain. Sound laik 'im anyway.'

They relaxed slightly, having learned to trust Reynold's hearing and intuition. A minute passed and Shaun Logan's Vauxhall appeared, bouncing toward them along the corrugated track.

'Must have forgotten to tell us somethin',' Jack said half to himself wondering why the priest would return.

'Funny bloke, that?' Reynold nodded at the approaching vehicle. 'That Logan 'e lot diff'rent 'n Father O'Malley … 'e never wear priest clobber, eh?'

Jack went to comment then stopped, noticing a passenger in the priest's car. 'Got someone with him. Wonder who that could be?'

The car came to a stop in a swirling cloud of red dust and Shaun Logan stepped from the driver's door. They couldn't see the passenger clearly as he came around the front of the vehicle but there was something vaguely familiar about the way he walked, or rather 'bounced' along beside the priest. Anna growled a warning until Harry said, 'sit, good girl.'

The two men paused at the foot of the slope. 'Is it OK to come on up?' Shaun Logan called.

'Rennol 'e not see that other fella before. Yu bloke know 'im? Sure got funny 'at on.'

Recognition hit both Jack and Harry at the same time and they gasped in disbelief. Reynold looked at them with a puzzled look and was about to ask again if they knew the stranger when his two friends took off down the slope waving their arms and yelling to the two men standing in the desert heat, one carrying a brown Gladstone bag.

◆◆◆◆◆◆◆◆◆◆◆◆

The police sergeant sat at his desk in the small office sorting through files and papers. He hated the drudgery of clerical work but, as it was a one-man station, he was required to do all the work, policing and administration. He reached for the phone when it rang, grateful for the interruption. 'Police station, Sergeant Carter.'

'Ron.' It was the sister from the first aid post. 'Glad I caught you; I need to have a chat about Bruno; any chance of calling in later?'He checked the time on the wall clock then looked at the papers strewn over his desk. 'Yeah Iris, give me half an hour or so and I'll be there. Put the kettle on.'

Iris Smith was a slightly built middle-aged widow who wore her hair in a tight bun. Iris never considered herself 'pretty' although she had a quality that drew people to her, her ready smile infectious and attractive. Miners and townspeople alike regarded her as an angel as she was never too busy to see anyone regardless of the time, day or night. Dedicated to her nursing she believed the role extended far beyond just caring for patients physically so became involved in many social and psychological issues as well. Iris, Ron Carter and Shaun Logan worked closely together as well as being firm friends.

They sat in the small clinic kitchenette at a yellow laminex table, with a pot of tea and a plate of home-baked scones between them. 'You bake these, Iris?' Ron Carter loved scones.

'They didn't rise as well as they should have, Ron, but there's plenty. I'll put a few aside for you to take home.'

The sergeant took another one and piled it with butter. 'What do you want to see me about, Iris?'

'It's Bruno. He doesn't seem to be responding at all. The only time he showed any animation was when those two young boys were here. You know … the ones that found him.'

'Young Ferguson and Turner. Good coupla kids those. Did you hear how they run off those blokes that tried to jump their claim?' He chuckled.

'Hmm,' she looked thoughtful and smiled knowingly. 'They look like butter wouldn't melt in their mouths but they must be tough young boys that's for sure. Where they from?'

'Don't know much about 'em, Perth, I think. Shaun says they're friends of the priest in Kalgoorlie and I noticed a little Irishman get off the bus today asking for directions to Shaun's place so there might be some connection. We'll find out in due course no doubt. Now, what are we gonna do about Bruno?'

'There's not a thing wrong with him physically that I can see but he's not eating and won't talk. He just lies there muttering quietly to himself in his own lingo and staring at the ceiling.'

'No reaction at all?'

'Not to me or anyone else. He gets very agitated at night so I leave a light on for him, poor fellow. The dark must remind him of being trapped underground for all those hours. I'm amazed he survived.'

'The drive collapsed behind him leaving him unscathed but trapped in about six feet of tunnel. Just had enough air to keep him alive but another coupla hours and he'd have been history.'

Iris shuddered. 'Not a nice way to go. I think he will have to go to hospital in Adelaide to get some professional help. I can't do any more for him here. Do you think you can help me arrange it?'

'No trouble, Iris; when?'

'As soon as we can. I'll let them know down in Adelaide. Does he have any family at all?'

'Not that I know of. I don't even know his surname. Have you asked him?'

'Of course!' Iris was indignant. 'But I can't get any information out of him at all.'

'That's part of the trouble 'round here. People come to town for lots of reasons but are very secretive. They never speak about their past, their families, what they've found, nothing. As long as they keep their noses clean here or I get a bulletin about them or a warrant from somewhere, I leave 'em alone but it makes a policeman's life hard.'

'Oh you poorly done by, overworked cop,' Iris ragged.

'Yeah, well, it does make it hard when something like this crops up. I'll go out and have a gander round his claim. You never know, there might be some papers in his shed or somewhere.'

'You could always check at the Department of Mines, they should have something.'

'Clever girl, want to work for me?' He laughed. 'Hope he comes good though, 'cause that opal he found's worth a bloody fortune I'd say. Biggest I've ever seen.'

'Is it safe?'

'It's locked away in a cell under a bunk.' He patted his pocket. 'Got the key right here.'

◆◆◆◆◆◆◆◆◆◆◆◆

After the emotional and excited reunion between the three friends, Shaun Logan left them alone to talk, knowing his presence would make them uncomfortable and restrict conversation. He couldn't help smiling as he drove off how Paddy and the two boys had linked arms and danced around in circle in the dust like three schoolkids with Reynold looking on in amazement. He sensed that Paddy O'Brien would be a positive influence in the boys' lives although he felt the little man with the big smile, bubbly personality and jaunty 'pork pie' hat had more than a touch of the 'blarney' about him.

'Now, be tellin' me, lads, what it is ye've been doin' these past months.' They were seated at the table in the dugout. 'This is a fine piece of engineerin' it is and that's for sure.' Paddy looked about him in wonder, amazed that these three boys could have achieved so much in such a short time.

When Reynold disappeared quietly the two boys excitedly spoke together, rushing to get all their news out at once. Paddy held up both hands in mock defence. 'Whoa on there, me lads. We've got all the time in the world to be talkin' so start from when ye left the fine Father at Mt Margaret. He's read your letters out to me but I want to be hearin' it all from you and ye can be fillin' in the gaps.'

They talked animatedly for the next hour, taking it in turns to tell Paddy briefly of their experiences on the trip through the centre of Australia with uncle Warri and the droving team. Paddy listened intently, smiling, nodding, raising his eyebrows and occasionally saying, 'is that right? To be sure, to be sure,' as they told of learning to ride, droving the herd and Harry's brush with death in the desert after the snake spooked his horse. They talked fondly of uncle Warri, how he had 'learned' Jack bushcraft and shooting skills and of Toffy with his bow tie.

Harry was wide eyed with excitement as he described how Wandoo had been hurt and how Jack had found them, leading them safely back to camp and they talked of Warri's magic with bush medicine. They described the stations, Christmas dinner and the presents. They told him their horses were stabled at a friend of Bruno's where they paid a few bob a week to keep them fed. Jack proudly showed Paddy the rifle and Harry tickled Anna's ears as she sat at his feet. Paddy laughed heartily when they described the brawl in the pub at Marree and how the boys reckoned Tom Cooper was the best fighter they had ever seen.

Paddy was fascinated when they talked about Ishmo with his camels, laughing as Harry did a little impersonation, bobbing his head saying, 'yes, yes, yes. No, no, no.' He was spellbound with wonder when they told him about finding their first opal and that the stones were sold for a considerable sum.

He sat forward on the old oil drum, wide-eyed as they explained about the claim jumpers and how Jack had shot the tin from the tree sending the blokes packing over the dunes with Anna in hot pursuit. 'That'll teach 'em to be messin' with me boys,' he said proudly.

Finally they described the cave-in and Bruno's rescue but modestly down played their roles, although Shaun Logan had already told Paddy of their courage in the situation.

'Well, well, well.' Paddy scratched his ear then stroked his stubbled chin. 'It's a grand time ye've had and all. Only five months it is since you left as a coupla green kids and look at ye now.' He stood up and stretched. 'Men it is that ye are and that's for sure. I'm proud of ye, lads, and if I had a wee drop of 'the doins' left I'd be havin' a little toast to you.'

Both boys were embarrassed at Paddy's praise so Harry quickly changed the subject. 'We better be gettin' over to Bruno's then. It's startin' to get on … be dark soon.'

Chapter Thirty One

Ron Carter found no clue to Bruno's identity or information on any family that might exist when he searched through the old tin shed at the mine. He did find a calico bag with some rough opals in it so decided to put them with the big rock in the cell at the station. Checking records at the Department of Mines, he learned that Bruno's surname was Boccelli but no other information was available.

Taking this small bit of information to Iris Smith they went to see Bruno who was still in a catatonic state. The policeman leant close to the man in the bed. 'Mr Boccelli? Bruno Boccelli?' Iris stood by, watching.

The Italian blinked and turned soulful eyes to the sergeant. 'Boccelli? Yes, thatsa me.' Then he mumbled unintelligible words that neither the policeman nor Iris could understand.

'We are going to send you down to Adelaide, Bruno … for some treatment.' Iris spoke slowly and distinctly. 'You'll be all right; they will look after you well.' There was a fluttering of eyelids but no other response from the man in the bed.

'Do you understand, Mr Boccelli? You're going to Adelaide.' Iris spoke firmly.

The mention of the name 'Boccelli' again prompted some mild reaction but the little man said nothing.

'Bruno ... Mr Boccelli?' The policeman decided using the surname had more effect. 'Your opal is safe, locked away where no one can find it.'

'Opla belonga to me.' The man became agitated again, rolling from side to side in the bed.

The sergeant took a long shot. 'Mr Boccelli. Jack and Harry are going to look after your mine while you're away.'

'Jack? Harry?' The Italian frowned in concentration then a small smile edged his lips. 'Good, good. They friendsa Bruno, they take good care.'

Iris raised her eyebrows encouragingly to the sergeant. 'Seems like there's a bit of a breakthrough. At least he's OK about the boys looking after things. Better get him ready to travel.'

'OK, Iris. Oh, I almost forgot.' The sergeant slapped his forehead. 'Shaun dropped a few things in he thought Bruno might need. You know? Undies, shaving gear, pyjamas ... few things like that. They're in the car; I'll grab 'em.' He left the room.

◆◆◆◆◆◆◆◆◆◆◆

'Bruno's been transferred down to Adelaide.' The sergeant had arrived at the nine-mile claim late in the afternoon, his appearance sending nervous fears into the boys before he explained why he had called.

'G'day to you, sir, name's Paddy O'Brien.' The Irishman stepped forward, introducing himself. 'I got in yesterday from Kalgoorlie.'

'Yes I know, on the bus. Ron Carter, I'm the sergeant-in-charge here.'

'And right on the ball if I may say so, Sergeant. Good to see it is and all,' Paddy beamed.

'You a friend of the boys?' Carter nodded to Jack and Harry.

'Came over special to see 'em I did. See if I could be lendin' them a hand but it seems to me that they're doin' pretty well on their own.'

'Yes, they're pretty capable young blokes.' Carter turned to the boys. 'Bruno's still not well but he did recognise your names and said he's pleased you're takin' care of his mine while he's away. I suppose you know not to do any mining there?'

'Wouldn't go down another bloke's shaft without permission or him bein' there,' Jack replied.

'Good lad.' He turned to Paddy. 'You got a driver's licence, Paddy?'

'That I have, sergeant, but it's a WA one.'

'We can sort that out later. In the meantime it might be handy if you bring Bruno's Landy over here to keep an eye on it. You can use it to run back and forth between claims. Bit of a walk otherwise.'

'We'll be takin' good care of it, sergeant.'

'I'm sure you will and if you don't know how she works … ask him.' He winked knowingly at Harry who felt his face flush. 'He can drive it pretty good. Used it to get help for Bruno. How old are you son?'

'Er … Fifteen … nearly.' Harry turned a deeper shade of red but the sergeant didn't comment.

'You, Jack?'

'I'm sixteen at the end of this month.'

'Drive a car do you?'

'I've had a go a few times in me dad's car, yes. But not on the roads though, Sergeant,' he added quickly

'Of course not.' He emphasised the 'of course'. 'Better pop down to the station and pick up your learner's permit, Jack. You can get a licence here in South Oz at sixteen.' He walked off down the slope to his vehicle. 'See you fellas soon. Have any trouble over at Bruno's you call me, OK?'

◆ ◆ ◆ ◆ ◆ ◆ ◆ ◆ ◆ ◆ ◆ ◆

The next week was busy and confusing until they developed a routine about minding Bruno's claim. Jack also got Paddy to drive him to the police station where the sergeant asked the appropriate questions and issued him with a learner's permit, telling him to come back in a week or so when he was confident enough to sit a driving test. The Land Rover was heavy to steer and the pedals stiff but he quickly got the hang of the vehicle and they retuned one week to the day for the test.

Jack was nervous with the policeman beside him as the test began but after having driven about half a mile the sergeant said, 'Turn around, Jack, head back to the station.'

'What'd I do wrong?' Jack was perplexed, believing he had done everything correctly.

'Nothing, you can handle her pretty well. Crunched the gears coupla times but I'll put that down to the car needing a service. I've kept an eye on you the past week anyhow and seen you driving Paddy around. Haven't had any accidents in that time and no complaints from other drivers, not that there too many of them around here, so just a couple more questions then you're on your way.'

'Gee thanks, Sergeant.'

Back at the station Jack was thrilled when the sergeant handed him a piece of paper and told him it was his interim licence and the official one would arrive some time later in the mail. 'We'll put your address as care of Father Shaun Logan. That OK with you?'

Jack nodded. 'Can I ask you a favour, Sergeant?'

'You can ask but it doesn't mean I'll do it.' The sergeant looked stern.

'Nah, doesn't matter then.' Jack went to leave.

'Hey, mate, only joking. Of course I'll help if I can, what is it?' He walked around the counter to Jack who had his hand on the door.

'It's just that Bruno took our opals to the buyer for us and now we don't know what to do. Paddy said he'd go if he knows where.'

'Paddy, eh?' The policeman checked to see if Paddy was out of earshot. 'Think you can trust him?'

'Paddy? No problem trusting Paddy.' Jack didn't tell him about the two-up game in Kalgoorlie. 'He might joke around a bit but Paddy's as honest as the day's long, Sergeant.'

'That's OK then, just wanted to make sure that's all. There's nothing suspicious about your friend, Jack, in fact he's a happy-go-lucky bloke and from what I can see, really likes you two. It's just a copper's natural curiosity, Jack … forget I asked.'

Jack left the police station proudly holding the piece of paper allowing him to officially drive. It wasn't until later when he examined the 'interim licence' more carefully that he noticed it was postdated to his birthday.

♦♦♦♦♦♦♦♦♦♦♦♦

Alice Ferguson could not accept that her son had seemingly vanished into thin air. Jack's letters continued to arrive, postmarked Kalgoorlie, yet all searches of that area by her husband and Harry's father Claude had turned up no positive leads. She never consciously blamed her husband for not finding their son but had distanced herself from him, busying herself with caring for the younger children.

She had become much closer to Jean Turner, though, who previously had only been an acquaintance but was now, because of shared grief and worry, an intimate friend and confidant. They met at least twice a week and still cried together often as they read their sons' letters over and over.

'This one says,' Alice read from the last letter received some days before, 'both Harry and I are in good health and getting real fit working in the mine. We have made a bit of money and hope to send some home for you and dad'. She had to stop reading when her voice caught.

Jean reached out to pat her arm. 'Harry's letter says much the same thing, Alice. It's incredible that they must sit down together when they decide to write. They must read each other's letters to make sure they say the same things before they mail them to us.'

'Yes, I'm sure they do.' She took a deep breath and blew her nose. 'They're so careful not to give any clues as to where they are. If only they knew they aren't wanted by the police and that everything's all right here.'

'What worries me, Alice, is that they've covered their tracks so carefully; are they being truthful when they say they're all right or are they just saying it to keep us from worrying.'

'That concerns me too, Jean. I hope they've got enough to eat as Jack is always hungry but can't boil water without getting lumps in it.'

Jean smiled. 'Their schooling concerns me, Alice. How are they ever going to get on in life, you know … get a decent job without an education, make a good living.'

'Yes, it makes me sick to think that that young Billy Munse who caused all of this is doing so well at school and plans to go on to university to study law then move into the family business. It just isn't fair, Jean.' There was a trace of bitterness in her tone.

'Always seems to be the case doesn't it? He'll be OK, he's got a good future but our boys will get left behind and have to struggle for the rest of their lives.'

◆◆◆◆◆◆◆◆◆◆◆◆

Paddy tipped the small pile of rough opal from the calico dilly bag onto the table in front of the visiting buyer. Carefully inspecting the stones with a poker player's face, the buyer finally half shrugged his shoulders and curled a disdainful lip. 'Not vorth much, three hundred ze lot.' The man spoke with a thick German accent.

'Tree hundred pounds?' Paddy blurted out, astounded by the amount and thought to himself, *Mother of God, tree hundred quid for a bit of rock*. He was about to speak when the buyer leaned over the table and began a closer, second appraisal of the opals.

'Hmm, I suppose zere are a couple zat might be vorth a bit more zan de udders.' The buyer deliberated a few moments longer. 'Three fifty, final offer.'

Paddy, with no knowledge of opals or the ability yet to value them, realised the game the buyer was playing so resorted to his gambler's instincts and, taking a punt, reached out and began to pick the stones up, dropping them one at a time into the drawstring bag.

The buyer, surprise on his face, squinted at Paddy through his horn rimmed glasses, eyes distorted by the thick lenses. Putting his hand out he stopped Paddy. 'You drive ze hard bargain, I'll be loosing money on zis but obviously you know ze values yes? Four hundred pounds zen, not vone penny more.'

Paddy found it hard to keep the smile from his face until he left the room but on the street he danced a little jig and whistled while he drove the Land Rover back to the mine. Passing the pub he licked his lips, the bundle of crisp ten and twenty pound notes bulging in his shirt pocket. Slowing the vehicle he began to pull in then mentally slapping himself on the wrist he accelerated and drove on. 'Ahh, Paddy, ye've a heart after all. I'd be doin' anythin' for a little bottle of 'the doins', except to be robbin' me mates.'

Jack peeled off two twenty-pound notes from the bundle and handed them to Paddy. Stunned, he protested. 'What in heaven's name are ye doin', lad?'

'You deserve it, Paddy. It's not just for sellin' the opals for us it's for bein' our mate and helpin' us. Harry and I decided on it while you were away.'

'Here, Reynold.' Harry handed him ten pounds. 'Do you want us to send the rest on to uncle Warri?'

'Not this time, Harry. Reynold tink 'e maybe save a little bit eh? Yu bloke keep 'im safe for me.'

Father Shaun Logan drove the Vauxhall out to see the boys and catch up with Paddy again. He didn't have to ask permission to come onto the claim because Harry saw him arrive. 'G'day, Shaun, come on up,' he yelled.

'Have you heard how Bruno's gettin' on?' They were seated around the table in the dugout away from the heat.

'No, Jack, except he got there all right and is being treated by the psychologists at the hospital. Iris Smith, you met her … the nurse, is telephoning them today and that's another reason for calling out to see you. You're all invited out for tea tonight.'

'Tea! Invited where?' Harry asked.

'To my place actually but Iris is cooking. Not just lamb chops and mashed spuds this time … it's a full roast dinner.'

'Oh. I dunno know, Shaun. We have to look after Bruno's place and we're pretty grubby.' Jack patted his pants and dust filled the air.

'Thought you could all come in a bit earlier and have a tub before tea. Come on, it'd do you good. It won't be a late night and you can go to Bruno's after tea.'

'Dunno, What d'ya reckon, Harry?'

'Iris bakes the best apple pie in Coober Pedy, be a shame to waste it. Makes great vanilla custard too.' The priest watched their eyes widen.

'Vanilla custard you said?'

'Yep.'

'Ok, We're in.'

Reynold spoke. 'Rennol 'e look after Bruno's while yu bloke 'ave tucker.'

'You're included too, Reynold.' The priest turned to him. 'Iris said to invite you all and she's looking forward to meeting you too, Paddy.'

'Is she now and all. It'll be a pleasure to be sure.' Paddy beamed. 'Do ye take a little drink, Father?'

The priest smiled and nodded. 'Father O'Malley said in his letter that you and he sometimes had a small drop now and then.' He winked. 'Just for medicinal purposes only though, I'm sure.'

'Rennol, 'e not come. I go look after eight-mile tonight.'

'Go on, Reynold, come with us.' Harry tried to persuade him.

'Nah, Harry.' Reynold shifted uneasily from foot to foot looking at the dirt floor. 'Don' laik white fella tucker too much.' He mumbled.

Bathed and dressed in clean clothes, their hair now in need of a trim but neatly combed, Jack and Harry felt quite respectable for a change, looking forward to the roast dinner and especially the apple pie with custard. Iris Smith greeted them warmly when Paddy dropped them off, saying he would just nip down to the pub and pick up a little something for the evening.

Father Shaun had a wireless tuned to the ABC and soft music was playing quietly in the background. The aroma of the meal cooking transported the boys back to Perth, reminding them of Sunday nights when a roast was always on the table. They didn't dwell on the memory but the thought made them feel warm and comfortable.

'Ron should be along shortly.' Iris was busy at the stove, an apron protecting her pale blue frock.

'The sergeant is coming?' Harry shot a nervous looked at Jack.

'Yes.' Iris wiped her hands on the apron then removed it and hung it near the stove. 'He's a good friend to Shaun and me. We get together pretty regularly, don't we, Shaun? He's a really nice man and I'm sure you will all get along well.'

Not knowing what to say and concerned by the prospect of spending time in a social situation with a policeman who might ask embarrassing questions, they were relieved when Paddy appeared at the door, carrying some bottles in brown paper bags.

Shaun introduced him to Iris and the boys giggled quietly when Paddy bowed graciously brushing his lips over her outstretched hand. 'A pleasure it is to be meetin' such a lovely lady.' It was unusual also to see Paddy not wearing his hat and they couldn't understand how he had bathed, was cleanly shaved and wearing cologne. They found out later that Paddy had paid to use a room at the pub for his ablutions.

Iris coloured slightly and became somewhat flustered by the compliment. Retrieving her hand from Paddy's grip she retreated to the kitchen saying she had to check the gravy. *What a stupid response,* she scolded herself, *check the gravy indeed!* She patted her hair, unsure of why she was blushing. *Incorrigible Irishman, coming here with all his blarney.* She smiled nonetheless.

Sergeant Ron Carter arrived a few minutes later. The boys were relieved to see he wasn't wearing his uniform as it made him seem less like a policeman so they relaxed a little more and, when dinner was served, conversation flowed easily around the table. It was noticeable to the visitors that Iris, Shaun and Ron were well acquainted and comfortable in each other's company. Paddy was charming, joked throughout the meal and when the apple pie had been consumed, with the boys having seconds, he insisted on helping Iris with the dishes. Shaun, Ron and the two boys moved outside into the fresh air, the two men to enjoy an after-dinner smoke and share another bottle of beer.

Iris and Paddy joined the four of them outside, where the night air was cool, when they had finished the washing-up and Iris brought a jug of lemonade on a tray and some home-baked biscuits for the boys.

'Well, Iris,' Ron Carter refilled his glass from the beer bottle as Paddy poured a healthy nip of whisky into his tumbler, 'any news today on Bruno?'

'I spoke with the hospital and they didn't have a lot to say but it seems he's responding well to treatment. Starting to communicate a bit and is at least eating now, although he complains about the food,' she laughed.

'Have they made a diagnosis yet?' The priest took another 'Turf' cigarette from the pack and lit it.

'They say it's trauma related. The time buried without light and with the air running out must have caused his mind to shut down. There aren't many case histories on this sort of thing so they are just playing it by ear a lot.'

'Do they think he'll recover?' The sergeant took a drink from his glass.

'Hard to say, Ron, but they think in time that the awful memory of the accident will fade and he'll come good. Could take months or even years though and they say he shouldn't go down a shaft again for a while as it could throw him right back to square one.'

'I would've thought it'd be worthwhile to get back down as soon as possible. You know … a bit like being thrown from a horse, get back on as soon as possible to conquer the fear.'

'You're far too simplistic, Ron,' Iris chided. 'Bruno's experience was a bit more traumatic than falling off a horse!' She turned to Jack and Harry. 'Seems he has asked about you two a couple of times. You must have made a big impression on him.'

The two boys looked sheepishly away, unsure of how to respond to the accolade. 'These Anzac bikkies are good stuff.' Harry's voice was muffled as he bit into the biscuit.

'That reminds me.' Ron Carter sat forward. 'The Anzac service this month … you officiating, Shaun?'

'Yes, I've been asked to take the memorial service again this year.'

'Do many returned soldiers turn up for the march?'

'Not a lot of ex-servicemen around here, Paddy, although there are more now than before. Lot of men came here four or five years back after the end of the war. They found it hard to settle into routine life I guess so tried their luck out here.' Iris poured herself a glass of lemonade. 'Bad move though because once you've spent time out here it's hard to go back to any normal way of life. Sort of gets into your blood, doesn't it, Ron?'

'Yeah, does have that effect on people. You're a case in point, Iris; how long you been out here now? A lot of years isn't it?'

'Longer than I'm prepared to say.' Iris looked coyly at Paddy who missed her glance as he was reaching again for the Irish whisky. 'We have a big turn out though, Paddy, and you don't have to be a returned serviceman to be involved in Anzac out here.'

'We used to march with the school at home on Anzac day.' Harry realised from Jack's dark look and slight shake of the head that he had said the wrong thing.

'What school was that, Harry?' The sergeant asked. 'You two go to the same school?'

'Yeah,' Jack said quickly then changed the subject. 'It's gettin' late; we must head off. Thanks for a great tea, Mrs Smith.' He stood up and Harry sprang to his feet, also anxious to get away from the uncomfortable line the conversation had taken.

'You're very welcome, boys.' Iris walked off to the kitchen. 'Hold on a minute.' She returned a short time later with a brown paper bag. 'A few Anzac biscuits to take home. Your friend … Reynold isn't it? He might like some.'

'Ahhh, Anzac Day,' Paddy said as they all walked to the Land Rover. 'Great Australian tradition it is to remember the fallen.'

'Do you march, Paddy?'

No, Shaun, but I've been known to take a small part in some of the celebrations that are traditionally associated with Anzac day.'

You wouldn't be meaning the two-up game now would you, Paddy?'

'Well of course not, sergeant.' Paddy was indignant. Two-up's illegal, everyone knows that to be sure.'

'You're perfectly right, Paddy, totally illegal.' The policeman winked at him. 'People say there's a game on here each Anzac night but even though I scour the town for it every year, I've never been able to find anything that even resembles 'tiddlywinks' let alone a two-up game.' Iris punched him on the shoulder and the four adults laughed but the boys couldn't understand why.

Ron Carter knew his innocent question about the school had spooked the boys and it puzzled him. They had already proved in their short time in Coober Pedy that they were capable and honest and his instinct, that rarely failed him, said they were good kids. 'Seeing as you two lads have marched before I'd be grateful if you'd march with me this Anzac day, how about it?' He was keen not to be the cause of spoiling their evening.

'Thanks, sergeant, we'll think about it.' Jack slipped behind the wheel of the Landy then remembered the help he had received from the policeman in getting his driver's licence. 'We should be able to make it don't you think, Harry? We'll let you know in a day or so.'

Chapter Thirty Two

The next two weeks sped quickly past and were spent upgrading the nine-mile dugout to make it more comfortable now that Paddy had joined them. With the money they had received from the German, added to what they had previously got from the sale of their opals, they were able to purchase timber and other building materials plus some basic tools. They also had a healthy cash reserve that they had buried in a safe place.

They were amazed at Paddy's versatility, as he seemed to be able to turn his hand to almost everything. He used some of his own money to buy some better cooking pots and he arrived home one day from town with a Coolgardie safe loaded in the back of the Land Rover. The boys asked how it could possibly work to keep things like salted beef or butter cool. Paddy explained that the gauze-covered frame, a bit like one of the meat safes Toffy had, kept the flies out and when the tray on top was filled up with water it dripped down hessian bags at the sides keeping them wet. Wind, and there was plenty of that, blew through the wet bags and kept the goods inside at a reasonable temperature.

'One day we'll buy a kerosene fridge.' Jack examined Paddy's new acquisition, 'Like Shaun's got.'

They helped Paddy build a frame around the entrance to the dugout, fitting a heavy planked door to it so they now had security and could leave it padlocked at night without concern that some moonlighter or pilferer could just walk in. This gave Reynold more freedom also and he would head off a couple of nights a week to meet his own people no to doubt eat some 'proper tucker' while Jack and Harry stayed over at Bruno's.

Paddy seemed in his element now, with purpose to his life and hardly ever touched 'the doins' although he kept a bottle cool inside the safe for a nightly nip. Jack wondered if he had many bottles and just kept replacing them as they were emptied but that was not the case. It seemed that Paddy had turned over a new leaf although he hadn't changed in any other way and was always gregarious, happy, quick with a joke and ready to lend a hand. The boys noticed that he shaved every morning and there were two evenings he changed out of his work clothes and, asking if it was OK to borrow the Land Rover, disappeared into town. Harry said he must have made friends with a couple of blokes from town and joined them for a drink at the pub but he was always sober, whistling happily to himself when he returned.

Jack tried to get out into the bush at least once a week. Brehardie looked good from his spell from droving and seemed certainly friskier but Jack ragged him. 'You've gone soft, Brehardie. Stables at night and chaff with oats.' Apart from wanting to feel the solitude of the desert, Jack usually brought home rabbits or occasionally a small kangaroo for the table. Paddy had a problem eating roo but Reynold loved it. They normally tried to supplement the salted beef and tinned food with game of some sort and Reynold often came back with a bungarra, or goanna as they were called in South Australia, and one time dropped a large brown snake beside the fire, its tail still twitching.

'Is it true what they say then?' Paddy kept as far from the writhing serpent as possible. 'That snakes don't die till the sun goes down.'

Jack and Harry laughed but Paddy went on. 'Ye may laugh but I've heard it said with me own ears from bushmen and miners alike. What do you say, Reynold, me lad?'

Reynold didn't laugh but simply shrugged his shoulders 'This fella 'e still kickin' 'n sun 'e still up. I seen 'em wriggle a bit until dark then not see 'em no more. Could be true.'

'It's just the nerve ends twitchin' away.' Jack poked the snake with a stick. 'The reason you can't see 'em when the sun goes down is because it's *dark*. You can't see nothin' in the dark.' He laughed again, pleased with his reasoning.

Harry joined him most times on the horses but would sometimes take a couple of hours by himself to saddle Brumby and ride out into the dunes and along the dry creek beds. There were no cattle to drove or rogue steers to turn back to the mob but the freedom of galloping through the desert dunes on the colt was exhilarating.

There was a time not long ago when they had considered droving 'hard work' but now that they had to gouge in the clay beneath the ground to earn a living, droving seemed like a long holiday and they both missed the unique excitement of the cattle camps. When they were out on their horses they imagined that Wandoo would come hurtling over the next ridge, or Tom Cooper would appear on his bay, standing straight in the stirrups and hand to eyes to shield the sun as he inspected his mob. Returning reluctantly to the mine they would conjure up images of Toffy in his work clobber and bow tie, stirring stew and ringing the metal triangle with a spoon to signal dinner.

They hoped that one day they would get the chance to be with them all again around a camp fire somewhere beside a waterhole surrounded by tall gum trees and drinking sweet black tea. They could picture uncle Warri sitting on his haunches rolling a smoke and telling everyone in earshot how he had 'learned' just about the whole world population everything they knew.

They often reminisced about one night when Tom Cooper and uncle Warri were in a particularly good mood, trying to outbrag each other across the fire with the whole crew listening and urging encouragement. Tom Cooper had bragged that he had taken a mob of four thousand head of cattle with only three blokes from Darwin to Adelaide but couldn't sell them so turned around and drove the mob all the way back to Darwin. He said that half the cows calved on the trip so he ended up back where he started with six thousand head.

No one believed Warri could top this story but he was not about to be beaten. 'That nothin', Tom. Sidney Kidman 'e say one day, 'Warri you best darn' drover I ever seen. Take this big mob for me will ya, over to Inglan for da quin.' So Warri take 'em sure 'nough, all way to Inglan.' He sat back a smug look on his face.

His smile faded quickly when Tom Cooper said, 'England, eh, Warri? Bet the Queen was pleased.' He paused for effect. 'Tell me, mate, how did you get the buggers across the sea?'

The crew sat waiting for Warri to admit defeat.

There was a breathless silence as Warri slowly licked the cigarette he was rolling, put it in his mouth and, lighting it ceremoniously, blew a cloud of blue smoke into the air. 'That easy, Tom. Warri din' take 'em *over* the sea mate. Warri not *that* silly, eh? Warri 'e drove 'em all way to Inglan' 'long the beach.' He spat into the fire as the whole droving crew burst into uproarious laughter.

Tom Cooper had stood and held his hand out to Warri. 'You win, old timer, I never woulda thought of that.'

◆◆◆◆◆◆◆◆◆◆◆◆

Sergeant Carter drove out to see the boys, bringing news from Iris that Bruno was progressing well in Adelaide. He apparently didn't have much recollection of the cave-in or the ordeal except that he still became irrationally agitated at night if there was no light in the room. A phobia, the doctor advised, that might stay with him for life. He did remember the opal he had found prior to the cave-in and asked every day if it was safe. The doctors reckoned that within a couple of weeks he would be fit enough to leave hospital.

'You fellas think about the Anzac Day march?' The sergeant reminded them of his previous conversation. 'It's on next week.'

'Yeah we'll come along I guess. Be a bit of a break from diggin', anyhow.'

'That's for sure, Jack. No need to ask you I suppose, Paddy.'

'I'll be there to be sure, Ron. Wouldn't be missin' it for quids.'

'Yeah, I bet you wouldn't,' the sergeant said, tongue in cheek.

'Shaun said for you boys to stay at his place the night before. Tub up and get dressed so we can be at the dawn service. It'll be an early start so no use driving in that morning.' He turned to Paddy 'You can bunk at my place, Paddy. The company will do me good and Iris said she'd cook tea for all of us at her joint so you won't have to put up with my burnt snags.'

Paddy's face lit up when Iris's name was mentioned and for the rest of the day he whistled happily, working with renewed vigour.

Jack began to put two and two together. 'Iris, eh, Paddy?' he said that night over the campfire.

'What's that ye're sayin' there, young Jack.'

'Iris. I said Iris. You a bit keen on her, Paddy?'

'Now I don't know what'd be givin' yer that idea now.'

'Hmm, just a thought.' He grinned at Harry who began to understand the reasons now for Paddy's little sojourns into town at night.

'Aaah, she's a fine lookin' woman an' all that's for sure. Not exactly a colleen you know, no … but close enough I should think. A fine heart it is that she's been blessed with, a fine heart indeed.' He looked dreamily into the coals.

♦ ♦ ♦ ♦ ♦ ♦ ♦ ♦ ♦ ♦ ♦ ♦

Ishmael Mohammed Hassan arrived on April twenty-four, the day before Anzac. He came up to the claim on his camel and on command the beast dropped to its knees, allowing Ishmo to jump lightly to the ground, his shirt tails whipped by the fierce wind making his thin legs look like skeletal bones beneath the threadbare fabric.

'Ishmo!' Reynold was the first to greet him. 'Yu come see Jack 'n Harry? They down the mine, I get 'em.' He ran into the dugout to find the boys he knew would be digging down in the drive with Paddy.

When Jack and Harry came out into the sunlight they saw Ishmo standing before them, a huge smile on his bearded face and his hands on his head. 'You dig big.' He pointed to the dugout mouth 'You make the home, yes?'

'It's good to see you, Ishmo.' Jack was happy to see their old friend again.

'We've been waitin' for you to turn up, Ishmo.' Harry walked to where the Afghan was standing. 'Have we got a lot to tell you!'

The Afghan looked about him in wonder at the mine entrance with its timber door and heavy chain, the bed base sieve, sorting table and the Land Rover parked near the corrugated iron shed.

'You do so much of the work. Good yes?' His face was beaming. 'Ishmo not dig this good.'

'Come inside outta the heat, Ishmo.' Jack pointed to the dugout and walked toward the entrance, motioning for the Afghan to follow. 'You wanna drink?' He handed a waterbag to him.

Taking a swig from the bag and placing the stopper back in the neck he handed it back to Jack. 'I call out on Bruno but no see him.' There was a concerned look on his face. 'Bruno always dig, dig. No dig today.'

They told him about the accident, explaining that Bruno was in hospital in Adelaide as they watched the tall man's face crease with concern for his friend. They assured him that the latest news was good and that Bruno should be back on the fields in a week or so.

They then said that they had found some opal and Jack went into the drive returning with a bag containing their cash. 'Now, Ishmo,' he said placing the bag on the table, 'we owe you some money.'

The Afghan held up his hands shrugging his shoulders and holding his arms to them palms outward. 'What for you owe Ishmo money, no, no. You do so much work to this place Ishmo should be pay you.'

'But we had a deal Ishmo, we work the claim and share what we find with you. We put some aside for ya.' Harry pulled a drum up to the table.

'Yes, yes. Deal yes, but no, no, no owe Ishmo.' He shook his head from side to side. 'What deal we decide?'

'Well ...' Harry thought for a second. 'We didn't agree on no actual amount, Ishmo.'

'Exactly, yes? No amount we work out. Ishmo now say you do work and dig mine so good that Ishmo have to pay you.'

The boys were astounded, not knowing how to deal with the situation. They expected to share their finds at least fifty-fifty after paying expenses and wages to Paddy and Reynold.

'Ishmo work camel, make little money long time. No spend, no reason. Ishmo not … how you say? … Rish, yes? But got money to live … care for camel. Camel only family Ishmo have but now you. Ishmo no ever dig mine, you dig, yes?'

Jack counted off two hundred pounds and handed it to the Afghan 'Go on, Ishmo, at least take somethin'.'

'Jack? Harry?' He waited till he had their complete attention. 'Bruno, he trap in mine, yes? Ishmo not want to be trap, no dig ever.' He shook his head sadly. 'Poor Bruno, good friend.'

Jack held out the money but Ishmo refused again to take it from him. 'Please, Ishmo, it's only fair. We wouldn't have anythin' if it weren't for you. We'd have to noodle in the mullock heaps or try to prospect a claim for ourselves.'

'Ishmo take money one condition only.'

'What condition, Ishmo?' Harry asked.

'Tomorrow you, me, we go to Mines of Department yes? Ishmo take two hundred pound, you take mine, yes? The last 'yes' was not a question but an affirmation.

'What do you mean, Ishmo?' Jack had a suspicion of what the Afghan was getting at.

'Ishmo sell mine to Jack and sell to Harry. Two hundred pound. Deal, yes?'

'It's worth a lot more than that, Ishmo.'

'Not you no find more opal,' he said with wisdom. 'And not you trap here one day. Two hundred, Ishmo sell to you. If you no want, then Ishmo sell anyway … to 'nother man maybe. You want?' He looked at them steadily, waiting for their answer.

Harry's eyes were wide with amazement. 'Jack? What d'ya reckon?'

'You sure about this, Ishmo?' Jack checked the offer again, finding it difficult to believe.

'We go Mines of Department tomorrow. Deal, yes?'

Jack looked at Harry who nodded. 'OK, deal. But on the condition that if we find more opal it's our choice if we want to give you a commission.'

Ishmo looked as if he was about to cry when he said softly …'Is deal.'

The boys could not believe that they had left Perth with nothing more than a dream and a few bob in their pockets and now, six months later, they owned a working opal mine.

◆◆◆◆◆◆◆◆◆◆◆

The six friends, Jack, Harry, Paddy, the police sergeant Ron Carter, Iris Smith, the nursing sister and the priest, Shaun Logan were sitting around the dining table at Iris's house having just eaten when Paddy reached into his coat pocket.

'I've got an apology to be makin', lads.' He passed a buff-coloured envelope across the table. 'Father O'Malley gave me this to pass on to you when I left Kalgoorlie but I dropped it into me Gladstone bag for safe keepin' and forgot all about it. It wasn't till I was lookin' for a clean shirt at Ron's place that I came across it. I'm real sorry.'

'What's in it, Paddy?' Jack studied the envelope. It had nothing written on it.

'I've not the faintest idea, lads. Open it up. I'm truly sorry, boys.' Paddy apologised again.

'I'll clear the table.' Iris began to collect the empty plates. 'You boys can read your mystery note.'

'How about a little nip of that whisky, Paddy?' Shaun Logan pushed his chair back and stood up. 'You feel like one, Ron?'

'Wouldn't say no.' He stood and moved away from the table. 'Let's go outside and have a smoke and let the boys read their letter in private eh? You need a hand with the dishes, Iris?'

'No. You men go and have your smoke ... there's not a lot to do. I'll join you in a bit.'

The three men left the room, Paddy brandishing the bottle of Irish whisky and Ron carrying three tumblers. Jack tore the end from the envelope and took a single sheet of paper from it. As he did so, a folded square of newspaper fell onto the table. Leaving it on the table he began to read the short note aloud.

'Hope he hasn't used all them big words again, Jack.'

> I will be asking Paddy to pass this on to you both. I've wanted to send it for some time now but, until recently, I didn't know where. I'm sure you will be interested in the newspaper article I clipped from the West Australian a couple of days after you left here in November last year. How you handle the news in it is up to you but I pray you will be sensible about it.
>
> Your friend,
> Timothy O'Malley.

♦♦♦♦♦♦♦♦♦♦♦♦

'Look at *this* will ya?' The weedy man with watery eyes slapped the *Adelaide Advertiser* onto the pub bar in front of his two companions. 'Read that, Andy.' He poked a finger at the open page.

'Read what? … Where?' Andy slurred, finding it hard to focus, the alcohol blurring his vision. The three men had been drinking heavily all afternoon.

'Oh, give it here, I'll read the damn thing.' The second man picked up the paper. 'The Prime Minister, Robert Menzies stated …'

'Not *that,* Cyril, you bloody idiot!' The watery-eyed man snatched the paper from him 'This! … I'll do it then.' He glared at his companions.

Opal miner recovers from cave in

He read the headline and continued.

Bruno Boccelli, the Coober Pedy opal miner who survived a cave- in when the roof of his mine collapsed trapping him under tons of rock for fourteen hours, forty feet underground, was today released from hospital. Mr Boccelli is staying with friends in Adelaide but plans to return to the opal fields in a few days time.

Mr Boccelli is lucky to be alive and without the quick thinking and brave actions of three teenage boys who discovered the accident, he would have suffocated in the mine. The boys raised the alarm and started digging to reach him while rescue teams were mobilised.

Mr Boccelli declined to be interviewed but a hospital spokesman said it was a miracle that he was not seriously injured and apart from having suffered trauma from the ordeal, he was in good health. A source in Coober Pedy told the Advertiser that the miner had apparently uncovered a huge opal just before the roof collapsed and was still clasping it to his body when pulled from the shaft.

The opal, one of the largest finds ever discovered in Coober Pedy, is under police security and is estimated to be worth many thousands of pounds. No decision has been made at this stage as to when the valuable gemstone will be offered for sale but considerable interest has already been generated from overseas investors.

'So what, Joe? So some bloody wog found an opal worth a fortune and escaped from a cave- in. What's that got to do with us?' Andy laughed and hiccupped before tossing the rest of his beer down and thumping the empty glass heavily on the bar.

'You blokes are dumber than I thought.' Joe spat the words out. 'Can't you see the connection?'

His two companions stared blankly at him without comprehension 'What connecshun?' Cyril swayed on the bar stool.

'Remember? … Coober Pedy, a few weeks back … three boys … a bloke named Bruno with a shotgun?' Joe began to shake with rage and embarrassment at the memory.

'You sayin' the kids that ran us off are the same ones that found the wog?' Cyril frowned trying to grasp the connection.

'Gotta be. I'll never forget that name 'Bruno' either. It was those kids that set those blokes onto us too. They were just lucky I was blinded by the spotlights otherwise I'da beat the livin' daylights outta them.' Joe's voice was shaking with anger.

'Yeah, sure.' Cyril nudged Andy 'Would thata been before or after you changed yer pants.' They both burst into laughter.

'Shut up, you morons!' Joe was seething. 'We're gonna get even somehow, mark my words.'

'How we gonna do that, Joe? We can't go back to Coober Pedy as they warned us not to ever go near the place again?'

'Dunno yet, dunno. But with that Bruno outta the way, the kids should be a pushover now that we know the lie of the land. We'll think carefully about it, work out a good plan and then when we're ready … maybe in a month or so, we'll head back up there. Get even with 'em all and grab some of that opal for ourselves.'

'By that time that Eyetie bloke might have sold his big opal and have a few thousand quid hangin' 'round as well.'

'Now yer thinkin', Andy.' Joe yelled at the barman to refill the glasses.

◆ ◆ ◆ ◆ ◆ ◆ ◆ ◆ ◆ ◆ ◆

Iris finished drying the dishes and put them away in the kitchen dresser. She filled the kettle and, placing it on the wood stove to boil, took the teapot from a shelf. Taking her apron off she hung it on a hook behind the door and walked into the dining room to see Jack and Harry sitting like statues, with shocked expressions on their faces.

'Whatever's the matter, boys?' She went to them immediately, sensing there was a problem and noticing that Jack held a newspaper clipping loosely in his hands. Without speaking he handed it to her.

Boys cleared.

The article began.

Two teenage boys reported missing after being charged with theft have had the summonses dropped after a school friend admitted he had falsely accused them of stealing his bicycle. The initial investigation led police on a grim search for the bodies of the two missing boys after the offending bicycle was discovered in bushes beside the bank of the Ashmorton River near their homes.

The two teenagers, fourteen year old Harold Turner and fifteen year old John Ferguson had been missing for over a week with all attempts to locate their whereabouts unsuccessful until letters written by the boys arrived at their parents' homes, postmarked Kalgoorlie.

The sergeant in charge of the Ashmorton police station commented that it was disgraceful that police had been misled but even more serious was the fact that two innocent kids had been forced to run away for no reason. The sergeant added that no charges for the false information had been laid at this stage but that the matter was under serious investigation.

Iris was stunned. She stared at the grainy photos included with the editorial of two boys smiling at her from the page. There was no mistaking that the photos were of the two young men now seated at her dining table but they looked like kids, much younger, with neat haircuts and wearing school uniforms, and not like the Jack and Harry that she knew at all.

'Oh, you poor things.' Iris moved between the boys and put her arms around their shoulders, expecting them to draw back from her touch but they both leaned their heads towards her and Harry began to sob. She felt Jack tremble but he kept control.

After a few moments, Harry sniffed and Jack looked up at her, eyes moist but without tears. He took a deep breath. 'Thanks, Iris, we'll be OK. Bit of a shock, that's all.' He attempted a weak smile.

The priest came back inside to find Iris sitting quietly with the two boys and sensed there was something not quite right. 'You blokes all right?' Shaun spoke to the three of them.

Iris held out the newspaper article and Shaun shook his head as he read. Finishing, he looked at the boys. 'Dear God, lads, you've been through a lot. Can we help somehow?'

'You already have helped.' Jack spoke quietly. 'Just bein' here helps.'

'I'll get Paddy and Ron. Does Paddy know about this?' The priest tapped the article.

'Not about the charges being dropped but he knows why we ran away. That's why he helped us. He's been a beaut friend and so has Father O'Malley.' Harry's voice was thick with emotion but he had wiped his tears away. 'They both believed we didn't pinch no bike.'

'Dear Mother of God.' Paddy glanced guiltily at Shaun Logan. 'I wished I'da been givin' you this long before now, boys.'

'That's OK, Paddy. I think you did the right thing. I'm glad you saved it till now when we had you'se here.'

'Thanks for that, Jack, but I was still remiss. What are we to be doin' now, lads?'

Both boys shrugged helplessly.

'You should let your parents know you're all right, boys.' The sergeant moved to them. 'They'll be worried sick.'

'We've been writin' regular but just haven't told 'em where we are in case the coppers ... er, sorry Sergeant,' Jack corrected, 'the police arrested us.'

'I understand your evasiveness now when I asked you about school and Perth. It must have been a bit scary for you having a copper around all the time.' Both boys smiled at his use of 'copper'.

'We could telephone to let them know you are here and that you're OK.' Iris was worried about the boys' parents, knowing what heartache they must be experiencing. 'I've got a daughter, Helen, in her final year boarding at St Mary's College in Adelaide and although we are in regular contact by post and telephone I still worry about her.' She imagined the pain that these boys' mothers must be suffering.

'Just give us a bit of time to think it through. A few more days won't make a lotta difference. We'll decide then what's the best thing to do.

'I know you will.' The priest handed the newspaper clipping back to them. 'We're here to help in any way we can.'

'That's right, we are … all of us.' Ron Carter confirmed Shaun Logan's comment.

Paddy nodded in agreement, moving close to Iris, putting his hand lightly on her arm. 'That we are, lads, that we are.' He spoke gently and Iris smiled, looking into his eyes but the boys missed the intimate exchange.

Chapter Thirty Three

The boys had a restless night at the priest's house. They didn't discuss the newspaper article in any depth, as they were too stunned to think clearly. Jack did say that Billy Munse had been a little mongrel, but that he had at least eventually owned up to lying about them.

'Bet he got a thrashin' from his, father.' Harry imagined the stern obnoxious Mr Munse and shuddered. 'Glad I'm not Billy.'

'Deserved it I'd say, Harry, but he did own up.'

'This means we can go back and not be in trouble with the police, Jack.'

'Yeah, I know. We'll be in trouble with our parents though.'

'Guess you're right, but it also means we didn't have to run away at all.'

'No we coulda stayed, but then again, Billy might not have owned up if we had. We wouldn't have seen what we have either, or made such good mates along the way. We'd still be gettin' a few bob a week pocket money too, instead of earnin' big quids.'

'Wouldn't own an opal mine either'. Harry checked to make sure the bag with their cash and mining lease was still under the pillow.

'It means, though, we can tell our parents the truth now, Harry. It's been hard havin' to watch everything we say in them letters.'

'We better write to 'em now, Jack. Let 'em know everythin's OK.'

'Not sure what's best, Harry. Let's sleep on it. We'll work it out tomorra.'

They didn't 'march' as such, the next morning, but gathered before dawn at the town hall for a service which their friend Father Logan officiated at. They then moved outside to the cenotaph where wreaths were layed and a bugler played the 'last Post' as the sun rose majestically out of the desert, bathing the scene with an amethyst glow.

A man, introduced as the shire president, read short accounts of what the troops had experienced and suffered, speaking of their bravery that fateful morning at Anzac Cove in far off Turkey. A prayer was said which finished with 'Lest we forget', then a bearded miner dressed in dungarees with a battered felt bush-hat on his head played a guitar and sang a song they had never heard before but which moved the crowd to reverent silence. A line in the song touched Jack deeply and he felt a lump rise in his throat and he was glad, when he looked furtively around, to see tears in many grown men's eyes.

The line in the song that affected Jack so profoundly was: 'And tears ran down my brother's face as he thought of loves in another place and I asked God to rescue me and my brother.'

◆◆◆◆◆◆◆◆◆◆◆◆

Anzac Day in Ashmorton was a very different affair from the small gathering in Coober Pedy. Jack Ferguson had served in the Royal Australian Army during World War Two as an artillery sergeant in the Middle East. Anzac Day was an emotional time for him, as memories of lost mates flooded back, but he didn't allow himself to dwell too much on the sadness but marched proudly dressed in his uniform and medals as a mark of respect for his fallen comrades.

The parade was well organised with military and pipe bands, vehicles and marching servicemen following a set route while spectators lined the streets cheering as they passed and waving miniature Australian flags. The service at the war memorial was structured with a number of dignitaries officiating. There were speeches and more speeches culminating with the 'Last Post' played by a solitary bugler signalling the end of the official remembrance. It was then, to Jack's way of thinking, that the real tribute to their mates began.

It was then time to meet up with mates that had fought together, regardless of the theatre of war they had been engaged in or the branch of the services they had been a part of. There was certainly some spirited good-natured rivalry however, between the Navy, Air Force and Army at bars across the nation.

Claude and Eric had served in Borneo with the light infantry and they and Jack always met up after the parade for a 'few beers' with their mates at the RSL club; that usually meant they stayed till stumps, got a taxi home and suffered hangovers for two days!

This Anzac day was dampened somewhat for Jack and Claude because of not knowing where their sons were and although they enjoyed the after service celebrations there was a subtle cloud over them. They had each determined not to mention the boys but as the night drew to a close and they were sitting quietly together reminiscing, the subject came up. 'Harry marched last year with the school … sort of missed him not being there today.'

'Jack too. Wonder if they kept up the tradition and marched somewhere in Kalgoorlie or Coolgardie or wherever they are, Claude.'

'Don't expect so,' Claude replied sadly. 'I think they only did it because the school involved them.' He took a swallow from his glass. 'One for the road, Jack?'

'Yeah, why not, mate.' Jack passed him his empty glass.

Although the boys wanted to head back out to the mine Iris insisted that they stay in town another night. Ron Carter agreed and said he'd take a run to check things out and make sure their diggings were OK. 'Another night'll do you good, not having to worry about things. Give you time to think through what you have to do.'

Father Logan was more than happy to have them stay another night. 'Everyone in town will be on the turps somewhere so we'll throw some snags on the barbecue at my place. It won't be flash but it'll be tucker. Can you make it, Ron?'

'No, I'll have to do the rounds tonight, mate, as there'll be a lot of mugs about but I might call in from time to time. Won't have a drink though, on duty.'

The boys turned in early leaving the priest, Iris and Paddy outside, relaxing in the cool night after a hectic day. Iris noticed Paddy was restless and smiled to herself. 'Paddy, why don't you take the Landy and have a look around town. Many interesting things to see on an Anzac night.' She winked at Shaun.

'Ahh, I'm content to be here. Don't know what it'd be I'd be lookin' for anyway.' He fidgeted on his seat.

'Paddy! Stop fooling around, man. I know what goes on and you'd be missing an Australian tradition if you didn't join in the ahh … celebrations! I'm about ready to turn in anyhow, as I'll probably have a busy day tomorrow dispensing aspirin in bucket loads. You can give me a lift home on your way, Paddy, if you like.'

'It's a marvellous woman that ye are, Iris. I get the feelin' it'd be hard to be pullin' the wool over yer eyes on anythin' at all, to be sure. You're not Irish somewhere way back are ye?'

'A dyed in the wool Aussie, Paddy, but I do know what makes a man tick. Just don't lose all your money.'

'Paddy O'Brien! Lose? There's a lot you're still to be knowin' about Paddy O'Brien, Iris, m'dear.'

'I'll be looking forward to that, Mr O'Brien.' She stood up. 'Thanks, Shaun, for the night. See you tomorrow no doubt and I hope those two dear boys can decide what's best for them.' She put her arm in Paddy's as they walked to the parked Land Rover.

The priest smiled in the darkness as he watched Paddy, the gentleman; graciously open the passenger door for her. *You best be reading up on the nuptial mass, Shaun,* the priest laughed to himself, *never done a marriage in Cobber Pedy.*

♦♦♦♦♦♦♦♦♦♦♦

'You awake, Harry?'

'Yep.'

'What're you thinkin' about?'

'Same as you I guess. The newspaper clippin', mum and dad … what we should do.'

'What do *you* think we should do, Harry?'

'We got a lot here now, good friends and makin' a go of things. You know, the mine and all.'

'We couldn't just go and leave it all then.' Jack lay on his back with his arms behind his head staring at the ceiling. '… Could we?'

'Not really, Jack.' Harry was silent for a time. 'But it'd be good to see everyone again.'

'Yeah, all except Billy Munse. I'd like to throttle that mongrel, Harry. Wonder what he's doin' now?'

359

'Polishin' his bike probably. Or hidin' from his father.' Harry giggled in the darkness.

Jack laid quietly thinking, his eyes wide open in the pitch darkness of the windowless bedroom. So many confusing and conflicting thoughts ran through his mind that he was unable to isolate or group them rationally enough to make a decision.

'Paddy could look after things for us, Harry, and Reynold would stay on.'

'I'm scared, Jack. If we go home my parents are gonna be real mad at me. Probably lock me away or send me to boardin' school or somethin' just to get even.'

'I think they'd be too glad to see you to do anythin' bad to ya.'

'Maybe.' Harry sounded unconvinced.

'So what do ya reckon we do then?'

'I'll leave it up to you, Jack, whatever *you* say.'

'That's not bloody fair, Harry, why me?'

'You're the oldest, Jack, that's why.'

'We always made the decisions together before, Harry, so why won't you make this one with me?'

'Because …' Jack heard the catch in his voice. 'Because I love it here, Jack, but I miss home too and I don't want to make a decision that could mean I'd lose either here or home depending on the decision. I don't think I can make such an important choice as that.' His last words were muffled and Jack realised Harry had buried his face in the pillow.

There was silence from Harry now so Jack just continued to stare into the darkness, his mind in turmoil. Lying in the stillness, his thoughts drifted back over the events of the last twenty-four hours or so. He saw the newspaper clipping vividly and recalled the contents, word for word. He felt the compassion of his friends as they consoled him and Iris's warm arms around his shoulders and the scent she wore as he leaned on her breast. He could see the anguish in Paddy's eyes as he apologised over and over for leaving the envelope in the Gladstone bag for so long. He experienced again the sunrise that morning as they stood in the piccaninny dawn, that pre-sunrise light, grouped together, men and boys, before the cenotaph. He pictured the soldiers clambering up the beaches at Anzac Cove being blasted to ribbons as the shire president had described and he heard the song the old miner sang.

The words came flooding back and he hummed along, silently mouthing them. 'And tears run down my brother's face as he thinks of loves in another place.' He stopped humming and sat bolt upright in the bed. 'You asleep yet, Harry?'

'No, Jack, just thinkin' about stuff.'

'We're goin' home, Harry, the song decided it for me.'

'Song! What song?'

'The one that was sung at the service this morning. You know, about thinking of loves in another place.'

'I didn't listen all that closely, Jack.'

'Well I did and we're goin' home, or at least I am. You can stay if you like. My 'Love' is me family and the 'other place' is back home in Perth so that's it.'

'You mean you don't love it here, Jack, rather be back in Perth?'

'No, I didn't say that. I think it's great here and I don't regret the decision we made to come here but until I put the guilt of runnin' away to rest and make up to my parents for the heartache I've caused 'em, this place can never be home. It's sort of like we're still on a journey, not permanent … do you know what I mean? I have to know where 'home' *really* is and until I go back I won't know if it's here, or back in Perth.'

'I think I understand what you mean, Jack, and I'm with you, so when do we leave then?'

'As soon as we can. It's our birthdays in a few days' time, Harry, so let's try to make it back by then.'

◆◆◆◆◆◆◆◆◆◆◆◆

The decision made, they were anxious to get things organised so were up, dressed and having a cuppa when Shaun woke. He listened attentively while they told him of their decision.

'I agree with your reasoning, Jack, very grown up. What can I do then to help you? You won't have to worry about the mine as Reynold is trustworthy and a good friend to you both and Paddy's on hand to manage things while you're away.' He paused and looked them both squarely in the eyes. 'I have to ask this … do you plan to come back?'

'You bet!' Harry answered immediately but Jack considered the question before he answered.

'I'm not sure, Father,' he said. 'I want to, of course, and would always return but whether or not it would be permanently or just to wind things up I won't know until I've been home.'

'Fair enough and you're being totally honest so I appreciate that. I also appreciate your sentiment, Harry. Now let's get things in motion.' He looked at the alarm clock on the sideboard, shrugged and reached for the telephone.

'Did I wake you, Ron? ... No, good. The boys have made a decision to get home to see their parents and want to get going as soon as they can. I agree with their decision; they've thought it through well, and I was wondering if you can help out with some advice or whatever?' The priest listened for a time 'Not sure, I guess they'll need to get to Pt Augusta somehow and train it to Kalgoorlie, then on to Perth.' More listening. 'That could work. OK ... Yes, sounds good. We'll wait for you then.' He put the receiver back on the cradle.

The boys looked at him expectantly and he explained. 'Ron says there's a surveyor bloke he knows in town that could be driving to Pt Augusta in the morning. He'll check if he can give you a lift and will be around here in half an hour to see what else he can do.'

Jack and Harry paced around as, now that the decision was made, they were anxious to get moving and knew there was a lot to organise in a short time.

The sergeant turned up with Paddy, and Iris arrived as they were walking to the door, having been telephoned by Ron Carter. 'Looks like a council of war then,' Iris joked as she joined them at the kitchen table.

Shaun Logan elected himself chairman of the organisation for their trip and went through the plans so far, sparing the boys from having to explain their decision. 'How'd you go with the surveyor, Ron?'

'Done. He's happy to have the company on the drive. Leaving at sun up in the morning.'

'Well then, not much more to be done. Do you want to call your parents and let them know to expect you? The priest pointed to the telephone.

'No!' Jack stated emphatically. 'Harry and I wouldn't know what to say and we want to surprise them anyhow. It's my birthday at the end of the month and Harry's two days later, we'd like to try to make it there by then.

'It seems like you'll be *giving* presents rather than getting them. What a great surprise for your families.' Iris was excited for them all.

'We'd like to call and see Father O'Malley on the way through if we can, maybe stop over a night. He's been real good to us so we want to thank him.'

'I'll call him for you.' Shaun offered. 'He can meet you at the train.'

'If his car will start!' Harry laughed. Paddy and Jack laughed with him but the others looked on blankly, not knowing the joke.

'We'll have to organise some money for you, Paddy, while we're away.'

'Money, Jack? What for?' Paddy patted his coat pocket and looked at the sergeant with a cheeky grin. 'You're not forgettin' now that Paddy O'Brien is a master at survival lads. Particularly when there's a little game of chance on that Ron here knows nothin' about.' The sergeant smiled at Paddy's jibe. 'There's no need to be worryin' about money for Paddy now. A few blokes last night made what could be only described as a handsome contribution to me welfare and all.'

'The horses, we need to make sure they're all right.'

'They'll be fine, Harry. I love horses and will check on them a couple of times a week. I know Ned at the stables well.'

'Gee thanks, Mrs Smith.'

'When are you going to stop calling me 'Mrs', Harry. We're all friends here and in Coober everyone uses first names. There are people here I've known for years and still couldn't tell you what their surnames are. Now, I suspect you might have a few clothes that could be in need of a wash and a press so drop them off and I'll have them ready for you to take with you.' She reached out and ruffled Harry's hair. 'Can't have you going back to Perth and having people think we live like hobos out here, can we?'

'Reynold can look after Anna OK but what about Bruno's claim?'

'I hear he's out of hospital,' Iris said. 'Should be back soon and Paddy can look after things till then.' She gave the little Irishman a questioning look and he nodded.

'I'll be pleased when that happens.' The sergeant looked relieved. 'Never heard of anyone breaking into a jail but it worries me having that huge stone in the cells. The sooner Bruno collects it the better.'

'Wonder what he'll do with it, Ron, must be worth a packet.'

'It's big all right, Shaun, and I imagine it'll be worth a small fortune.'

'Just as well. I don't think Bruno will be doing much digging after this and he's worked hard out there so he deserves some reward.'

'You're right, Iris.' The sergeant agreed.

'OK then! You don't mind if I recap on what everyone needs to do, Shaun?' Without waiting for an answer Ron Carter stood up signalling an end to the meeting, then, with military like precision said, 'let's get on with it. Paddy, you drive the boys out to get their laundry and so they can explain to Reynold what's going on. Shaun, you're going to call the priest in Kalgoorlie, is that right?' The priest nodded. 'Right then, I'll confirm with the surveyor to make sure there's no hitch. I'll also call a mate of mine at the cop shop in

Pt Augusta and get him to book tickets on the train for you blokes. He'll take care of you too when you get there. Good fella, you'll like him. Got kids about your own age as well.' He looked at both the boys with a wry grin. 'Don't suppose you're wanted in Pt Augusta for knocking off bikes are you?'

'Ron,' Iris scolded, 'don't be mean.'

'You may be thinkin' that me and the good Father in Kalgoorlie were doin' the wrong thing by shieldin' the boys but when I met 'em on the train I knew in me heart they were good lads. Then when they told us why they were runnin' away, Timothy and me believed their story. I'm real glad you're goin' to be seein' your families again but Paddy'll miss you and all, to be sure.' There was a thickness in his voice so he added brightly, 'Now, Iris, would you be likin' another cuppa before we head off on our missions.'

Chapter Thirty Four

The surveyor pulled up in front of the priest's house just before dawn in a black Ford utility and the boys threw their bags containing the clean and neatly ironed clothes with their other belongings into the back. The surveyor was introduced only as Gordon. 'Hop in, lads, got a long drive,' he said, revving the motor.

With the bulk of the money split between them and carried inside their shirts and spending money for the trip secure in their button down pockets, they couldn't help but think about the start of their last long journey when they only had a few quid between them. This time they had several hundred pounds.

Reynold had come to see them off and they shook hands with him, Shaun Logan and Sergeant Carter, but Iris hugged them tightly without speaking and they noticed when she drew back that she was dabbing at her eyes with a small lace handkerchief.

Turning to Paddy, they were ready to shake hands when the little man held his arms wide. 'Aargh, come here, ye young rascals.' Paddy put his arms around them briefly then stood back. 'You be takin' good care of yourselves now ye hear, and say hello to me old mate Timothy for me. Give him this would you. Say it's an investment that I'll collect interest on one day.' He handed them a wrapped bottle he had taken from the Land Rover. He also gave them an envelope. 'Tell the old rogue that this is for the plate. He'll be knowin' what I mean.'

'Take good care and don't get lost along the way. It'd be a shame after all you've been through to lose your way, get on the wrong train and end up in Melbourne instead of Perth.' Shaun Logan tried to keep the moment light.

The sergeant stood holding the Ford's passenger door open and as they got into the vehicle he shut it, speaking through the window. 'You won't get lost as Ned Wilson, the sergeant at Pt Augusta, has booked your tickets on the train and he's waiting for you; spoke with him again this morning. Gordon here'll drop you off at the police station. Don't worry about things, have a good time and stay out of trouble.'

Gordon accelerated and the powerful car leapt away. Pressing the horn he turned left at the end of the street leaving the small group standing forlornly beside the roadway. They were on their way.

Having to farewell their friends overshadowed the excitement about the trip and the prospect of seeing their families again so Gordon's impatience to be on the road suited them. What the reception at home would be like, or how they would feel about being away from the life they had led for the past six months and the friends they had made, was anybody's guess. At that moment Jack and Harry were feeling numb, as alone as they had felt when they boarded the train at Northam a lifetime away.

Gordon drove fast, the big Ford sitting firmly on the gravel, trailing a cloud of dust that was whipped away by the desert wind. The boys tried to talk to him a couple of times but found that Gordon was very economical when it came to conversation and was happy to drive in total concentrated silence.

The trip took several hours. The only stops were to refill the tank from drums of petrol lashed in the back of the ute, a call of nature and to change a punctured tyre. The Ford pulled into the outskirts of Pt Augusta just after lunchtime. The boys, having been in remote locations since leaving Kalgoorlie months before, stared at the shops, cars and more people than they had seen in one place for a long time.

Gordon pulled the dust-coated Ford up in front of the police station and left the motor running. 'We're here,' was all he said. Taking their bags from the back of the ute they thanked Gordon for the ride. 'Good on ya, see ya again sometime,' he said, and was gone, the V8 motor growling into the distance.

'Better find this Ned Wilson bloke, eh?' Jack started toward the police station when a giant of a man in police uniform walked out of the front entrance and flashed a friendly smile. 'You must be Jack and Harry, been expectin' ya. Ned Wilson,' he introduced himself.

His handshake was crushing then he picked up their heavily packed blueys in one hand like they were filled with feathers. 'Follow me, you had any lunch? Guess not.' He answered his own question. 'The missus has got some cold meat and salad ready at home.'

He led them through the station, introducing them to the two constables on duty and out the back door to where a police car was parked. 'Jump in fellas, it's not far. I've got your train tickets at home.'

'Thanks, sergeant, we'll fix you up for them when we get there.'

'No worries, Jack, and call me Ned. Everyone else does 'round here.'

Ned pulled into the driveway of a freshly painted weatherboard home with neat lawns and large trees dominating the front garden. 'Used to be in the police house next to the station but the senior connie's in that now because we bought this one.' He pressed the horn to announce their arrival. 'Good for the family to be a bit away from the station.'

As Ned switched off the engine and stepped from the car a woman came out the front door and down the steps to meet them. She was slim and neatly dressed in a floral frock with fair bobbed hair.

369

Clear hazel eyes twinkled when she smiled. 'I'm Rosemary,' she said, 'welcome. How was your trip?'

'Pretty good, thanks,' Harry Replied.

'Long, but good, thanks, Mrs Wilson.' Jack noticed movement behind her on the porch and glanced up to see a young girl, around his own age, come skipping down the steps. As she approached, Jack was sure his mouth fell open because she was the prettiest creature he had ever seen. Her skin was like honeyed cream with a sprinkling of freckles across her nose that gave her a tomboyish air. Blonde hair tumbled to her shoulders and her eyes, almost violet, shone with warmth as she spoke. 'Hello, you're the two from Coober Pedy. Dad told us all about you.' Her voice tinkled like music to Jack and he just nodded dumbly, not trusting himself to speak in case it came out like a squeak.

'I didn't tell her *all* about you.' Her father opened the car boot and grabbed the two bags. 'My daughter, Naomi,' he said by way of introduction. 'Nomes, this is Jack Ferguson and Harry Turner. Don't know a lot to tell anyhow only that Ron up at Coober said you needed to get to Perth in a hurry, something about a birthday in a few days?' He walked ahead toward the house. 'Come on in then. Lunch ready, Rose?'

As the boys washed up for lunch in the bathroom, Harry whispered to Jack. 'You looked like a fish out there, Jack, your mouth open like that.'

'Shut up, Harry.' Jack sluiced water onto his face and reached for a towel. 'You gotta admit though, she's good-lookin', mate.'

'Yeah … OK for a blonde, I suppose. She's pretty skinny though.'

'She is not!' Jack snapped back at him.

'Ahh, got ya!' Harry ducked as Jack threw a friendly punch at him.

There was cold lamb with lettuce, tomato, cucumber and onions plated up when they came to the table. 'Help yourself to bread and butter, there's home-made mayonnaise in the jar there ... would you like sauce, or mint jelly?' Rosemary Wilson fussed. 'Don't expect you get to eat all that well batching up at the mine so tuck in.'

Jack was seated opposite Naomi and found it hard to meet her eyes so concentrated on the lunch aware that she was looking steadily across the table at him. Each time he chanced to glance up her eyes locked on his but he looked quickly back at the plate, sure his face was bright red. He heard Harry snicker beside him, which made him even more uncomfortable, and was glad when her father broke the silence. 'So tell us, boys, what's it like living in Coober Pedy?'

Jack let Harry carry most of the conversation but Naomi was determined to include him. 'Jack, tell me, are there many girls in Coober Pedy?' There was a sneaky smile on her lips and he felt like jelly.

'Er, no. Haven't seen any. We work pretty hard up there and it's no place for girls.'

'What do you mean by no place for girls? Don't you think girls can work hard?' There was challenge in her voice.

'Crikey, you've done it now, Jack.' Ned jerked a thumb towards his daughter. 'We've got two daughters, Claire's away at present and I'm glad we don't have a son because he'd have a hard time keeping up with Nomes here. She reckons there's nothing a bloke can do that a Sheila can't do just as well'

'Dad!' Naomi sounded offended. 'You make me out to be an ogre. I'm not that at all and I'm certainly not a 'Sheila' either.' She shot an indignant look at her father, wrinkling her nose.

'I know, honey. But you'd rather be off in the bush somewhere on a horse than sitting at home sewing.' He then spoke to Jack. 'She can ride pretty well and shoots like a trooper.' Ned was obviously very fond of his daughter.

'You *shoot*?' Jack sounded incredulous.

"What's wrong with shooting?' Naomi was defensive.

'Nothing, nothing at all.' Jack bit into a slice of bread.

'Jack's a top shot.' Harry lauded his mate. 'Can read the bush well too; an old aboriginal drover taught him.'

'Wow! What do you shoot, Jack?' Naomi was immediately animated.

'Oh nothin' much. Rabbits, the odd kangaroo, stuff like that, but not for sport, only for food. We had to for a long while to survive on the cattle drive.'

'You've been droving too.' Her eyes lit up. 'Where? … When?'

'Come on, young lady; don't ask the lads *too* many questions now.' Her mother took the empty plates from the table.

'Harry's the real stockman, got a magnificent colt at home.' Jack didn't realise he had unconsciously called Coober Pedy 'home'.

'A colt, great.' Naomi smiled across at Harry briefly but her interest was obviously on Jack. 'You own a horse too, Jack?'

'Yeah, I got a big bay gelding. He's gettin' on a bit now but a good horse. He's called Brehardie.'

'That's an unusual name, Jack.' Mrs Wilson joined in.

'It's an Aboriginal name. Uncle Warri, that's what we call him, gave him to me.'

'You two seem to have led an interesting life.' Ned reached for the teapot, filling his cup.'

'Well, only for the past few months. Up till then we lived in Perth.'

'Tell me more about shooting, Jack.' Naomi fixed her gaze on him over the table.

'Not much to tell really.'

'Do you have your own gun, Jack?'

'Got one for Christmas, yes. Tom Cooper, the boss on the cattle drive, and uncle Warri, gave me a Winchester lever action.'

'Jack ran some claim jumpers off our mine with his rifle, shot right past their ears and blew a tin aw ...' Harry stopped in mid-sentence. Flushing a pink colour, he looked at the police sergeant and stammered. 'Er, he ... er ... wasn't aimin' at them, he ...'

'That's OK.' The sergeant rescued Harry 'Bloody claim jumpers deserve all they get.'

'Ned! No swearing at the table.' His wife gave him a scalding look.

'Sorry dear. Well lads, we better get going if we want to catch this train. Be through in a while; I'll get your tickets.' They stood from the table and Ned handed Harry the tickets that Jack paid cash for, unaware of the surprised look on the policeman's face at the size of the bankroll Jack buttoned back in his top pocket.

'Mind if I come and see you off?' Naomi looked directly at Jack.

He nodded, pleased because this vibrant, beautiful girl fascinated him, but unnerved nonetheless by her forthrightness.

The train whistle blew. 'Have a good trip, fellas,' the sergeant said.

'Thanks for all your help.'

'Think nothing of it, Jack. You're mates of Ron's and that's good enough for me. See ya, Harry. Make sure you both keep in touch with us now and let us know how you go. You know where we are.' He stepped back to make way for his daughter.

Harry said, 'Bye' to Naomi then jumped up the steps into the carriage but Jack lingered a moment. Ned chuckled to himself and withdrew a few feet, aware that there was some sort of chemistry brewing between his headstrong daughter and the well built modest young man with the dark hair and blue eyes. *Poor bugger,* he said to himself. *If she's set her mind on you you've got no chance, son.*

Jack stood shyly on the platform with Naomi. 'Thank your mum again for the lunch, Naomi' He spoke her name for the first time and thrilled at the sound of it inside his head.

'That's all right, Jack, nice to meet you … and Harry,' she added.
'You too, bye for now.' Putting a foot on the step and about to haul himself into the carriage to join Harry, he paused when Naomi held a piece of paper out to him.

'Dad said for you to keep in touch but how can you without the address. Here.' She pushed a note towards him 'I wrote our telephone number on it too. Bye.' She turned and joined her father as the train began to move away from the platform, gathering speed.

Jack stood at the open window for a time until Naomi faded from view, swallowed up by the steam and smoke from the engine.

◆◆◆◆◆◆◆◆◆◆◆◆

374

Alice and Jean were seated on the back verandah of the Ferguson home, enjoying the afternoon sunshine. Autumn in Perth could be quite cold and overnight rain had made the morning chilly, so they took the chance when the clouds broke to have afternoon tea outside, sheltered from the wind by the timber lattice enclosure that Jack had built over the Christmas break.

'It's nice out here, Alice.'

'It is, yes.' She poured tea into delicate china cups.

'Heard from Jack, Alice?'

'Not for a while.' Her smile faded at the mention of her son's name and she had hoped that maybe today Jean would not raise the subject of the boys as she had determined to get on with her life as best she could, but he was always close to her consciousness. Only a thought or a name mention or a glance at a mantelpiece photo away. She had even begun to call her husband by his proper name 'John' instead of the familiar 'Jack' to help her cope.

'It's his birthday this week, Jean. Sixteen; couple of years and he'll be a man.'

'I know. Harry'll be fifteen two days later.' She looked wistfully into the garden, 'Remember last year when we had a combined little party for them here on Jack's birthday? Harry said he couldn't wait another two days for his presents, seeing that Jack would have his before him. Had a few of their schoolmates over.'

'I know.' Alice took a deep breath to shake off the memory. 'Why don't we do the same thing again this year, Jean?' she said with a burst of bravado. 'It's still their birthdays whether they're here or not. We won't have a kid's party or invite anybody; just you, Claude and your kids can join us all here in the evening for a barbecue. Be one of the last chances to cook outside with the weather turning colder. What do you say?'

'Oh, I don't know if I could cope, Alice.'

"Yes you can,' she urged. Despite Alice's sorrow, she was still stronger than Jean and also felt a little guilty that Jack, being a year older, might have influenced Harry to run away. 'We'll celebrate *for* them Jean instead of *with* them this year.'

Jean thought for a minute and, encouraged by Alice's enthusiasm, warmed to the idea. 'All right, Alice, why not? She sounded more cheerful. 'I'll bake a cake and we can sing 'Happy birthday' and hope wherever they are at that moment they may hear us in spirit.'

◆ ◆ ◆ ◆ ◆ ◆ ◆ ◆ ◆ ◆ ◆ ◆

The train journey was uneventful. The boys had comfortable seats and they nonchalantly watched the vastness of the almost treeless and flat Nullarbor Plain blur past the picture windows of the carriage. It surprised them to see fellow passengers sitting glued to the window in awe of the scenery that to them was now commonplace. Kids pointed and became excited as various animals came into view then, seconds later, vanished as the train sped past.

'Look, dad! A camel, it's a camel.' One young boy screamed in delight at a wild dromedary grazing peacefully in the distance, its front legs spread slightly, long neck bent to the grass.

'You know, Harry, we were like that not so long ago. Remember how we jumped up and down on the train when we saw the emus and you couldn't believe that eagle when it dived down and grabbed the rabbit just out of Coolgardie?'

'We couldn't have been as silly as that, surely?' Harry pointed at the boy who now had his nose pressed closely against the window glass.

'I think we were.' Jack stretched his legs and pressed his head back into the cushion. 'Seen a lot, haven't we, Harry?'

'Yeah … done a lot to.'

'You lookin' forward to bein' home, Harry?'

'I think so. It'll be good to see mum and dad again. Do you think we've changed much, Jack?'

'Nah, not much. Got a bit browner but we're still the same blokes, Harry. Haven't been away long enough to change all that much.'

'I suppose you're right. We can go and catch some yabbies when we get back.'

'I can't wait to see the creek. Water! What a change that'll be! A big stream and tall trees. We can maybe catch a feed of fish too.'

'We'll be able to go to the pictures, Jack. I miss the pictures, don't you?'

'You bet, wonder what's on?'

'Dunno. You know somethin' else I'm lookin' forward to?'

'What?' Jack shook his head.

'Fish 'n chips. A big feed of crispy-battered fish and those chips with all the crunchy bits at the bottom.'

'With heaps of vinegar sprinkled on 'em, Harry'

'Do ya think we'll see Billy Munse, Jack?'

'We'll make sure we do, Harry, we'll make sure we do. You hungry?'

'The thought of fish and chips *has* made me a bit peckish.' Licking his lips he said, 'let's go down to the dinin' car.'

They walked through two carriages to reach the buffet carriage with its long counter down one side, padded stools bolted to the floor, and dining tables in neat tableclothed rows. Entering the carriage they saw it was packed, with no spare tables, and were about to turn around when a porter spotted them. 'Table for two?'

'There's no room, you're full up,' Harry replied looking around the carriage.

'Two seats this way … follow me.' the man walked off and they trailed behind him, swaying with the movement of the speeding train.

'Oh no!' Harry grunted and baulked so that Jack ran into him. 'Not there!'

Jack looked past him to see a table for four with two vacant seats. The problem that Harry spotted and Jack concurred with, was that two girls occupied the other two seats. Their intention to turn tail out of the dining room was ambushed by the porter.

'Two young gentleman to join you if you don't mind,' he said to the girls and handing Jack and Harry a menu he guided them expertly into the seats before they could protest further.

The two girls of average looks were dressed almost identically in frilly dresses and giggled and nudged each other as the two boys sat down opposite them.

'G'day,' Jack said but Harry just nodded. The girls giggled again.

They had ordered their meal and were sitting self-consciously, both toying with the table napkins, when one of the girls plucked up the courage to speak. 'My name's Mary and this is my sister, Theresa. What's yours?'

'I'm Jack and this is me mate, Harry.'

The girls took in the clean but faded dungarees and cotton drill shirts they were wearing and had noticed the scuffed riding boots as the boys seated themselves. 'You work on a station? You ringers or something?' Mary asked.

'No we're not ringers.' Harry answered but Jack said nothing.

There was an awkward silence. 'What do you do then?' Theresa asked.

The question staggered the boys, as they had never thought about what they did. It occurred to them at that moment that they were not just a couple of schoolboys on the run any more, nor were they greenhorns learning to ride and shoot and drove cattle, but that they were in fact opal miners. Not *just* opal miners but the owners of a mine purchased from Ishmo for two hundred pounds with the deed tucked securely in the bundle of notes beneath their shirts.

'Ahh … we live in Coober Pedy,' Jack stated.

'Coober Pedy!' Both girls said at once their eyes widening. Are you miners or something?' Mary asked.

'We dig around a bit.' Harry was relieved when the waiter arrived carrying the roast beef they had ordered. 'Enjoy your meal, sir,' he said to each of them as he placed their meals on the table.

'Coober Pedy, that's a coincidence.' Mary tucked into the apple pie. 'Isn't it, Theresa?'

'Amazing,' her sister said, 'simply amazing. Who'd have thought we'd meet someone *else* from Coober Pedy.'

'Someone else?' Jack stopped eating, fork poised. 'Who else do you know from Coober?'

'We have a close friend whose mother lives in Coober Pedy, don't we, Theresa?'

'Whose mother?' Harry asked.

'We board with her at St Mary's, Helen Smith.'

'Helen Smith. Doesn't ring a bell with us does it Harry?'

Harry pursed his lips thoughtfully 'No … Helen Smith … What's her mother's name?'

'Don't know what her name is … Mrs Smith I suppose!' Both girls laughed at Mary's joke. Gaining control of her mirth Theresa said, 'she's a nurse or something up there.'

'A nurse! You can't mean Iris?' Harry was flabbergasted.

'Not sure, is Helen's mum's name Iris, Mary?'

'Could be, I can't remember.'

'There's only one nurse in Coober Pedy and that's Iris,' Jack said. 'What's she look like, you know … this Helen?'

'We've got a school photo here. She's in the same class as us. We're on our way over to Perth for our brother's wedding so have some time off school … almost the holidays anyhow.' Theresa babbled on as she rummaged through the large carryall bag on her lap. 'Here it is.' She triumphantly flourished a photograph that she placed on the table facing the two boys. 'That's her.' She put a finger on the picture'

'Well I'll be darned.' Harry was stunned 'Look, Jack. If that girl had her hair pulled back in a bun and was a few years older who would it be?'

Jack leaned over the table, picked up the photo and angled it to avoid the glare from the overhead lamps 'Iris. It'd be Iris,' he said emphatically.

Chapter Thirty Five

Father O'Malley couldn't remember last when he was so excited. He kept glancing at the wall clock in his study and had telephoned the railway station asking for the arrival time of the Pt Augusta train.

'You mean the *Adelaide* train, sir?' A clerk with a nasal problem had said but as Jack and Harry were boarding at Pt Augusta, Father O'Malley couldn't have cared less if it had originated at Timbuktu.

He began to pace, little doubts niggling at him. *What if they'd been delayed on the way down from Coober Pedy and missed the train? What if they'd changed their minds and were still in Coober Pedy?* He contemplated calling Shaun Logan to check if they had actually left but dismissed the notion and filled and lit a pipe of tobacco, something that always had a calming effect but for some reason didn't work today.

Mrs Lacey, as dour as she was, had bustled about, made up the spare beds in the room where they stayed last time and cooked Anzac biscuits and a peach crumble for sweets. She had also prepared a large leg of lamb that was in the refrigerator, decorated with sprigs of rosemary for the night's main course. Vegetables were peeled and ready for the roasting dish in a water-filled bowl covered with a tea towel.

Finishing his pipe, the priest placed it in a large cut-glass ashtray to cool and looked again at the clock. Very little time had passed so he decided he would get the car out and warm up the motor as he hadn't driven it for a day or so. Slipping behind the wheel and patting the dashboard affectionately he savoured the smell of leather seats mingled with the aroma of pipe tobacco and petrol fumes. He couldn't remember exactly how long he had been driving this car but he loved it and, turning on the ignition switch, he pressed the starter. There was a high pitched churning sound as the battery spun the starter motor, the engine fired twice, backfired loudly, burst into life momentarily then instantly died, a pall of blue smoke filling the shed.

'You cantankerous old beast, why do I put up with you?' The priest slammed the door and lifted the bonnet, fiddling with the spark plug leads. Timothy O'Malley was in no way mechanical but felt better doing *something*, although he suspected spark plugs were the least of this car's problems.

 He was surprised when at the second attempt the motor burst into life, misfired a couple of time but then settled down to a steady purr. 'You're a beautiful Old Girl, you are.' He patted the dashboard again and reversed from the shed.

◆◆◆◆◆◆◆◆◆◆◆◆

The boys were glad the two sisters, Mary and Theresa, were travelling in a different carriage from theirs as, although they were friendly enough, they appeared immature and giggled incessantly. The girls said they would tell Helen Smith that they had met miner friends of her mothers on the train and gave Jack and Harry a Perth contact address. The boys politely said they'd be in touch if they got a chance but knew they wouldn't bother.

'That Helen looks a lot like Iris, eh, Jack? Except she's better lookin' don't ya think?' They had returned to their seats.

Jack realised that Harry was quite taken with the girl in the photo as he had asked for a second look at it before they left the dining car. 'That's just because she's younger than her mother is, Harry. Looks pretty skinny too, needs a good feed,' he teased.

'She's not skinny, she's just …' He woke up that Jack was ribbing him. 'OK, evens,' he said remembering his 'skinny' comment about Naomi in the bathroom at the Wilson house. 'You gotta admit though, Jack, she's not too bad,' he persisted.

'There's no doubtin' she looks like her mother, Harry, and if, like Iris, her face lights up when she smiles then she'd be a bit of a looker for sure.'

'Wonder if we'll ever get to meet her?' Harry looked wistfully out the window into the passing night.

They slept for most of the journey, emotionally drained from the events of the last forty-eight hours and the speed at which they had made the decision to return to Perth. Small, lonely railway sidings flashed by the train, most of them just rough timber platforms supporting tin sheds and signboards with names like 'Zanthus', 'Coonara', 'Chifley' and 'Karonie' painted on them.

A man seated across the aisle from them was also reading the signs. 'Not far to Kalgoorlie now,' he commented to the lady travelling with him as 'Randell' appeared briefly into view. Passengers, obviously leaving the train at Kalgoorlie, started to pack books into carry-bags, gather their belongings and visit bathrooms to freshen up and the boys noticed that the terrain had changed from the vast openness of the Nullarbor to more undulating mulga-studded country.

With 'blueys' slung over their shoulders they stepped from the train onto the platform at Kalgoorlie for the second time in six months and dodged people milling around them hauling large suitcases, and groups hugging and greeting each other.

They noticed the two sisters leave the train, heading for the cafeteria and were thankful that they were obscured from view by throngs of people as they searched for Father O'Malley.

♦ ♦ ♦ ♦ ♦ ♦ ♦ ♦ ♦ ♦ ♦ ♦

The priest couldn't believe it. His old black Chev, running like a clock when he'd left the presbytery heading for the railway station, had begun to misfire after travelling a few hundred yards. It had stalled at an intersection and a motorist behind him had started honking impatiently and Father O'Malley could hear the colourful language the driver hurled at the stranded vehicle blocking the road. Stepping from the car the priest was smugly pleased when, noticing his clerical garb, the man left his vehicle with the engine running and walked up to the Chev. 'Can I help you, Father? The man sheepishly asked.

'I've got to meet the train to pick two friends up and my old car is being temperamental again.' He gave the Chev a withering look as if it could understand him. 'I'm going to be late now I'm afraid.'

The man considered the situation for a moment. 'Let,s push her out the way, Father. 'I'm heading that way so, if you like, I'll take you to meet your friends and give you all a lift back.'

'But it'd be taking up too much of your time, you seemed to be in a bit of a hurry.' Father O'Malley couldn't help taking a snipe at the man's previous impatience.

What? Oh yeah … sorry. It's no trouble really. I'd be glad to help out,' He replied guiltily.

With little choice, the priest readily agreed. Thanking the man profusely he got into the passenger seat and the driver sped off toward the station, the priest noticing that a number of cars were passing them from that direction. He was concerned that Jack and Harry would be getting anxious, being two small boys arriving at a strange destination with nobody to meet them. He left the man to park his vehicle and hurried onto the station as he heard the train pull out for Perth. The platform was now almost deserted except for some railway employees and a smattering of straggling passengers. Jack and Harry were nowhere to be seen.

Worried now and muttering under his breath, blaming the old Chev abandoned in the street, he walked the length of the platform checking small alcoves and even went into the men's room in case they were there. Deciding to check the canteen he found it almost empty except for three ladies seated at a table and, by their dress and demeanour, two young stockmen leafing through a rack of magazines. He almost walked out before he realised it was Jack and Harry. He stood shaking his head in disbelief as he had been expecting two kids like the ones he'd left at Mt Margaret Mission and instead he was meeting two people he almost mistook for grown men.

'My goodness, just take a look at you two!' He was beaming as he went to them.

Recognising the rich brogue, the boys spun around to see the tall stooped figure of Father O'Malley, his arms wide in greeting, swooping toward them across the polished lino of the canteen watched by three curious ladies sipping tea at one of the tables.

The boys stood stiffly; slightly embarrassed by the pipe tobacco and cologne hug they received from a delighted Father O'Malley. Recognising their unease, the embrace was brief and the priest stood back to look at them. 'I declare that you've grown a couple of inches at least or maybe it's the hats that make you look so tall.' He shook his head in wonder. 'Come on then, the old Chevvie is broken down and a kind man is giving us a lift. Better not keep him waiting.'

They all piled into the man's car and he drove them to where the black saloon was parked. 'Do you think we can get her started?' he asked the priest as they pulled up behind it.

'There's a chance, yes,' Father O'Malley said. 'Perhaps if you lads give her a push she just might start.'

The roadway was level and, although the vehicle was heavy, with the stranger helping them they easily got the car rolling and laughed when the priest let out the clutch and the motor backfired before starting, enveloping them in a cloud of smoke. Letting the motor idle, the priest stepped out and thanked the man for his assistance and the boys transferred their belongings into the Chev.

'I think you should take her to a garage and get her checked over. Do you know a good mechanic?' the stranger asked.

'I'm afraid I don't. Been a little while since I had her serviced,' the priest said sheepishly.

'Hmm, I can tell. Look, I've got a mate that owns a workshop not far from here. Follow me and we'll see if he can take a look at her. He's very good and because he knows me, and you being a man of the cloth, I'm sure he won't overcharge you.'

'Well … I don't know, it could be a bit of work that she's needing I'm afraid.'

'You can't keep driving it like it is, Father. At least get an idea what's wrong; might be something simple.' the stranger urged. 'I can run you home if he has to keep it for while.'

'Well …' Father O'Malley stroked his chin thoughtfully. 'Perhaps it won't hurt. You're most kind.'

The mechanic lifted the bonnet, checked a couple of things and listened closely to the misfiring motor. 'Could be a coupla things. Spark, maybe, and it's in dire need of a tune as that carbie's pourin' fuel out …' he tapped it with a screwdriver '… and there's oil everywhere … probably needs a coupla gaskets. When was the last time you had her serviced, Father?'

'Well … I can't quite remember that now … last year sometime I believe. I changed the oil myself and cleaned the spark plugs too, couple of things like that.'

The man lifted his eyebrows. 'You need a proper service then, Father, and a couple of replacement bits and pieces. Those tyres are nearly down to the rims too.' He kicked the front wheel.'

'I can't be affording new tyres I'm afraid, on top of everything else.' Father O'Malley looked concerned. 'How much will the tune up be then?'

'Hard to say off hand. Depends on what bits I need to put in but I'll do it as cheaply as I can for you seeing you're a friend of Sam here.' He indicated the stranger.

The priest continued to procrastinate about leaving his car at the garage. 'Lovely car isn't she?' the man said giving the Chev a pat on the hood. 'Don't make 'em like this any more. Solid as a rock and once she's runnin' sweet again she'll be right for another twenty thousand miles or more I reckon.' Father O'Malley basked in the praise of his car and agreed immediately to let the man work on it.

The priest gave the man his telephone number, instructing him not to do anything major unless he called first, and they walked out to Sam's car.

'Can you hang on a minute, sorry?' Jack said as they got in. 'I left somethin' in your car, Father, won't be a second.' He ran back into the garage and walked quickly up to the mechanic. 'Excuse me, I'd like you to do whatever work needs to be done on this car. Also put a set of tyres on it and anythin' else you feel's necessary.'

The man wiped his hands on a rag and grinned, 'Yeah, sure son, and how're you goin' to pay for all of that?'

'With this.' Jack pulled a roll of notes from his shirt pocket, watching the man's eyes widen in surprise. 'Do you want me to leave you a deposit now?

'Er … that won't be necessary, no.' The mechanic was chastened, 'It's the weekend and we don't usually work but if you're prepared to pay a bit of overtime I'll get a couple of the boys to start on her straight away. Probably won't be ready until tomorrow, though. We'll work into the night.'

'The cost's no problem. See ya then.' Jack returned to the others and jumped in the car.

'Did you find what you were looking for?' the priest asked

'Yep, everythin's OK. Sorry to hold ya up.'

They spent the evening that night after dinner, seated in the cane chairs on the presbytery verandah, where they enthralled Father O'Malley with tales of their trip after leaving Mt Margaret and filled in the gaps between the letters they had written. He interrupted often with many questions, particularly about Coober Pedy and opal mining. Pipe smoke swirling around his head he chuckled when they described the bar room brawl in Marree and he sat forward captivated as they relayed the events that led up to the cave-in and Bruno's rescue.

He was thrilled with the present Paddy had sent, savouring the whisky as they talked, and, when he opened the envelope after the boys passed on Paddy's message about 'the plate', he sat staring at the money it contained. He then asked a number of questions about his friend, particularly interested when Jack let it slip that he seemed to have more than a passing interest in Iris Smith and that he seemed to be less interested in 'the doins' than he had before.

They then told him about meeting the girls on the train and about the coincidence that they went to school with Iris's daughter.

'Harry thought she looked pretty good didn't ya, Harry?' Jack thought he'd have a little fun at Harry's expense but failed to anticipate the response.

'I didn't go all googly-eyed like you did over Naomi Wilson,' Harry shot back.

'Hmm, a girl you're keen on up at Coober Pedy, is there, Jack?'

'Not in Coober, Father,' Harry said. 'The police sergeant's daughter in Pt Augusta'

Jack turned bright red. 'We just happen to like shootin' that's all,' he snapped at Harry.

'Shooting indeed.' The priest raised his eyebrows. 'An unusual pursuit for a girl I must say. You told me you got a rifle for Christmas in one of your letters. I was a little worried about that.'

Jack, pleased to be presented with a diversion, described his rifle and the shooting he had done to keep the drovers supplied with fresh meat, glaring at Harry as he did so.

They talked about many things that night but said little about their claim and the gems they had dug from it, unconsciously guarding their activities, even from a close friend, like any other 'Cooberite' would do when it came to opal. Father O'Malley politely didn't question them on how much they had found or what it was worth, knowing from his experiences with the miners of the Goldfields that this was a taboo subject. He sensed that Jack and Harry, even after only such a short time, had absorbed the culture with its secrecy and respect for another man's business.

'Reynold is still with you then; that's marvellous. I knew he was a good lad and that you'd get along. It's good that you've included him, as not many young men would have, you know. It'll be many years before the gap between black and white is bridged, unfortunately,' he said sadly. 'It'll take a lot of effort by both sides to build the trust.'

'If it wasn't for Reynold and uncle Warri we'd have probably got lost somewhere out in the scrub. They made us feel a part of their family and taught us so much,' Harry commented.

'It was uncle Warri that saved Harry's life when he was lost in the desert and he also treated him with bush medicine to make him better. He taught me bushcraft and trackin' and how to shoot.' The priest couldn't help but notice the respect these two boys had for their aboriginal friends and it gladdened his heart to think there could be some hope for future generations to put aside the misunderstandings.

'That reminds me.' Father O'Malley lit his pipe. 'I heard that your uncle Warri's back in Warburton and as fit as ever after being in hospital for a while.'

'No doubt he 'learned' all those doctors everything they knew.' The two boys laughed at Jack's joke but the priest looked on, baffled by the comment.

They made a pot of tea for themselves and nibbled on Mrs Lacey's Anzac biscuits for a time then Father O'Malley poured a final nip of whisky into the tumbler 'A nightcap, lads, before I turn in. You must be getting tired as well.'

'I'm a little weary, Father.' Harry yawned

When the priest stood and placed the remainder of Paddy's present on the mantelpiece saying, 'you're an incorrigible rogue you are, but you've a heart of gold,' to his absent friend, the two boys gathered up the teapot, cups and plate to take to the kitchen.
'Father,' Jack said, 'we really want to thank you for believin' in us and for bein' such a good friend.'

'Aahh think nothing of it, lads, it does me good to see you in such good health. The life certainly seems to suit you. I hardly recognised you today at the station and I just hope that your parents forgive me for my deceit.'

'We got a present for you too, Father, but you'll have to wait till tomorrow for it.' Jack said.

'There's no need to be giving me anything now. It's a pleasure it is to be helping you.' The priest nonetheless was a little curious about what the boys could be giving him that would have to wait until tomorrow.

'I hope me old car's all right down there in that garage,' Father O'Malley said as they walked down the corridor to the kitchen. 'She's never been away from home before.'

Harry looked at Jack and they wondered if he suspected anything but then dismissed the thought.

'I was hoping she'd hold together for a while longer because I was planning to drive you two down to Perth and meet your parents and explain how I was involved in all of the goings on over the past months.' He looked at the boys. 'That is, if you want me to?'

'Gee, that'd be great. We've been a bit nervous about explaining things to them and you being with us would help a lot. We were gonna ask you to come with us on the train but thought you might be too busy. I want to get home for my birthday on Monday.

'Well, Jack, if the mechanic can keep the old girl going we'll do that. Have to wait and see. I hope he can fix her enough to drive to Perth, otherwise we will have to take the train.'

'I've got a feeling ...' Jack put the dirty cups in the sink and turned the tap on '... that she'll be as good as new when we pick her up tomorra.' The priest missed the wink he gave Harry.

Chapter Thirty Six

Father O'Malley was busy conducting mass on the Sunday morning and even though he invited the boys to go along to the service they declined and waited until he was well gone before they asked Mrs Lacey if they could use the telephone.

'Well, I don't know.' She hesitated to give permission, fiercely protecting Father O'Malley and his domain 'Where are you calling?'

Jack explained that they were going to pay for the repairs to the car and wanted to call the garage but not to tell Father O'Malley as it was a surprise. 'My goodness,' was all she said but she nodded approval and pointed to the telephone.

Jack spoke to the mechanic who told him that he had replaced the distributor and spark plugs, overhauled the carburettor and adjusted the timing. He said he'd also replaced the fan belt, put some new gaskets on the sump and gearbox, given the car a grease and oil change and put four new tyres on. 'It drives like a new car.' He seemed well pleased with the results of his work.

'Would it be OK to drive to Perth?'

'Drive around Australia if you wanted to.'

Jack asked that, if he and Harry walked to the workshop and paid for the repairs; would the man drive them back to the presbytery, as they wanted to surprise the priest. 'The work on his car is a present.'

'It's come to a few quid, son,' the man said.

Jack didn't comment on the cost. 'We'll be around in about half an hour. Will it be ready then?'

◆◆◆◆◆◆◆◆◆◆◆◆

Father O'Malley looked at his pocket watch and frowned. He had completed mass for the morning and was surprised that the boys were not in the presbytery when he returned. 'Have they been gone long? He asked his housekeeper when she told him they had gone off and would be back soon.

'Not long.' She was intent on avoiding saying too much.

'Where did they say they were going?'

'Going? … Oh, I'm not sure … they didn't really say. You see they …' Mrs Lacey sighed in relief when Harry burst into the room.

'Your car's back, Father,' he said breathlessly.

'Back? What do you mean by back, Harry?'

'In the shed. The man drove it round earlier.'

'I don't understand. It's a Sunday. They don't usually work on Sunday and what about the bill? Did he say anything about the bill?'

Harry shook his head, finding it difficult to keep a straight face. 'Dunno, but it's parked in the shed.'

He followed the priest out the door but held back, allowing him to reach the shed alone. Jack joined Harry and they sneaked closer, waiting outside the double doors. They heard Father O'Malley muttering to himself as he got into the car and pressed the starter. The motor sprang into instant life, no backfire, no smoke and no shuddering. Father O'Malley backed the vehicle from the shed a smile creasing his face when he saw the boys standing by the open doors. 'Now …*this* is what she *used* to be like, perfect.' They saw him pat the dashboard. 'Coming for a test spin, lads? Hop in. I've got to go round to the garage and fix up the bill. Very good of that fellow to deliver it … amazing.' He wore a puzzled expression.

'We've already been for a test spin, Father.'

'What do you mean, Jack?'

'In the car. We were with him when he brought it round.'

'I don't understand.' Father O'Malley left the motor ticking over and stepped from the vehicle. He then noticed the new tyres and his face went a shade of green. 'Oh my Lord. He was supposed to call me before he …'

Jack waved the receipt at him. 'It's all been taken care of, Father.' He reached out and put his arm around Harry's shoulder. 'Our way of sayin' thanks.' They handed him the receipt marked 'paid in full'.

◆ ◆ ◆ ◆ ◆ ◆ ◆ ◆ ◆ ◆ ◆

Naomi Wilson badgered her father. 'Can we go up and visit Ron Carter one of these days, dad?'

'What for?' He knew the answer but played a game with her. 'You wouldn't like Coober Pedy much, you know. Full of dust, wind, flies and snakes. Dirty opal miners too.' He watched her reaction.

'I don't care about the *miners,* dad,' she snapped, a tinge of disgust in her voice. 'I'd just like to find a couple of opals that's all. You know Mr Carter has invited us up to stay. Said we had an open invitation anytime we wanted to go.' She then pulled out the big guns. 'You know mum wants to go, don't you?'

'You been harassing your mother as well as me have you?'

'Dad!' She was exasperated.

'You haven't told me why you really want to go, Nomes.'

'Yes I have.' She pouted and stormed off from where he was edging the lawn, her blonde hair glinting in the sunlight.

Ned knew ever since the two boys had left on the train that his daughter had strong feelings for the dark-haired lad Jack Ferguson. He concurred with her choice, as the lad seemed to be a decent sort of bloke, quiet and in control … except around his daughter.

He felt that Naomi was far too young to be getting seriously involved with any boy but when he had mentioned this fact to Rosemary she had reminded him how old she had been when they started courting.

'That's different,' he had said defensively but his wife just looked at him. 'Yeah, well. I still think she's too young and we know nothin' about him,' he grunted.

'Ron seems to think that Jack and his friend are really good young lads. Says they work hard and are honest and dependable. They were the two that helped get that trapped miner out, what was his name? … Bruno, wasn't it?'

'Must say they're a cut above the other young blokes around here. Seem a lot maturer for their age. I suppose that's because of where they live. Got to be tough to last up in Coober,' he grudgingly admitted. 'How long did they say they were staying in Perth?'

'They didn't, but I suppose it's only for a holiday to see their parents, isn't it?'

'Maybe. Well … I'll consider it. Perhaps we could go up in a month or so when it gets a bit cooler. Got some holidays due so I'll think about it'

'Good,' his wife said. 'I'll call Ron tomorrow and let him know we'll take up his offer.'

Ned Wilson couldn't help but think how alike Naomi and her mother were. *Get any damn thing they want, those two,* he thought lovingly.

♦ ♦ ♦ ♦ ♦ ♦ ♦ ♦ ♦ ♦ ♦ ♦

They left Kalgoorlie on the morning of Jack's birthday, heading home to Perth. Mrs Lacey had packed a picnic lunch of cold roast chicken and salad in a hamper with a thermos of tea. 'See how you go then.' She farewelled them as they drove out of the yard, her plump arms folded over her matronly apron-clad bosom.

The car ran beautifully and Father O'Malley was in his element behind the wheel of his treasured old Chev, with some hundreds of miles ahead of the bonnet with its chrome emblem glinting in the sunshine. He had been overwhelmed at the generosity of Jack and Harry in repairing his car, knowing he could never have afforded to pay the bill himself, at least not in one lump. To feel the car beneath him, smooth as the day he'd bought her, was one of life's little pleasures he allowed himself. That and a small flutter on the horses now and then and, of course, a little drop of 'the doins' with his friend Paddy, but he felt that could be a rare treat now.
They had stopped to eat lunch beside the road under a clum
p of tall trees and Jack couldn't help but stroke the trunk of a large tuart. 'I just love big trees,' he said by way of explanation. 'No big trees like this in Coober Pedy, Father.'

Harry was content to sit and devour chicken legs; trees didn't interest him all that much. He was waiting to get home and tuck into some fish and chips though, and head off to Cottesloe. He also wondered if he'd get a swim at the beach because the autumn weather was getting quite cool, unlike Coober where it was certainly cold at night but the sun still packed a punch during the day.

Excitement, mixed with trepidation, settled on the boys the closer they got to Perth and when they passed through Northam and headed down the range toward the city, the sun low in the sky before them, the reality of being back silenced them. Father O'Malley sensed their anxiety and understood, to a degree, what they must be feeling.

I hope this all goes well. He thought. He was nervous himself about meeting the parents and concerned that the boys might find their reception not as easy as he knew they were expecting, or at least hoping, it would be.

♦ ♦ ♦ ♦ ♦ ♦ ♦ ♦ ♦ ♦ ♦

Jean and Claude arrived at the Fergusons just as the sun was setting. It had taken Jean a while to convince her husband about having a get-together but he eventually concurred, agreeing that they had to get on with their lives and that there was no harm in celebrating the boys' birthdays in their absence.

The night was unusually warm for the time of year with a promise of rain in the air. Jack Ferguson had set wood in the barbecue and had run a power lead out to a tree where he had hung a light to shine on the area. He figured he would keep the fire stoked up as the night got cooler, to save them all having to go inside, and the kids could eat their tea on the newly enclosed verandah. Alice had a table set up especially for them with cordial, home-made sausage rolls and cheerios.

'Want a beer, Claude?' Jack took a bottle from the ice and snapped the top off, pouring a tall glass for his friend. 'What would you like, Jean?'

'Tea's fine with me for now but I might have a brandy and ginger ale in a bit. I'll give Alice a hand first.' She went into the house, leaving the two men to discuss work, football and the Korean war situation that was headlining the newspapers, anything but their missing sons.

'Been off buying cattle lately, Jack?'

'No interstate trips for a while. Been up north a few times. The last big trip was over to Marree in South Australia. Big mob of cattle, that one.'

The two women joined them 'What are you blokes telling lies about now?' Alice jibed. 'They usually tell some tall stories when we're not here to water them down, Jean, eh?'

'No lies, Alice, honest.' Claude held up two hands in mock surrender, then arranged two chairs for the women. 'Jack was just mentioning his trip across to Marree buying cattle.'

'That's somewhere near Coober Pedy isn't it?' Jean asked

'Yeah, not too far away.'

'I'd like to see that country one of these days, dear.'

'Not much to see, Alice. It's flat, dry, red sand, hot and as rough as guts. We got to Marree and pulled up in front of the pub to find the front windows boarded up. Seems there was brawl in the bar the night before we got there between the drovers and some ringers. Tom Cooper, the bloke who brought the mob down we inspected, was involved and there was a big hole in the ceiling where the publican had fired a shotgun to stop the fight.'

'How do people live like that?' Jean said. 'They sound like animals.'

'No, not really,' Jack replied. 'Just tough.'

'Remember last time we were here for a barbecue we talked about opals and Coober Pedy and ....' Jean stopped in mid sentence. 'Oh I am sorry,' she said softly.

'Hey, that's all right, Jean,' Jack said, 'There's no sense in beating around the bush, too frightened to talk about anything in case it upsets us. After all, we're here tonight to celebrate Jack and Harry's birthdays and by God we're gonna do it.' He stood up. 'It's high time we put all the rot aside. I miss Jack like hell and worry about him but he made the choice and from the letters we get they both seem to be enjoying life and getting on with things. Not that I agree with it and I'd like to know exactly where they are right now but that's how it is.' He stopped to take a breath. It was a long speech for Jack and he noticed that the other three were staring at him in amazement. 'Well.' he went on, 'I mean it.' He topped up his beer glass and refilled Claude's. 'Get a sherry or something for you and Jean, Alice, so we can all drink to Jack and Harry's health ...wherever they may be.'

As Alice returned from the kitchen with a bottle of cream sherry and two crystal glasses, they all wondered who could be arriving when headlights flashed down the driveway onto the garage and they heard a car pull up in front of the wooden picket gates.

♦ ♦ ♦ ♦ ♦ ♦ ♦ ♦ ♦ ♦ ♦

Joe rubbed his watery eyes and leafed through the newspaper, gasping when he saw the headline. 'Opal sells for record sum.' He continued to read, envy boiling in him as the article went on to state that the large opal discovered by the rescued miner, Bruno Boccelli in Coober Pedy, had been sold for an undisclosed figure, said to be the highest ever paid for a single gemstone.

He walked to the lounge where Cyril was sleeping, empty beer bottles and an overflowing ashtray beside him on the floor. He poked him hard in the ribs. 'Cyril … wake up ya lazy slob.'

'What?' Cyril opened his eyes and coughed. 'What's up?' He rolled over and reached for his tobacco.

'That opal the wog found has been sold for a fortune,' Joe said bitterly, waving the newspaper in Cyril's face. 'I think it's time we looked to heading back up to Coober Pedy and exacting a bit of revenge on that mongrel and those bloody smart-arse kids.'

'Why don't you let it rest, Joe, I think it's a mistake to go back there.'

'Mistake! What do ya mean, mistake?' he snarled. 'I reckon I deserve some of that opal money after what that bloke did. If he hadn't of run us off we could have found some opal ourselves and made a quid, so it's his fault that we didn't.'

'Suppose you're right.' Cyril yawned. 'When do you want to go?'

'We'll get Andy over and work out a plan. I reckon we'll leave it a week or two and let this Bruno bloke settle in, then we'll strike'

'What sorta plan, Joe?'

'How the hell do I know? We haven't worked it out yet! You certainly are a dumb bugger aren't ya?'

'We'll need another car, Joe. The old truck's had it and I don't think it'll make it up there; besides, people will recognise it.'

'Perhaps yer not as dumb as ya make out. Shouldn't be a problem gettin' a car, Cyril, Andy's pretty good at that.' He laughed sarcastically.

'Yeah.' Cyril's face lit up 'Wonder if he could pinch one of those new Studebakers; they're pretty flash?'

'No, we need something that doesn't stand out. Once we've got our hands on some of that lovely cash you can buy whatever you like, mate.'

'Yeah,' Cyril said again.

'Let's get Andy over then and we'll work it all out. We can take our time, as there's no need to rush because that wog'll never be able to spend all that cash in a hurry so there'll be plenty left for us. We need to get hold of a coupla guns too. I wanna have somethin' a bit more persuasive than a tyre lever this time.'

◆ ◆ ◆ ◆ ◆ ◆ ◆ ◆ ◆ ◆ ◆ ◆

Bruno Boccelli arrived back in Coober Pedy richer than he had ever dreamed he would be, richer in fact than most people in the fields. When he was discharged from hospital he had organised for Ron Carter to have the gemstone escorted down to Adelaide and he sold it to the highest bidder. He was disappointed that it went to an overseas buyer, as he would have liked to see it remain in Australia, but nobody could match the price.

His purpose for going back to Coober was to tidy things up there and sell the mine. There had been a lot of interest shown now that there was a distinct possibility that there was more high quality opal still buried there. He knew he would never go underground again so selling was the sensible option. He had no memory of what had happened after he found the stone early that fateful morning before the drive collapsed. It seemed his mind had blanketed out a section of his life between finding the stone and a week or so before he was released from hospital. It was his intention to sell his claim, farewell the few friends he had, say hello to the boys and give them his Land Rover, as he heard they had been minding his claim while he was away. He then planned to leave the fields forever.

It was a surprise to him when Ron Carter said that Jack and Harry had returned to Perth. The policeman explained about how they had ended up in Coober Pedy, that Paddy O'Brien was taking care of things for them and sharing the work of looking after the claims with Reynold and that the boys had returned home to square things off with their parents.

'You're a lucky man, Bruno,' Carter said. 'Lucky to have found that gemstone and sold it for a fortune and lucky that you're alive to tell the tale.'

'I musta thank alla those men who digga me out.'

'You need to thank the boys more than anyone, Bruno. If it weren't for them you'd be dead, mate.'

'Howsa that?' He looked puzzled.

'They were the first to discover the cave-in, Bruno. Harry took off and raised the alarm and got the rescuers out to you. Jack and young Reynold headed back down the shaft despite the danger and started to dig for you with their bare hands until help arrived. Didn't you know that?'

Tears welled up in the Italian's eyes. 'Those boys they doa that for me?'

'Yes, mate, they did. By the way, Bruno, I still have a dilly bag here with some Opals in it. I found it in your shed and brought it with me for safekeeping.'

The Italian spread the stones on the sergeant's desk and, selecting the largest one from the pile, he handed it to him 'To saya thanks.'

'I can't accept it, Bruno.'

'Yesa you can. You helpa me out, you take care of the opla for Bruno, its just a littla thank you.'

'I appreciate the thought, Bruno, but I can't accept a gift like that. What I did was in the line of duty and it'd be against all the rules. You could think about maybe giving a couple to the lads,' he suggested. 'They deserve it more than anyone.'

'Yes, I thinka something, yes. Do you know how I get inna touch with them?'

'I don't, but you can check with Paddy O'Brien. He should know where they are in Perth. I'll run you out now and introduce you to him.'

'You mind if you bringa him here, Ron? I notta want to look onna da mine ever again.'

Chapter Thirty Seven

The three people in the black Chevrolet were as nervous as each other when they pulled into the Ferguson driveway at Ashmorton. The closer they had got to Jack's street the more concerned Jack and Harry had become about what sort of reaction they would receive from their parents and the anxiety was so infectious that Father O'Malley also had sweaty palms. Harry had insisted that they go to Jack's place first. That way, he figured, the brunt of the reaction would be over by the time they contacted his parents but his plan backfired when they saw Claude Turner's car parked on the roadway in front of the Ferguson house.

Jack sucked in a sharp breath. 'That's dad. It's me dad,' he whispered as a figure walked around the side of the house towards them to investigate the visitors, his hand to his eyes, shielding them from the glare of the headlights.

'Just settle down, lads. Everything will be fine.' The priest spoke with a confidence he didn't feel, 'let's work to the plan, you stay here for a bit.'

The headlights went out, leaving Jack Ferguson temporarily blinded as his eyes adjusted to the sudden blackness. He saw a dark figure step from the driver's side and come to meet him and wondered who the stranger was, unable to recognise either what appeared to be an older model saloon or the tall stooped figure walking towards him. 'Hello,' Jack called, 'Can I help you?'

'Mr Ferguson?' A voice asked from the darkness.

'That's right, who are you?' His eyes began to focus and he recognised the clerical garb of a catholic priest as the man opened the gates to enter his front yard. 'What do you want?' Jack's tone became challenging and slightly angry at the gall of this man to walk onto his property uninvited.

'Do you mind if I come in, Mr Ferguson? I'm sorry to turn up unannounced but I have some news about your son, Jack. Good news, sir, I assure you, so please don't be alarmed.' He saw Ferguson flinch.

'Jack? You've got news about Jack? You better come in then.' Ferguson peered into the darkness past the priest to the car. 'Have you got someone with you, er … Father?' Jack was unaccustomed to talking to priests

'They'll be fine,' the priest said quickly. 'I'll only take a minute or so of your time.' He walked forward into the yard in case Jack decided to go closer to the car and held out his hand to introduce himself. 'Timothy O'Malley, Mr Ferguson.'

'Call me Jack. Come on in then, we've got Claude and Jean Turner here so they'll be interested in any news you have. You see their son disappeared with our boy.'

'I know, I've got news of Harry also.' He saw Jack Ferguson throw him a sharp puzzled look.

The two boys were trembling as they watched the shadowy scene played out through the windscreen but unable to hear the conversation clearly. They had shrunk down into the seats when they thought that Jack's father was going to come to the car and watched with trepidation as Father O'Malley disappeared from view with him around the corner of the house.

'Alice, this is Father O' Shan … er … sorry, O' …' Jack had forgotten the priest's name.

'Timothy O'Malley.' The priest rescued Jack and he was beginning to get control of his fear. 'Nice to meet you, Mrs Ferguson.' He turned to Claude and Jean 'You must be Harry's parents, how do you do?' He nodded to Jean and shook hands with Claude who looked at him suspiciously.

Alice stared at the priest blankly. 'How do you know Jean and Claude?'

'I don't, Mrs Ferguson, but I know Harry. I know Jack also.'

Alice looked as if she was about to collapse and Jean gasped, her hand to her mouth. The two men stood side by side, staring at the priest silently. 'Have we met somewhere before? Jack said.'

'No, I don't believe so.' The priest replied thoughtfully.

'You do look sorta familiar, Father.' Claude looked at him closely 'You haven't said where you're from.'

'I'm the parish priest in Kalgoorlie, been there a number of years now.'

'My God, that's it!' Claude became animated. 'Jack, remember? The priest, the old broken down Chevy we push-started and …'

'Forget the car, Claude.' Alice came to life. 'What's the news you have, Father, about our boys?'

'Yes, you say you know Harry?' Jean joined in.

The priest was assailed with questions from the four of them speaking at once so he held up his hands to quieten them. 'I think you better sit down and I'll explain some things to you. Rest assured though they are in good health …and safe.' He anticipated the next question.

'So, where in Kalgoorlie are they?' Claude pressed.

'Let the good Father explain.' Jean put her hand on Claude's arm. 'Sit down and listen. Please tell us about our boys, Father.'

Father O'Malley explained as briefly as he could that Jack and Harry had been brought to his home by Paddy O'Brien but before he could explain further Alice broke in, 'Who's Paddy O'Brien?'

'I know you're anxious to know everything at once but please …' He paused, waiting for their full attention. 'Let me explain briefly first, then you can ask questions. The lads wanted me to clarify some things to you as they are very concerned about your reaction to what they did by running away from home.'

He waited until he thought they would be quiet enough for him to continue without major interruption, then went on to give them a thumbnail sketch of the events, watching their eyes become wider and wider and mouths slack open with shock. He told them briefly that the boys had gone from Kalgoorlie, joined a droving team in the Territory and travelled down into South Australia ending up in Coober Pedy where they had been for some months.

'You mean they're not in Kalgoorlie after all?'

'No, Alice, I'm afraid they're not. In fact they were only there for a day.'

'But the letters we received were all postmarked Kalgoorlie. How could …' She shook her head in a daze, 'I don't understand.'

'There's an explanation for that.' Father O'Malley felt guilty but decided he would explain that at a later time. 'The major thing is that both the lads love you very much. They are wonderful young men and would have let you know their whereabouts long before now except they believed they were still wanted by the police until quite recently. The reason I'm here is to break the ice as they were afraid you would be angry with them. I understand if you are but for their sakes please consider what they've been through before you react to them.

Alice burst into tears and sobbed. 'I don't care what Jack's done, I just want to hold him. I'm not angry, just worried.'

'Me too.' Jean also started to cry putting her arms around Alice. 'I couldn't care less where they've been or what they've done, I just want to see my son again.'

The priest looked at the two fathers standing together beside the barbecue. 'You, Jack? Claude? How do you both feel?'

'I could have strangled the little buggers, oh … sorry, Father, when they just up and left but that's well past. I'm just glad to know they're safe. There'll be no recriminations. Tell them they can come home and that we love 'em.' Jack Ferguson's voice was thick with emotion.

'I feel the same as Jack,' Claude said. 'We searched high and low for them but not to punish them, just to let them know they could come home and that they'd been proved innocent of any crime.'

Alice sniffed, gaining control of her tears. 'So they're in Coober Pedy, I can't believe it. We were just talking about that area tonight.'

'Well no,' Father O'Malley said, 'they're not in Coober Pedy at the moment.'

'They're not?' Jack Ferguson was exasperated. 'Where the hell are they then?'

'Sitting in my car out the front of your house.'

There was stunned silence for some seconds until the news registered and then with shrieks and yells, the four grown adults ran like little children, scrambling over each other, to greet their sons.

◆◆◆◆◆◆◆◆◆◆◆◆

Father O'Malley was relegated to an ignored onlooker, standing off to one side as the families were reunited. It was mayhem, tears, laughter, hugs and rowdy conversation. Jack's five brothers and sisters and Harry's siblings ran wild, shouting and tugging at their brothers for attention while the adults plied them with questions. Jack and Harry were overwhelmed with the attention and found it impossible to answer any of the questions completely as, before they could compose a reply, another question was fired at them, so anxious were their families to get all the information immediately.

After the initial uproar the younger children began to lose interest and drift off one by one until only Jack's brother, Tim remained with the adults, a look of sheer adulation on his face. Eventually, the initial shock and reaction waned and quietness fell on the group of seven as Father O'Malley watched, feeling somewhat of an intruder on this very personal moment in the families' lives.

The priest moved closer to the group still all standing around the barbecue and coughed softly to gain attention. 'Excuse me, I'm sorry to intrude but I best be heading off now and leave you all to catch up on the past few months. I'm sure you've got a lot to talk about.'

'Oh, I am sorry, Father,' Alice said, her arm around her son's shoulders. 'We are being rude. Please stay for a while and join us. I'm sure the boys are hungry and you must be too. Jack ...' She turned to her husband. 'Fire the barbecue up so we can get the food cooking.'

'Yes, you will stay won't you, Father?' Jean pressed 'I'm sure the boys would like you too.'

'I don't know how we can ever thank you.' Jack senior walked forward and drew the priest into the group 'We owe you a lot for bringing our sons back.'

'I didn't do much more than drive the car, the lads brought themselves back.' Father O'Malley smiled.

'I think without you goin' in first to break the news, Father, we woulda bolted,' Jack said with a grin. 'Don't you, Harry?'

'It was pretty scary, mate, yes. Come on Father, stay for a bit.'

'Its done my heart good to see you all so happy and I'd love to stay but you need time together alone and I have to get to where I'm staying otherwise they'll think I got lost …or my car broke down. He turned to the boys. 'Not much chance of that now though thanks to you two.'

Jack looked at his son. 'How's that, Jack? You do some work on it, you and Harry?'

'Its nothin', dad. The old Chevy ran like a clock didn't she, Father?'

'It did indeed, Jack. Well, I'll be off then, lads.' He turned to the parents. 'Nice to have met you and I'll have that barbecue again some other day perhaps.'

The two sets of parents watched as their sons went to the priest and couldn't fail to notice the friendly intimacy they shared as they shook hands warmly in farewell. 'You two have a great time now,' the priest said. 'You have my telephone number so call and tell me what your plans are.'

'Plans?' Claude asked. 'They're home now where they belong and the only plans will be to settle down and get back to school.' He moved closer to his son. 'Finish out that Leaving Certificate, eh, son?' He punched Harry affectionately on the arm, missing the alarmed reaction on Harry's face that Father O'Malley noticed.

They all walked the priest to his car where the boys retrieved their blueys from the boot and taking their hats from the back seat placed them on their heads. Alice couldn't help but think how grown up they appeared with the hats, dungarees and riding boots as they slung the packs over their shoulders, watching the priest back from the driveway.

'You're right, Claude,' Jack said as he watched the Chev drive off 'That's the same darned car we push started in Kalgoorlie all right.'

◆ ◆ ◆ ◆ ◆ ◆ ◆ ◆ ◆ ◆ ◆

Jack woke well before sun up and after lying in bed for some minutes, couldn't settle, so got up, dressed quickly, stoked the stove and had the kettle almost boiling when his father appeared wearing striped pyjamas and brown slippers.

'What are you doing up so early son? You're making a racket out here, wake the whole family you will.'

'Sorry, dad. I'm normally up about this time at home.' He realised the slip immediately.

'Home, eh? This is 'home', mate.' His father yawned and looked at the clock. 'Good heavens it's still the middle of the night but it's so darn good to see you, Jack. You had us so worried.'

'Like a cuppa, dad?' Jack refused to be drawn in the 'home' issue.

'May as well, seeing I'm up.' He sat at the laminex kitchen table opposite his son and couldn't help noticing how well developed his son had become, muscles rippling under the tanned skin of his bare arms.

'Tell me, Jack, I know why you blokes bolted but what made you decide to go to Coober Pedy of all places?'

'We overheard you talking about the 'fire in the stone' the night the police came round and figured we'd go out there and make our fortune.'

'Make a fortune, eh?' His father grinned and took a sip from the cup. 'More people go broke out there than find anything worthwhile. Bet you slogged away and found nothing of any real value.'

Jack didn't respond and his father took it for agreement. 'How did you get there? The priest told us you joined a droving team in the territory, which is bloody amazing. Did you travel in the wagon or what?'

'No, dad, we leaned to ride. Got a horse now too. Big bay gelding named Brehardie. Uncle Warri, he's our aboriginal mate that taught me to ride, gave him to me. Harry's got a colt too, named Brumby, and we've got a packhorse, Dolly, as well.' Jack said conversationally.

His father looked at him in amazement unable to believe what he was hearing. 'Really? That's incredible, and the priest said you went down to South Australia with some droving team, that right?'

'Yes, dad, that's right. Joined Tom Cooper's team in the territory and drove with them all the way to Marree.'

Jack's father almost choked on his tea. 'Tom Cooper, the drover? Big Tom Cooper, you're kidding?'

'No, you know him, dad?

'Ahh, sort of. I went over to Marree to inspect a mob of cattle just after Christmas. Met him and the camp cook. Can't remember his name. Funny bloke … wore a bow tie.'

'Toffy,' Jack said.

His father turned pale, realising that his son was not making up any stories as he spoke in a matter of fact manner and obviously knew these men. 'Bill, the bloke from Adelaide office and I went up there and stayed the night in the Marree pub. Pretty rough joint that. Had the front window boarded up as it had been smashed the night before in some wild brawl.'

Jack laughed and refilled his cup from the teapot. 'Some fight that, dad. You shoulda seen Tom Cooper, he took on the whole bar. Did you see the hole in the ceiling? Bert the publican blasted it with a shotgun to stop the fight. Great night!' he chuckled.

'You ... you were there?' His father was incredulous. 'They took you to the pub in Marree? Good God! What sort of blokes would take two kids to a rough joint like that?'

'Yeah, we were there. There's always a celebration at the end of a drove.' Jack couldn't understand why his father seemed so upset and angry.

◆◆◆◆◆◆◆◆◆◆◆◆

Harry was also up well before anyone else in the Turner household. He boiled the kettle, made tea and cooked toast that he took outside onto the back verandah. It was chilly, but not as cold as an autumn desert morning and he was still in shirtsleeves when his mother came out, dressed in slacks and a thick woollen cardigan.

'What on earth are you doing out here, Harry? Come inside before you catch a death of cold.' His mother fussed over him.

'I'm all right, mum. Used to this weather and it's not all that cold anyhow.'

'At least put a jumper on.' She shivered. 'Why are you up so early, I heard you moving around an hour ago?'

'This isn't early, mum, normally started shovelling by now. Got to before the sun gets too hot, then about lunchtime we go underground where it's cooler and work down there for the afternoon.'

'Goodness me, it all sounds so dangerous, is it?'

'Can be, I suppose.' He didn't say anything about the cave-in 'It's safe enough if you're careful.'

'Well, it's certainly made you a lot fitter. You must have grown a couple of inches in a few months and you've filled out too. At least it's been an experience you can talk about in years to come,' she said with a smile '… the time you spent months out in the wilds of the outback.'

Harry didn't know how to respond and was even more stunned when she added, 'You will be able to write a good composition for your English class about your time out there.'

'English class? What? … You mean at school?'

'Well, of course, dear. Your teacher asks about you often and you will want to finish your education. You're smart, Harry, and you will soon catch up on the lost time.'

Going back to school was an option Harry had never contemplated. He and Jack in fact had never discussed it and the thought of being back in a classroom again disturbed him. 'I think I might go and see what Jack's up to a bit later, mum, what are your plans?'

'I have to run the children to school. I thought you might like to come with me and see the headmaster. Haven't you seen enough of Jack for a while?'

'No, mum. We're good mates and I'd like to have a week or so to just catch me breath before I go to see any headmaster,' Harry said in an attempt to defer the issue.

'Well, all right. I suppose you do need to rest up, you poor dear, living such a rugged life all these months but I don't think it's a good idea for you to spend too much time with Jack, dear. He's not a very good influence on you, causing you to run off like that.'

'Jack didn't make me do it, mum, we decided it together.'

'Whatever you say, Harry, but you need to have an education as you won't get anywhere in life without it.'

◆◆◆◆◆◆◆◆◆◆◆◆

Jack spoke to his wife quietly in the bedroom after sharing the early morning cuppa with his son and was still disturbed by what Jack had told him about Tom Cooper and the bar brawl. He wondered what other situations his son had been in while he was away, with no discipline and able to run wild with a bunch of uncouth bushmen. 'The sooner young Jack gets settled down the better, Alice. I don't think we'll be able to talk him into going back to school as I think it would only put him off being here. He's changed you know.'

'How do you mean, Jack?'

'I don't know exactly but he seems a lot more mature and has obviously been exposed to a lot of things other kids of his age aren't. He's got self-assurance about him, that's good in one way but could cause him to be a bit wayward.'

'What do you suggest then, Jack, if he doesn't go back to school?'

'Well, it seems he can ride a horse. Owns one apparently, that some old aboriginal gave him.' Jack shook his head in wonder 'He was also on a cattle drive so obviously knows a bit about stock, I suppose, so I thought I might have a talk with the boss at Elders. I'm sure I could get him into a job at the saleyards. It'd be a start anyhow.'

'That sounds like a good idea but don't push him too quickly, dear; let him get used to being at home first.'

'I'm afraid if we don't get him involved in something pretty quickly he won't get used to being home at all.'

A knock at the bedroom door interrupted their conversation. 'Come in,' Jack called and their son, carrying a bottle wrapped in brown paper, entered and sat on the edge of the bed.

'Dad, I got this present for you. Sorry it's only in a paper bag but Paddy says it's the best and I know you like a drop of whisky now and then.'

His father was speechless for a moment. 'How did you buy whisky, Jack, you're too young to go into a pub?' He then remembered Marree and the brawl.

'Father O'Malley bought if for me. Got one for Harry to give to his dad as well. Paddy calls it 'the doins'. Hope you like it.'

'The *priest* bought it?'

'Yeah, but we gave him the money.'

'I see.' Jack didn't know what else to say until Alice prompted him. 'Oh yes, thanks, son … very good.'

'Got somethin' for you too, mum.' Jack reached into a pocket and brought out a small cloth-wrapped item that he handed to his mother.

'Whatever is this, Jack? You shouldn't have spent all your money on presents for us' She began to unwrap the cloth. 'After all, that whisky must have cost you enough to ...' Her mouth gaped open as the opal fell onto the bed cover and glowed with rainbow colours in the overhead lamplight.

'Take it out into the sunlight later, mum,' Jack said, 'then you can *really* see it flash. Do ya like it?'

'Oh, darling.' The opal transfixed her. 'It's ... It's beautiful. It must have cost you a small fortune. Jack you shouldn't have.'

'Didn't cost me anythin',' Jack said proudly. 'Oh! I guess a bit of sweat.' His mother and father both looked at him with astonished expressions. 'You see I found it, mum ... in our mine.'

'*Your* mine?' Jack's father gasped. 'What do you mean *your* mine?'

'Me and Harry. We own a mine at the nine-mile in Coober Pedy, dad. Ishmo, he's the Afghan camel driver that took us over from Marree, had this claim and we bought it from him for two hundred quid.' Jack was unaware of the stunned looks on his parents' faces as he fondled the opal.

'You bought a mine for two hundred quid? Where the hell did you get two hundred quid?'

'Sold some of the opal we found, dad.'

'You just said some Afghan, this er ... Ishmo, is that right?' Jack Nodded. 'Took you from Marree to Coober Pedy with a camel train, when was that?'

'The day after the cattle drive ended.'

Jack's father couldn't speak at all. He took the stone from his wife, examined it closely, then, handing it back to her without a word, he patted Jack on the shoulder and walked from the room.

As he closed the door his memory flashed a picture across his mind of a camel train silhouetted against a late afternoon sky and three horsemen trailing a pack animal as he and Bill Martin drove into Marree.

Chapter Thirty Eight

'Good, eh, Jack? Harry spoke through battered flake and chips he had just stuffed into his mouth.

'Better than I remembered, mate.'

Sitting beside the creek at their old favourite spot in the park they had the newspaper-wrapped meal between them.

'Blimey I'm full, Harry. Can't eat another thing.' Jack up-ended a coke bottle to wash the salty fish away then lay back on the grass, staring at the sky.

'How's your mum and dad now that yer home?'

'OK, I guess.' Harry didn't sound convincing. 'They act a bit strange though. I mean it's good to be here and all, but they treat me like I'm a little kid.' Harry drained his coke and layed beside Jack on the grass.

'How do you mean, Harry?'

'Oh, just little stuff … you know, 'don't forget to clean your teeth son,' or 'make sure you wash your hands as you've been pattin' the dog.' Mum and dad want me to go back to school too.'

'They what?' Jack sat up. 'School, ya must be jokin.' Glad my mum hasn't said that to me. What are ya gonna do?'

'Dunno. Mum insists that I go to see the headmaster. She got an appointment for tomorrow so I suppose I'll have to go along. Don't wanna go to school but.'

'Me neither. Dad says he wants to talk to me tonight about me future so I hope he doesn't suggest school. After all we got a mine to run.'

'Do you think we'll ever get back there, Jack? To Coober.'

He didn't answer and they were quiet for a time watching the brown water flow sluggishly past their feet, ducks paddling in wary circles just out of reach, hoping for a tossed crumb. They could hear traffic on the streets and watched two council workers weeding garden beds while another stabbed loose paper and lolly wrappings with a pointed stick like some hunter gathering food with a spear then tucking his catch into a big green bag slung over his shoulder. A man with a mower was noisily cutting grass and red and green parrots called 'twenty eights' explored branches above them for seeds but their foraging sounds were lost in the noise of passing cars. Although the sun was shining and the day warm, a haze in the sky gave it a grey appearance rather than the vibrant blue they had become accustomed to.

Jack looked around him. 'This place doesn't seem as big as I thought it was, Harry. I never remembered seein' the cars or the buildings so close did you?'

'I thought the creek was bigger than this. It's pretty tame compared to some of the waterholes we camped on and the rivers we seen out back. Do you think we should try for some yabbies later?'

'Maybe. You goin' out to the beach, Harry?'

'Not sure. I asked dad but he said it was too cool for beach weather. Said he'd take me when the weather warmed up. What say we go to the pictures tomorrow after I get this school appointment over with?' Jack agreed, saying that they might as well, as there was not much else to do.

♦ ♦ ♦ ♦ ♦ ♦ ♦ ♦ ♦ ♦ ♦

The family finished tea and Jack's brothers and sisters were plying him with questions about his adventures and what it was like in Coober Pedy, as they had done most nights since he had arrived back. Tim was especially interested in the droving but when Jack began to describe the mob and the drovers in detail his father stood up. 'That's enough about your time away, Jack. Go and do your homework, Tim, I need to have a discussion with your brother.' He nodded at Alice who hustled the younger children from the table and went out to the kitchen.

'What are your plans then, son?' He nervously tapped fingers on the tabletop.

'Probably go and see a movie tomorrow with Harry after he's finished down at the school. He's got an appointment with the headmaster.'

'I didn't mean just tomorrow, Jack, but it's good that Harry's going to finish his education.'

'I didn't say he was goin' to go back to school, just seein' the headmaster 'cause his mother made the appointment.'

His father scowled 'You should be going back to school too, Jack, but I suppose you're old enough to leave and I don't see much point in it, but you have to plan a future.' Jack went to speak but his father held up a hand. 'Wait till I finish, son I've got some good news for you.'

'Good news? What, dad?'

'You start next Monday at Elders. You have à job, mate, in the stockyards.' He saw concern crease Jack's expression. 'Don't worry, Jack, I know you're a bit nervous about working but they won't expect a lot until you find your feet. The money's not bad either, as you should start on almost a quid a week. You'll have to pay a bit of board to mum, say five bob a week but you'll be able to put some away and make a future for yourself.'

'But, dad.' Jack shifted uneasily on the vinyl chair. 'I told you, Harry and me, we got a mine back in Coober Pedy.'

'Yeah, so you mentioned but that's a mug's game, Jack. Hot, dirty and a huge gamble. You blokes had a bit of beginner's luck that's all. Don't expect it to last.' He shook his head knowingly. 'Anyway, those blokes out there are a rough lot and you don't need to get mixed up with that kind.'

'They're tough, sure, but not rough, dad and they've become good friends and …'

'Don't argue, Jack! Your mother and I have discussed it and we know what's best for you. Elders it is. You can have a few days to relax and have some fun until you start working for a living.'

'But, dad, you don't understand, we …'

'Don't tell me I don't understand. It's you who don't understand. You've had your little adventure while your mother and I worried sick about you. Now I've been able to offer you the chance of a good solid job. A job, by the way, that a lot of young blokes your age would die to get. This 'whatshisname' … Paddy, he can look after it for you no doubt. Sounds like it's more his type of lifestyle than yours and the young black kid can help him out.'

'Reynold, his name's Reynold, dad.'

'Yeah, Reynold. Don't get me wrong son, I don't have a thing against aboriginals, Jack, come across a lot of them in the stock game, but you don't have to mix with them.'

Jack stared blankly at the table. His father took his silence for agreement and standing up, pushed the chair back. 'Well that's settled then. I'll tell your mother … she'll be pleased about it. Congratulations, Jack, you'll love it once you get started. Good bunch of blokes to work with.'

Jack was staggered and when his father left him he went out past the back verandah and onto the grassed area beside the barbecue where he sat to think. He unconsciously reached into his pocket and brought out the tobacco pouch and papers and expertly rolled a cigarette. He hadn't smoked in front of his parents since being home and hadn't told them that he'd been rolling smokes since half way out on the drove when Tom Cooper offered him his tobacco after Wandoo's accident. He sat looking at the sky, smoke drifting lazily about his head in the cool night air. *Why can't I see the stars?* He thought. *There are hardly any stars here.* He had never been aware before that the glow of the city lights dimmed their brilliance unlike the desert where, at night, the sky was a mantle of intense and vivid sparks.

♦♦♦♦♦♦♦♦♦♦♦

Mr Wallace, the school principal, was bald except for a few strands of greying brown hair he kept plastered with Brylcream so they wouldn't blow out of place. It was a joke amongst the students that his hair wouldn't budge in a cyclone as it was glued down. He had a perpetual nasal quality to his voice and rimless glasses that he constantly pushed with the tip of a forefinger to slide them back up his long nose.

'So, Turner, you want to come back to school do you?' Wallace shuffled with a file on the desk. Harry said nothing so he looked up. 'Well? Answer me, young man.'

Jean Turner frowned at Harry and replied for him. 'Of course he does, Mr Wallace. Harry knows he'll have to work hard to catch up on his lessons don't you, dear?'

Harry had objected strongly that morning about wearing his old school uniform to the meeting with the headmaster and was glad when his mother eventually agreed. 'Wear something decent though, Harry,' she had said. 'After all, it's important that you impress the man because we want him to see that you haven't changed and are still the same boy so he'll let you back into classes.' Sitting on the uncomfortable wooden chair in front of the principal's desk, Harry was pleased he had worn a long-sleeved check work shirt tucked into dungarees secured with a leather belt. He had made two concessions though; he hadn't worn his bush hat and he had polished his riding boots. His mother hadn't commented but clicked her tongue in disapproval at his mode of dress as they left for the appointment.

It had felt strange walking back into the schoolyard and Harry had been glad that lessons were in progress so none of the kids were outside to talk with him. As they had walked down the path toward the office past classrooms, many familiar smells had drifted to him. Smells like orange peel mixed with stale sandwich crusts in the bins, blackboard dust and unwashed, sweaty kids' bodies. It was strange, he thought at the time, how a smell could remind you of something, transport you to another place, another time. Now, seated at the headmaster's desk, Harry caught a whiff of the leather dressing he had used on his boots that morning and it immediately reminded him of his saddle and bridle and his mind placed him on Brumby galloping through the desert in hot pursuit of a runaway steer.

A nudge brought him back to reality. 'Harry, Mr Wallace asked you a question.'

'Er … sorry. What was that again?'

'Again, sir!' Wallace glared over his glasses. 'Let me tell you something, young man, it is a privilege to be allowed back here. A privilege you don't seem to appreciate and if it wasn't for your good results previously and ...' he smiled without warmth at Jean, '... your mother's wishes, I wouldn't be considering taking this unusual step. I had to convince the board to accept you after your mother spoke to me.'

Harry looked at the floor, wishing he could become invisible as Mr Wallace went on. 'Now, if you promise to be punctual, not discuss your misdemeanour with the other students and ...'

'What misdemeanour? We didn't steal no bike.'

'*Any* bike, Harry, not *no* bike and I was referring to you running away, not the bicycle incident. Another thing, you must promise not to take any revenge against young William Munse. He's a model student here and plans to go on to university. If you can work hard I dare say you could follow in young William's footsteps. Make your mother and father proud.'

'I wouldn't want to be like him, Mr Wallace, that's for sure,' Harry replied with disdain. 'He's nothin' but a liar.'

'I'll have none of that here, Turner. You will agree right this instant that there will be no more talk of this nature. There will be no more criticising a fellow student.'

Harry was angry 'You only think he's good because his dad's a solicitor and got lots of money. He's also on the school board isn't he?'

The headmaster turned purple and tugged at his collar as if his tie was choking him. Almost standing he glanced at Jean Turner, then regained control of his anger and sat back in the chair but when he spoke there was vehemence in his tone, 'Young man, I'll disregard that comment. It's obvious by your conduct that you've been exposed to ruffians wherever it is you've been and I will do all in my power ...' he looked at Jean with a forced, thin lipped smile '... to bring about a change in your manner that will be necessary if you are to make any future for yourself at this school ... and in life.'

'I don't know what's come over him, Mr Wallace. He's a good boy but I think older children influence him.' She refrained from saying 'like Jack Ferguson'.

'Quite understandable in the circumstances, Mrs Turner.' His voice had taken on a reconciliatory manner and he stood to indicate the interview had concluded. 'I'll be expecting you in class on Monday morning, Harry,' he said nasally.

The office door had hardly shut behind them when the smile his mother had farewelled Wallace with vanished and she turned angrily on her son. 'Harry, that was most embarrassing. What's come over you all of a sudden? You're not the same boy.'

'You seem to blame Jack for what's happened and everybody thinks that Billy Munse is a bloody hero because he's goin' on to university. Big deal! I can make more money now in a day than Billy Munse'll make in a year.' He unbuttoned his top pocket and pulled a roll of notes from his shirt and waved them in front of his mother. 'There's a few hundred quid here and Jack's got the same.'

Jean was taken aback at the size of the bankroll and could only say weakly, 'don't swear, Harry, it's not nice.'

They didn't go to the pictures as planned. When Jack telephoned Mrs Turner she said that Harry had gone to visit his aunty and wouldn't be back until later that evening. 'I'll tell him you called, Jack,' she said sweetly and hung up, but she never did.

He moped about the yard for the rest of the afternoon then went down to the creek but found it didn't feel the same without Harry so he returned home. Taking a shovel he began to dig up the vegetable patch behind the garage to fill in time. The tomatoes and other summer crops were withering so he pulled them out and turned the soil over quickly wishing, as he did so, that the dirt at Coober was as easy to sink a shovel into as this was.

Even though it was coolish it was sheltered behind the garage so he worked up a sweat and took his shirt off, hanging it on the fence, working only in his trousers. Raking the tilled soil into rows he stood back surveying his work when his mother walked around the corner. 'Good heavens, Jack, aren't you cold working bare chested.' She took in the well-developed muscles and was surprised by his mature physique.

'No, mum, it's good to be able to take the shirt off. Too darned hot where I live to take your shirt off.'

'You don't live *there*, Jack, *this* is your home.' She picked his shirt up from the fence. 'I'll pop this in the washing for you, son.'

'No, that's OK.' Jack reached out quickly for his shirt. 'My money's in there.'

Before he could retrieve the garment, his mother pulled out a wad of notes from the pocket that she gaped at unbelievingly. 'My God, Jack, where did you get this?'

'Told you, we sold a few stones, mum.'

'There must be …'

'About three hundred quid, mum.' He took the notes from his mother, unaware that she reached into the other pocket after feeling something in it.

'What's this then, Jack?' She held out a leather tobacco pouch. 'Who does this belong to?'

427

'It's mine, mum.'

'Don't tell me you smoke? Oh, Jack, what's happened to you?' There was anguish mingled with anger as she stood there, the tobacco pouch in her hand.

'Been rollin' smokes for months now, mum. All the blokes smoke on the drovin' team.'

'Children don't smoke, Jack. How could they let you smoke? What irresponsible people they must be.'

'They never thought of us as kids, mum. We did a man's work and were treated as such, me and Harry.'

'Well!' She turned on her heel, taking the pouch with her 'You are still a child here and I won't tolerate smoking. I'm glad your father doesn't know as he'd be ropable. And as for the money, you best give it to your father for safekeeping. You're too young to have that amount of cash on you.' Jack stood in shock as his mother stormed off toward the house.

♦♦♦♦♦♦♦♦♦♦♦

It was Saturday and Alice had just returned from shopping with her husband and they were packing the groceries away when there was a knock at the front door. 'Can you get that, son.' Jack called.

'He's down the back yard digging in the vegie patch, Jack, I'll get it.'

'No, you're busy there, Alice, I'll go.'

He opened the door to see a stranger, immaculately dressed in a cream suit with a blue shirt and wearing a Panama hat. The man was short but solidly built and was smiling broadly as he whipped the hat from his head with a flourish. 'Meesta Fergoosun?'

'Yes, I'm Jack Ferguson what can I do for you?'

'I'ma look for Jack. You musta be the father. He tella me you name Jack too.'

'Pardon me? You're looking for my son? Who are you?' Jack stood with his arms folded in front of the man.

'My name isa Bruno Boccelli.' The man held out his hand but Jack ignored it. 'What do you want my son for?' He noticed a hardening in the man's eyes that disturbed him a little.

'Isa Jack here, sir.' Bruno spoke politely but there was a hard edge to his voice. 'I would lika to discuss business with him.'

'I don't understand. Why would you want to discuss business with my son, he's only just turned sixteen? Still only a lad and if you want to do any discussing you'll do it with me.'

'Perhaps to you Jack isa boy but to me Jack isa man. You see Jack and his friend Harry they sava my life. Now can I talka to him plis? Is he at home or do I comma back?' There was a determination in the man's tone that made Jack aware that he would persist.

At that moment Alice came out the door behind her husband. 'What's the problem, Jack?'

'No problem. This bloke says he's a friend of Jack's and wants to talk business to him but he won't tell me what it's about.'

Alice smiled politely at the man and was about to agree with her husband when there was a shout behind her and Jack burst through the door and onto the verandah. Pushing past his parents, to their utter amazement, he launched himself at the stranger and threw his arms around him, 'Bruno! It's you. You're OK, mate.'

'Jack, itsa so good to see you, my friend. The police sergeant he tella me what you do inna mine, Jack. You anda Harry anda Rennol. You sava Bruno life.'

'Ahh it was nothin', mate.' Jack dismissed the praise and stood back, taking in the suit and hat. 'Hey, Bruno, you look sharp, mate. Bought some new clobber, eh?'

'You like?' The small man turned a complete circle. 'You think maybe I getta nice lady inna Napoli, eh, Jack?'

'Dunno, Bruno, you look like a bloody Mafia gangster.' The two laughed uproariously and Jack's parents stood open-mouthed at the obvious rapport between their young son and this swarthy Italian with the thick accent.

Alice was first to recover. 'Ah, Mr …?'

'Boccelli' Jack senior said.

'Mr Boccelli … please come inside. It seems you and Jack here know each other well.' She reached out and took her husband's arm, guiding him aside, allowing the Italian entrance to the front door.

As soon as they were inside the house Bruno asked Jack a question. 'Harry. You know where Harry is? I need talka you both. Very important.'

'I'll call him on the phone, Bruno, wait here.' Jack went to the telephone, leaving Bruno and the Ferguson's standing in the hallway, the Italian twirling his hat awkwardly in his fingers.

Alice ushered him into the lounge room and seated him on the lounge. 'What's this about saving your life?'

'Jack he notta say nothing?' When they shook their heads Bruno relayed to them what Ron Carter had told him about the boys initiating the rescue and how Reynold and Jack had dug frantically for him with bare hands forty feet underground while Harry drove off for help.

430

'Bruno!' Jack returned from the telephone. 'Don't scare them with that sorta talk. It wasn't all that dangerous,' he said, playing down their roles in the rescue. 'Harry's on his way. Couldn't believe it when I said you were here. How did ya find us?'

Bruno explained that Ron Carter brought Paddy O'Brien to the station but he didn't know where Jack lived in Perth so Iris Smith drove him round to Shaun Logan who contacted Father O'Malley to get the Ferguson address. Jack's father sat in an easy chair with Alice perched on the arm, her hand on her husband's shoulder, and both of them were bewildered by the conversation and the names of people they didn't know.

Some minutes later Harry came bursting through the door and there was a replay of the reunion that Jack had had with Bruno. When it had settled down Bruno became serious. 'Jack, Harry we musta talk business. Where we go?'

'You can talk here, Mr Boccelli.' Jack's father indicated the lounge chairs.

'Thank you so much but this issa business between us. We talka private.' He stood up. 'Where we go, Jack?'

'Down to the creek I suppose. Best place, eh, Harry?

'Yep. Nobody can hear us there.'

Bruno made a move toward the door and apologised for interrupting the family.

'We'll see you when you come back then, Mr Boccelli,' Alice said as they walked into the hallway.

'No, Meesus Fergoosun, I go on fromma this ... creek, only have little time inna Perth.'

Bruno farewelled Alice and Jack Ferguson leaving them standing on the front verandah watching the two boys and the well dressed Italian walk off down the street. 'We have a lot to find out about what they got up to while they were away, Alice.'

'I can't believe it, Jack. They rescued that man from a cave-in. Our Jack and young Harry, that's incredible.' Her voice caught and she began to cry softly, 'Oh, Jack, to think they could have all been killed. I'm so glad they're not out there now and are safe here at home.'

'Yes, Alice, I know what you mean.' He reached out and drew his wife to him. 'But I think they grew up pretty quickly out there.' He watched as the unlikely three figures disappeared down the street. 'Remember what I said a few nights ago, about a maturity that I couldn't put my finger on?'

'I do remember you saying that, Jack, and I'm so glad Harry's going back to school and our Jack's starting with Elders after the weekend. At least we'll know where he is and that he's safe. Not scrambling around some godforsaken mine in the middle of Australia risking his life with all those strange people.'

Chapter Thirty Nine

The boys led Bruno through the park gates and down to the creek. They didn't sit on the ground as usual, due to Bruno being dressed in a suit, so they chose one of the benches under a spreading Morton Bay fig tree. Even so, Bruno produced a handkerchief that he placed carefully on the wooden slats to protect his new clothes before sitting down, a gesture which made the boys grin to themselves, as this was so unlike the Bruno they were accustomed to: the Bruno with the collarless shirt and waistcoat with patched trousers that he kept hitched up with a piece of frayed rope, and a beanie he wore when he went underground, the Bruno with the dust-caked face and dirt beneath his fingernails.

'I need to thank you for a save my life. Sergeant Roy he tella me all about it. I no remember, justa know that I scare now of ...' their friend shuddered visibly, beads of perspiration dotting his forehead '... of have to go underground. I no canna do that no more, boys.'

They didn't know what to say but realised he trusted them enough to allow them to witness this open display of his fear. Jack reached out tentatively and touched his shoulder 'That's OK, Bruno, I think I understand.'

'It musta been real scary, Bruno.' Harry attempted to reassure the Italian.

'Yes, Harry, I a very scared, I not think I get out. I sit with this bigga opla with so mucha dust all round inna air like I no breath no more and the silence, not a sound. I think this issa Bruno grave and I looka at the opla, big ...' He held his hands up to indicate its size, ' anna I say, 'Bruno, you find what you looka for alla you life and now you die here with her.' I cry then fora longa time before the light go out anna darkness issa so black lika the tomb. I shake anna shake anna cry anna pray anna think of my family back inna Napoli. I know I notta see them no more and then fall asleep I think. No remember no more from then.' There were tears in his eyes when he turned to look at the boys and they saw the fear deep inside him and knew that he believed he had come back from the dead.

He coughed and retrieved the handkerchief from beneath him, unconcerned now about the dirty seat, and blew his nose noisily. He smiled self-consciously. 'You thinka Bruno loosa his mind no?' He took a deep breath before continuing. 'That'sa why I never go backa down. I make the decision to go home, seea my family anna maybe Bruno finda nice lady to settle down. I sella the opla, no want to be a remind of that day. She bringa big money, more thanna Bruno need, anna now I say thank you for save my life.'

'Did you sell your mine then, Bruno, if you're not gonna go back there?'

'Someone else they worka him now, Jack, yes. Not belonga to Bruno no more.'

The Italian took an envelope from an inside jacket pocket and handed it to them. 'For you both.'

What's this, Bruno?' Jack took the envelope and turned it over in his hands. 'You don't need to give us anything, Bruno, we didn't do much, mate.'

'What in envelope issa for you Jack anna you Harry, but plis, you open him when I longa gone, otherwise I cry again. Maybe you open when you go backa your house, OK? I also leave something inna Coober for Rennol with Ron Carter.' He stood up. 'Buon giorno my friends, Bruno he never forgeta you.' He hugged each of the boys in turn for a moment then quickly spun on his heel to hide his tears and walked away up the path towards the exit, leaving the two boys standing beside the bench staring after their friend, knowing they would never see him again.

♦♦♦♦♦♦♦♦♦♦♦♦

Sergeant Ron Carter put the telephone down in the Coober Pedy police station after talking with Rosemary Wilson. She had asked him if they could take up his offer to stay with him and spend a holiday fossicking around the mullock heaps. Rosemary told him that the two lads, Jack and Harry, had lunched with them on the way to Perth and seemed like nice young men. He had agreed they were good young blokes that had been accepted quickly by the locals for their hard work and honesty.

Rosemary told him that Naomi had taken a shine to young Jack and she had badgered them into going up to Coober. 'She vehemently denies, of course, it's in order to see Jack Ferguson again.'

'Not sure if she *will* see him, Rose,' He had told her. 'We haven't heard anything from the boys although it hasn't been that long since they left. I was talking with Iris Smith and she tends to think that they'll get absorbed back into Perth life pretty easily as they had only been gone from there for about six months. She reckons their parents will talk them into staying but Paddy O'Brien, he's their Irish mate from Kalgoorlie, says they'll be back … hard to say. Be a shame though if they don't.'

He had also told her that Bruno Boccelli, the miner whose life they had saved, had been through to finalise a few things and was disappointed when he discovered they had left and were back in

Western Australia. Ron told her Bruno had managed to get Jack's address in Perth by a roundabout way from the priest in Kalgoorlie. 'If the boys don't return to Coober, Rose, Naomi could probably track Jack down through the priest. Not sure exactly why Bruno wants to see them but I guess it'll be to thank them in some way. Strange sorta bloke but who isn't up here? Says he's going back to Italy and left a parcel for me to give to Reynold.'

'He's their mate, young aboriginal lad that helped with the rescue,' he explained when Rose asked who Reynold was.

◆ ◆ ◆ ◆ ◆ ◆ ◆ ◆ ◆ ◆ ◆ ◆

The telephone rang and Alice answered it. 'Have you seen Harry?' It was Jean Turner.

'Yes, Jean, he was here a while ago. Didn't he tell you he was coming over?'

'No. I asked him not to leave the house. I was down the shops and when I got back he was gone. Is he off somewhere with Jack?' She sounded agitated.

Yes, Jean, down at the creek. They went off with an Italian who turned up from Coober Pedy.'

'They what? Who … what Italian? Alice, this is not good enough.' Her voice had an angry edge 'I don't want Harry mixing with Jack and all these strange people. Claude's here and we're coming around. We need to settle this thing.' She hung up, leaving Alice staring dumbly at the receiver in her hand.

Claude drove into the Ferguson driveway with Jean. 'I know you're upset and worried about Harry, Jean. I am too, but don't get too uppity and say something you may regret later. They're good friends and to be honest, I don't think Jack influenced Harry at all. I believe they were both a party to running off.'

'That may have been so at the time but Harry's going back to being a schoolboy again and Jack's starting work on Monday. I know Harry would rather be with Jack than at school so keeping them apart for a while will help the situation.'

'You'll find when they both get settled into their own routines that they'll naturally grow apart anyhow. With one working and one at school, their lives will be heading in different directions. We better go in; we look stupid sitting here in the car arguing.'

'What about this Italian and off down the creek with him?'

'We'll find out, Jean, just calm down.'

Harry baulked when he spotted his father's car outside the Fergusons, like he had done the night they arrived with Father O'Malley. 'What're they doin' here?'

'Dunno, let's find out.' Jack pushed through the back gauze door with Harry at his heels to find both their parents sitting at the kitchen table, staring at them.

'You didn't tell us about rescuing some miner from a cave-in.' Claude Turner opened up the conversation. 'Jack and Alice just explained that the man who arrived here earlier was the one you two rescued, is that right?'

Harry explained briefly about how Bruno had become trapped and described the rescue but played down their parts in it. He completed the brief story by saying that Bruno had called by to say thanks.

'Where is he now, Harry, this Bruno?'

'Gone, mum. Gone off to Italy. Says he won't be back'

'That's a relief then,' she said. 'What's that you've got?' Jean pointed to the envelope Jack was holding

'This? Oh, just a card sayin' thanks I think. We haven't bothered to open it yet have we, Harry?'

'No, just a card to say goodbye.'

'Well, that was good of the man but I'm glad he's gone. You're both too young to be mixing with that type of person.' Jean noticed the dark expressions cloud both boys' eyes. 'Probably a very nice man, pity we didn't meet him, Claude, isn't it?'

Her weak rescue attempt didn't work so Alice came to her assistance 'Now, I'm sure there are a lot of nice people up in Coober Pedy and you had some exciting times while you were away but it's time now to get on with your lives. There's no need to forget those people, you can write to them. Telephone Father O'Malley now and then. You know, keep in touch.'

'That's a grand idea, Alice.' Jean agreed, hoping that after a time the boys would forget all about Coober Pedy and Italians and drovers and priests and opals.

When they were ready to leave, the Turners called to Harry and both he and Jack appeared from the bedroom down the hallway.

'Dad?' Jack spoke. 'Mr Turner?' The men looked expectantly at the boys.

'Tomorrow's Sunday and if Harry goes to school and I go to work on Monday we wouldn't have much chance to catch up for a while so we were wonderin' … how about we all have a day out tomorrow? Maybe go to the beach or somethin', maybe have a picnic?'

The parents looked at each other and shrugged 'Why not? What do you think, Jean?'

'Sounds OK to me, Alice. Makes a lot of sense seeing they won't have much time together after Monday. Claude, that OK with you?'

'You bet.' Claude welcomed the decision the boys had come to themselves, knowing it would relieve his wife's anxiety. 'We'll have to take both cars. That's if everyone's coming?'

'Yeah, let's make it a two family affair. Been a while since we all got together,' Jack's father said, ' and we'll finish the day off here with a couple of beers and maybe fire up the barbie.'

'It should be our turn, Jack so we'll bring the meat. Come on, Jean, let's head home and get organised for tomorrow. Come on, Harry.'

'Can I hang in for a bit with Jack, dad? We thought we might go down to the creek. Promise I won't be late.'

Claude looked at his wife who hesitated but then smiled. 'Yes, why not. Be a while before you'll get the chance again.'

♦♦♦♦♦♦♦♦♦♦♦♦

The two boys sauntered through the park entrance. They had only walked a few yards when a bicycle came hurtling up the path, the rider with his head down and pedalling hard. Looking up at the last moment and seeing two people on the path the rider braked and skidded to a stop, narrowly avoiding hitting them.

'Sorry I didn't ….' The rider's voice trailed away in shock.

'Well, well, well. Look who it is, Harry?' The boy on the bike made to ride off but Jack grabbed the seat and held it firmly.

Harry took hold of the handlebars, further preventing the bike from moving. 'Hello, Billy, fancy seein' you here.'

'Surprised ya still have this bike, Billy. Thought somebody woulda stolen it by now,' Jack said with a wicked smile, watching Billy Munse squirm. 'Hop off, Billy and let's have a bit of a yarn. Ya wouldn't want to ignore a coupla old mates would ya?'

Billy Munse looked nervously about him, hoping other people would be nearby but they were alone.

'What! No witnesses, Billy?' Jack was enjoying the moment.

'Er … you blokes better let me go or …'

'Or what, Billy?' Jack spat at him. 'You and ya father'll make up some more bloody lies about us.'

'No. I ahh … I just meant that I'll be in trouble that's all. Gotta get home. Good to see ya, Jack … Harry.' Billy was shaking with fear, his hands sweaty on the handlebars. He had initially thought it was two men he had almost collided with, not recognising Jack and Harry with their jeans, work shirts and riding boots. He could see fierceness in their eyes that shocked him and he was afraid his bladder might give way.

'Get off the bike, Billy,' Harry ordered firmly. Billy obeyed and stood looking at the ground.

'You better not hurt me. I'll have ya charged with assault.'

'Nobody'd believe ya, mate. Not after the last time ya lied. What do ya reckon we should do with him, Harry? Pity there's not a shaft around we could chuck him down, eh?'

'There's the creek, Jack. We could throw both him *and* his bike into one of them deep holes.'

Billy was really afraid now and started to blubber, tears brimming in his eyes and bottom lip quivering. 'I … I didn't mean no harm, honest,' he choked. 'My dad said he'd lock me bike away and …'

440

'And ya lied to protect yourself, eh? That's a real man's way of handlin' things isn't it, Harry?'

They stood watching Billy quake for a minute before realising that he was nothing but a scared little child. 'So you're the hope of the school, Billy? Top student goin' on to university. God help us,' Harry sneered.

'We're not gonna belt ya, Billy. We don't hit little kids do we, Harry?' Jack actually began to feel sorry for Billy, with his runny nose and tear-stained face. 'Let him go, mate, before he pees his pants.'

Billy Munse immediately stopped sniffling and, alert to Jack's change of attitude, made an attempt to ingratiate himself with the two boys who he realised would be better friends to have, than enemies. 'I'm real sorry about what happened, honest,' he whined. 'You know, with the bike and all. Now that you're home we can be friends again, eh? I've got a billycart now, Jack, like yours and …'

'We're not home, Billy. Home's Coober Pedy. We're just visitin' for a while aren't we, Jack? And I don't think we're gonna be friends somehow.'

'Yeah, we can, sure.' Billy thought desperately for a way he could win the two antagonists over. 'Look, I got an idea.' He indicated his bike. 'Dad's away playin' golf this weekend so you blokes could borrow my bike and ride it around. As long as you had it back by tomorrow lunch time he'd never know and …'

'Borrow your bike?' Jack scoffed. 'We don't need to borrow your bike.' He leant against the gatepost and unconsciously took the makings from his pocket to roll a cigarette.

Harry sniggered 'Do ya think we'd ever touch ya bike again? Except to maybe chuck it in the creek.'

Billy watched wide-eyed as Jack rolled the cigarette with one hand, licked the gummed paper and stuck it in his mouth. 'Gee whiz, Jack, that's a good trick.' Billy looked about nervously, hoping no one would see him with another boy, smoking in the park.

'What trick? Oh, this?' Jack struck a match and lit his smoke. 'Have to learn to roll 'em one handed when you smoke and ride a horse drovin', Billy.'

'You rode a horse, Jack?' He turned to Harry 'How about you, you ride one too?'

'Harry's a gun horseman, Billy. He owns a big black colt called Brumby. He was cut from a mob of wild horses by Tom Cooper and his crew out near Angus Downs station in the Territory.'

'That right? Gee. I rode a pony at the show last year. Dad says I went well and he might get me one so I can join the pony club.'

Jack glanced at Harry but didn't ridicule the kid in the short grey pants holding the blue bicycle. 'That's great, Billy. Should be a lotta fun. Well, we better be gettin' on home, Billy.' He stubbed the butt out, grinding it under his boot. 'See ya 'round.'

'You sure ya don't wanna borrow me bike? No problem ya know.' Billy offered once more but knew in his heart as he watched his old friends walk away that they were well past ever wanting a ride on his bike.

'Everythin's not the same back here any more, Jack, is it?' Harry commented as they walked out of the park.

'Yes, it is, Harry, that's the problem. Everythin' *is* the same ... but we're not.'

Sunday was a warm autumn day with clear skies and a light breeze that dropped off by mid-morning. The boys were glad to see their mothers in particular, smiling and happy as they packed the picnic hampers into the vehicles. The two families started to squeeze into the cars with the smaller kids squabbling and vying for position, giggling and laughing together.

'Let's make this a good day, Harry.'

'It will be, Jack, I can tell.'

It was. There was only light traffic and the beach at Cottesloe was sparsely occupied. Jack's father said that they should only come to the beach at this time of year instead of in the summer when it was packed. 'Bit too cold for a swim though,' he added.

'Not for me.' Jack pulled his shirt over his head and flung it onto the sand. 'Race ya to the water, Harry. Last one in's a rotten egg,' he yelled over his shoulder as he sped off toward the light surf with Harry in close pursuit.

The younger children splashed around in the shallows, oblivious of the coolish weather, while Timothy kept up with the two older lads out in the deeper swell, body surfing to the beach. Alice watched her two oldest sons proudly but a phantom of concern flickered across her mind as she realised that Timothy was only a few months younger than Harry had been when he and Jack had left home. She shook her head, dismissing the thought, watching her husband and Claude on their knees helping the younger kids build sand castles at the water's edge and laughing as the littlies squealed with delight and feigned terror when a wave rolled in.

They picnicked on the lawn overlooking the water and Jack and Harry spoiled their brothers and sisters by buying hot chips, ice cream and soft drinks for them. 'You shouldn't go wasting your money like that,' Alice scolded but was proud, nonetheless, of the boys' generosity.

Back at the Ferguson home Jack and Harry set the fire and lit it while the two fathers sat back having a couple of beers. 'We'll cook tonight,' Harry said.

'Won't object to that, eh, Claude?'

'Can you cook?' Claude asked with a laugh, 'or do you burn the snags like your father, Jack?'

The younger children were tired from the day's activities, sun and fresh air so, after they had eaten, Alice decided to put them to bed. 'OK, baths everyone.' She herded the protesting kids into the house.

'Yeah, we should be off too.' Claude picked up empty beer bottles and put them in the rubbish bin. 'Tomorrow's Monday and an early start for everyone. You two …' He spoke directly to Jack and Harry '… have new adventures starting tomorrow, eh?'

'I suppose we do, yes,' Harry agreed.

'It's been a top day, Jack.' Claude clapped his friend on the back. 'Must do it more often.'

'Sure was, Claude. Nice to have all the family together too. It was a lot of fun but I think we might wait until the summer kicks in before we do it again, as I don't mind a swim but I'm not as hardy as these young fellas.'

◆◆◆◆◆◆◆◆◆◆◆

Alice snuggled close to Jack that night after putting all the kids to bed and looking in on Jack asleep in his old bed in the room he shared with his younger brother Timmy.

'That was a beautiful day, Jack.' Alice sighed and yawned.

'Mmm, it was,' He replied sleepily.

'Nice to see Jack joining in and helping so much. He's certainly grown up a lot since he's been away. Maybe Coober Pedy didn't do them all that much harm after all, dear.'

'No, probably not. There was a purposeful attitude in both of them today I hadn't seen since they came home. I think they've made up their minds at last as to where their futures lie.'

The alarm clock jangled Alice awake. Reaching out, she hit the button and the ringing stopped. Her husband stirred. 'What time is it, Alice?'

'Six o'clock, dear. You stay there for a bit and I'll put the kettle on and wake Jack up so he can get ready for work. You'll take him in of course?'

'Yeah. I'll introduce him to the blokes down at the yards. He'll be OK.' He turned over burying his head in the pillow. 'Bring me a cuppa please, Alice?'

'You lazy beggar,' she laughed, slipped from the covers and put her dressing gown on. 'Bbrrr,' she shivered, 'it's chilly this morning.'

Jack dozed, waiting for Alice to return with his cup of tea when he heard her cry out. 'What is it, Alice?' He jumped from the bed hearing her gasp again and ran to the kitchen, fearing she had burnt herself on the stove but when he found her she was standing beside the table holding a piece of paper in her hand.

'What is it, Alice, what's the matter?' She didn't reply but shakily handed him the paper and his heart leapt when he recognised his son's handwriting.

Dear mum and dad

Harry and I have thought this through long and hard. We
don't fit in back here any more. I know you and dad have
tried to do all you can for me and are worried about my
future but you have to understand that I already have a
future. A future that came by accident the day Billy Munse
said we stole his bike.

I'm sorry about the Elders job dad and I don't want to
disappoint you but there's something you need to know.
Harry and me own a claim at the nine-mile diggings. We
bought it from Ishmo the Afghan for two hundred pounds
and it's showing a lot of promise. We have found enough
so far to pay for the mine, keep us in tucker and help
Reynold out with a small share. We also paid for our trip
over and still have a few hundred between us to go back
with.

Jack sat down at the table, a lump in his throat as he read. Alice
was sobbing quietly beside him, reading over his shoulder.

When Bruno called the other day it was not only to say
thanks. When we opened the envelope it wasn't a card as
we thought, but there was a note in it saying he'd been to
the Department of Mines and transferred the ownership of
his mine over to us as a reward for saving his life. He also
put the certificate in the envelope as proof. I know you are
worried but it was just an unfortunate and uncommon
accident that the drive caved in and we can shore it up and
keep mining. Bruno sold the opal he found for over
twenty five thousand pounds and there has to be more
there. Maybe not as big but just as valuable. Paddy can't do
it on his own and even with Reynold to help they can't
work

Please don't worry about us. I know you think everyone out at Coober is running from something and we were like that too once. But there are many people who are there because they want to be there and we have really good friends. If you are worried you can talk to Ron Carter the police sergeant. He's our friend and also Iris Smith the nurse who fusses after us a bit like you do mum. Shaun Logan is the catholic priest and although we don't go to church he's become a good mate to us all. We have horses, a dog, a Land Rover, two working mines and real good friends. I know it's not what you had planned for me but I've learned in the past months that plans alone don't make futures but opportunities do.

Mr and Mrs Turner will be reading a letter almost the same as this and I know they'll be upset so hope you can get together with them and help them understand why we have to return home to Coober Pedy.

At least this time you will know where I am and you can write c/- the police station and I promise to telephone when I can.

I hope you forgive me but ask you again to understand. It's a fact that when you've spent time out there it gets in your blood and your life changes forever and there's no turning back. Nothing else compares to chasing the fire in the stone. Say goodbye to Timmy and the kids. Tell them I'll write soon.

Your loving son, Jack.

Jack placed the letter gently on the tabletop and stared at it. Alice had stopped crying but her voice was thick with emotion. 'He's gone, Jack, my boy has gone again.'

Jack didn't comment immediately but continued to stare at the carefully composed note then, taking a deep breath he stood, placed his arms around his wife and, drawing her gently to him, he stroked her hair. 'Yes, he's gone. But not your *boy*, Alice, your *man*. Jack's no longer a boy.'

The telephone's strident bell was insolently loud in the morning quietness. They knew before they answered that it was the Turners and that they too had found an empty bed with a note from their son saying he and Jack had returned to search for the elusive 'Fire in the Stone.'